EDISON BEAKER

CREATURE SEEKER

THE NIGHT DOOR

BY FRANK CAMMUSO

VIKING

For the Reverend Adrian Amaya
— F.C.

Special thanks to Ngoc Huynh, Khai Cammuso, Kathy Leonardo,
Nancy Iacovelli, Mai Huynh, Min Hong, Ai Vy Hong, Van Hong, Hart Seely,
Tom Peyer, Randy Elliot, Sheila Keenan, Denise Cronin, and Judy Hansen.

VIKING
Penguin Young Readers
An imprint of Penguin Random House LLC
375 Hudson Street
New York, New York 10014

First published in the United States of America by Viking,
an imprint of Penguin Random House LLC, 2018

LIBRARY OF CONGRESS CATALOGING-IN-PUBLICATION DATA IS AVAILABLE.
ISBN 9780425291924 (hardcover); 9780425291931 (paperback)

Manufactured in China

1 3 5 7 9 10 8 6 4 2

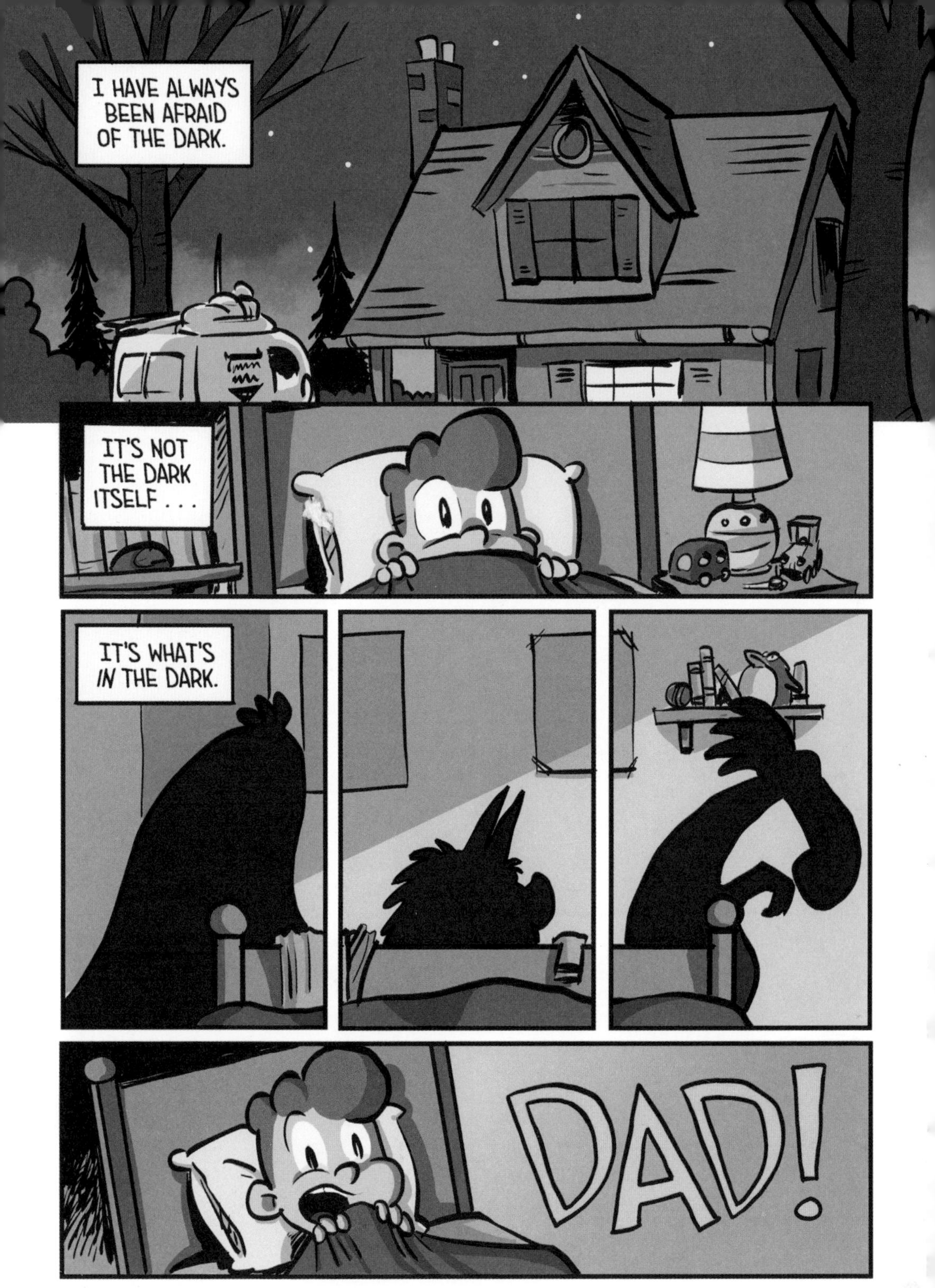
I HAVE ALWAYS BEEN AFRAID OF THE DARK.
IT'S NOT THE DARK ITSELF . . .
IT'S WHAT'S *IN* THE DARK.
DAD!

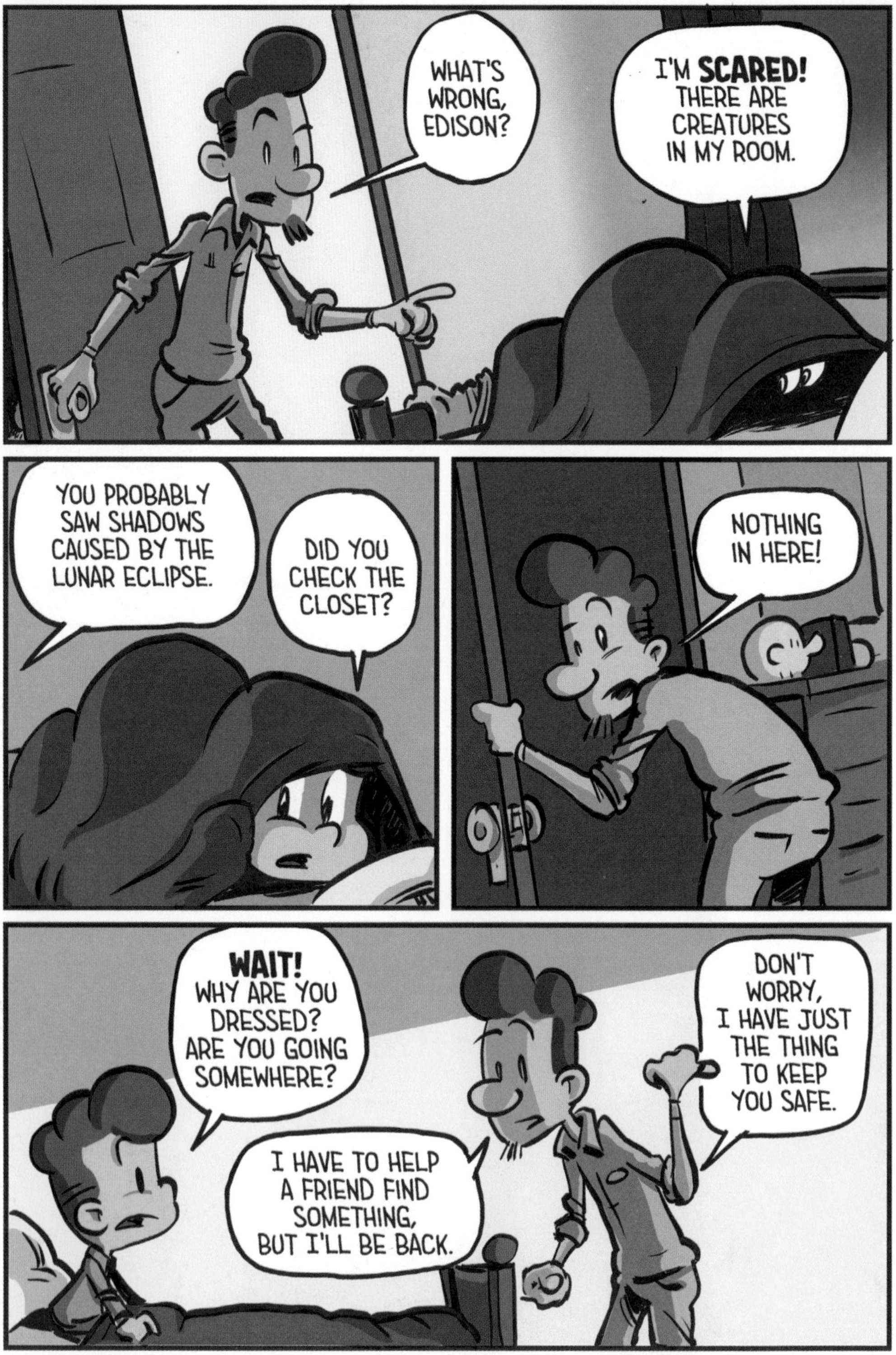
WHAT'S WRONG, EDISON?
I'M **SCARED!** THERE ARE CREATURES IN MY ROOM.
YOU PROBABLY SAW SHADOWS CAUSED BY THE LUNAR ECLIPSE.
DID YOU CHECK THE CLOSET?
NOTHING IN HERE!
WAIT! WHY ARE YOU DRESSED? ARE YOU GOING SOMEWHERE?
I HAVE TO HELP A FRIEND FIND SOMETHING, BUT I'LL BE BACK.
DON'T WORRY, I HAVE JUST THE THING TO KEEP YOU SAFE.

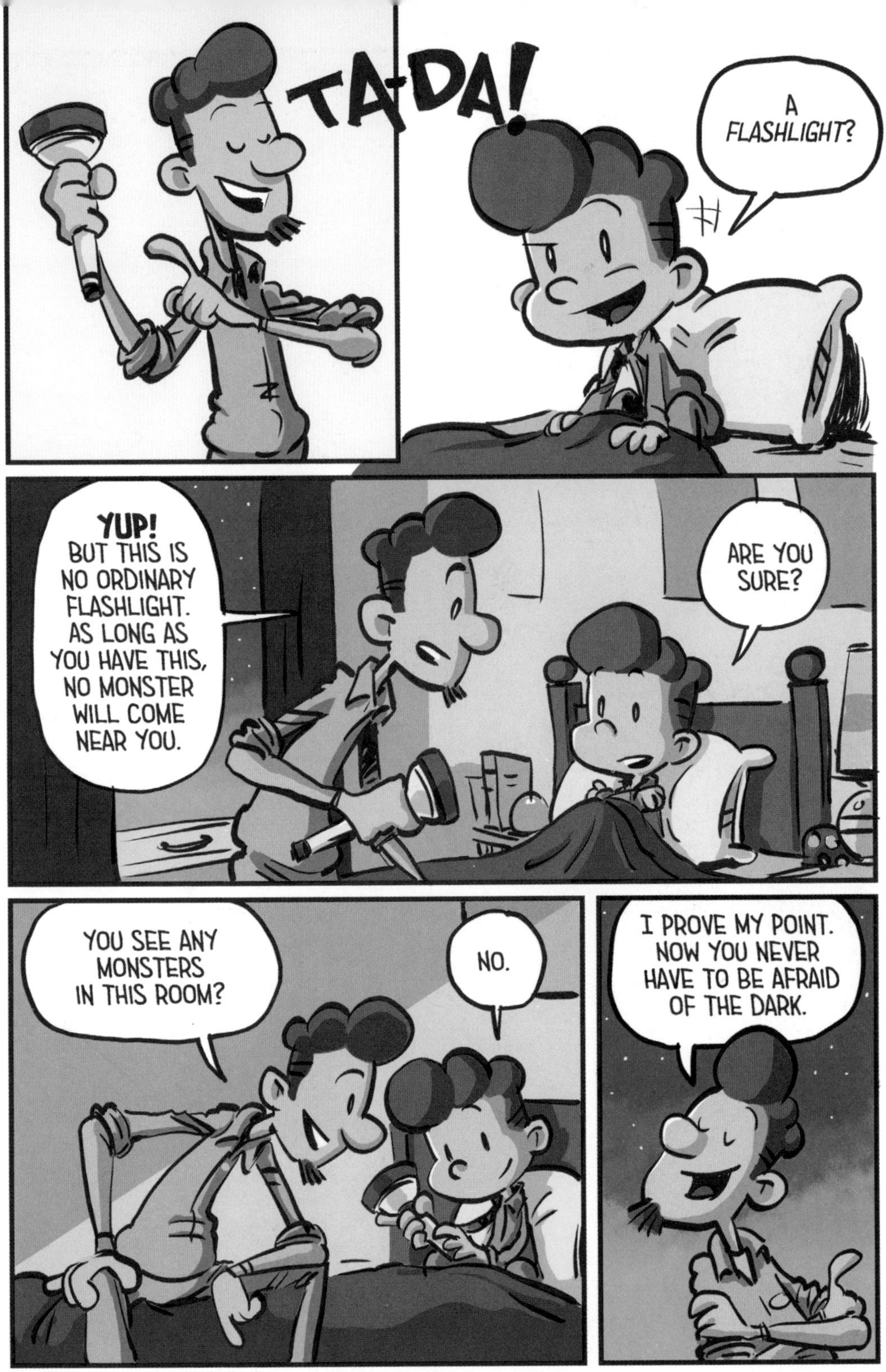
TA-DA!
A FLASHLIGHT?
YUP! BUT THIS IS NO ORDINARY FLASHLIGHT. AS LONG AS YOU HAVE THIS, NO MONSTER WILL COME NEAR YOU.
ARE YOU SURE?
YOU SEE ANY MONSTERS IN THIS ROOM?
NO.
I PROVE MY POINT. NOW YOU NEVER HAVE TO BE AFRAID OF THE DARK.

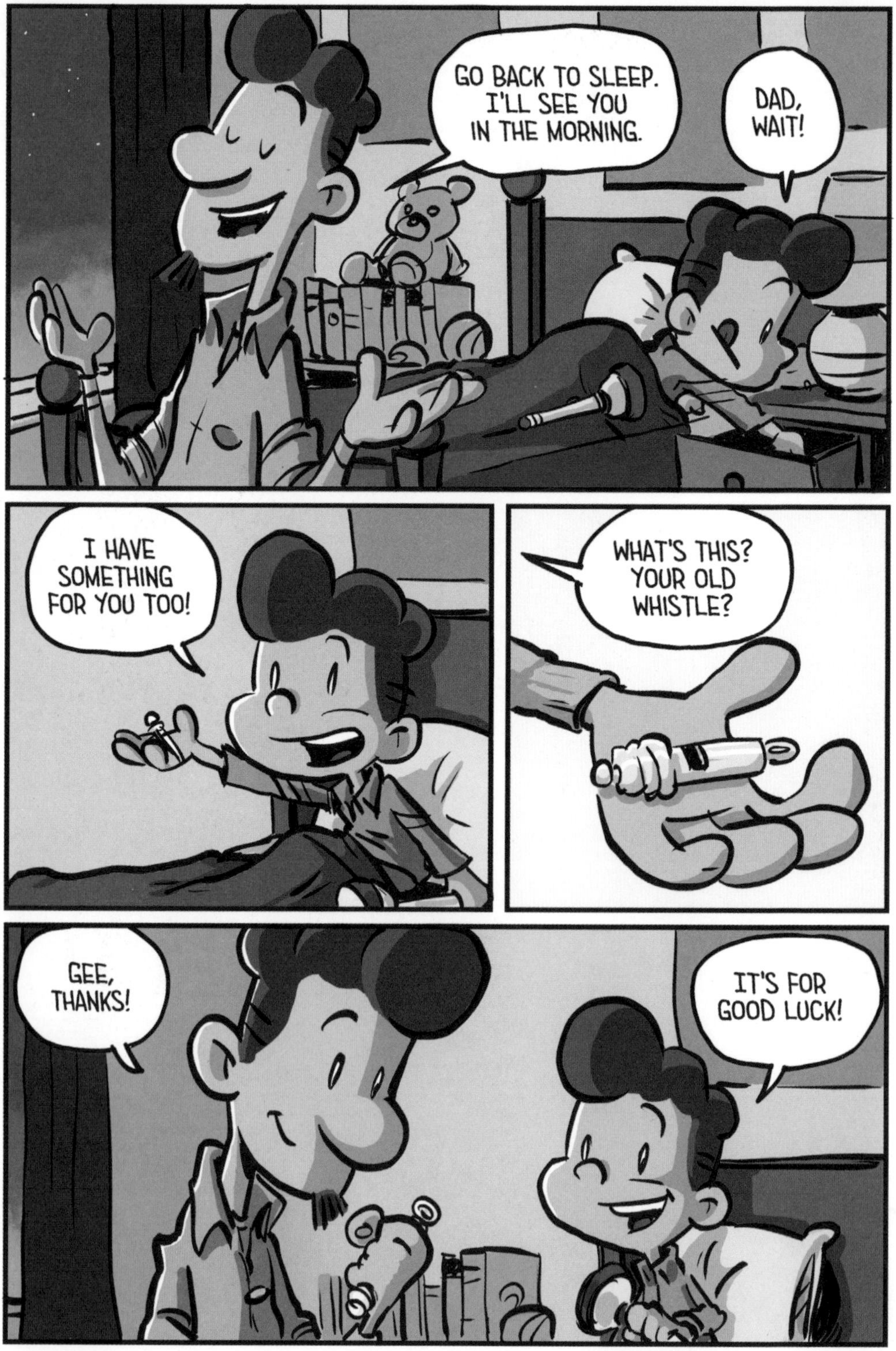
GO BACK TO SLEEP. I'LL SEE YOU IN THE MORNING.
DAD, WAIT!
I HAVE SOMETHING FOR YOU TOO!
WHAT'S THIS? YOUR OLD WHISTLE?
GEE, THANKS!
IT'S FOR GOOD LUCK!

GOOD NIGHT, BUDDY.

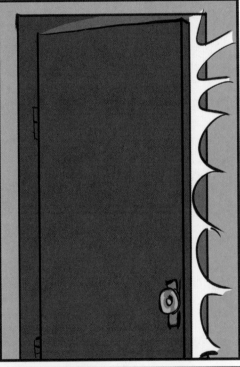

THAT WAS THE LAST TIME I SAW MY DAD.

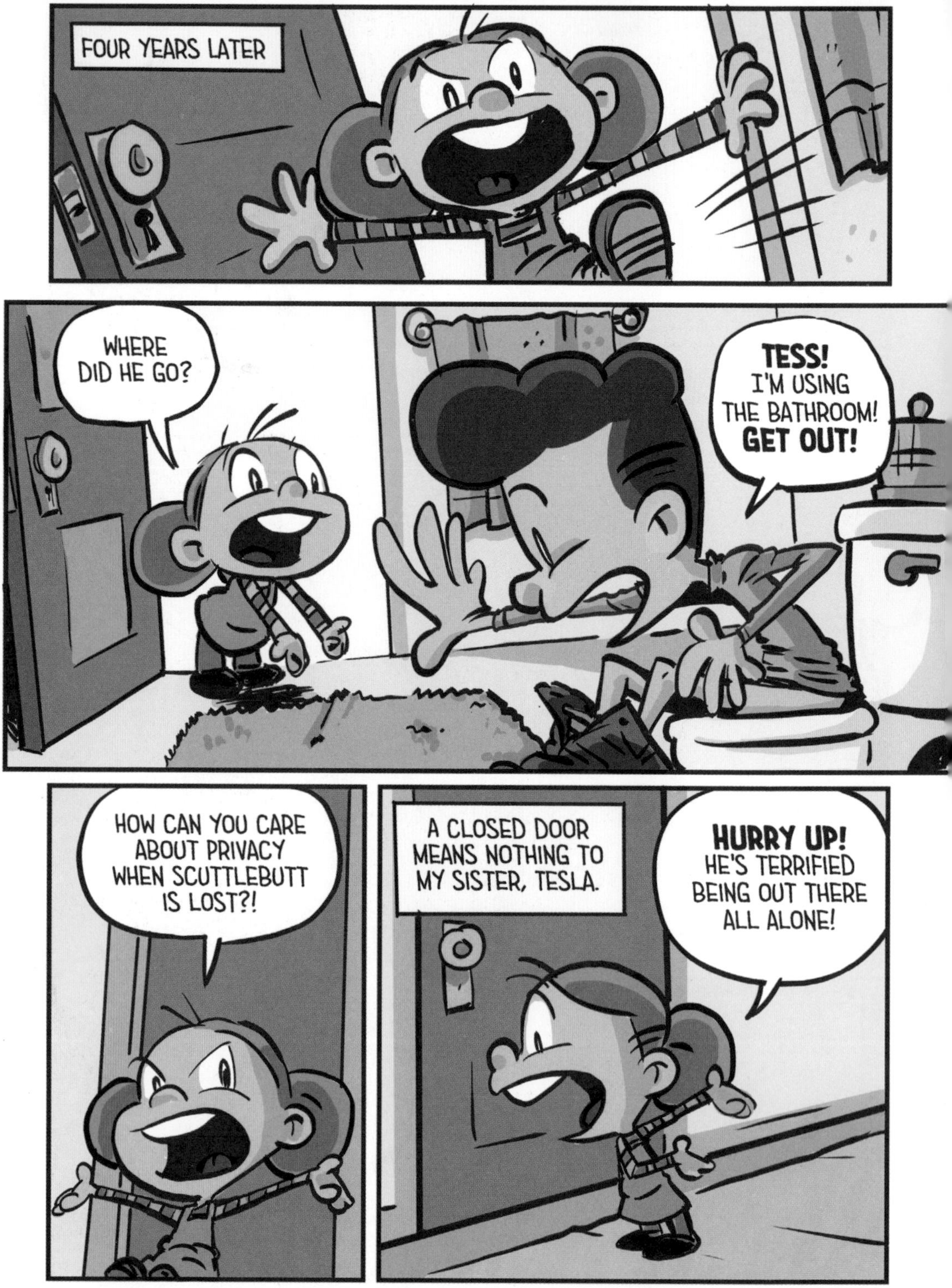
FOUR YEARS LATER
WHERE DID HE GO?
TESS! I'M USING THE BATHROOM! GET OUT!
HOW CAN YOU CARE ABOUT PRIVACY WHEN SCUTTLEBUTT IS LOST?!
A CLOSED DOOR MEANS NOTHING TO MY SISTER, TESLA.
HURRY UP! HE'S TERRIFIED BEING OUT THERE ALL ALONE!

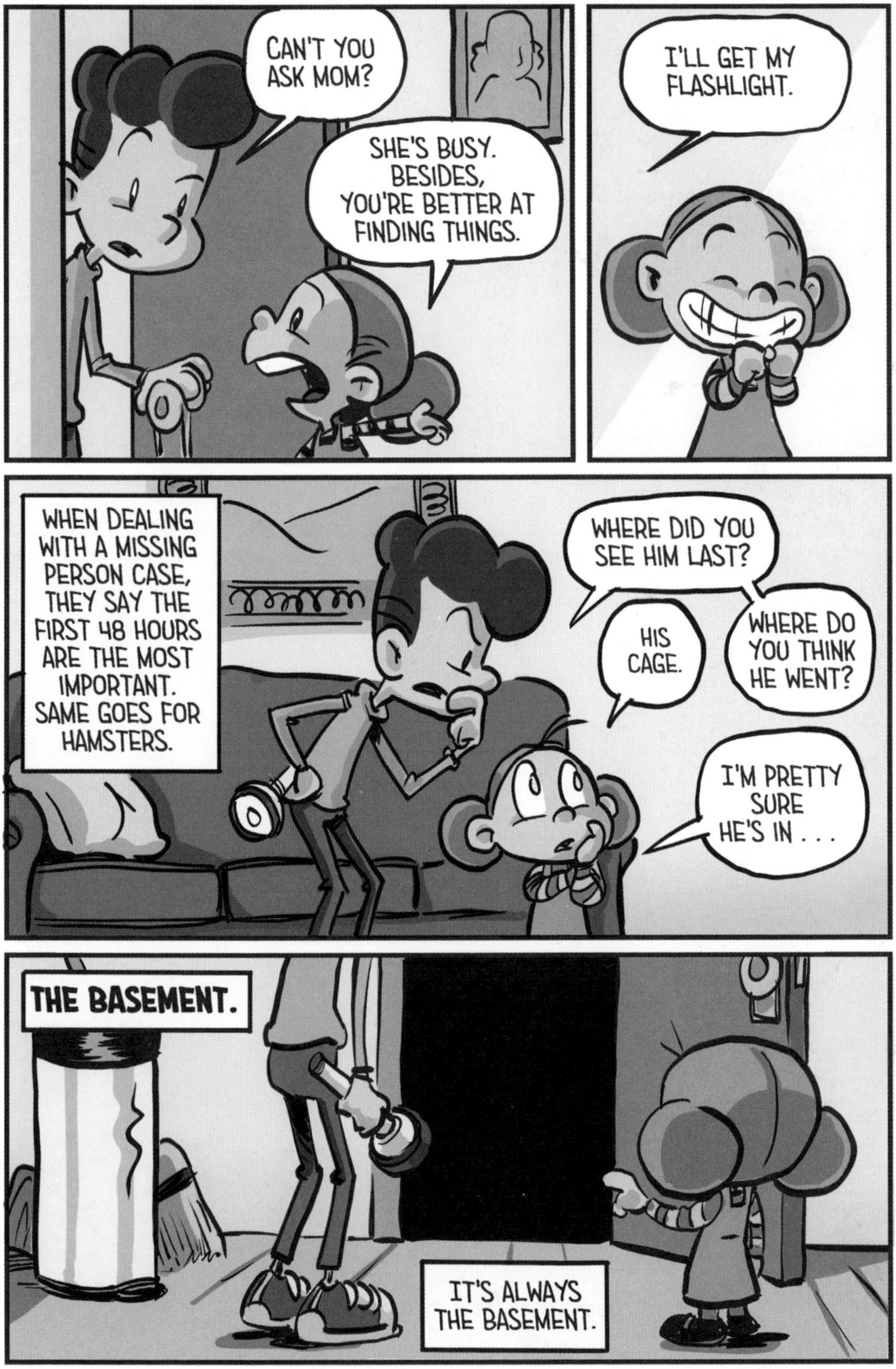
CAN'T YOU ASK MOM?
SHE'S BUSY. BESIDES, YOU'RE BETTER AT FINDING THINGS.
I'LL GET MY FLASHLIGHT.
WHEN DEALING WITH A MISSING PERSON CASE, THEY SAY THE FIRST 48 HOURS ARE THE MOST IMPORTANT. SAME GOES FOR HAMSTERS.
WHERE DID YOU SEE HIM LAST?
HIS CAGE.
WHERE DO YOU THINK HE WENT?
I'M PRETTY SURE HE'S IN . . .
THE BASEMENT.
IT'S ALWAYS THE BASEMENT.

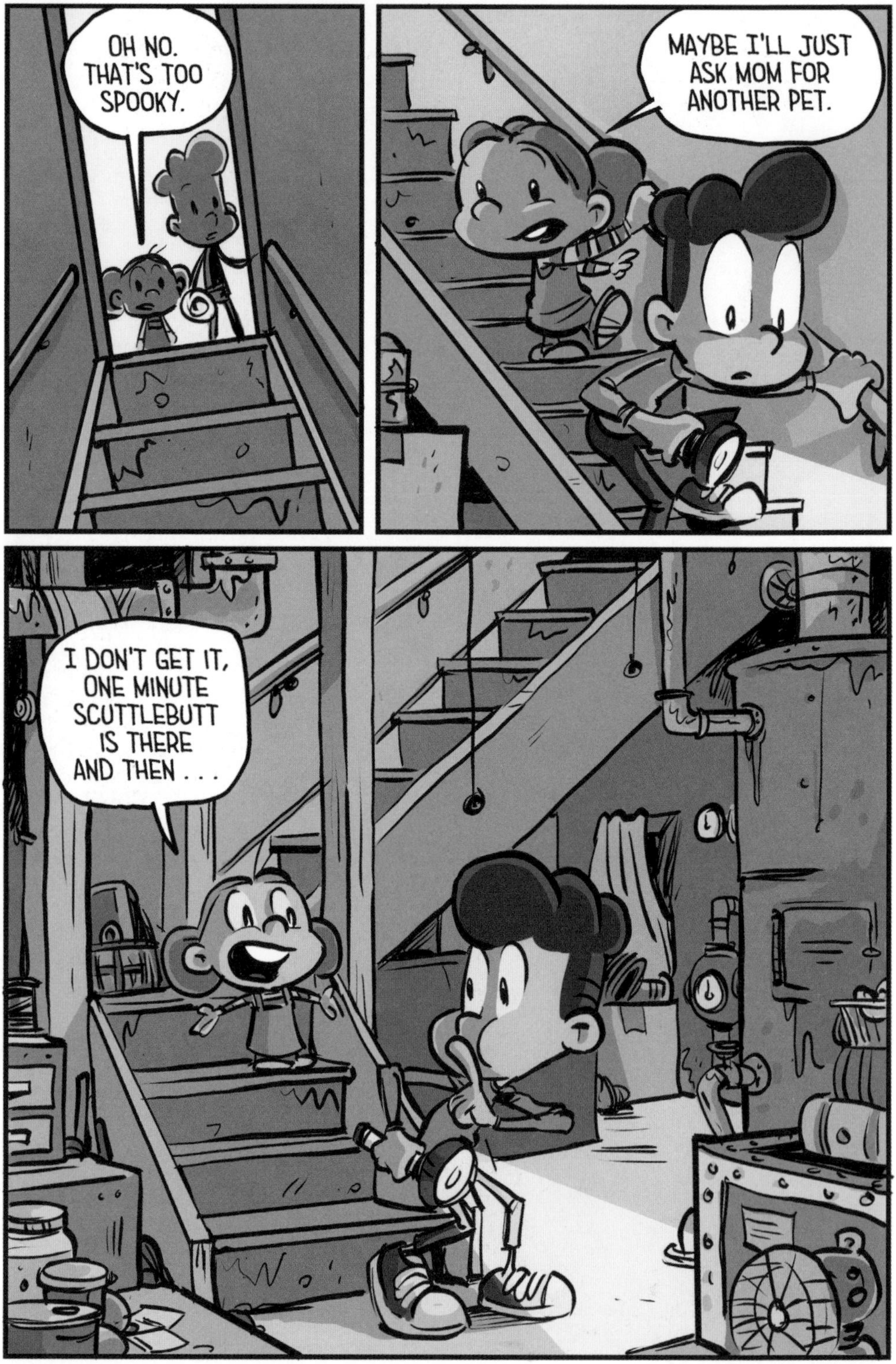
OH NO. THAT'S TOO SPOOKY.
MAYBE I'LL JUST ASK MOM FOR ANOTHER PET.
I DON'T GET IT, ONE MINUTE SCUTTLEBUTT IS THERE AND THEN . . .

I THINK HE'S UNDER THE WORKBENCH!

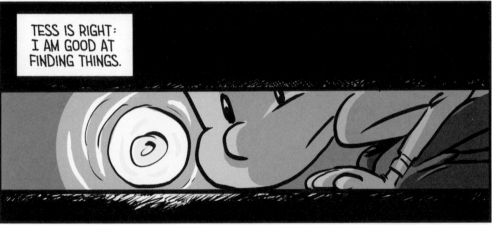

TESS IS RIGHT: I AM GOOD AT FINDING THINGS.

OR RATHER . . .

THINGS ARE GOOD . . .

AT FINDING ME!

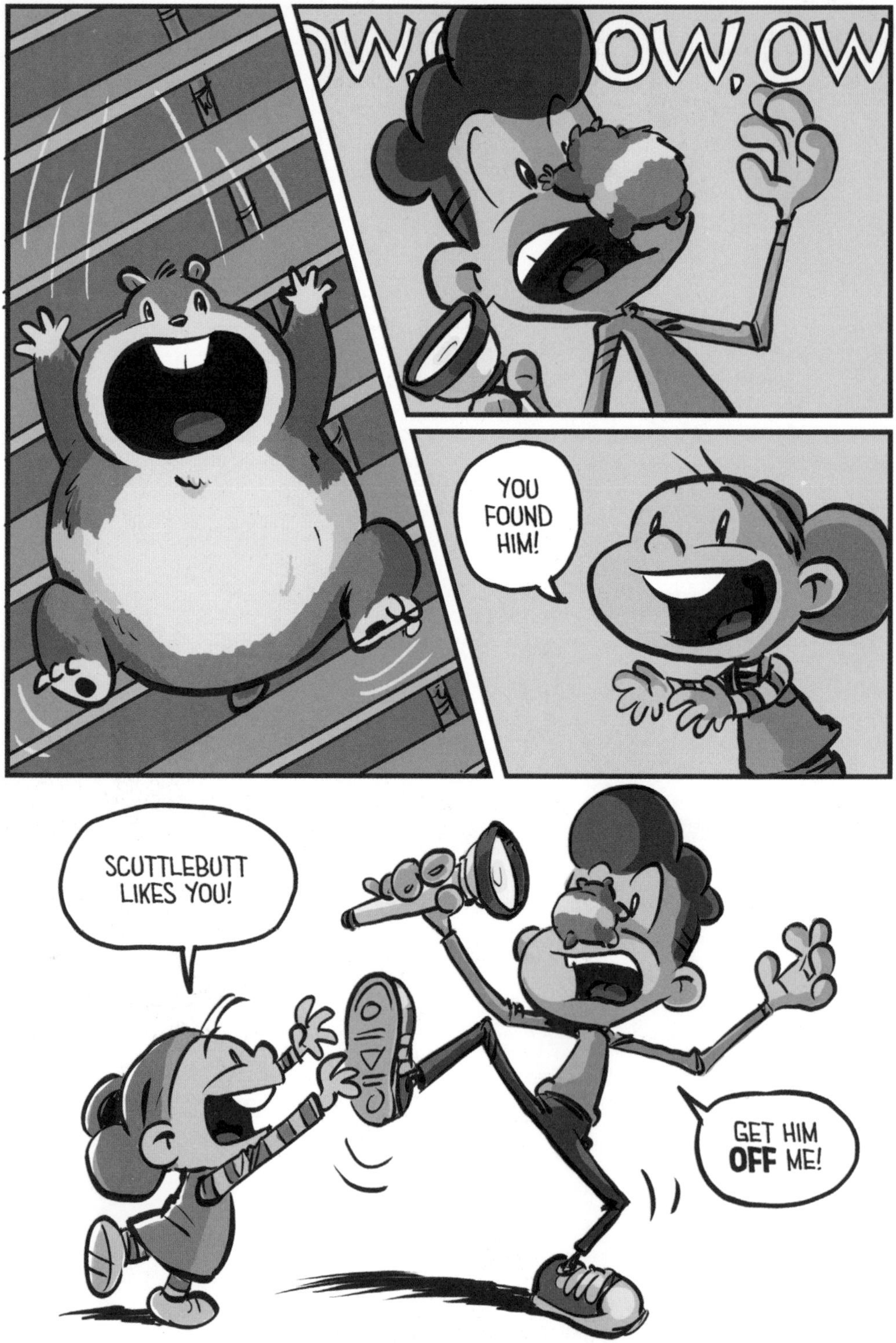
OW
OW, OW
YOU FOUND HIM!
SCUTTLEBUTT LIKES YOU!
GET HIM **OFF** ME!

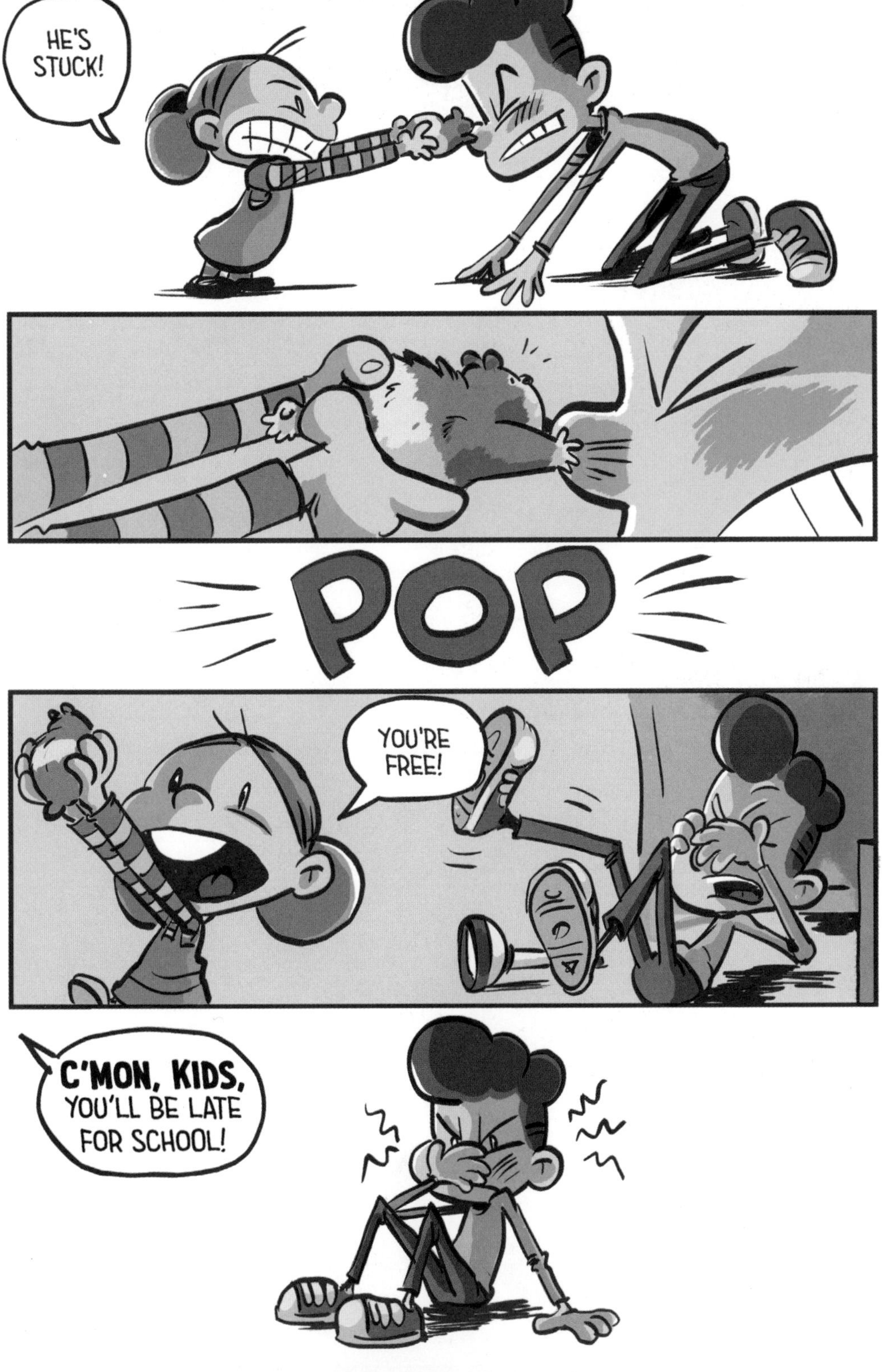
HE'S STUCK!
POP
YOU'RE FREE!
C'MON, KIDS, YOU'LL BE LATE FOR SCHOOL!

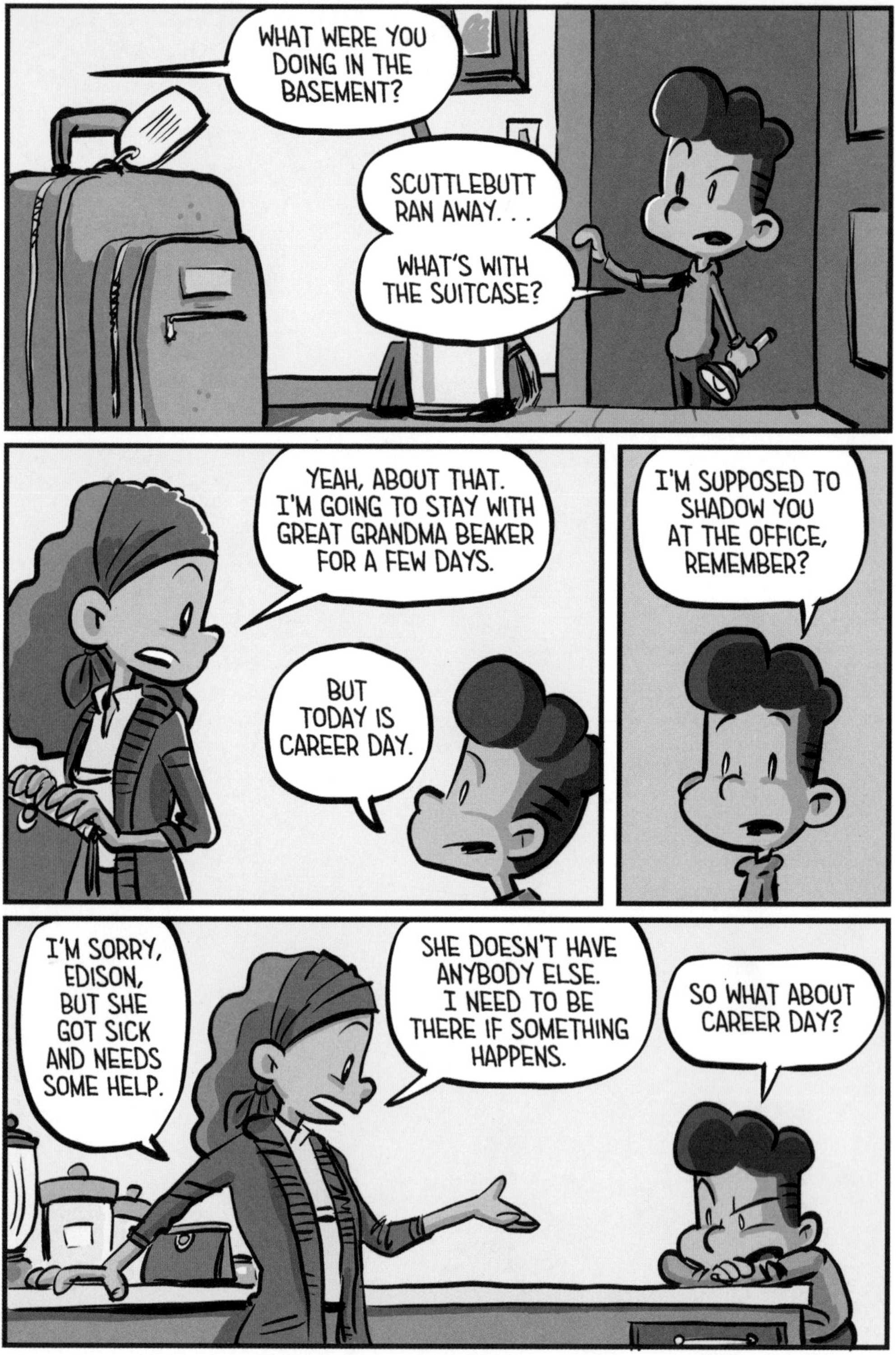
WHAT WERE YOU DOING IN THE BASEMENT?
SCUTTLEBUTT RAN AWAY. . .
WHAT'S WITH THE SUITCASE?
YEAH, ABOUT THAT. I'M GOING TO STAY WITH GREAT GRANDMA BEAKER FOR A FEW DAYS.
BUT TODAY IS CAREER DAY.
I'M SUPPOSED TO SHADOW YOU AT THE OFFICE, REMEMBER?
I'M SORRY, EDISON, BUT SHE GOT SICK AND NEEDS SOME HELP.
SHE DOESN'T HAVE ANYBODY ELSE. I NEED TO BE THERE IF SOMETHING HAPPENS.
SO WHAT ABOUT CAREER DAY?

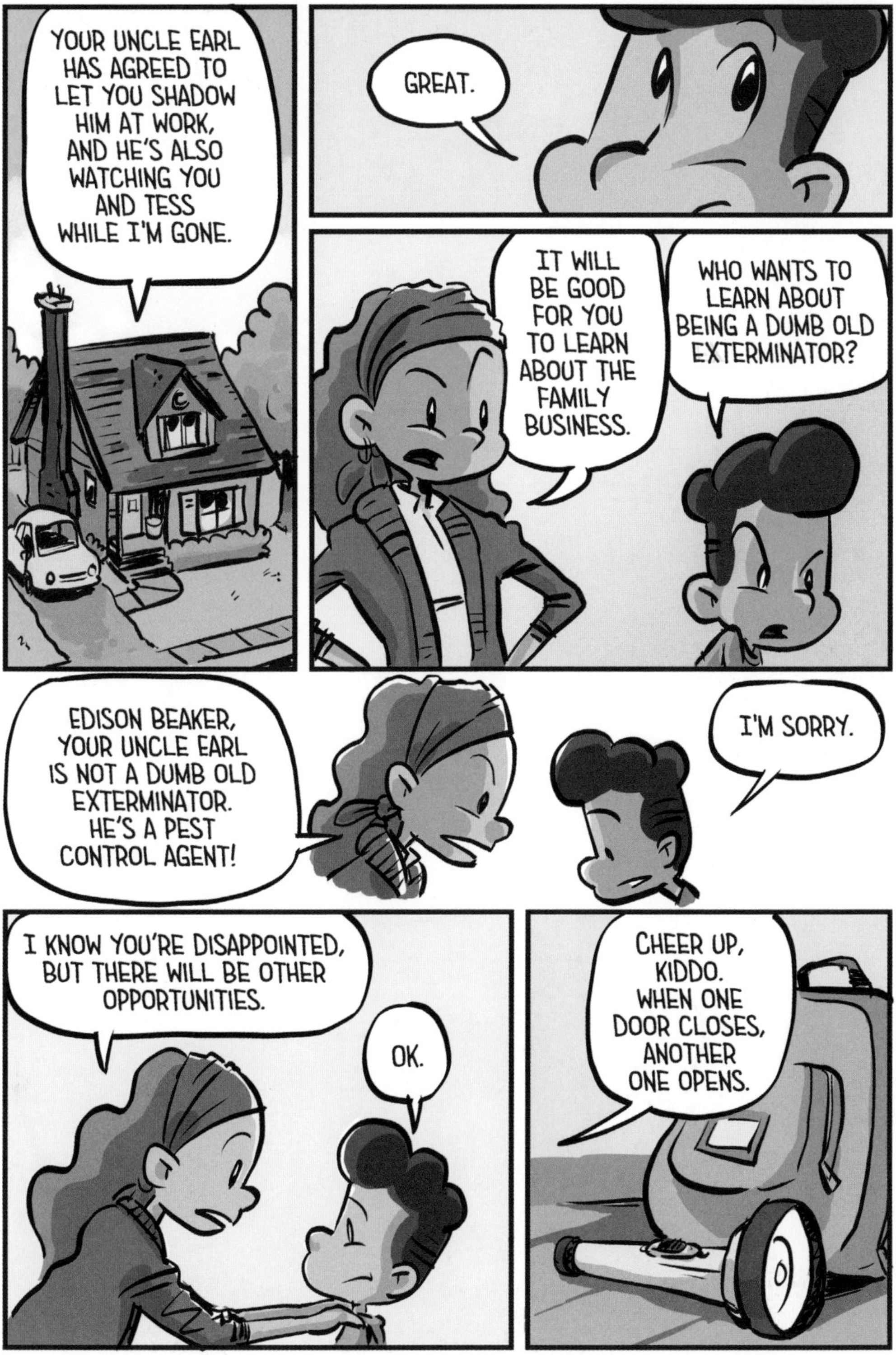
YOUR UNCLE EARL HAS AGREED TO LET YOU SHADOW HIM AT WORK, AND HE'S ALSO WATCHING YOU AND TESS WHILE I'M GONE.
GREAT.
IT WILL BE GOOD FOR YOU TO LEARN ABOUT THE FAMILY BUSINESS.
WHO WANTS TO LEARN ABOUT BEING A DUMB OLD EXTERMINATOR?
EDISON BEAKER, YOUR UNCLE EARL IS NOT A DUMB OLD EXTERMINATOR. HE'S A PEST CONTROL AGENT!
I'M SORRY.
I KNOW YOU'RE DISAPPOINTED, BUT THERE WILL BE OTHER OPPORTUNITIES.
OK.
CHEER UP, KIDDO. WHEN ONE DOOR CLOSES, ANOTHER ONE OPENS.

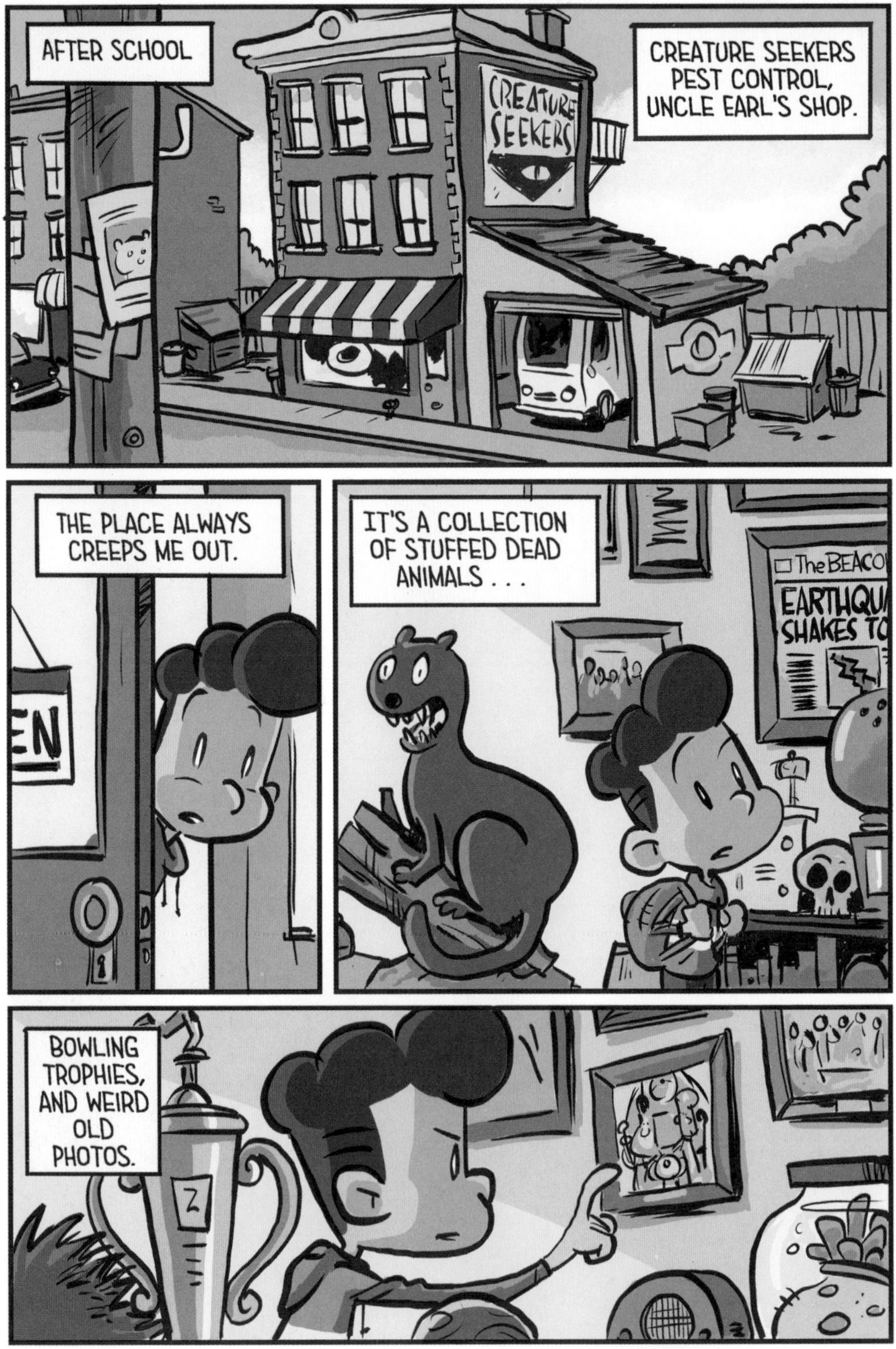
AFTER SCHOOL
CREATURE SEEKERS PEST CONTROL, UNCLE EARL'S SHOP.
CREATURE SEEKERS
THE PLACE ALWAYS CREEPS ME OUT.
IT'S A COLLECTION OF STUFFED DEAD ANIMALS . . .
BOWLING TROPHIES, AND WEIRD OLD PHOTOS.

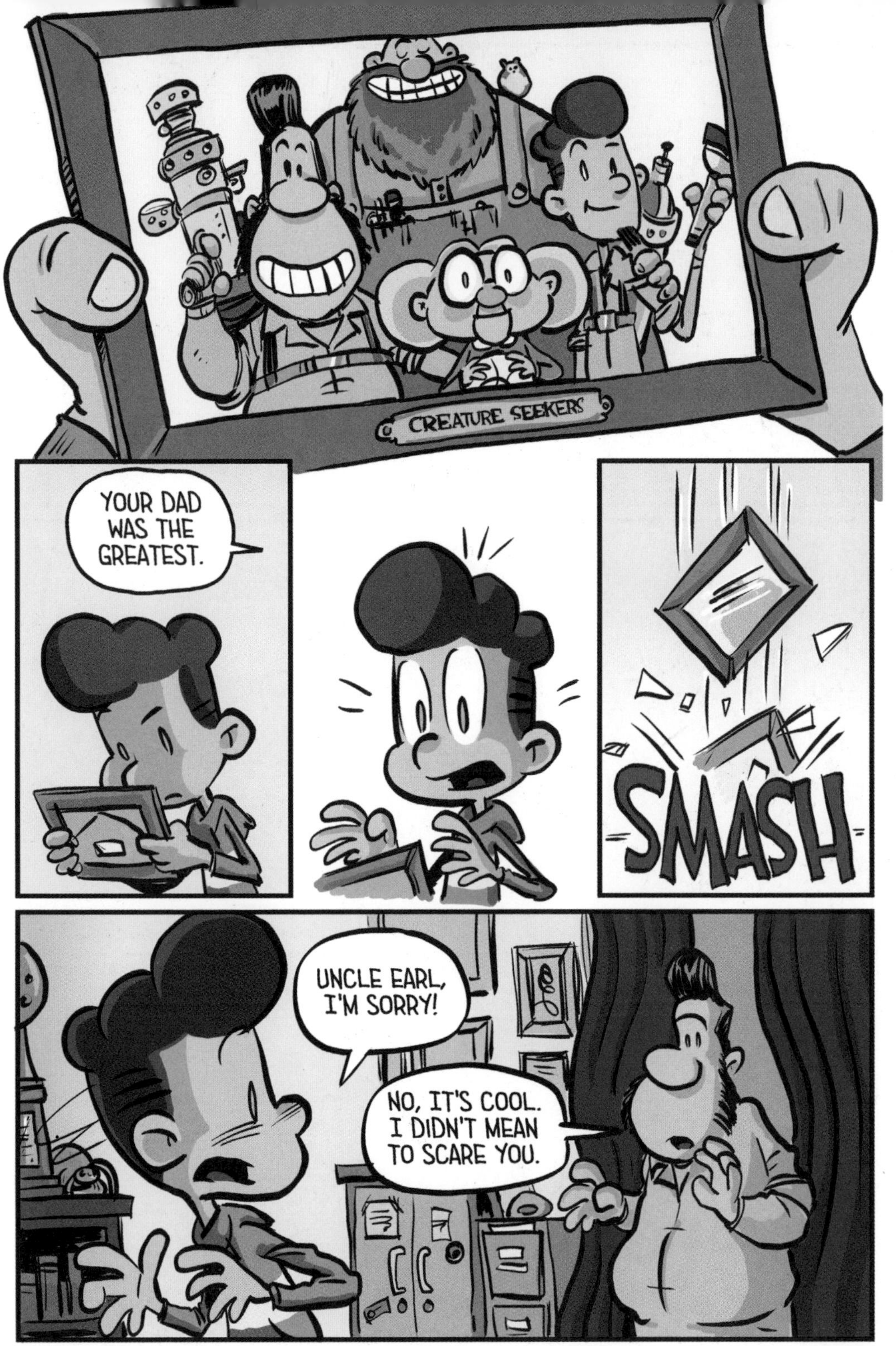
CREATURE SEEKERS
YOUR DAD WAS THE GREATEST.
SMASH
UNCLE EARL, I'M SORRY!
NO, IT'S COOL. I DIDN'T MEAN TO SCARE YOU.

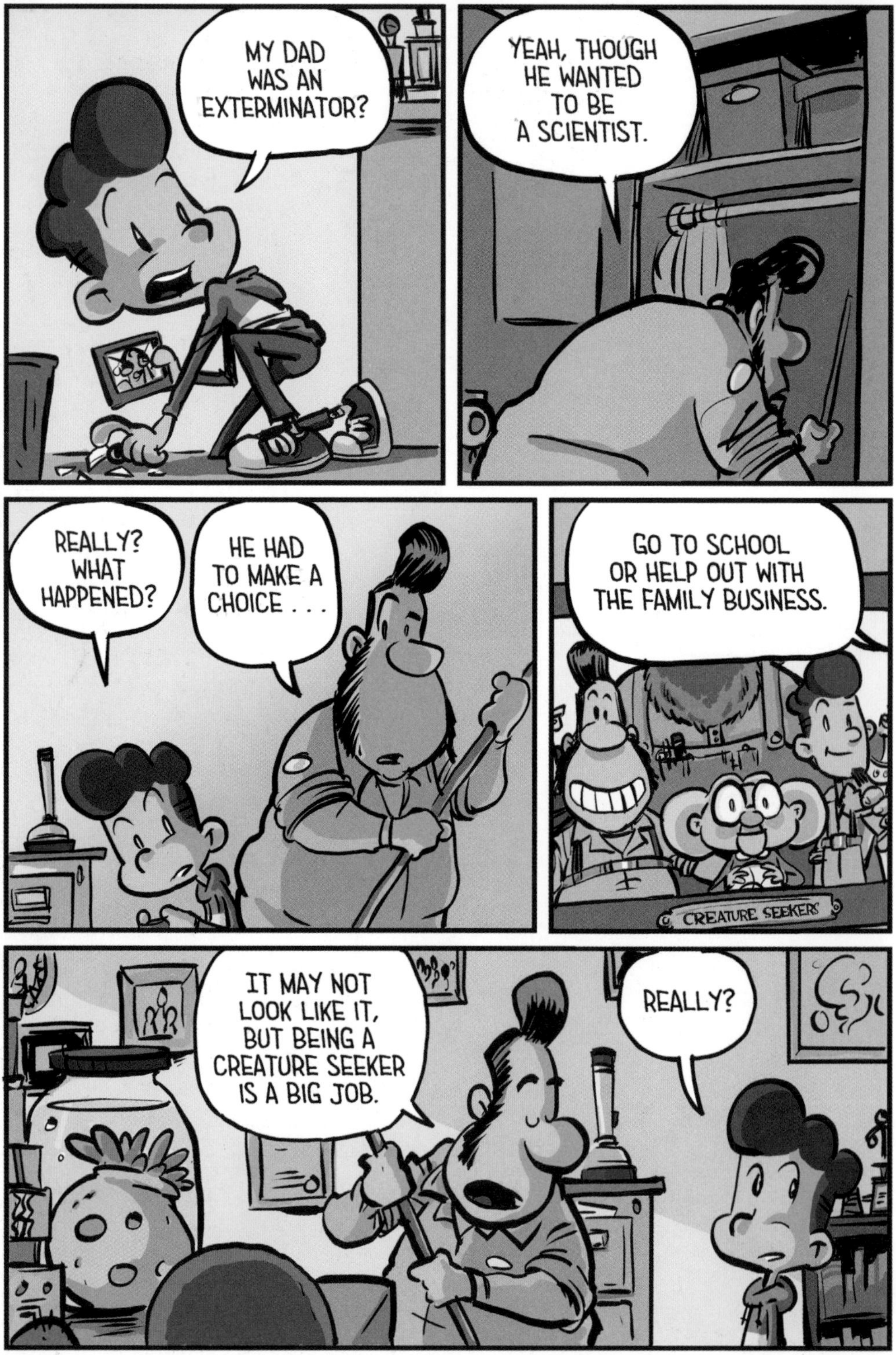
MY DAD WAS AN EXTERMINATOR?
YEAH, THOUGH HE WANTED TO BE A SCIENTIST.
REALLY? WHAT HAPPENED?
HE HAD TO MAKE A CHOICE . . .
GO TO SCHOOL OR HELP OUT WITH THE FAMILY BUSINESS.
CREATURE SEEKERS
IT MAY NOT LOOK LIKE IT, BUT BEING A CREATURE SEEKER IS A BIG JOB.
REALLY?

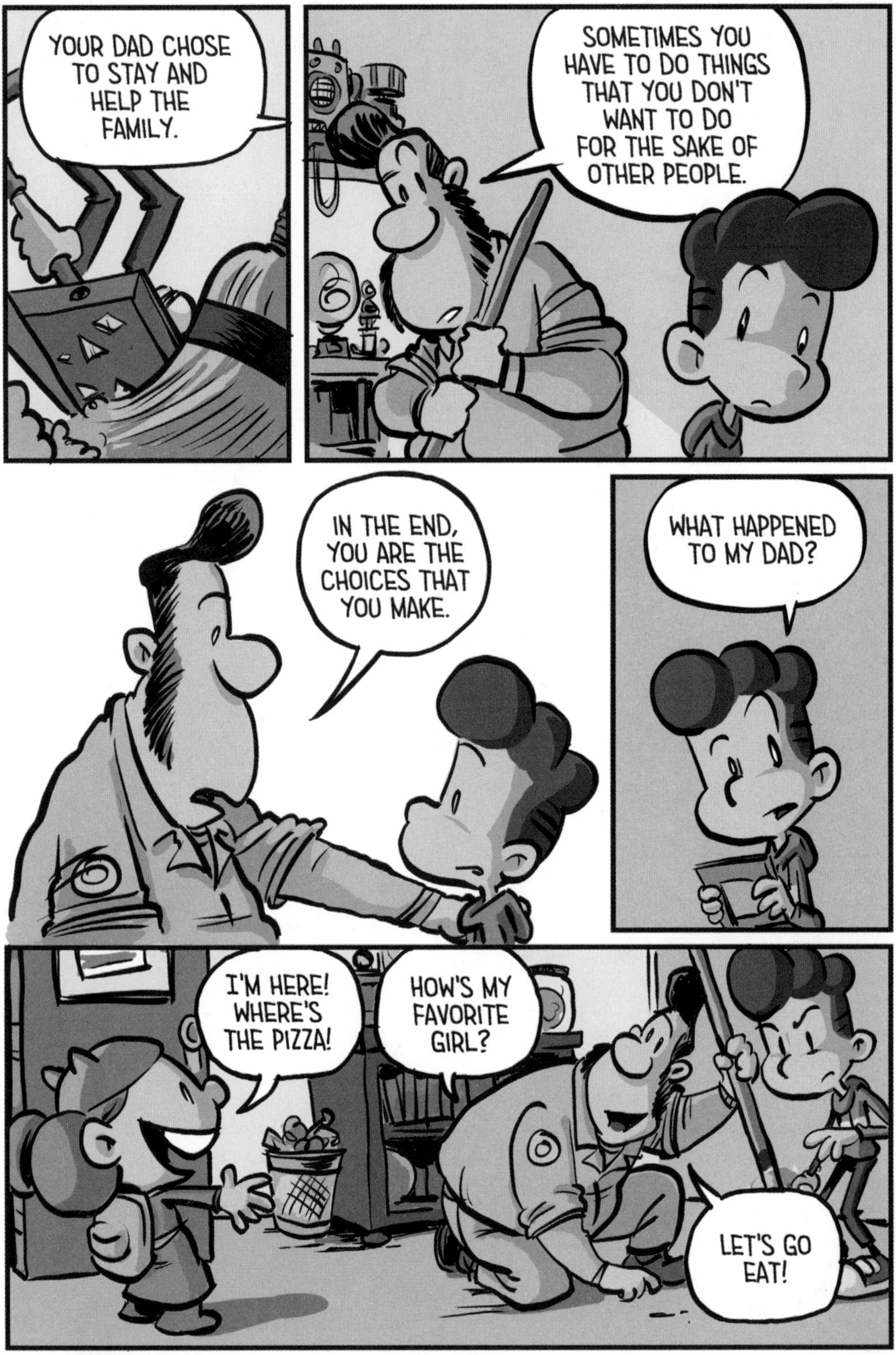
YOUR DAD CHOSE TO STAY AND HELP THE FAMILY.
SOMETIMES YOU HAVE TO DO THINGS THAT YOU DON'T WANT TO DO FOR THE SAKE OF OTHER PEOPLE.
IN THE END, YOU ARE THE CHOICES THAT YOU MAKE.
WHAT HAPPENED TO MY DAD?
I'M HERE! WHERE'S THE PIZZA!
HOW'S MY FAVORITE GIRL?
LET'S GO EAT!

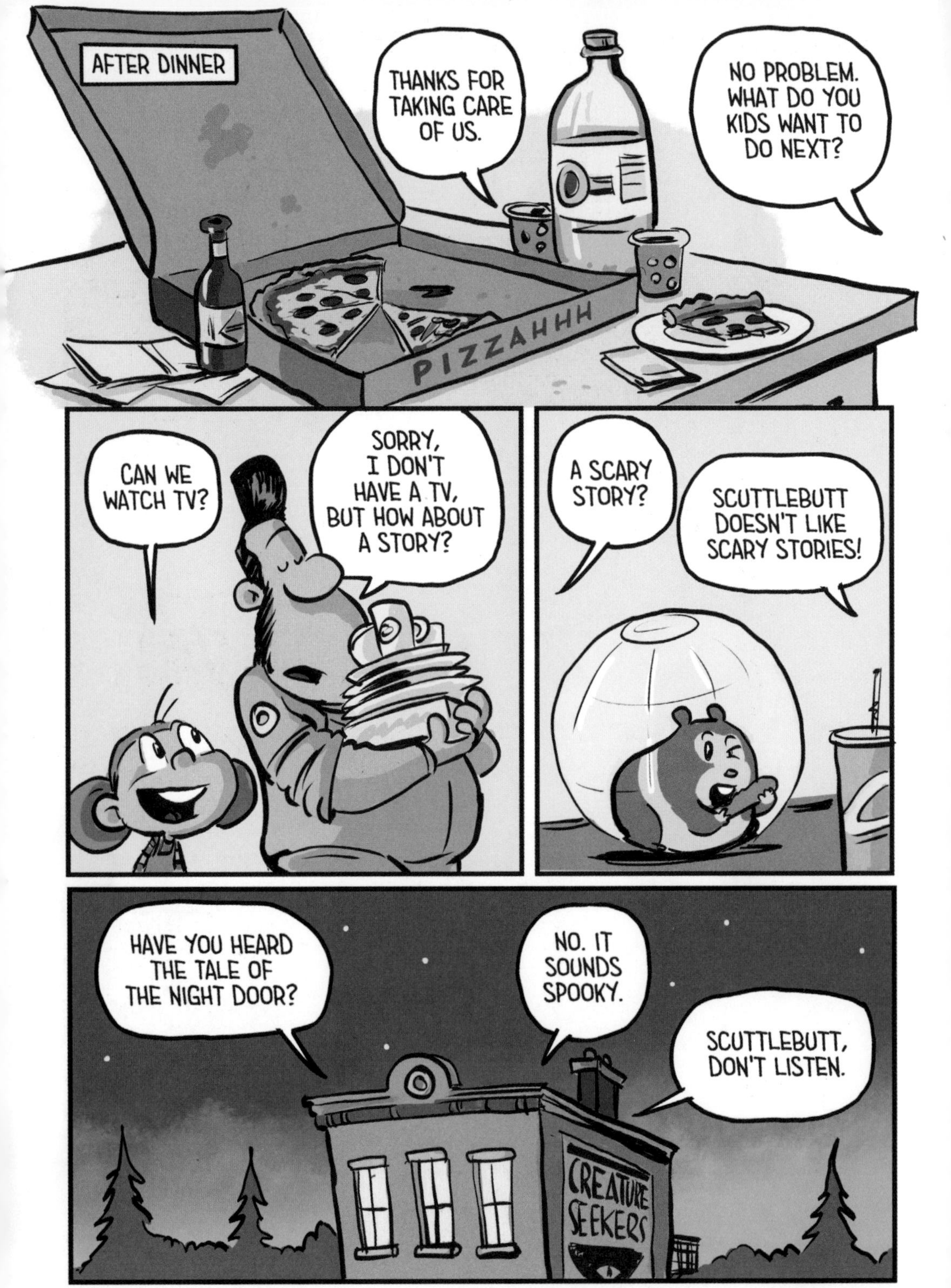
AFTER DINNER
THANKS FOR TAKING CARE OF US.
NO PROBLEM. WHAT DO YOU KIDS WANT TO DO NEXT?
PIZZAHHH
CAN WE WATCH TV?
SORRY, I DON'T HAVE A TV, BUT HOW ABOUT A STORY?
A SCARY STORY?
SCUTTLEBUTT DOESN'T LIKE SCARY STORIES!
HAVE YOU HEARD THE TALE OF THE NIGHT DOOR?
NO. IT SOUNDS SPOOKY.
SCUTTLEBUTT, DON'T LISTEN.
CREATURE SEEKERS

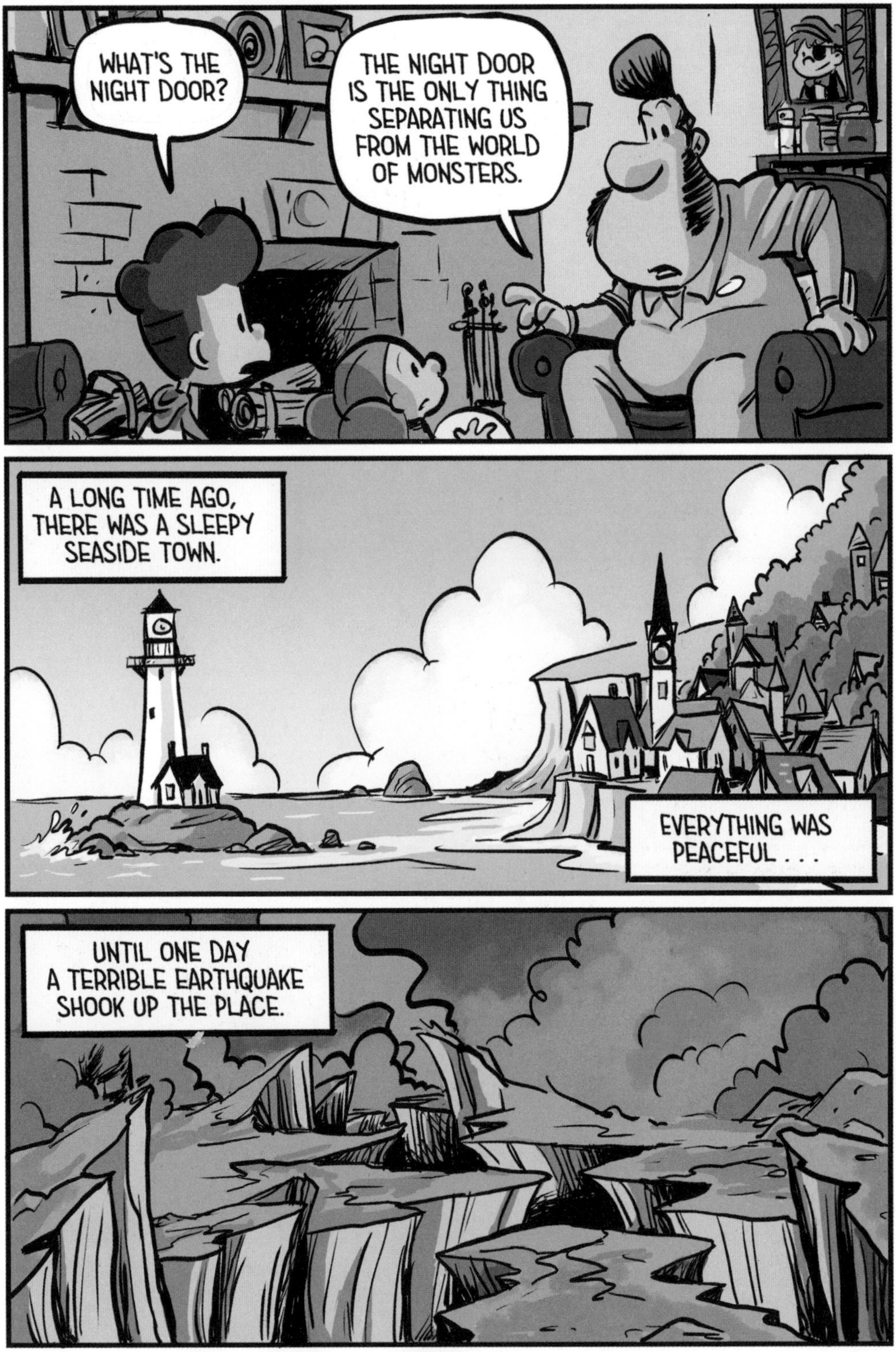
WHAT'S THE NIGHT DOOR?
THE NIGHT DOOR IS THE ONLY THING SEPARATING US FROM THE WORLD OF MONSTERS.
A LONG TIME AGO, THERE WAS A SLEEPY SEASIDE TOWN.
EVERYTHING WAS PEACEFUL . . .
UNTIL ONE DAY A TERRIBLE EARTHQUAKE SHOOK UP THE PLACE.

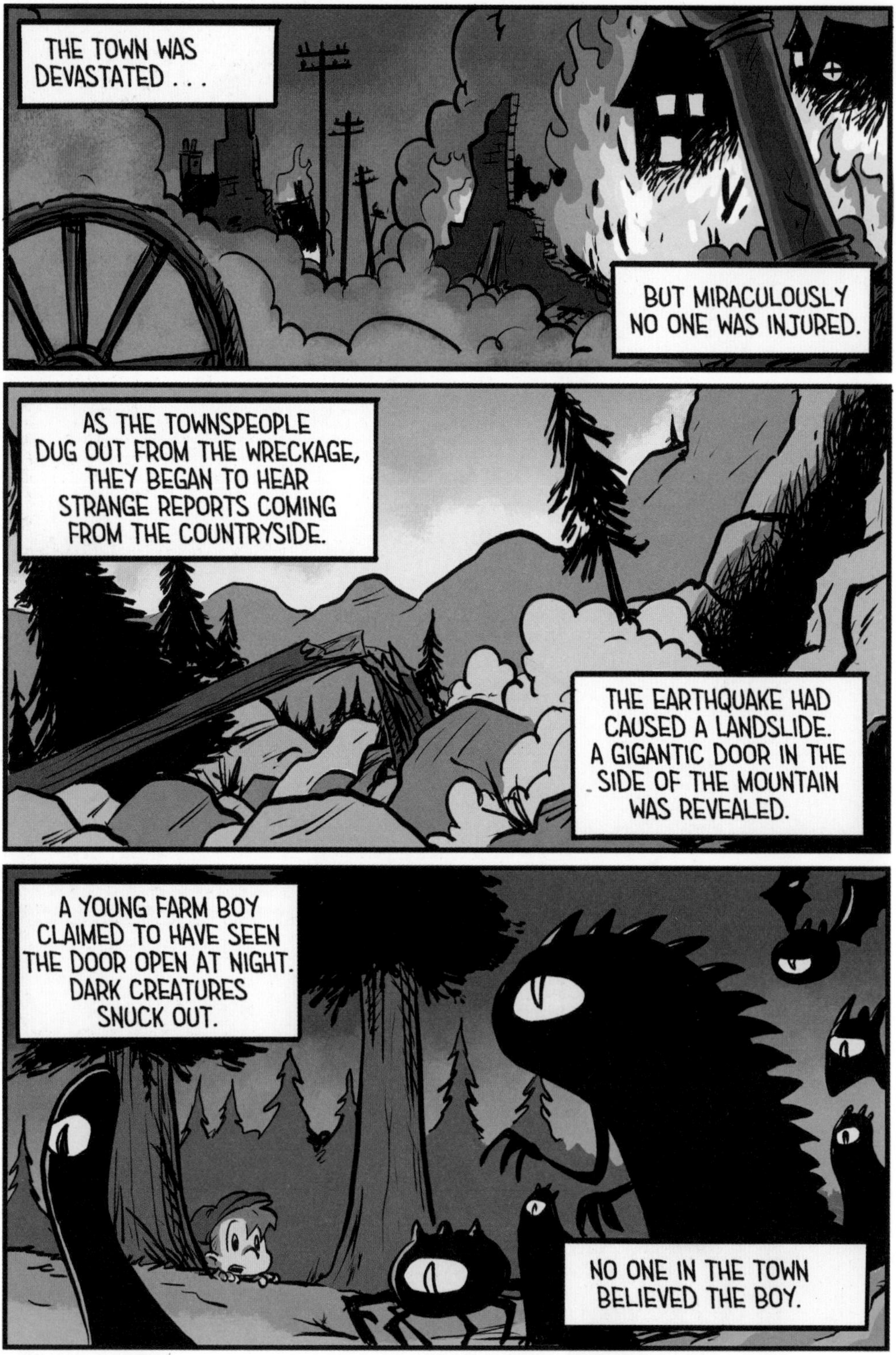
THE TOWN WAS DEVASTATED . . .
BUT MIRACULOUSLY NO ONE WAS INJURED.
AS THE TOWNSPEOPLE DUG OUT FROM THE WRECKAGE, THEY BEGAN TO HEAR STRANGE REPORTS COMING FROM THE COUNTRYSIDE.
THE EARTHQUAKE HAD CAUSED A LANDSLIDE. A GIGANTIC DOOR IN THE SIDE OF THE MOUNTAIN WAS REVEALED.
A YOUNG FARM BOY CLAIMED TO HAVE SEEN THE DOOR OPEN AT NIGHT. DARK CREATURES SNUCK OUT.
NO ONE IN THE TOWN BELIEVED THE BOY.

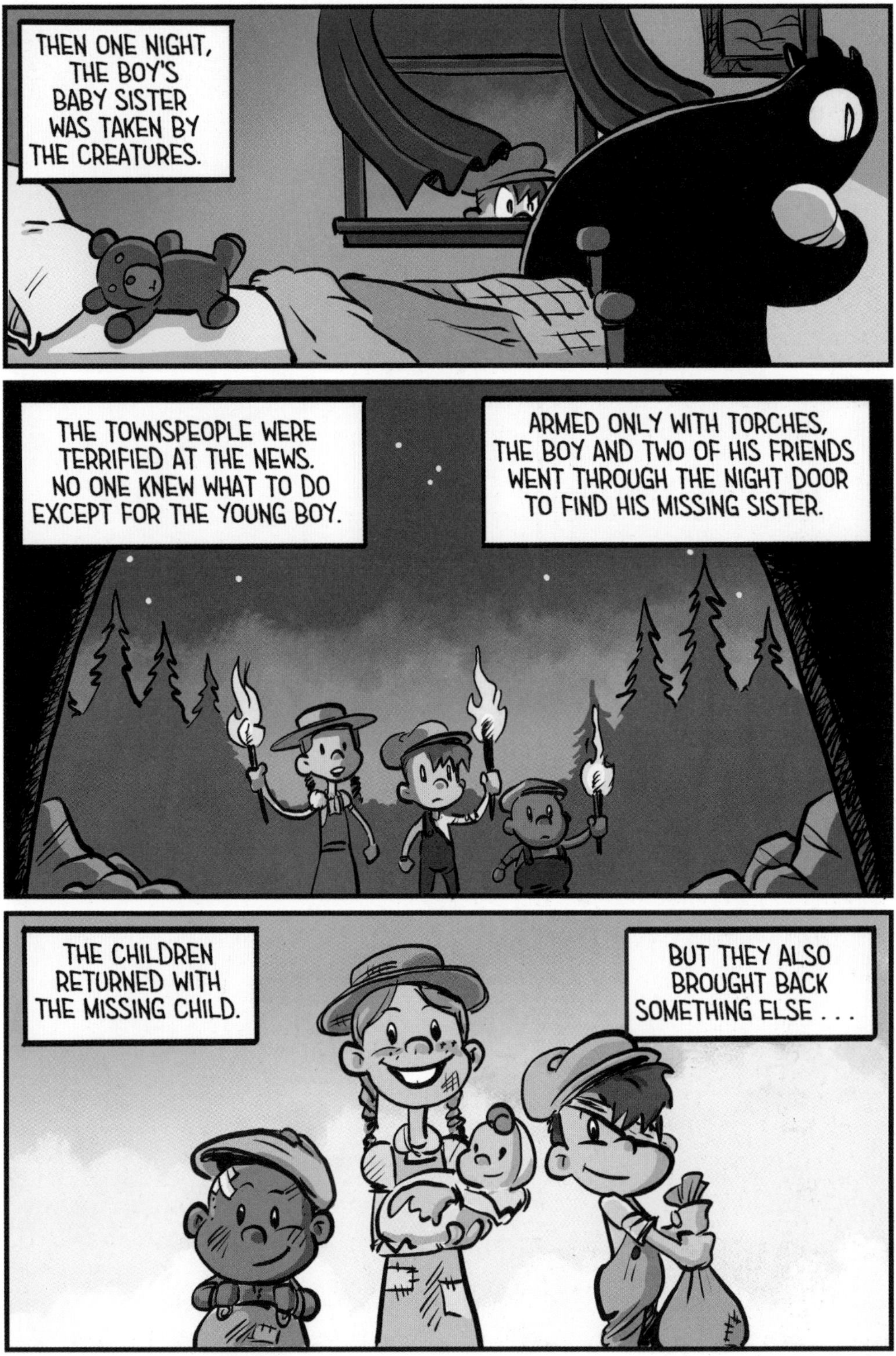
THEN ONE NIGHT, THE BOY'S BABY SISTER WAS TAKEN BY THE CREATURES.
THE TOWNSPEOPLE WERE TERRIFIED AT THE NEWS. NO ONE KNEW WHAT TO DO EXCEPT FOR THE YOUNG BOY.
ARMED ONLY WITH TORCHES, THE BOY AND TWO OF HIS FRIENDS WENT THROUGH THE NIGHT DOOR TO FIND HIS MISSING SISTER.
THE CHILDREN RETURNED WITH THE MISSING CHILD.
BUT THEY ALSO BROUGHT BACK SOMETHING ELSE . . .

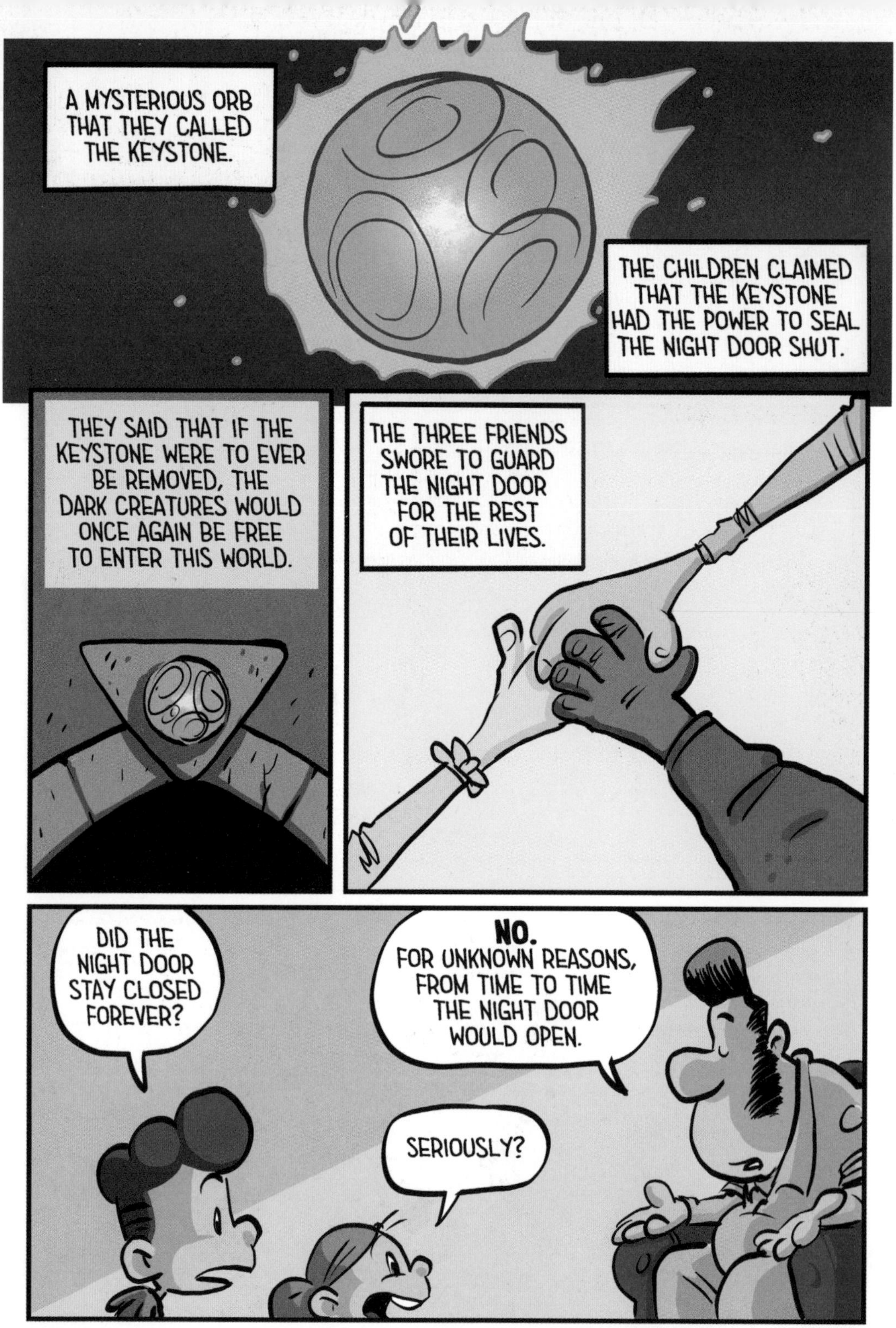

A MYSTERIOUS ORB THAT THEY CALLED THE KEYSTONE.
THE CHILDREN CLAIMED THAT THE KEYSTONE HAD THE POWER TO SEAL THE NIGHT DOOR SHUT.
THEY SAID THAT IF THE KEYSTONE WERE TO EVER BE REMOVED, THE DARK CREATURES WOULD ONCE AGAIN BE FREE TO ENTER THIS WORLD.
THE THREE FRIENDS SWORE TO GUARD THE NIGHT DOOR FOR THE REST OF THEIR LIVES.
DID THE NIGHT DOOR STAY CLOSED FOREVER?
NO. FOR UNKNOWN REASONS, FROM TIME TO TIME THE NIGHT DOOR WOULD OPEN.
SERIOUSLY?

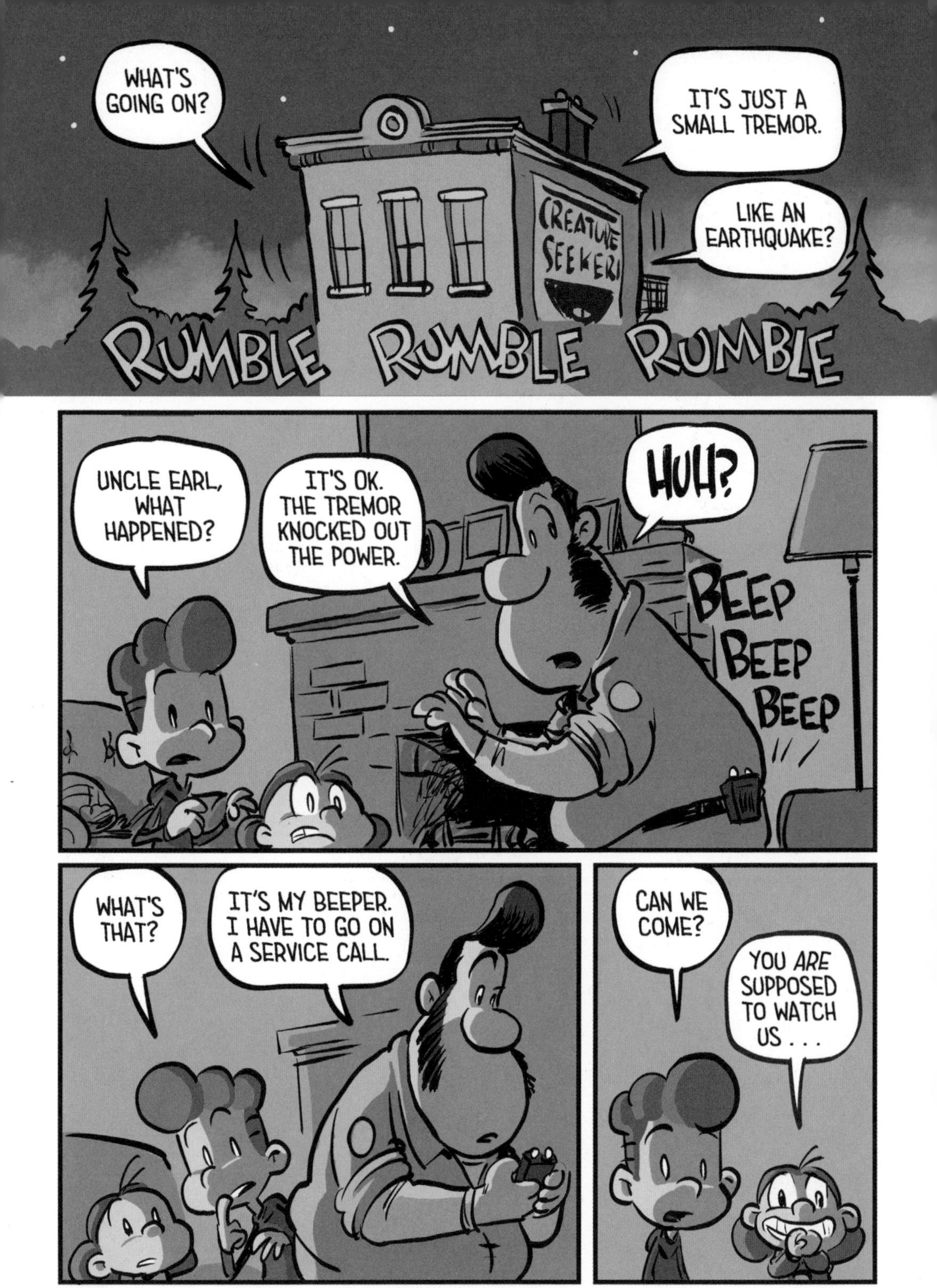
WHAT'S GOING ON?
IT'S JUST A SMALL TREMOR.
CREATURE SEEKER!
LIKE AN EARTHQUAKE?
RUMBLE RUMBLE RUMBLE
UNCLE EARL, WHAT HAPPENED?
IT'S OK. THE TREMOR KNOCKED OUT THE POWER.
HUH?
BEEP BEEP BEEP
WHAT'S THAT?
IT'S MY BEEPER. I HAVE TO GO ON A SERVICE CALL.
CAN WE COME?
YOU *ARE* SUPPOSED TO WATCH US . . .

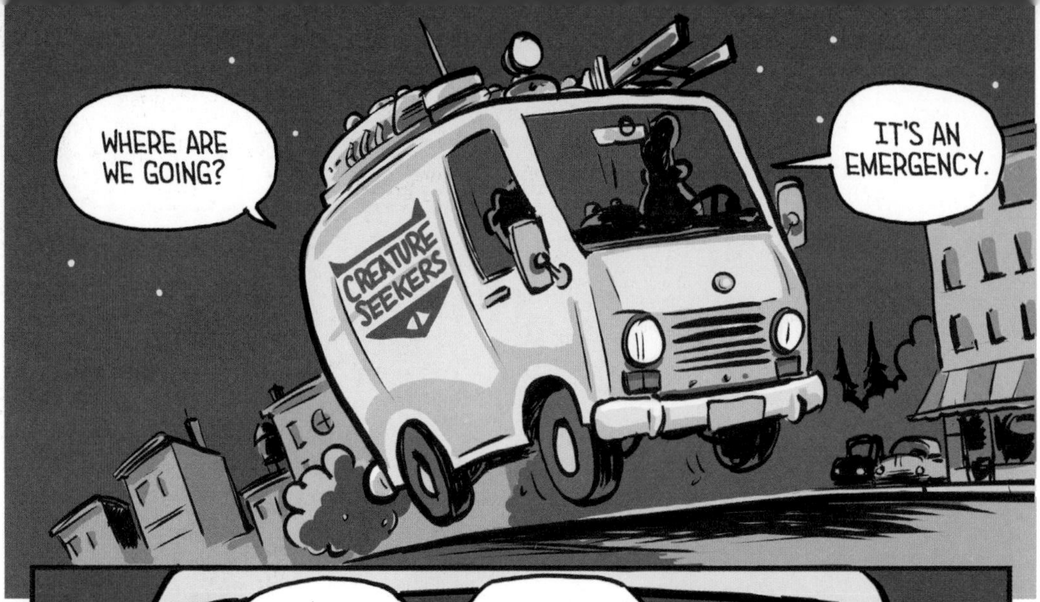
WHERE ARE WE GOING?
IT'S AN EMERGENCY.
CREATURE SEEKERS

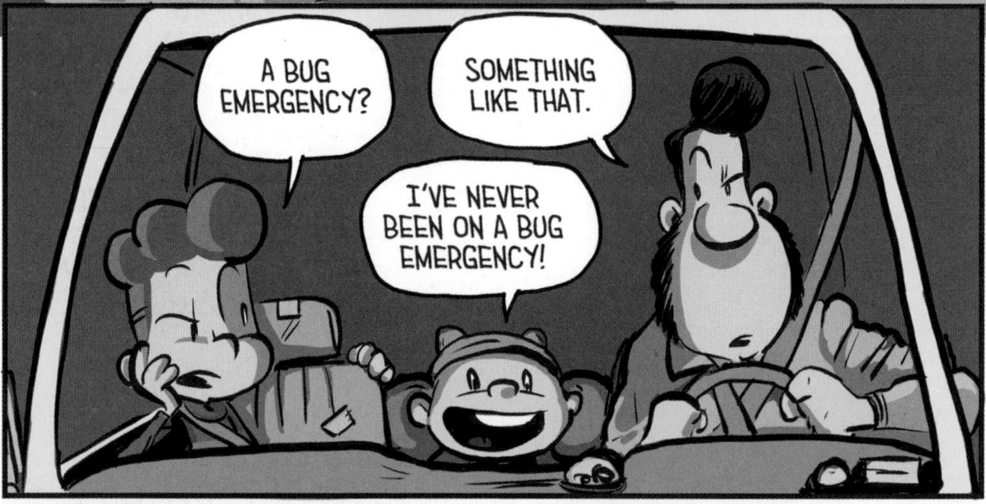
A BUG EMERGENCY?
SOMETHING LIKE THAT.
I'VE NEVER BEEN ON A BUG EMERGENCY!

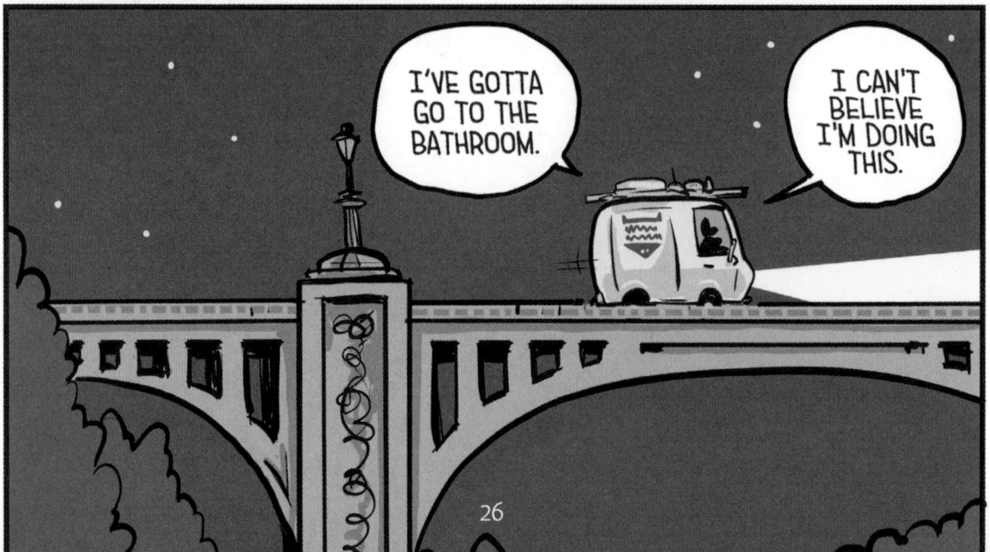
I'VE GOTTA GO TO THE BATHROOM.
I CAN'T BELIEVE I'M DOING THIS.

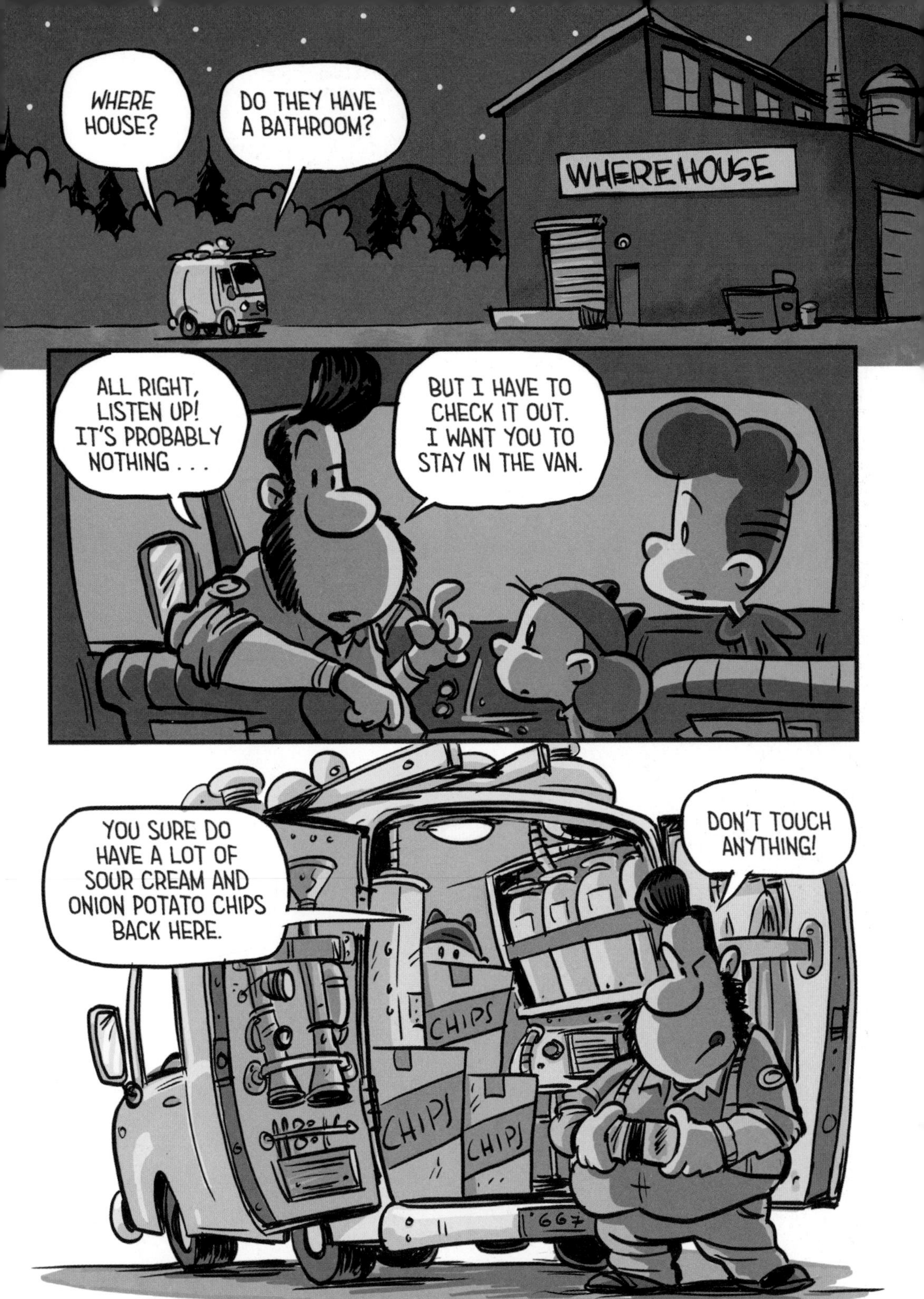
WHERE HOUSE?
DO THEY HAVE A BATHROOM?
WHEREHOUSE
ALL RIGHT, LISTEN UP! IT'S PROBABLY NOTHING . . .
BUT I HAVE TO CHECK IT OUT. I WANT YOU TO STAY IN THE VAN.
YOU SURE DO HAVE A LOT OF SOUR CREAM AND ONION POTATO CHIPS BACK HERE.
DON'T TOUCH ANYTHING!
CHIPS
CHIPS
CHIPS
667

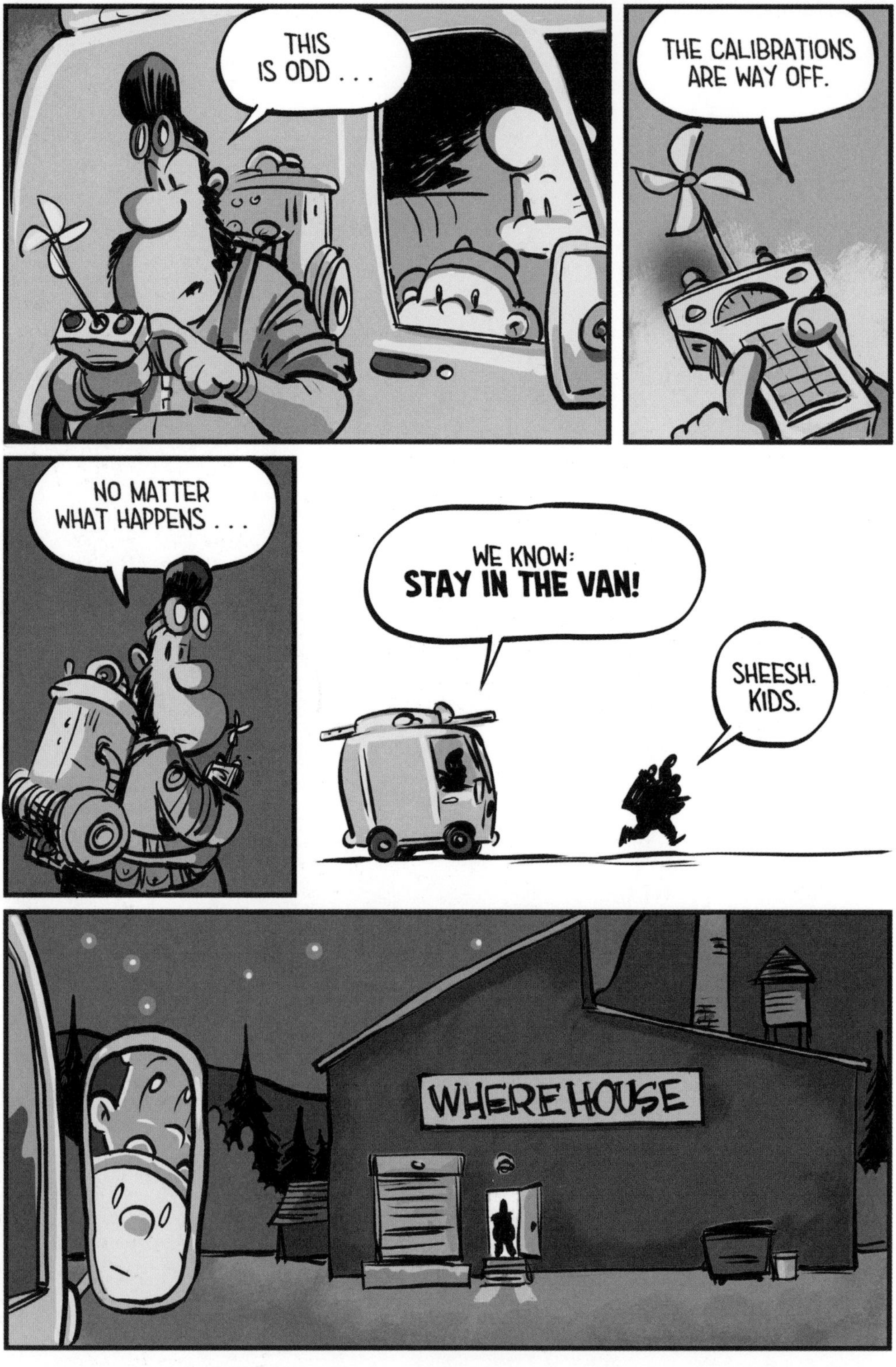
THIS IS ODD . . .
THE CALIBRATIONS ARE WAY OFF.
NO MATTER WHAT HAPPENS . . .
WE KNOW: **STAY IN THE VAN!**
SHEESH. KIDS.
WHEREHOUSE

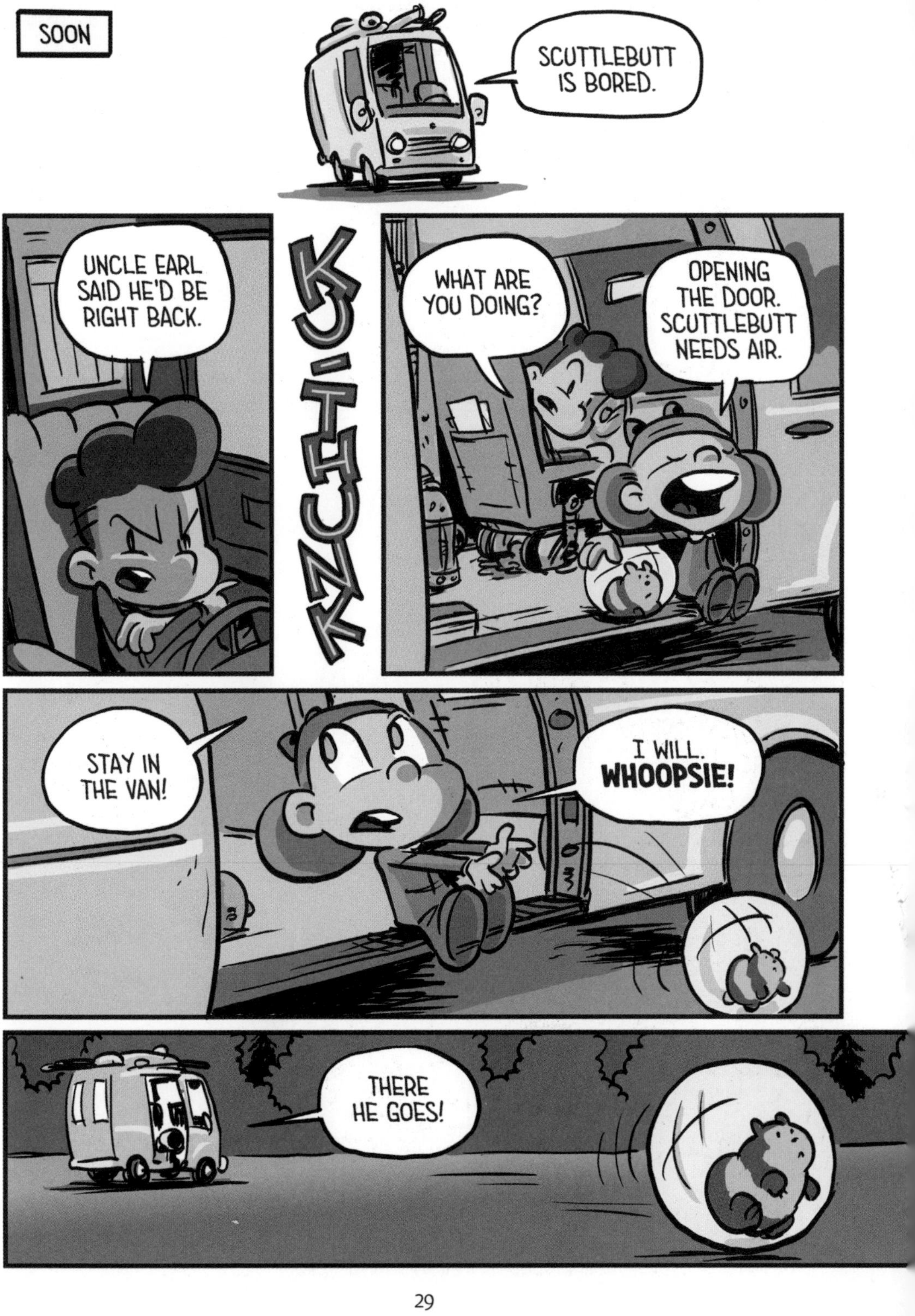
SOON
SCUTTLEBUTT IS BORED.
UNCLE EARL SAID HE'D BE RIGHT BACK.
KA-THUNK
WHAT ARE YOU DOING?
OPENING THE DOOR. SCUTTLEBUTT NEEDS AIR.
STAY IN THE VAN!
I WILL. **WHOOPSIE!**
THERE HE GOES!

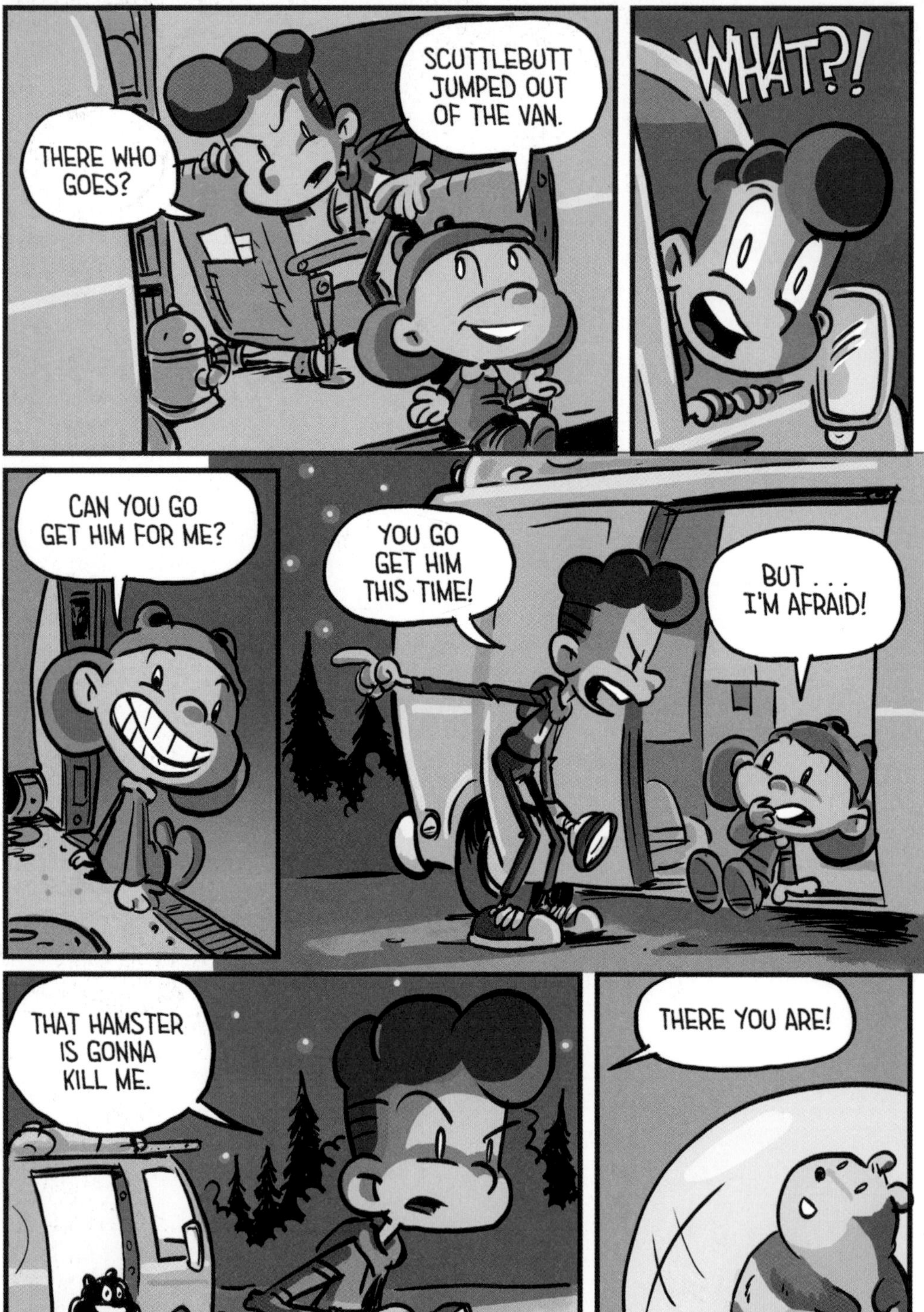
SCUTTLEBUTT JUMPED OUT OF THE VAN.
THERE WHO GOES?
WHAT?!
CAN YOU GO GET HIM FOR ME?
YOU GO GET HIM THIS TIME!
BUT . . . I'M AFRAID!
THAT HAMSTER IS GONNA KILL ME.
THERE YOU ARE!

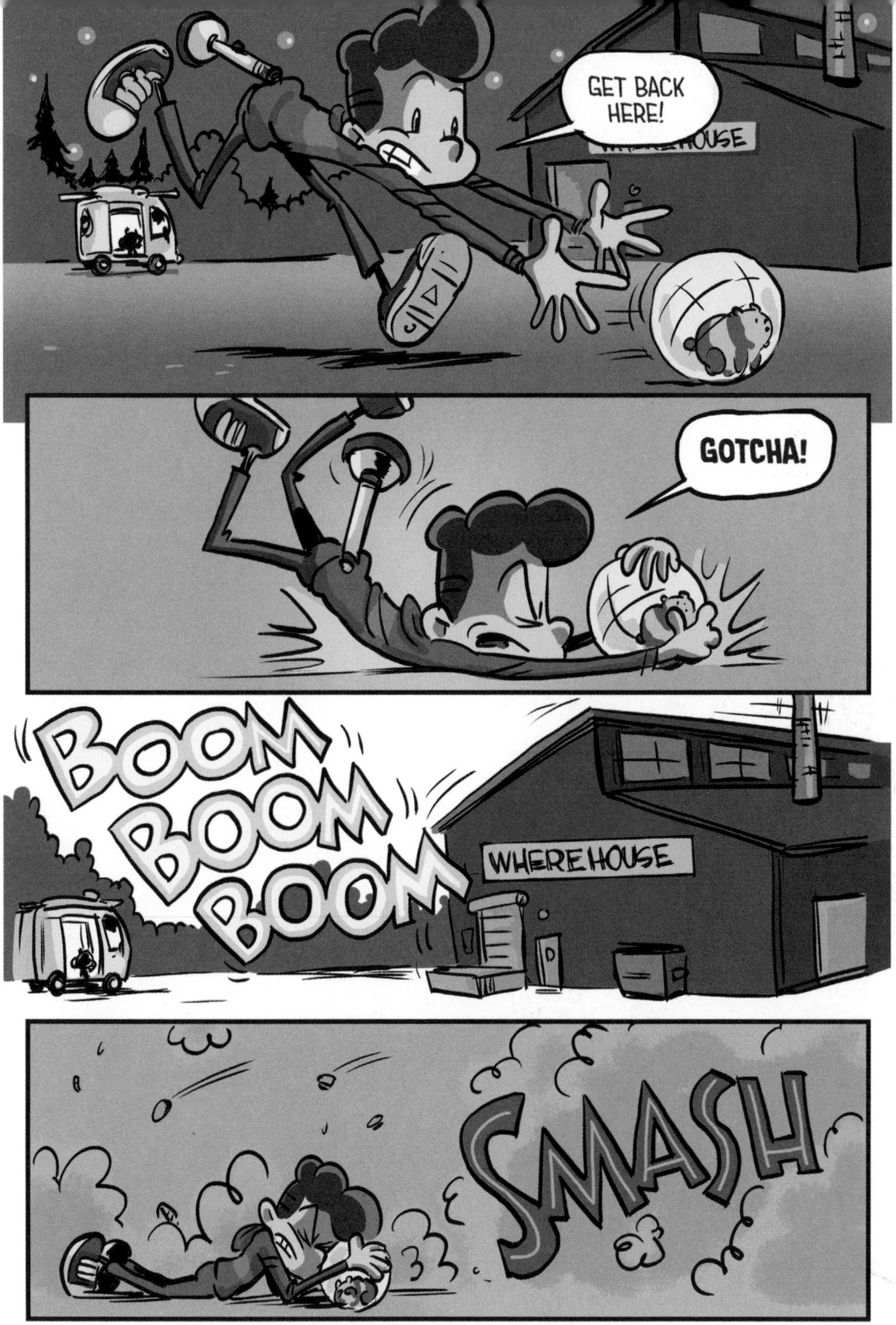
GET BACK HERE!
WHEREHOUSE
GOTCHA!
BOOM BOOM BOOM
WHEREHOUSE
SMASH

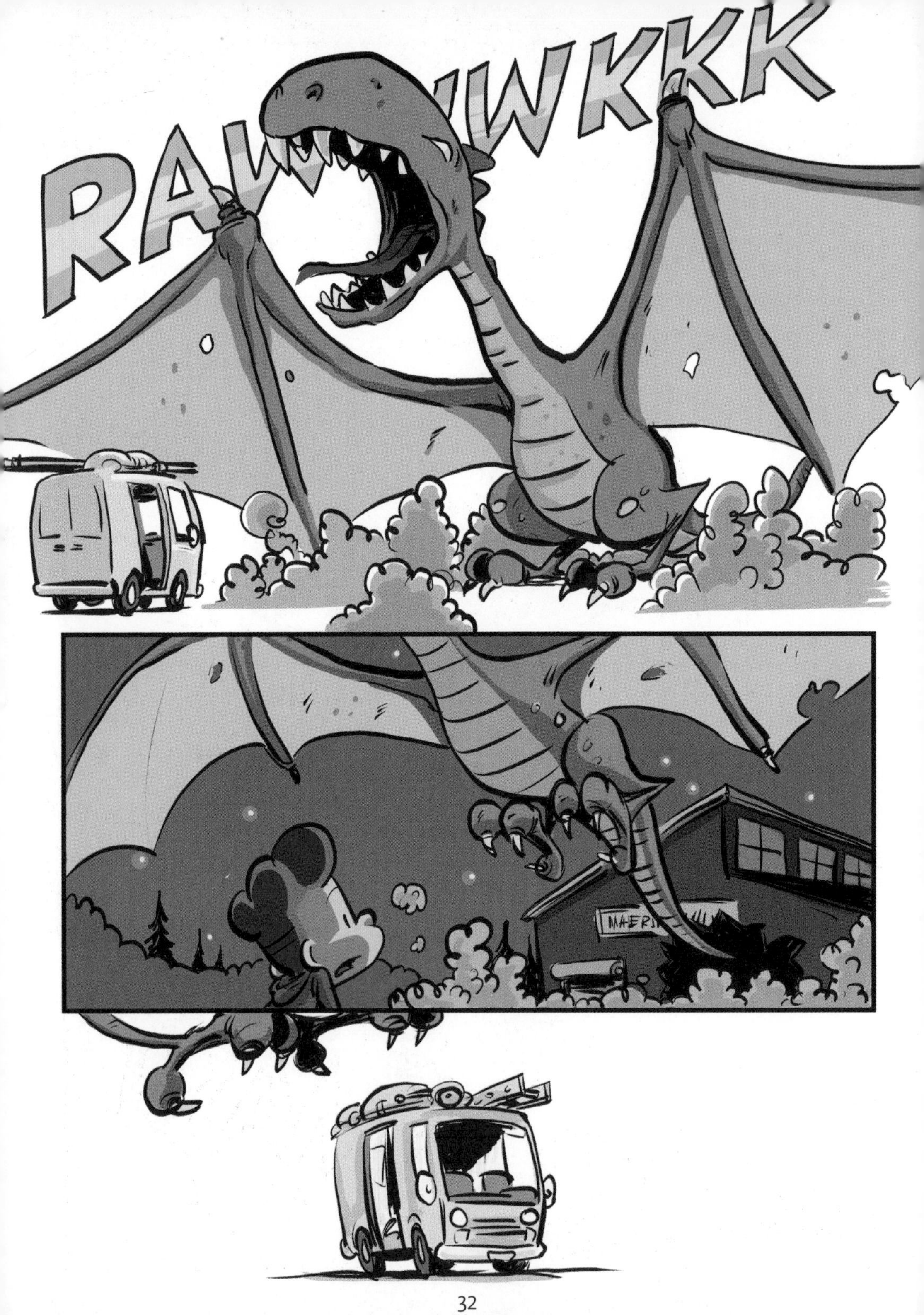
RA WKKK

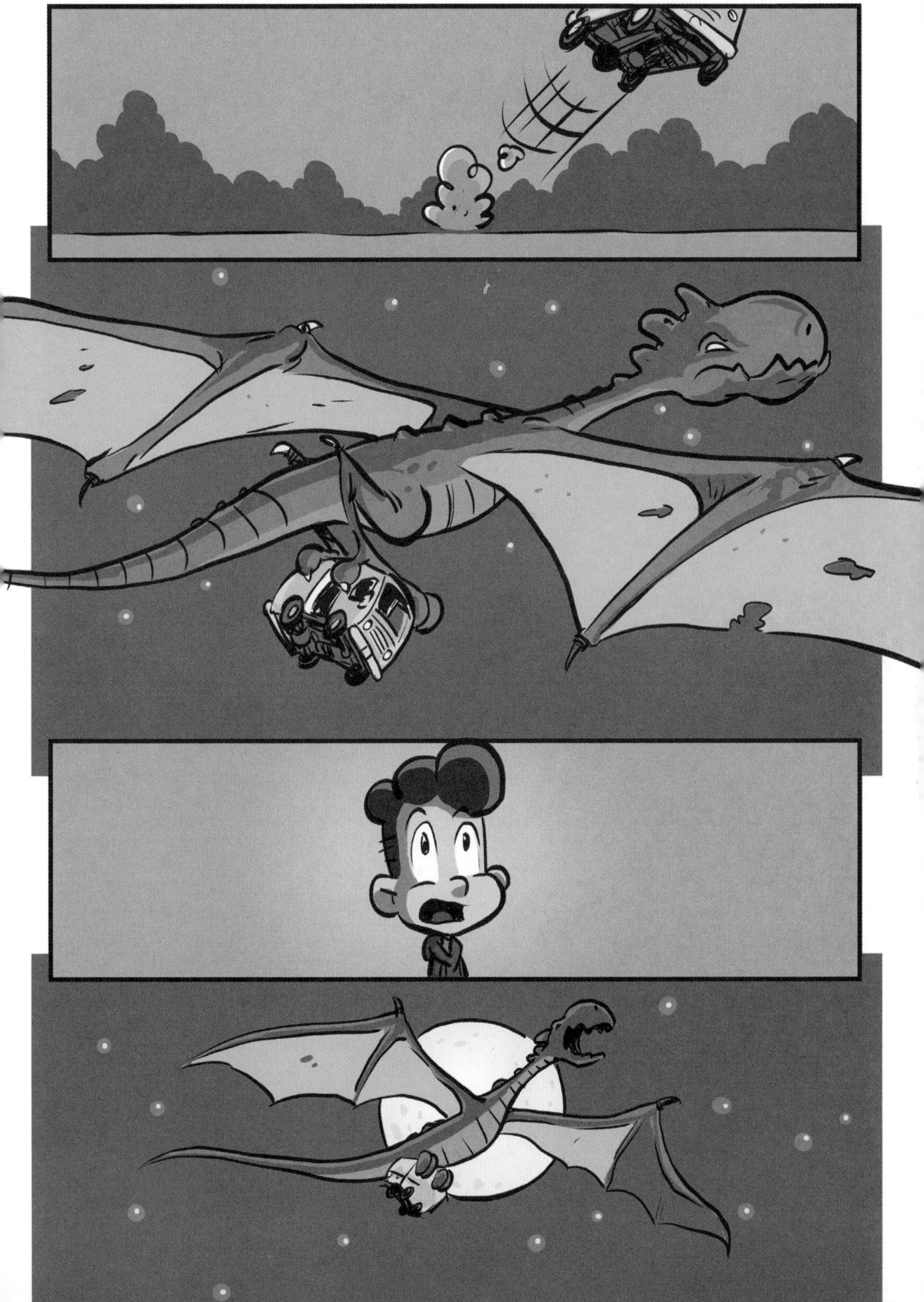

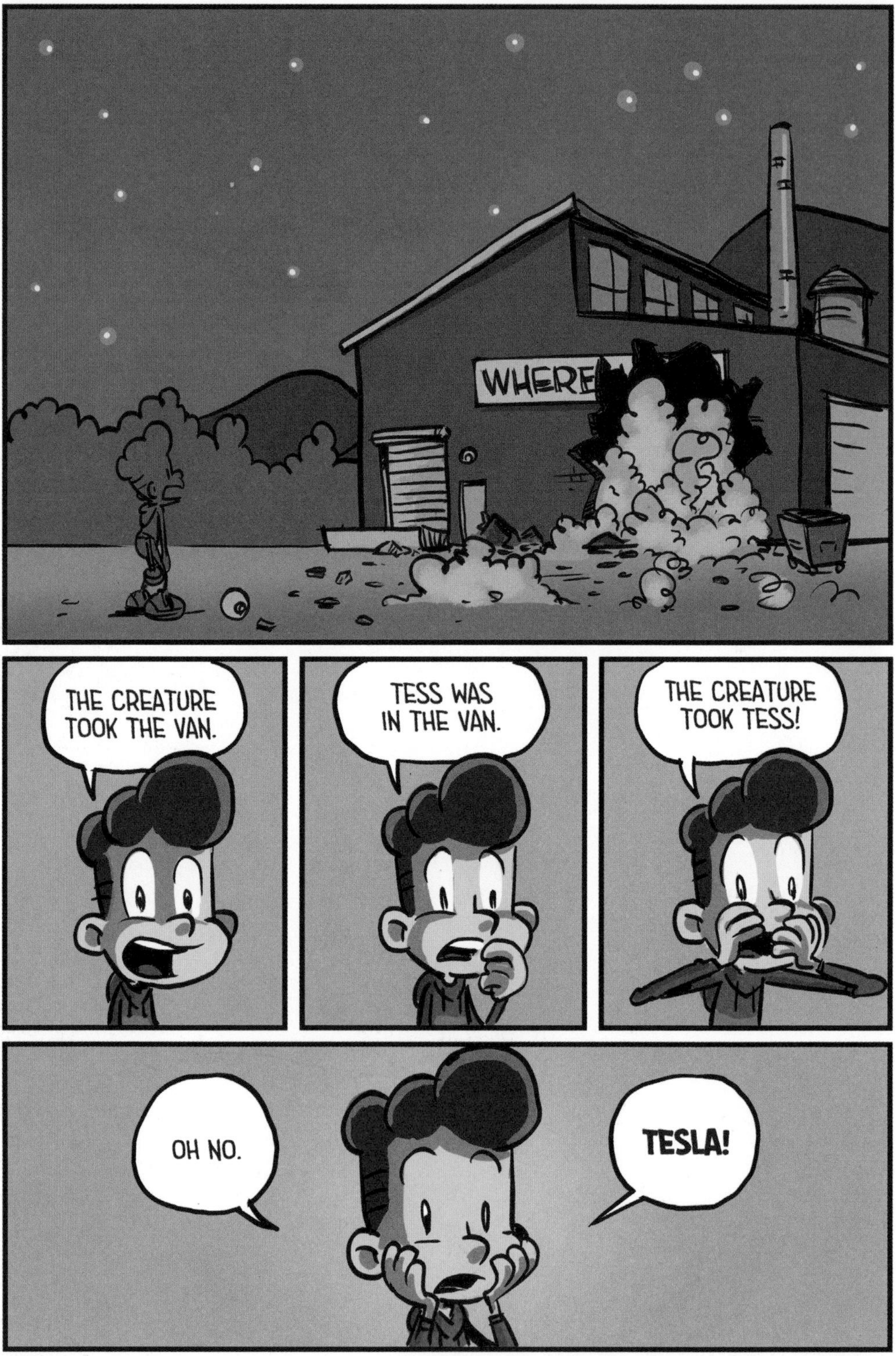
WHERE
THE CREATURE TOOK THE VAN.
TESS WAS IN THE VAN.
THE CREATURE TOOK TESS!
OH NO.
TESLA!

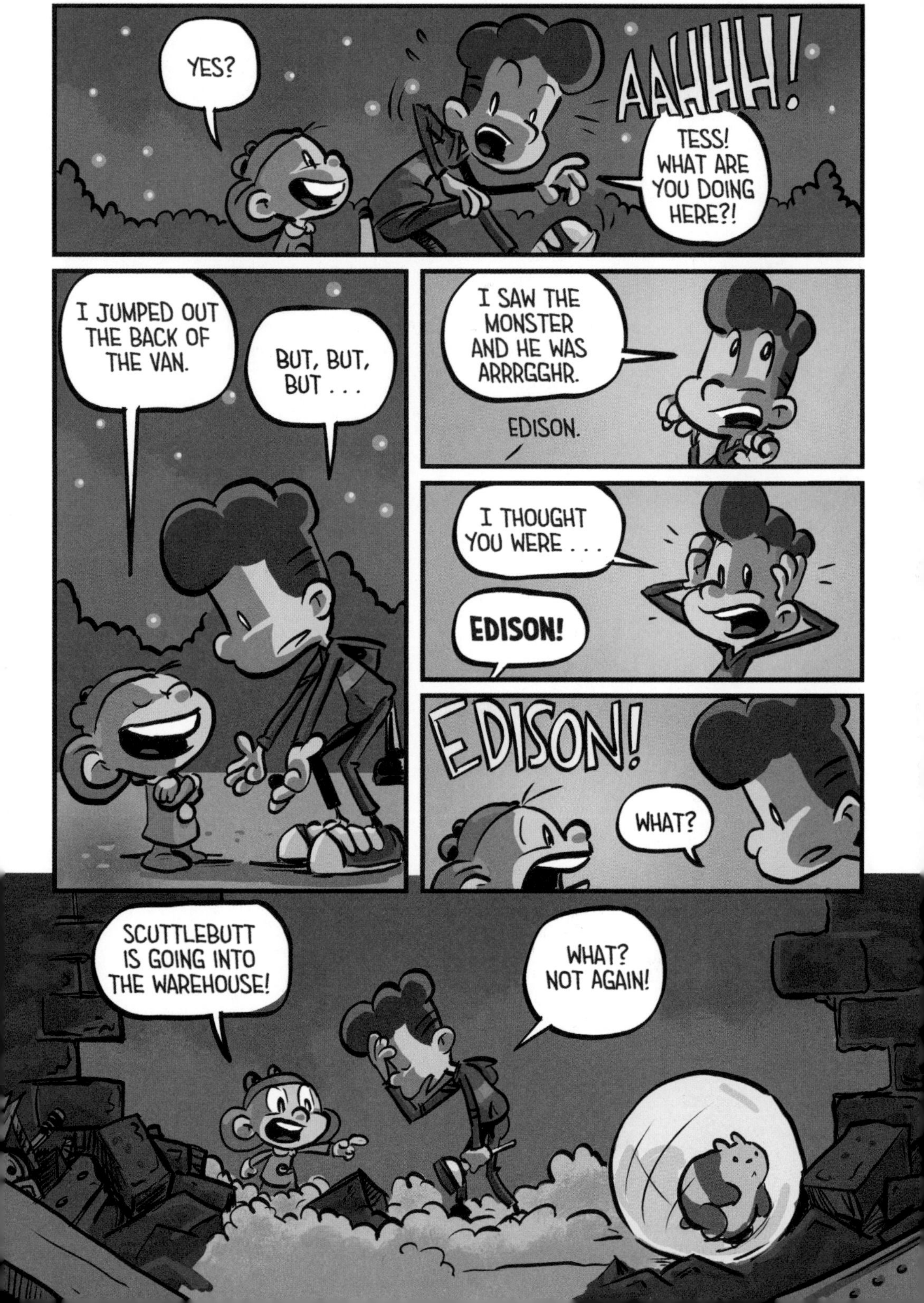
YES?
AAHHH!
TESS! WHAT ARE YOU DOING HERE?!
I JUMPED OUT THE BACK OF THE VAN.
BUT, BUT, BUT . . .
I SAW THE MONSTER AND HE WAS ARRRGGHR.
EDISON.
I THOUGHT YOU WERE . . .
EDISON!
EDISON!
WHAT?
SCUTTLEBUTT IS GOING INTO THE WAREHOUSE!
WHAT? NOT AGAIN!

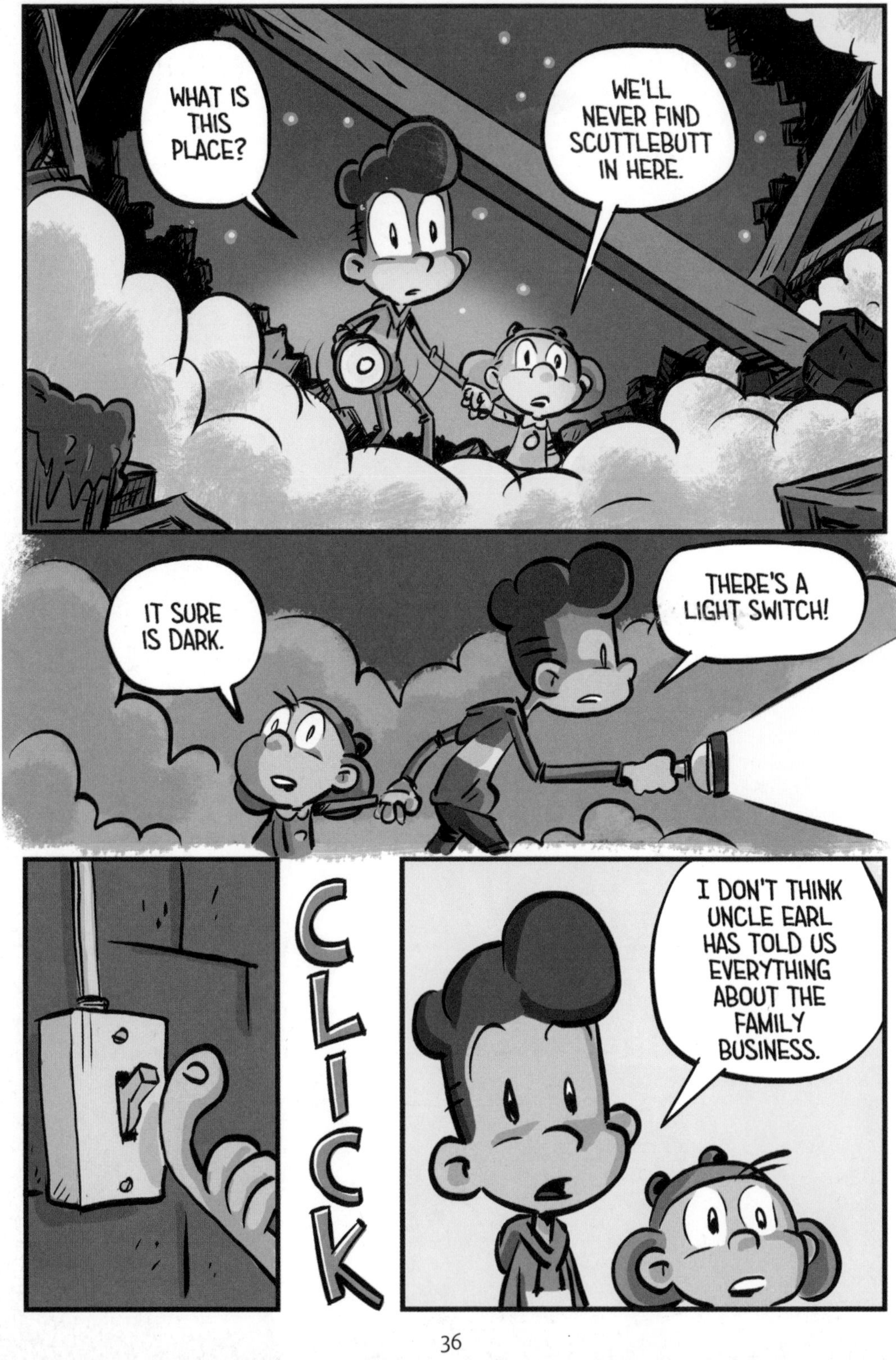
WHAT IS THIS PLACE?
WE'LL NEVER FIND SCUTTLEBUTT IN HERE.
IT SURE IS DARK.
THERE'S A LIGHT SWITCH!
CLICK
I DON'T THINK UNCLE EARL HAS TOLD US EVERYTHING ABOUT THE FAMILY BUSINESS.

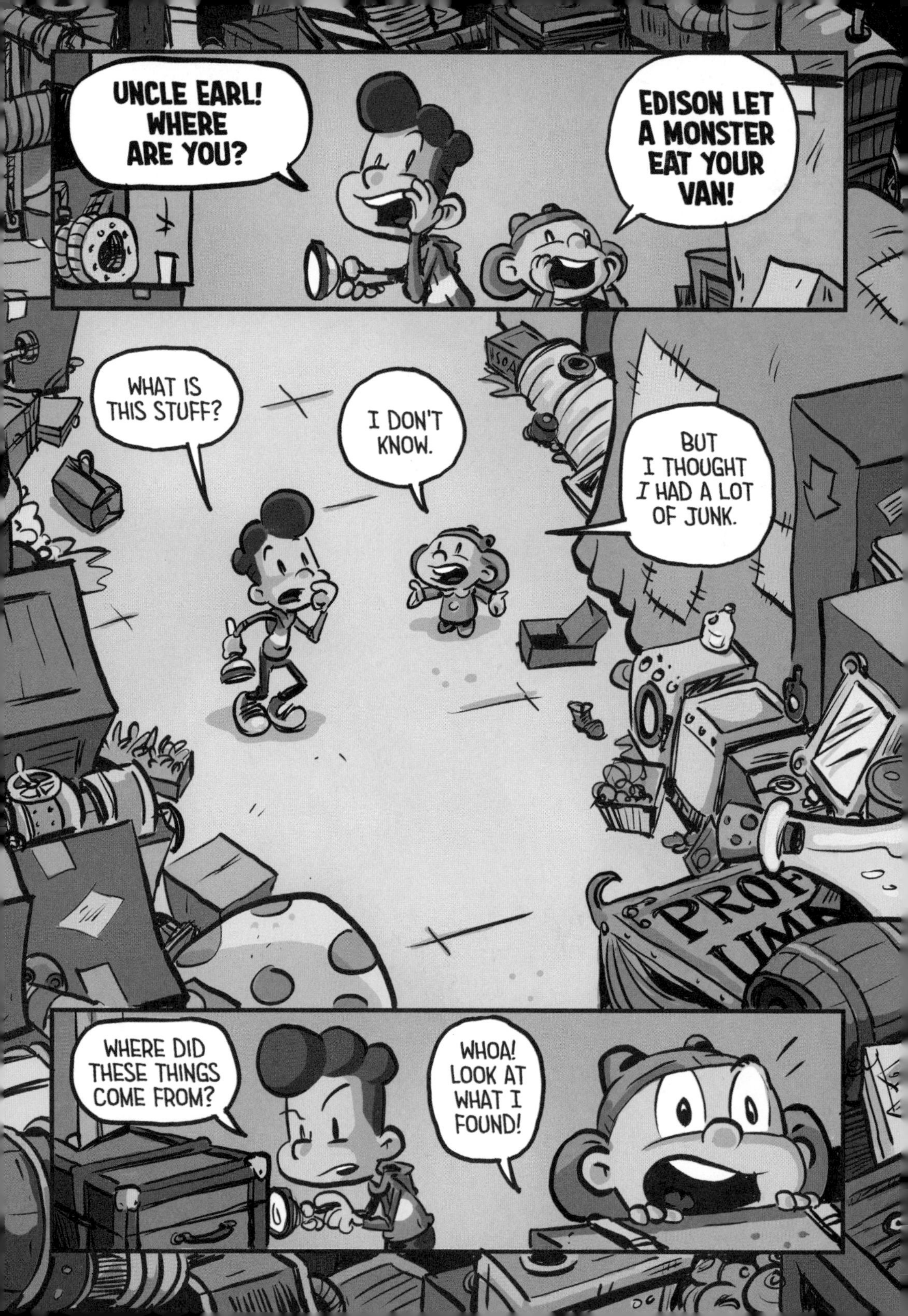
UNCLE EARL! WHERE ARE YOU?
EDISON LET A MONSTER EAT YOUR VAN!
WHAT IS THIS STUFF?
I DON'T KNOW.
BUT I THOUGHT *I* HAD A LOT OF JUNK.
WHERE DID THESE THINGS COME FROM?
WHOA! LOOK AT WHAT I FOUND!

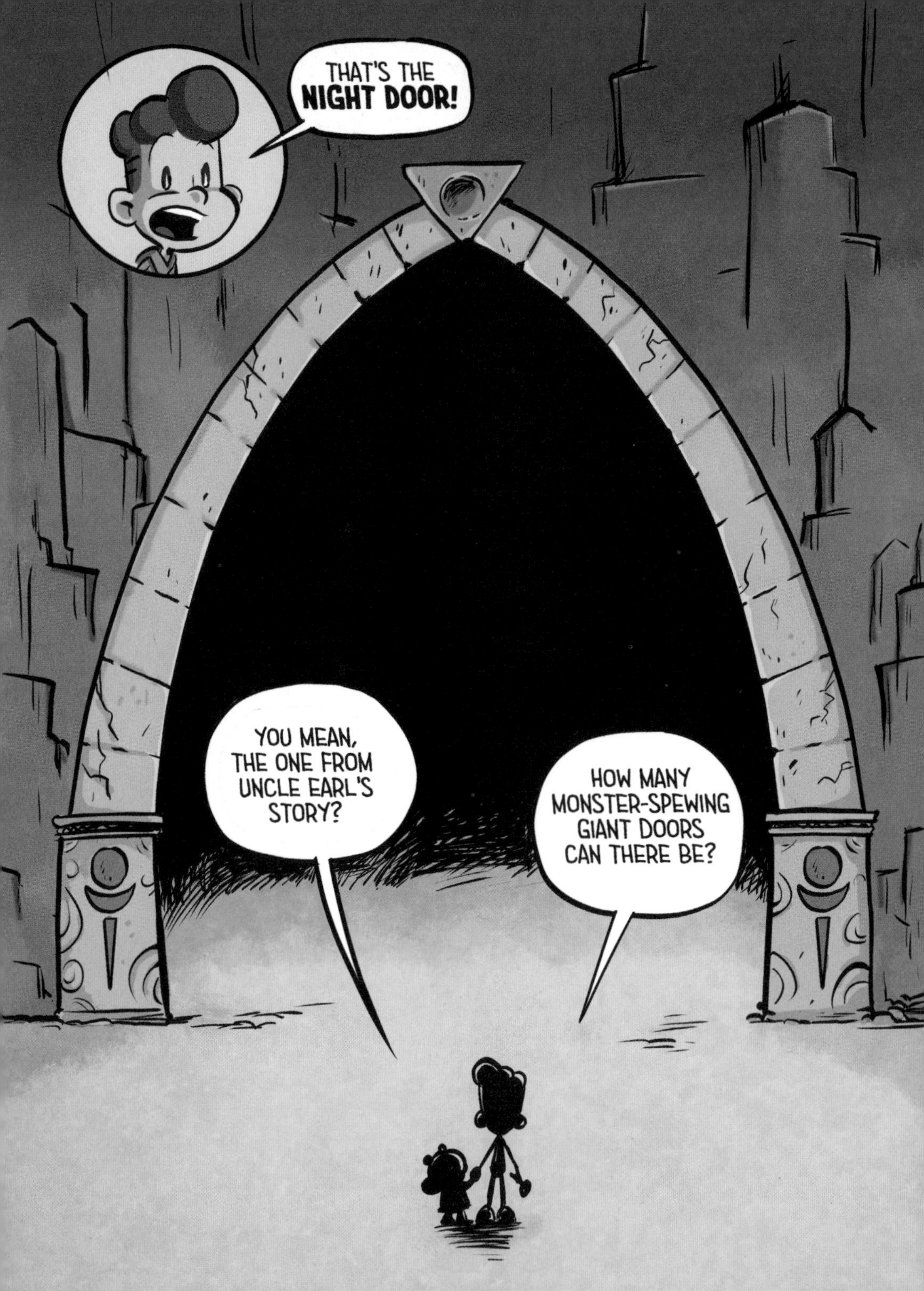
THAT'S THE **NIGHT DOOR!**
YOU MEAN, THE ONE FROM UNCLE EARL'S STORY?
HOW MANY MONSTER-SPEWING GIANT DOORS CAN THERE BE?

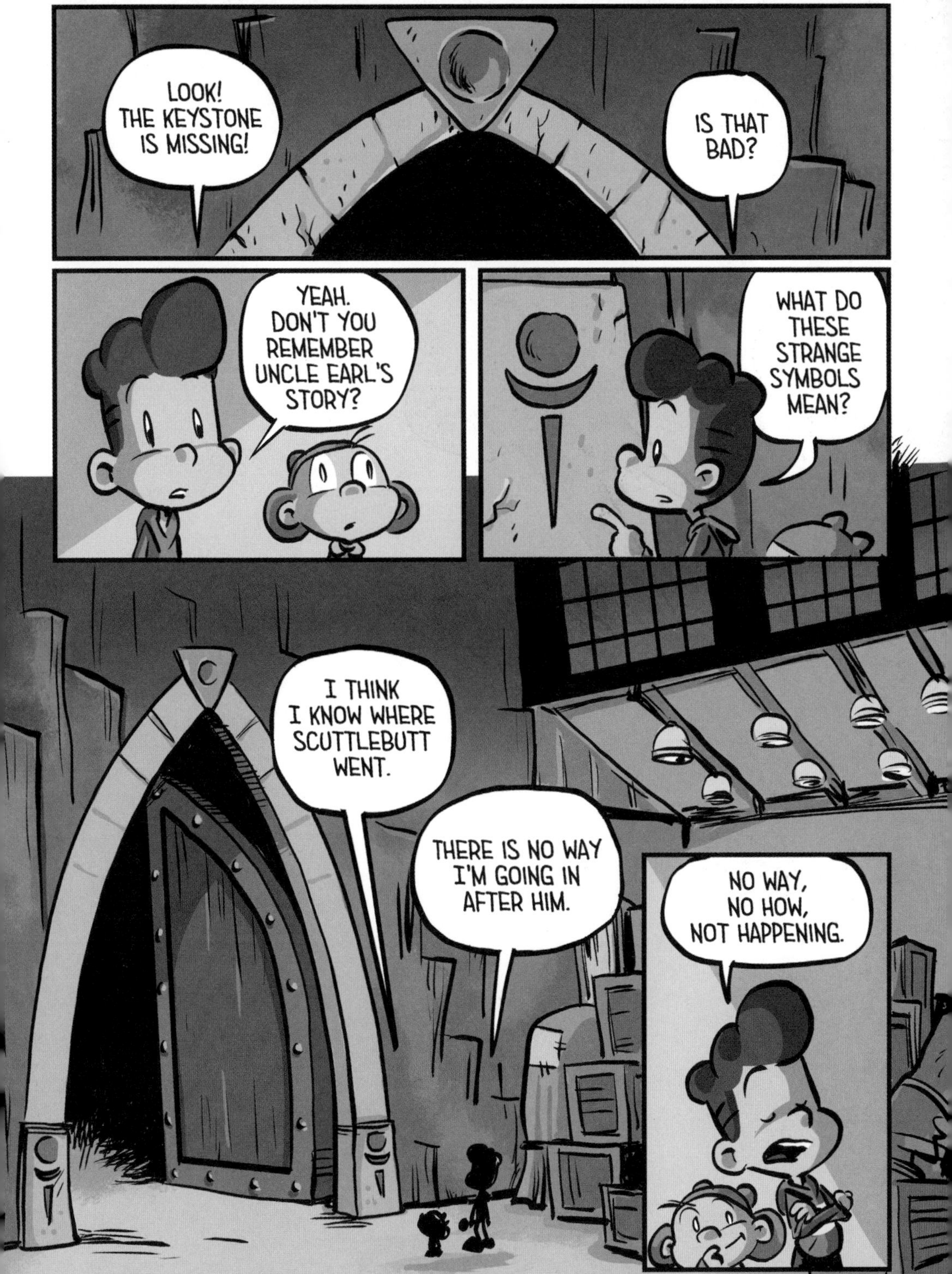
LOOK! THE KEYSTONE IS MISSING!
IS THAT BAD?
YEAH. DON'T YOU REMEMBER UNCLE EARL'S STORY?
WHAT DO THESE STRANGE SYMBOLS MEAN?
I THINK I KNOW WHERE SCUTTLEBUTT WENT.
THERE IS NO WAY I'M GOING IN AFTER HIM.
NO WAY, NO HOW, NOT HAPPENING.

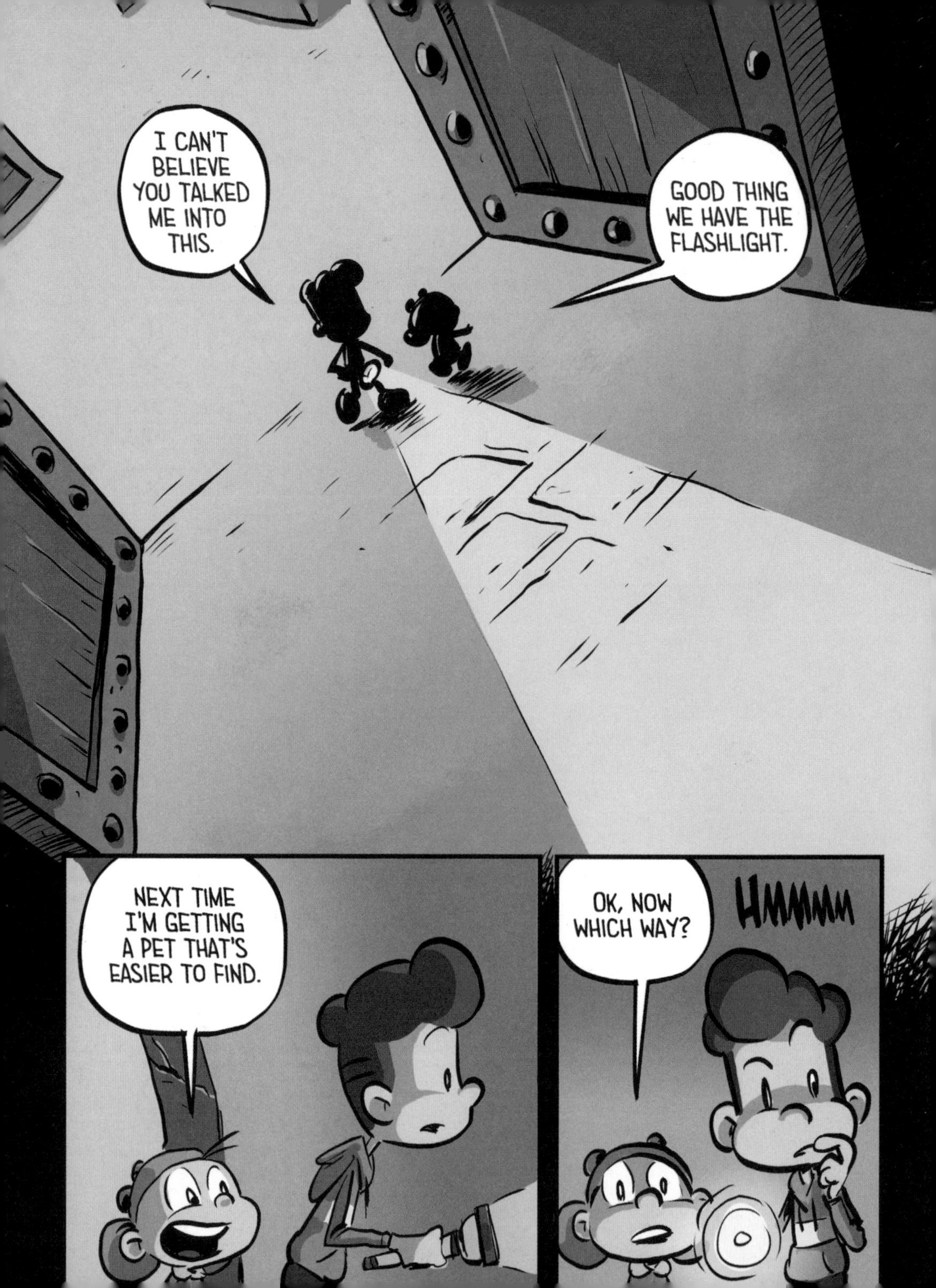
I CAN'T BELIEVE YOU TALKED ME INTO THIS.
GOOD THING WE HAVE THE FLASHLIGHT.
NEXT TIME I'M GETTING A PET THAT'S EASIER TO FIND.
OK, NOW WHICH WAY?
HMMMM

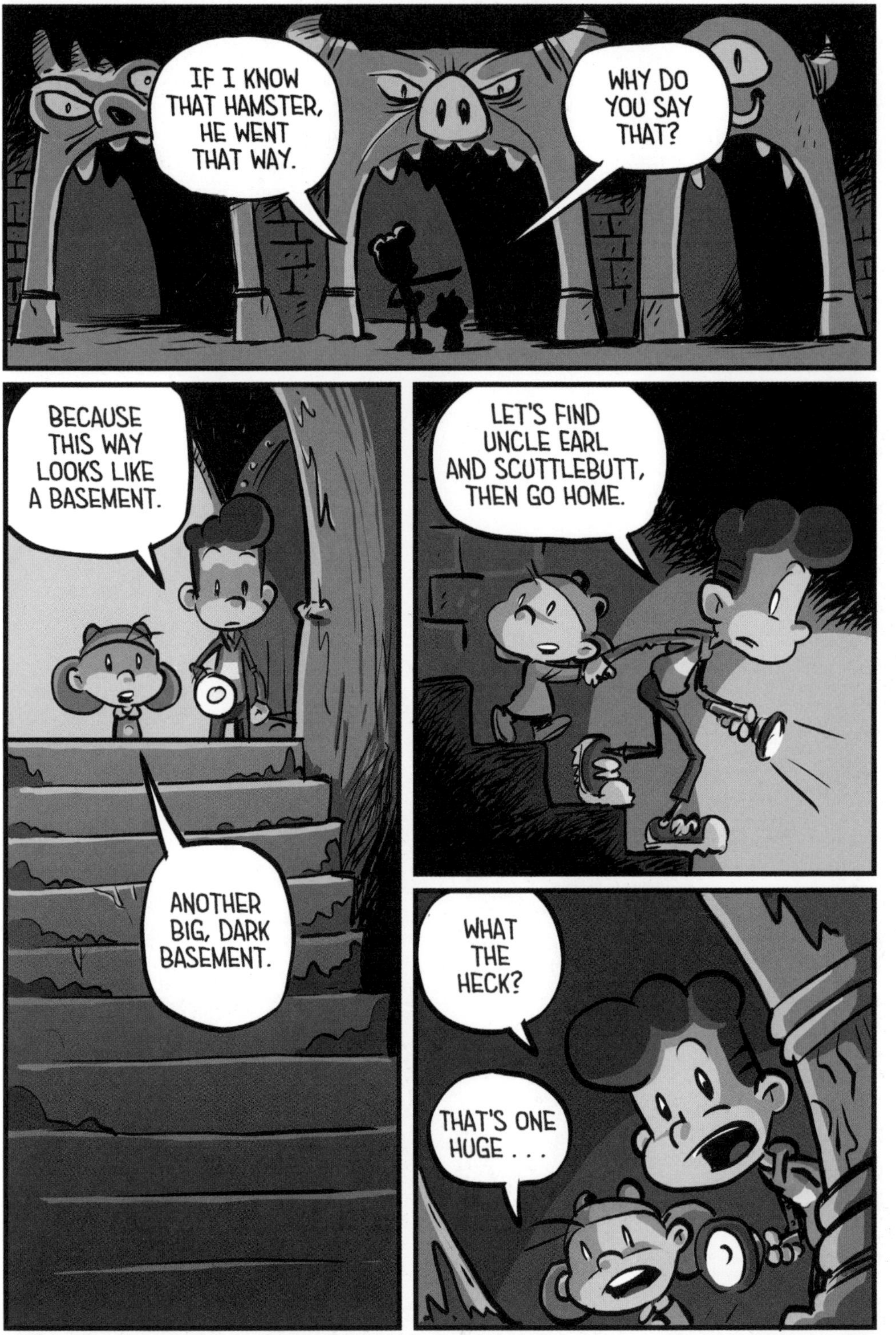
IF I KNOW THAT HAMSTER, HE WENT THAT WAY.
WHY DO YOU SAY THAT?
BECAUSE THIS WAY LOOKS LIKE A BASEMENT.
ANOTHER BIG, DARK BASEMENT.
LET'S FIND UNCLE EARL AND SCUTTLEBUTT, THEN GO HOME.
WHAT THE HECK?
THAT'S ONE HUGE . . .

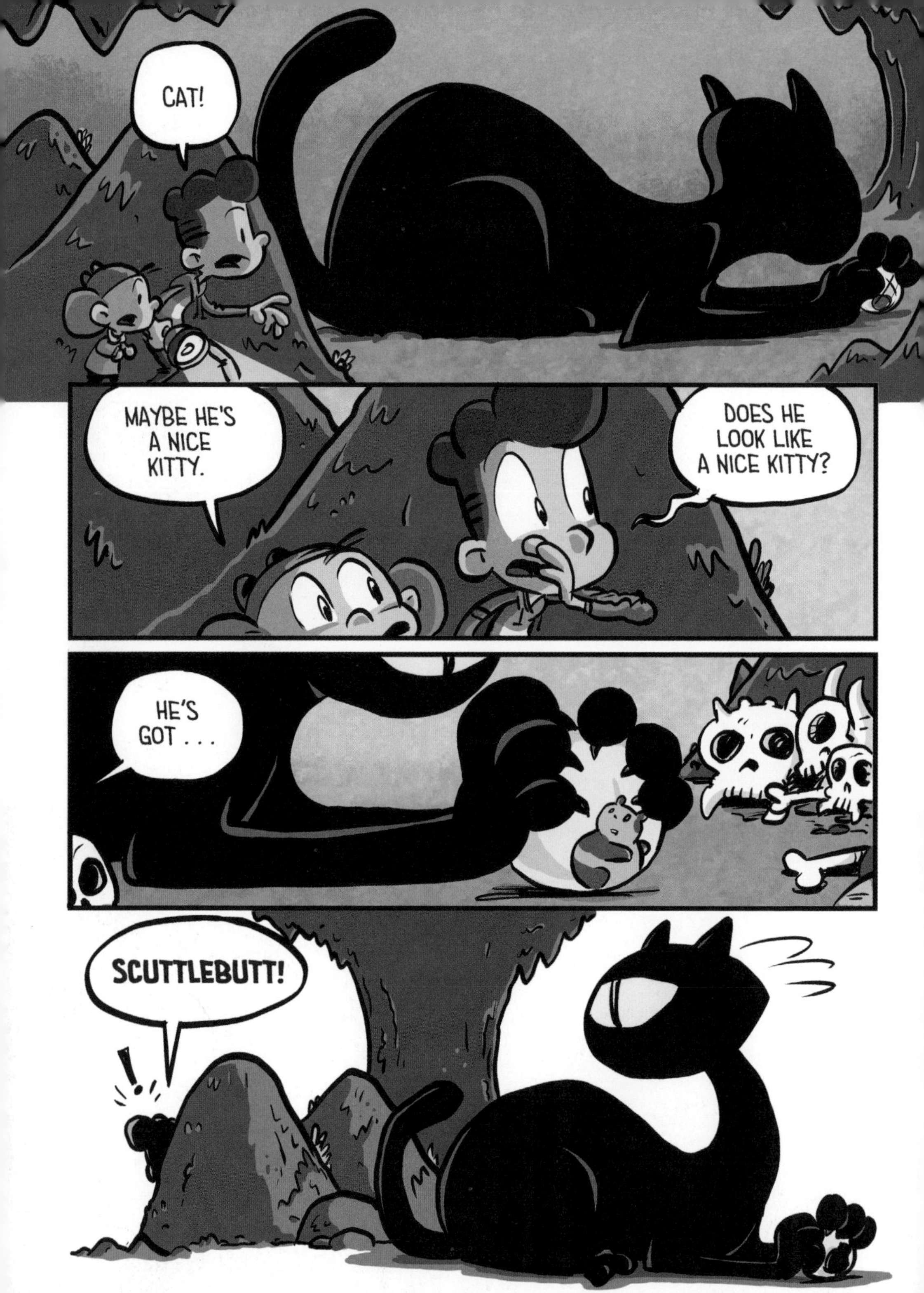
CAT!
MAYBE HE'S A NICE KITTY.
DOES HE LOOK LIKE A NICE KITTY?
HE'S GOT . . .
SCUTTLEBUTT!
!

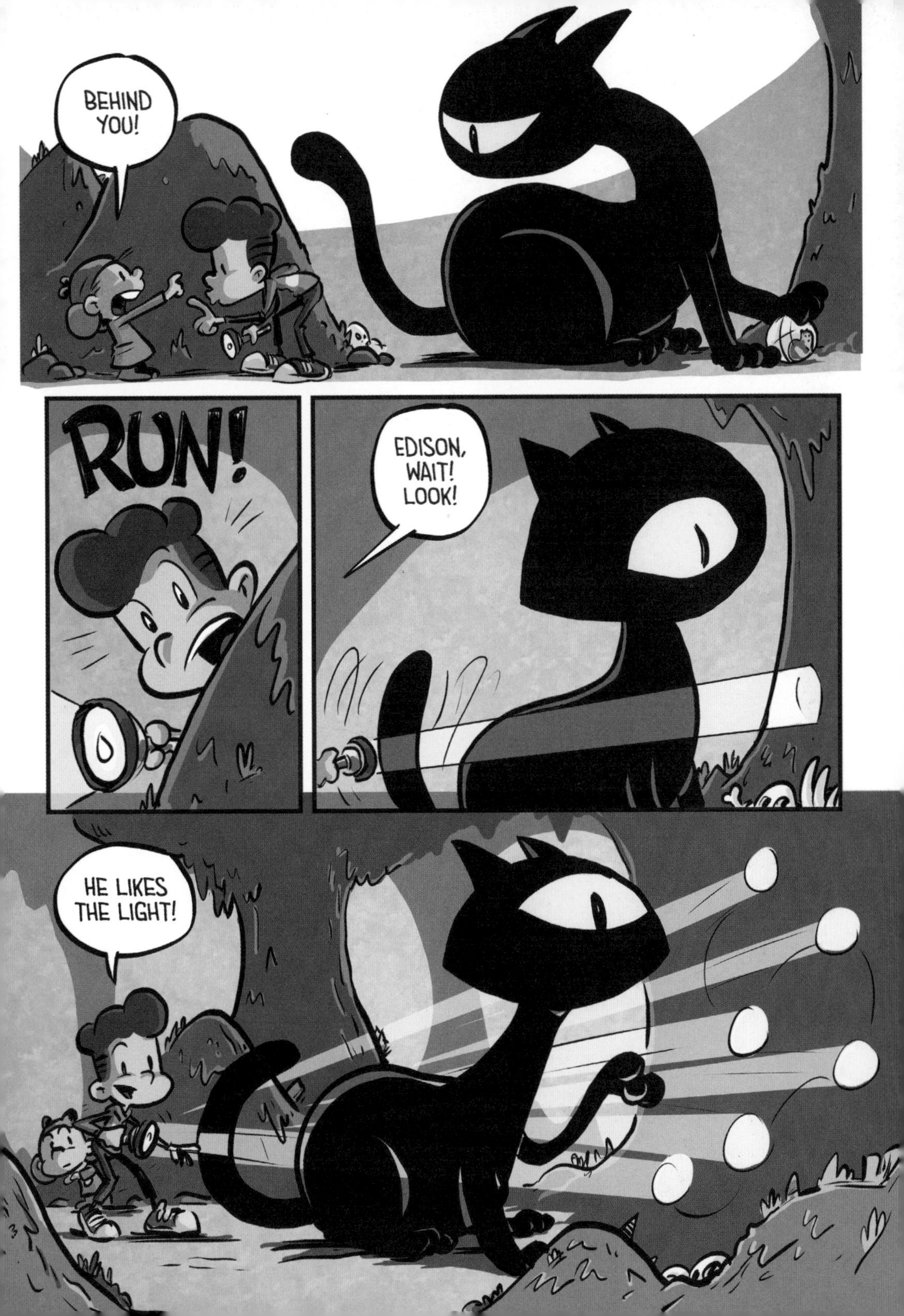
BEHIND YOU!
RUN!
EDISON, WAIT! LOOK!
HE LIKES THE LIGHT!

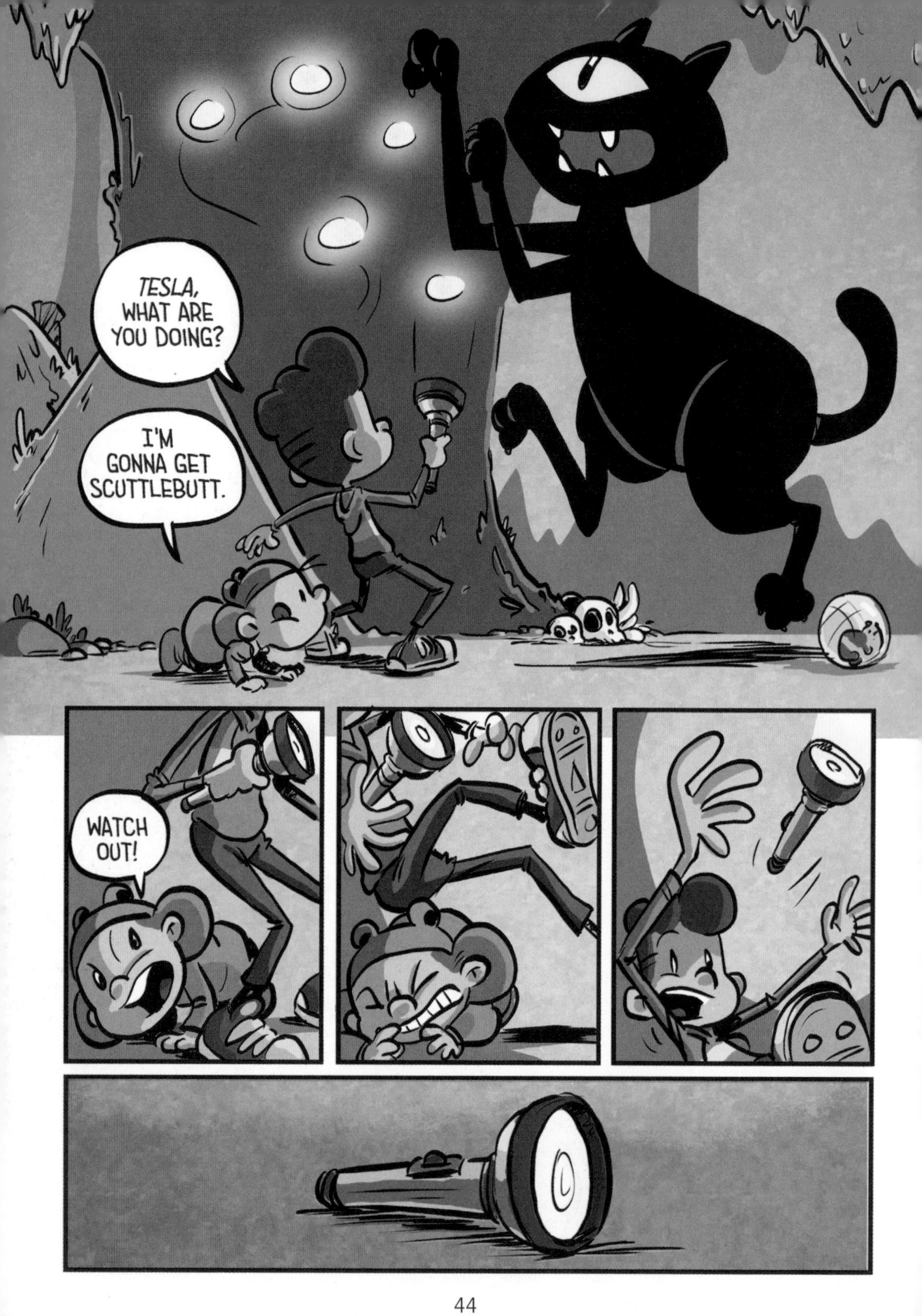
TESLA, WHAT ARE YOU DOING?
I'M GONNA GET SCUTTLEBUTT.
WATCH OUT!

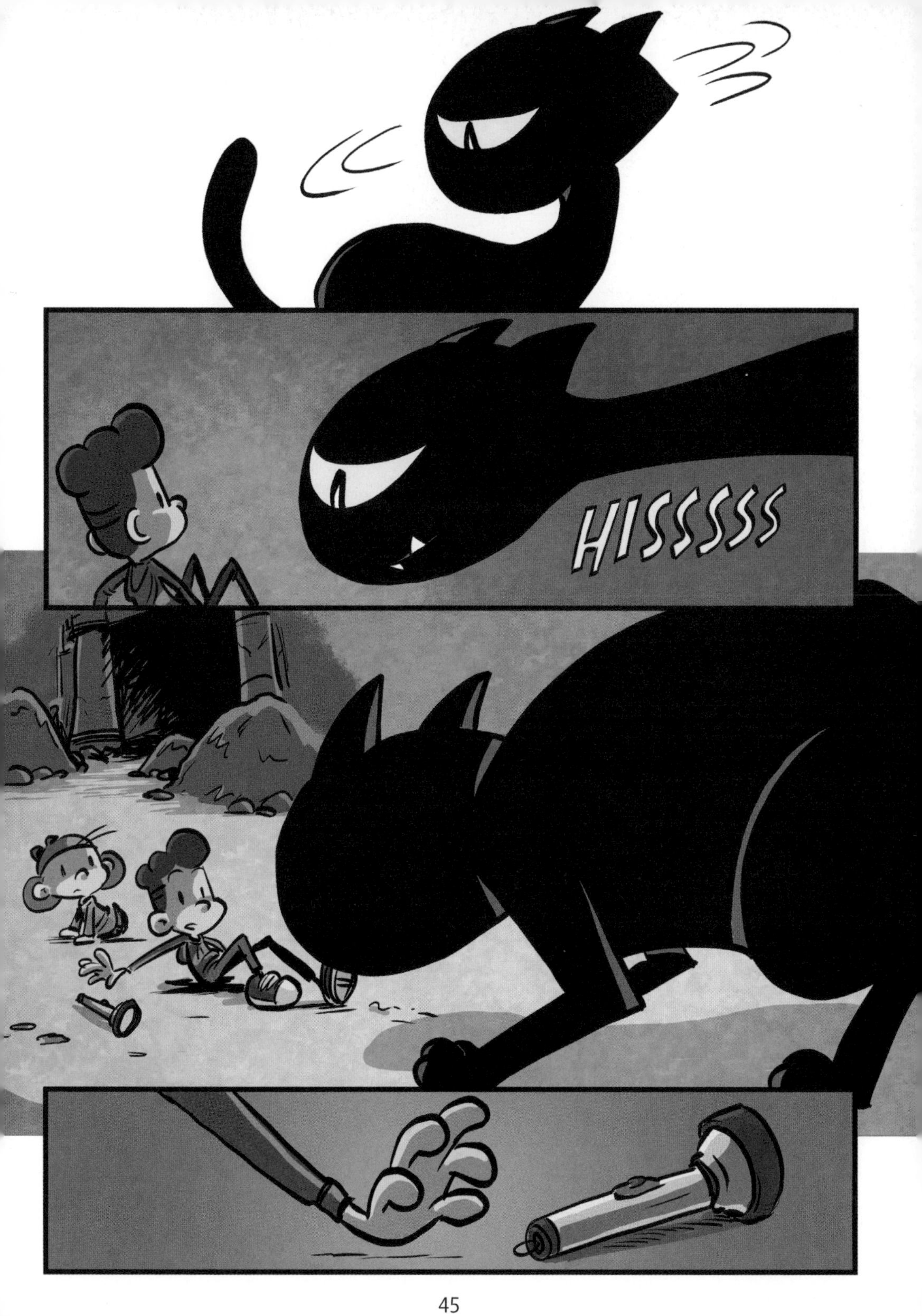
HISSSSS

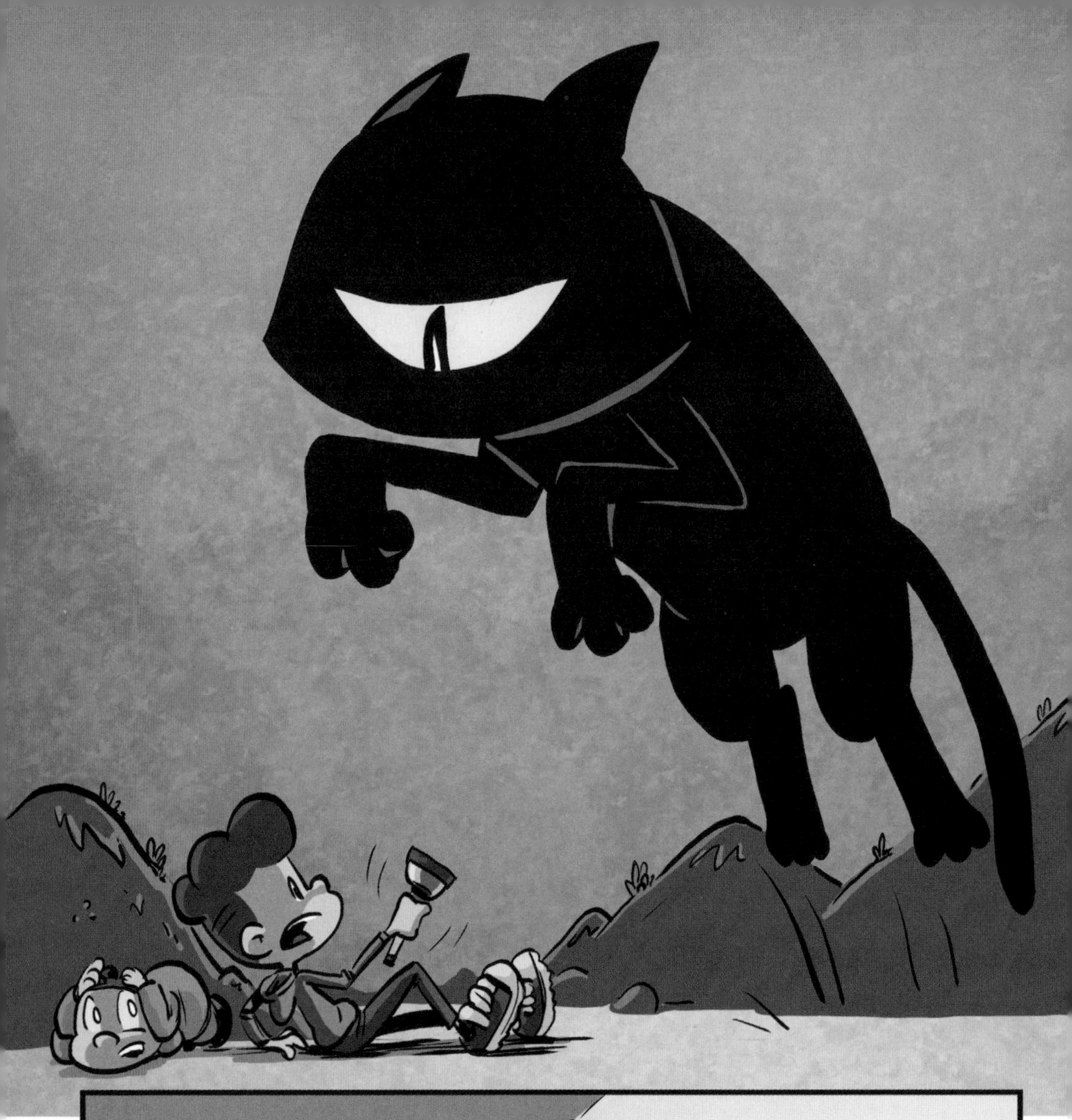

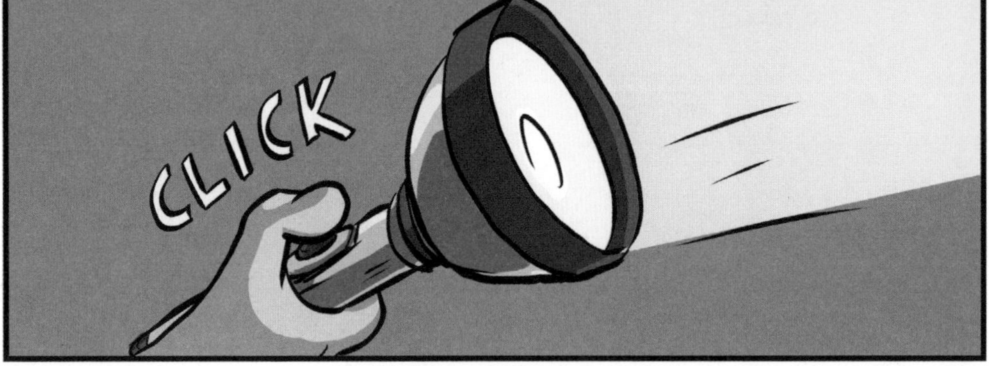
CLICK

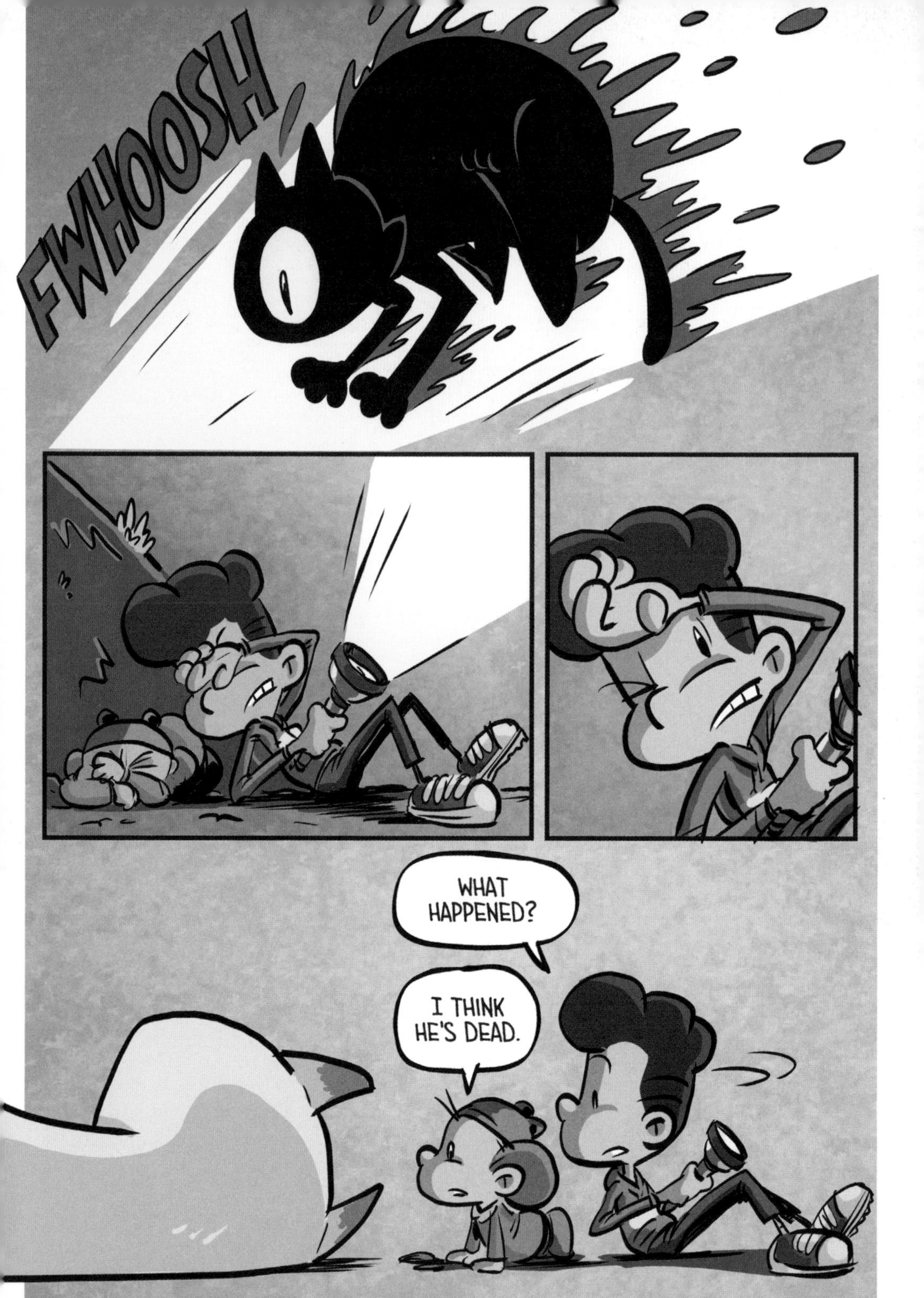
FWHOOSH
WHAT HAPPENED?
I THINK HE'S DEAD.

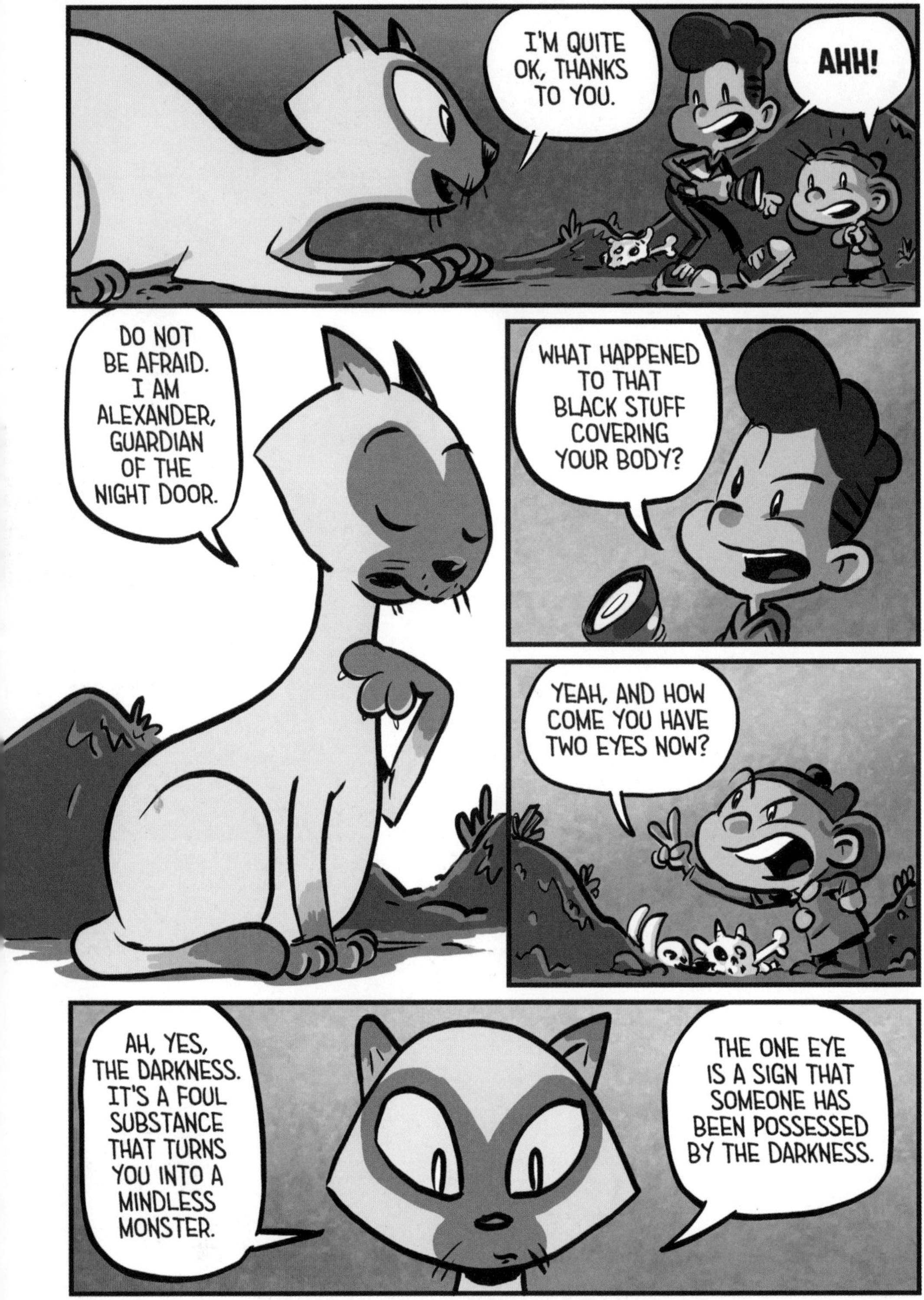

I'M QUITE OK, THANKS TO YOU.
AHH!
DO NOT BE AFRAID. I AM ALEXANDER, GUARDIAN OF THE NIGHT DOOR.
WHAT HAPPENED TO THAT BLACK STUFF COVERING YOUR BODY?
YEAH, AND HOW COME YOU HAVE TWO EYES NOW?
AH, YES, THE DARKNESS. IT'S A FOUL SUBSTANCE THAT TURNS YOU INTO A MINDLESS MONSTER.
THE ONE EYE IS A SIGN THAT SOMEONE HAS BEEN POSSESSED BY THE DARKNESS.

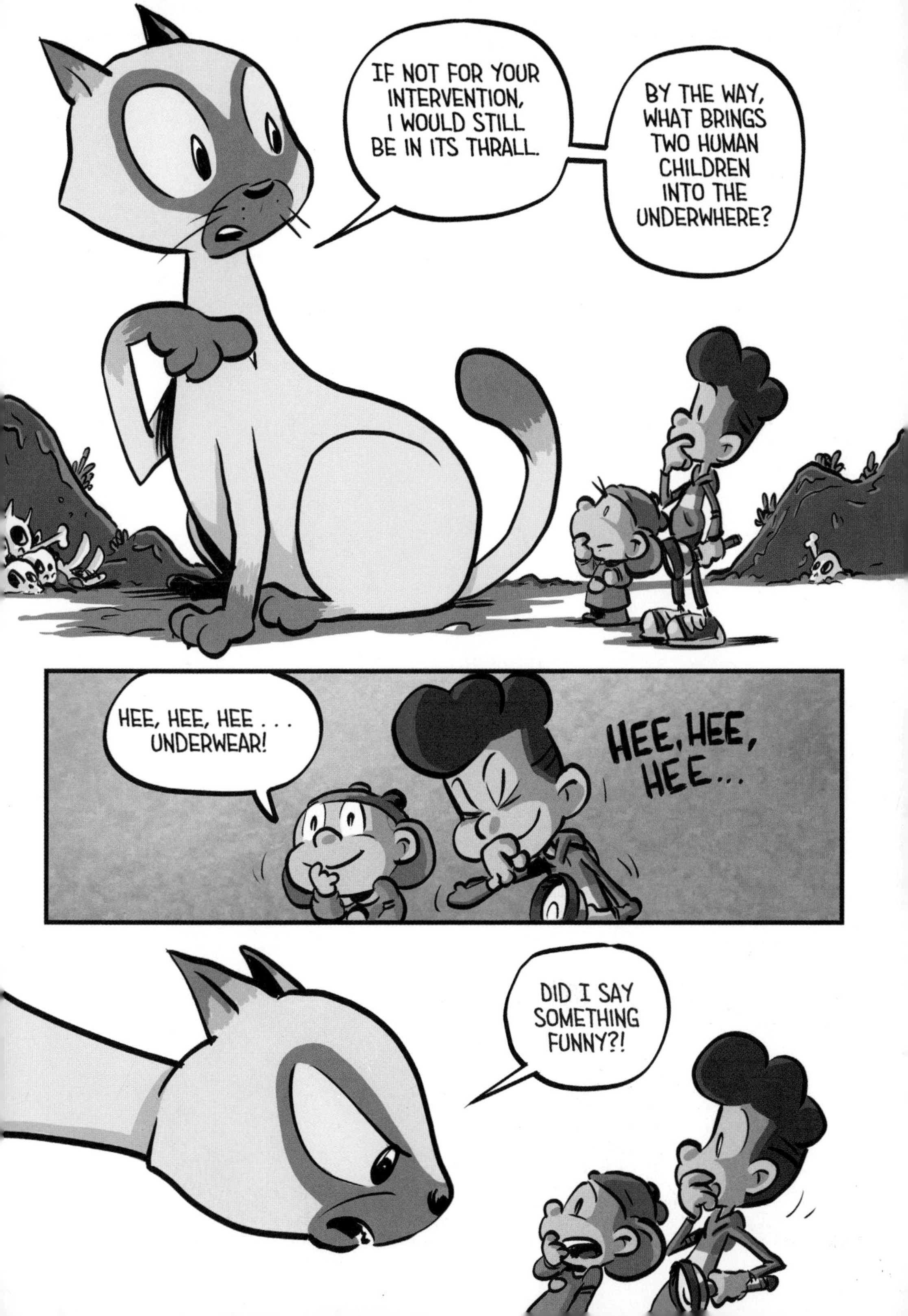
IF NOT FOR YOUR INTERVENTION, I WOULD STILL BE IN ITS THRALL.
BY THE WAY, WHAT BRINGS TWO HUMAN CHILDREN INTO THE UNDERWHERE?
HEE, HEE, HEE . . . UNDERWEAR!
HEE, HEE, HEE...
DID I SAY SOMETHING FUNNY?!

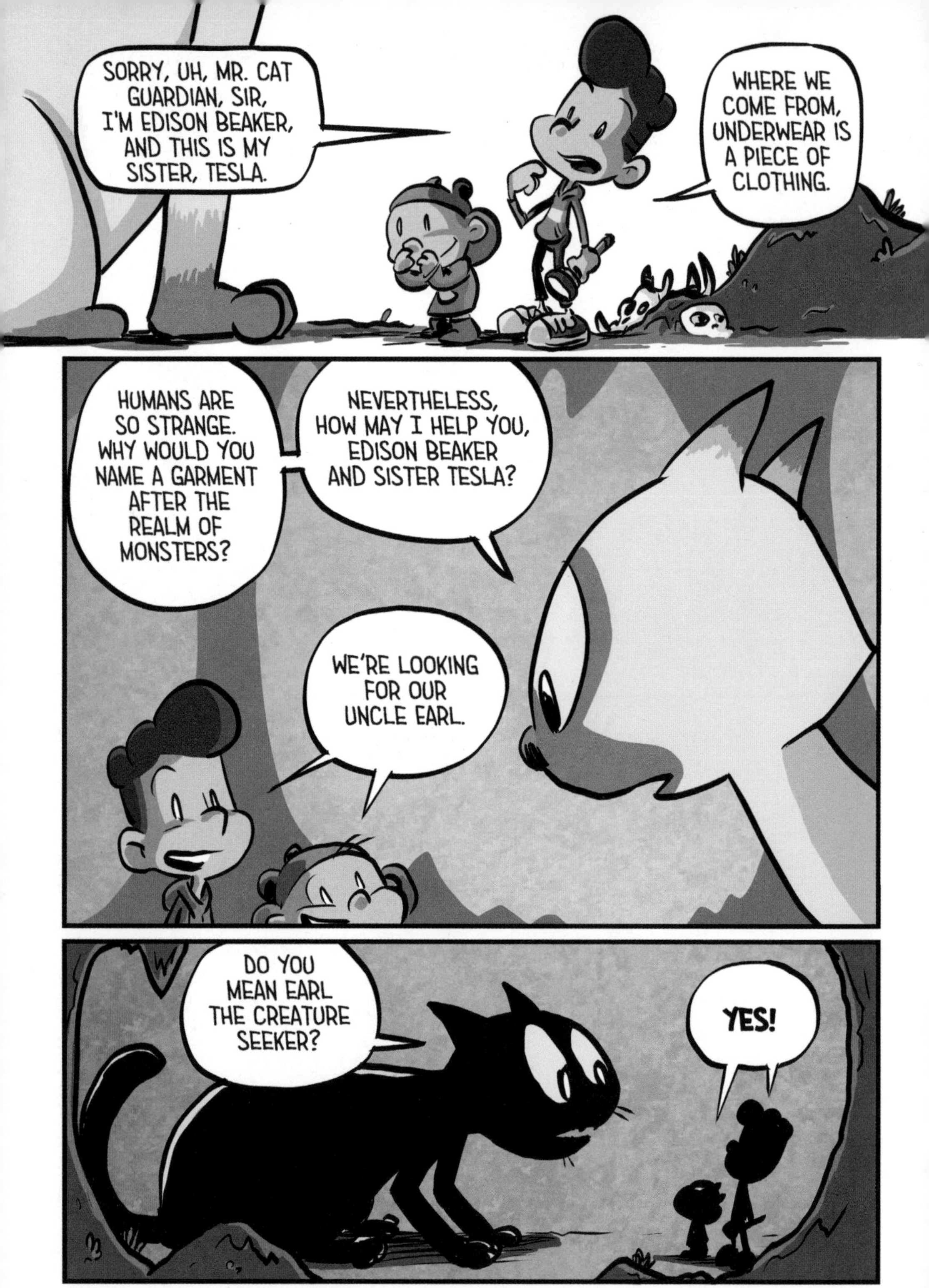
SORRY, UH, MR. CAT GUARDIAN, SIR, I'M EDISON BEAKER, AND THIS IS MY SISTER, TESLA.
WHERE WE COME FROM, UNDERWEAR IS A PIECE OF CLOTHING.
HUMANS ARE SO STRANGE. WHY WOULD YOU NAME A GARMENT AFTER THE REALM OF MONSTERS?
NEVERTHELESS, HOW MAY I HELP YOU, EDISON BEAKER AND SISTER TESLA?
WE'RE LOOKING FOR OUR UNCLE EARL.
DO YOU MEAN EARL THE CREATURE SEEKER?
YES!

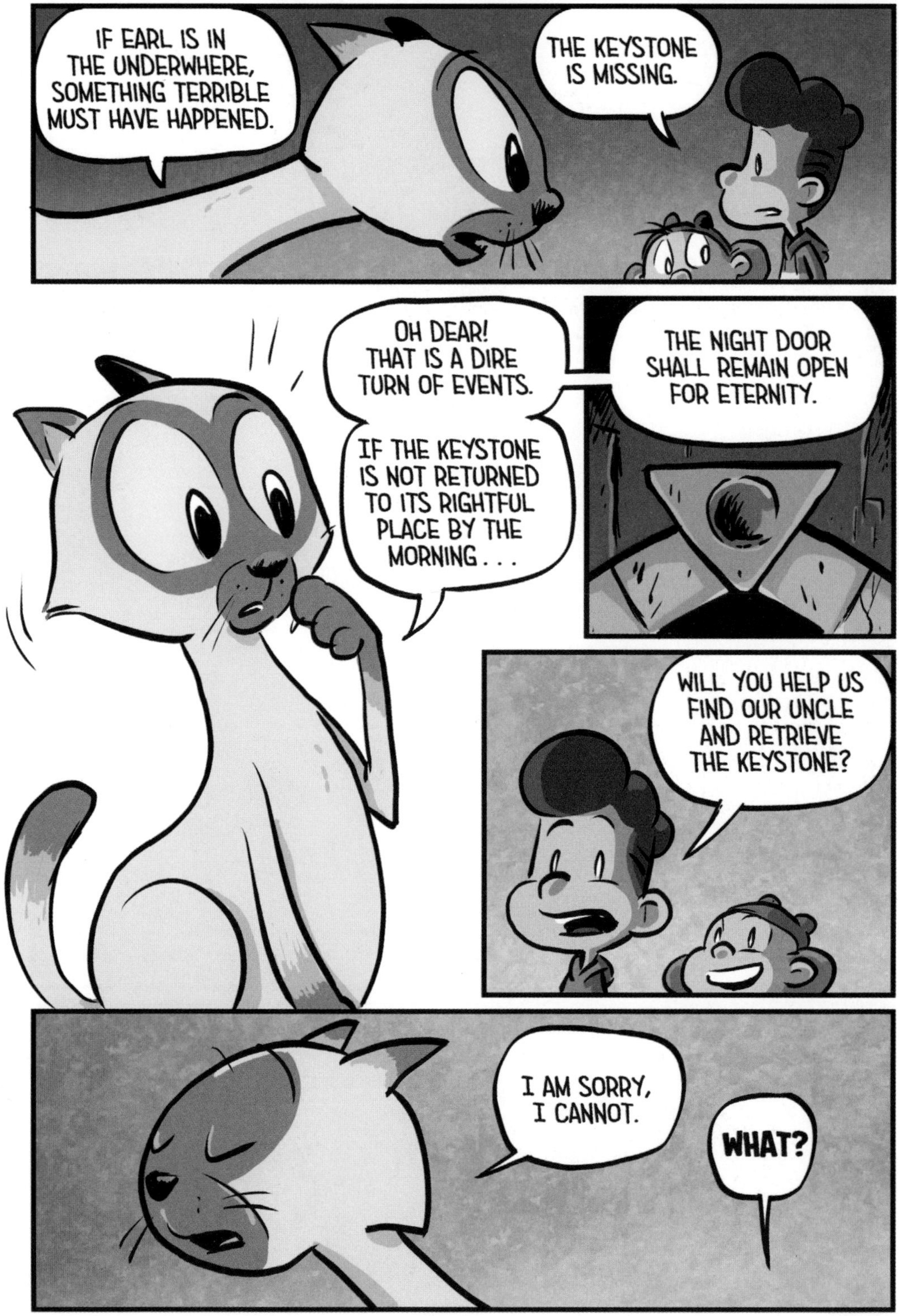
IF EARL IS IN THE UNDERWHERE, SOMETHING TERRIBLE MUST HAVE HAPPENED.
THE KEYSTONE IS MISSING.
OH DEAR! THAT IS A DIRE TURN OF EVENTS.
THE NIGHT DOOR SHALL REMAIN OPEN FOR ETERNITY.
IF THE KEYSTONE IS NOT RETURNED TO ITS RIGHTFUL PLACE BY THE MORNING . . .
WILL YOU HELP US FIND OUR UNCLE AND RETRIEVE THE KEYSTONE?
I AM SORRY, I CANNOT.
WHAT?

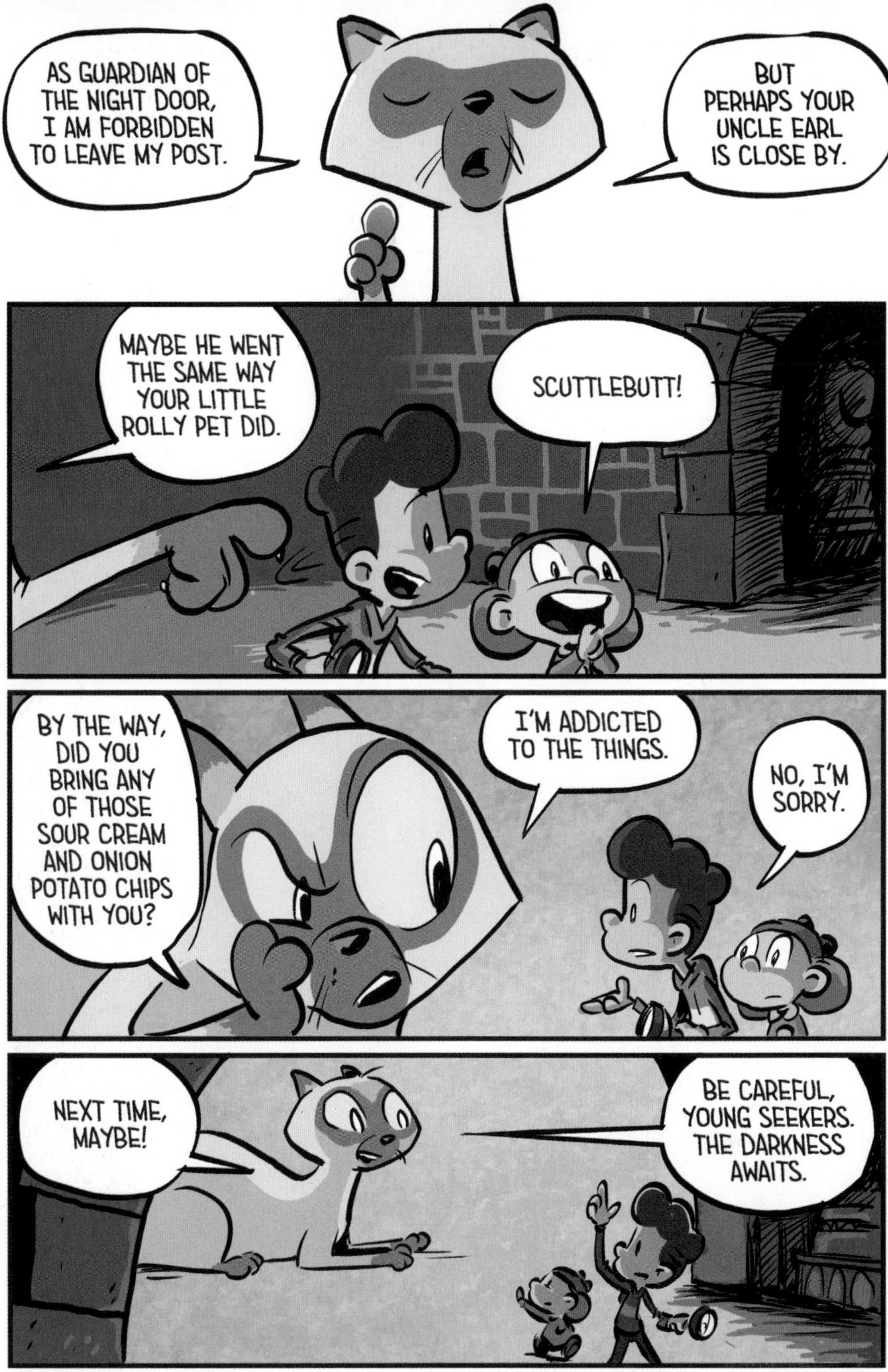
AS GUARDIAN OF THE NIGHT DOOR, I AM FORBIDDEN TO LEAVE MY POST.
BUT PERHAPS YOUR UNCLE EARL IS CLOSE BY.
MAYBE HE WENT THE SAME WAY YOUR LITTLE ROLLY PET DID.
SCUTTLEBUTT!
BY THE WAY, DID YOU BRING ANY OF THOSE SOUR CREAM AND ONION POTATO CHIPS WITH YOU?
I'M ADDICTED TO THE THINGS.
NO, I'M SORRY.
NEXT TIME, MAYBE!
BE CAREFUL, YOUNG SEEKERS. THE DARKNESS AWAITS.

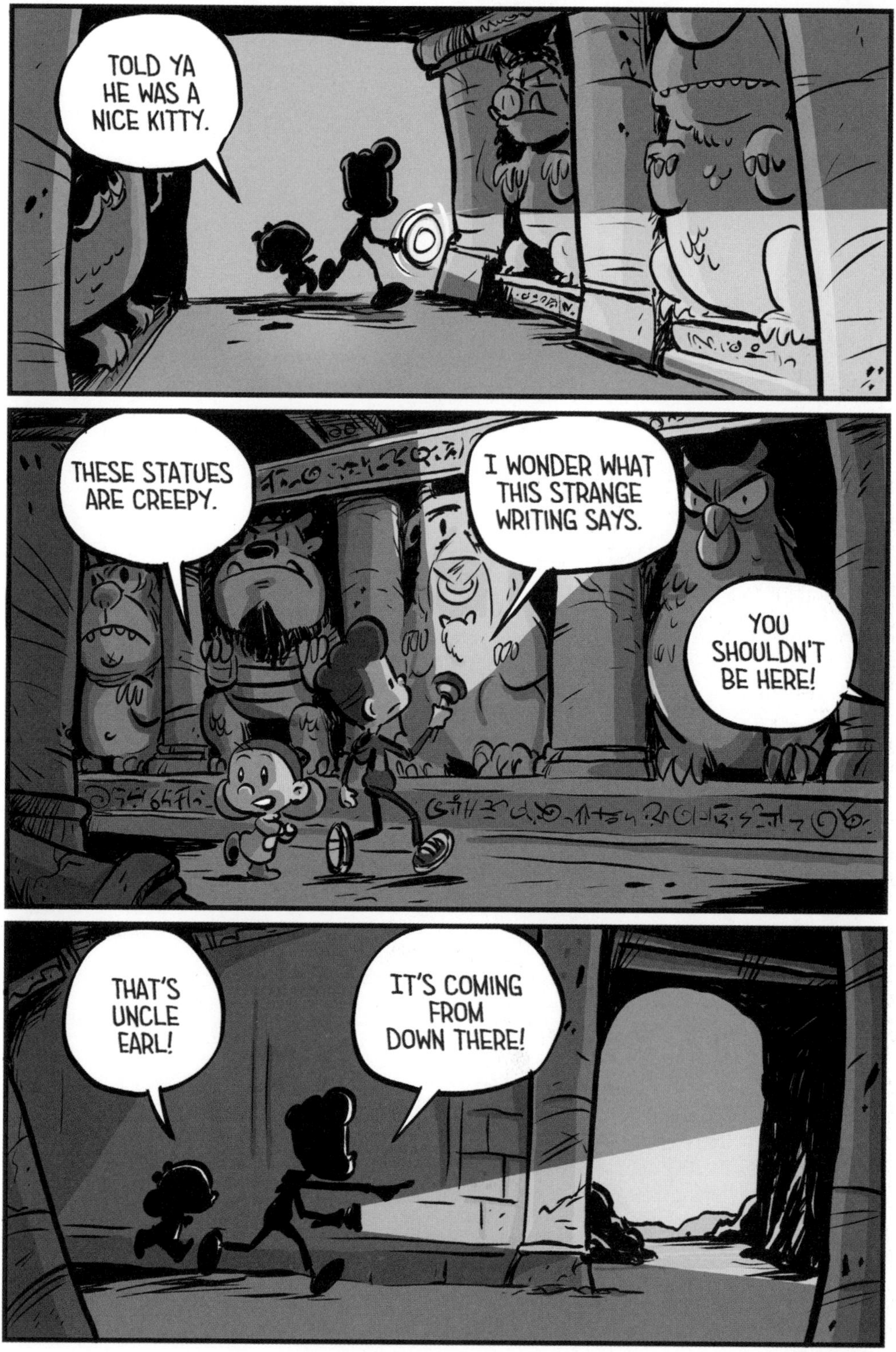
TOLD YA HE WAS A NICE KITTY.
THESE STATUES ARE CREEPY.
I WONDER WHAT THIS STRANGE WRITING SAYS.
YOU SHOULDN'T BE HERE!
THAT'S UNCLE EARL!
IT'S COMING FROM DOWN THERE!

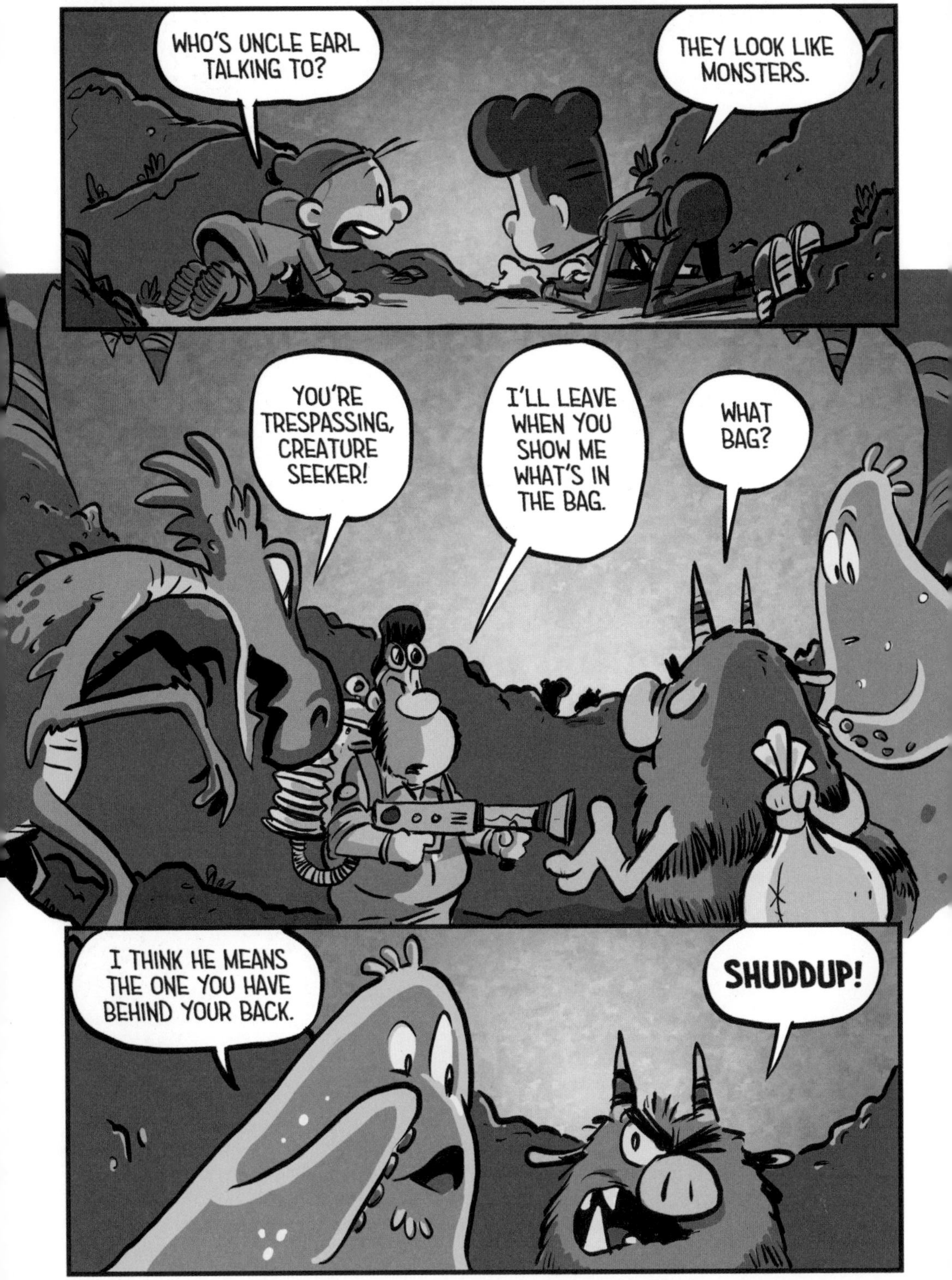
WHO'S UNCLE EARL TALKING TO?
THEY LOOK LIKE MONSTERS.
YOU'RE TRESPASSING, CREATURE SEEKER!
I'LL LEAVE WHEN YOU SHOW ME WHAT'S IN THE BAG.
WHAT BAG?
I THINK HE MEANS THE ONE YOU HAVE BEHIND YOUR BACK.
SHUDDUP!

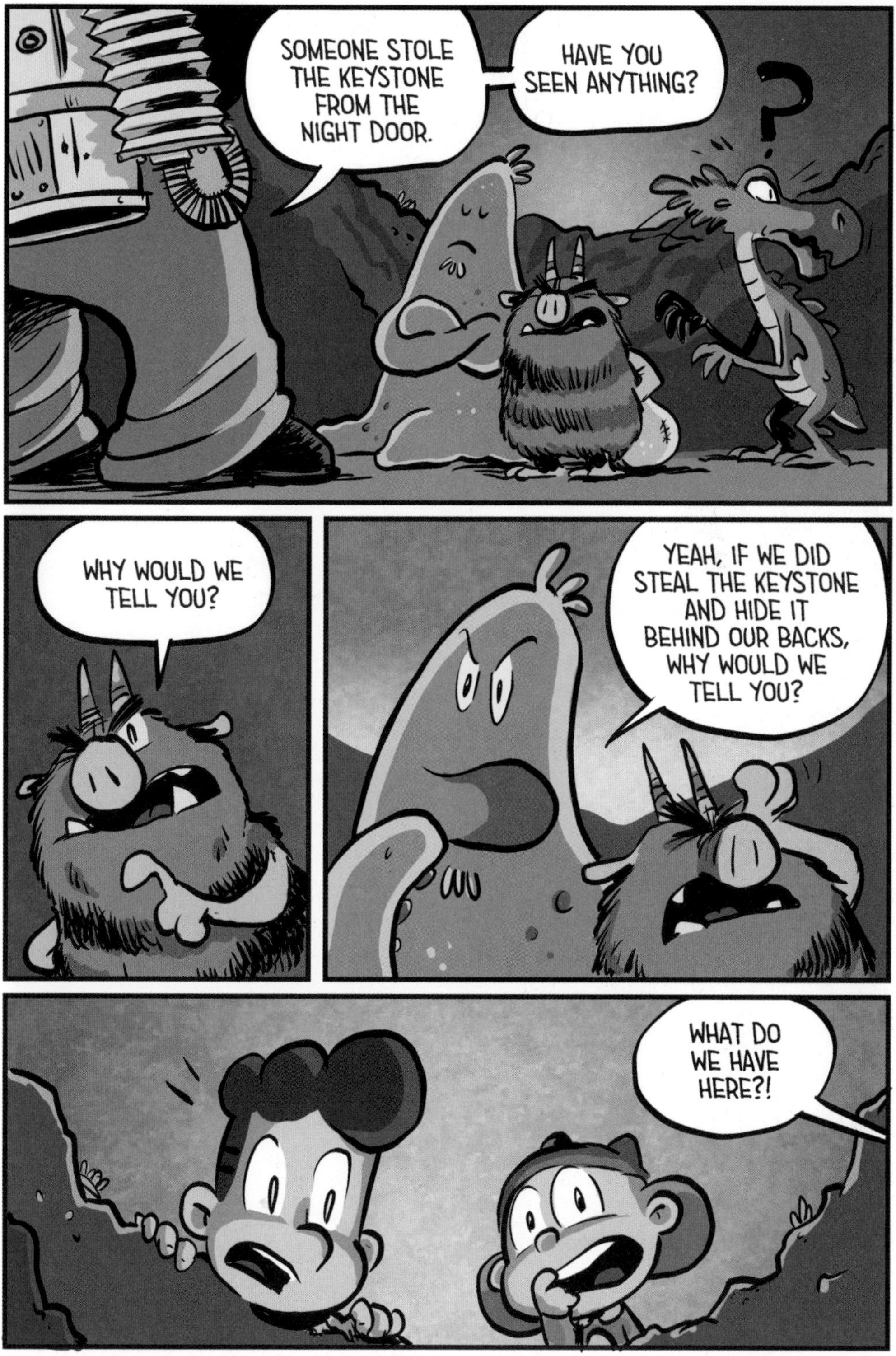
SOMEONE STOLE THE KEYSTONE FROM THE NIGHT DOOR.
HAVE YOU SEEN ANYTHING?
?
WHY WOULD WE TELL YOU?
YEAH, IF WE DID STEAL THE KEYSTONE AND HIDE IT BEHIND OUR BACKS, WHY WOULD WE TELL YOU?
WHAT DO WE HAVE HERE?!

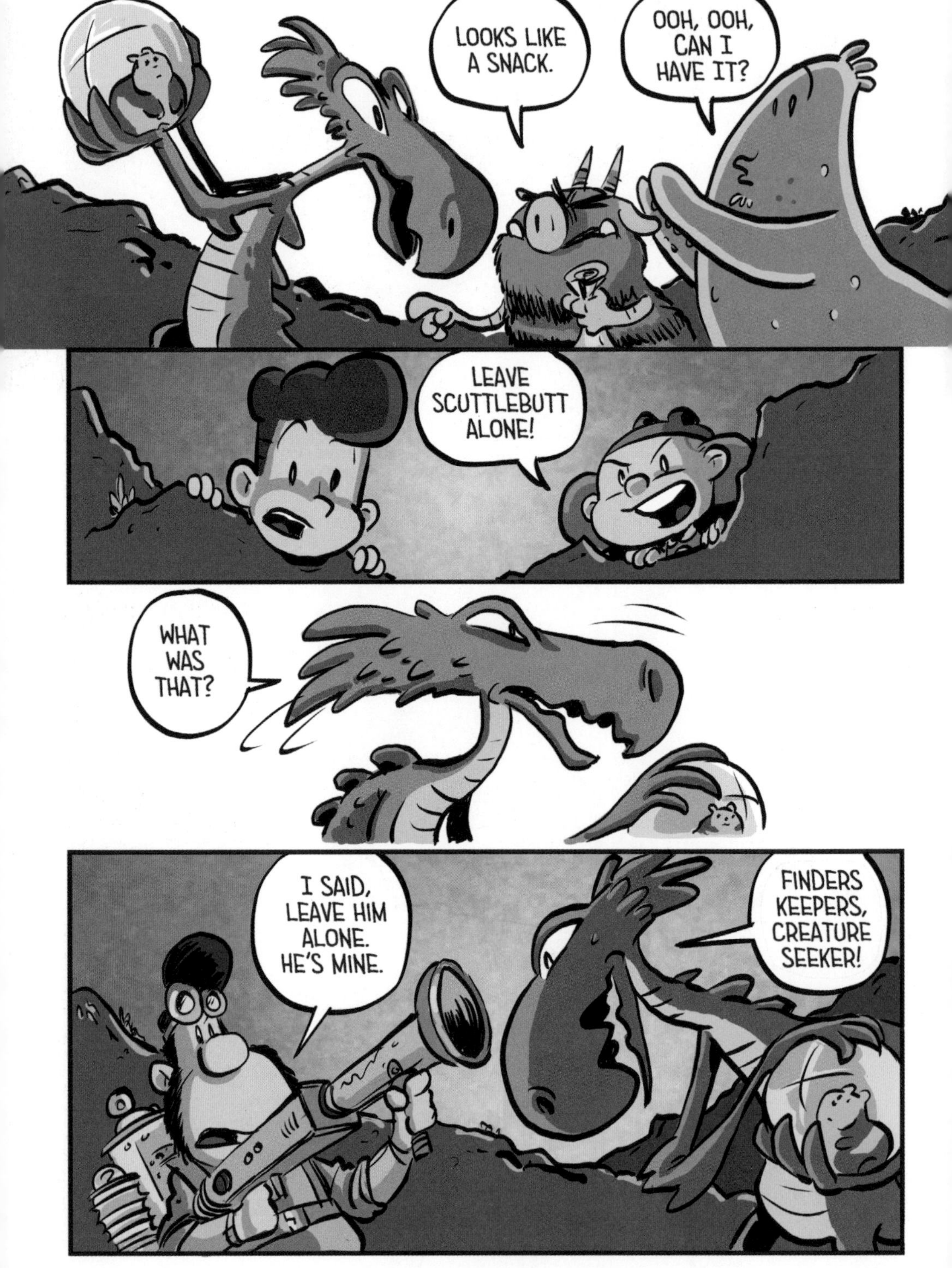
LOOKS LIKE A SNACK.
OOH, OOH, CAN I HAVE IT?
LEAVE SCUTTLEBUTT ALONE!
WHAT WAS THAT?
I SAID, LEAVE HIM ALONE. HE'S MINE.
FINDERS KEEPERS, CREATURE SEEKER!

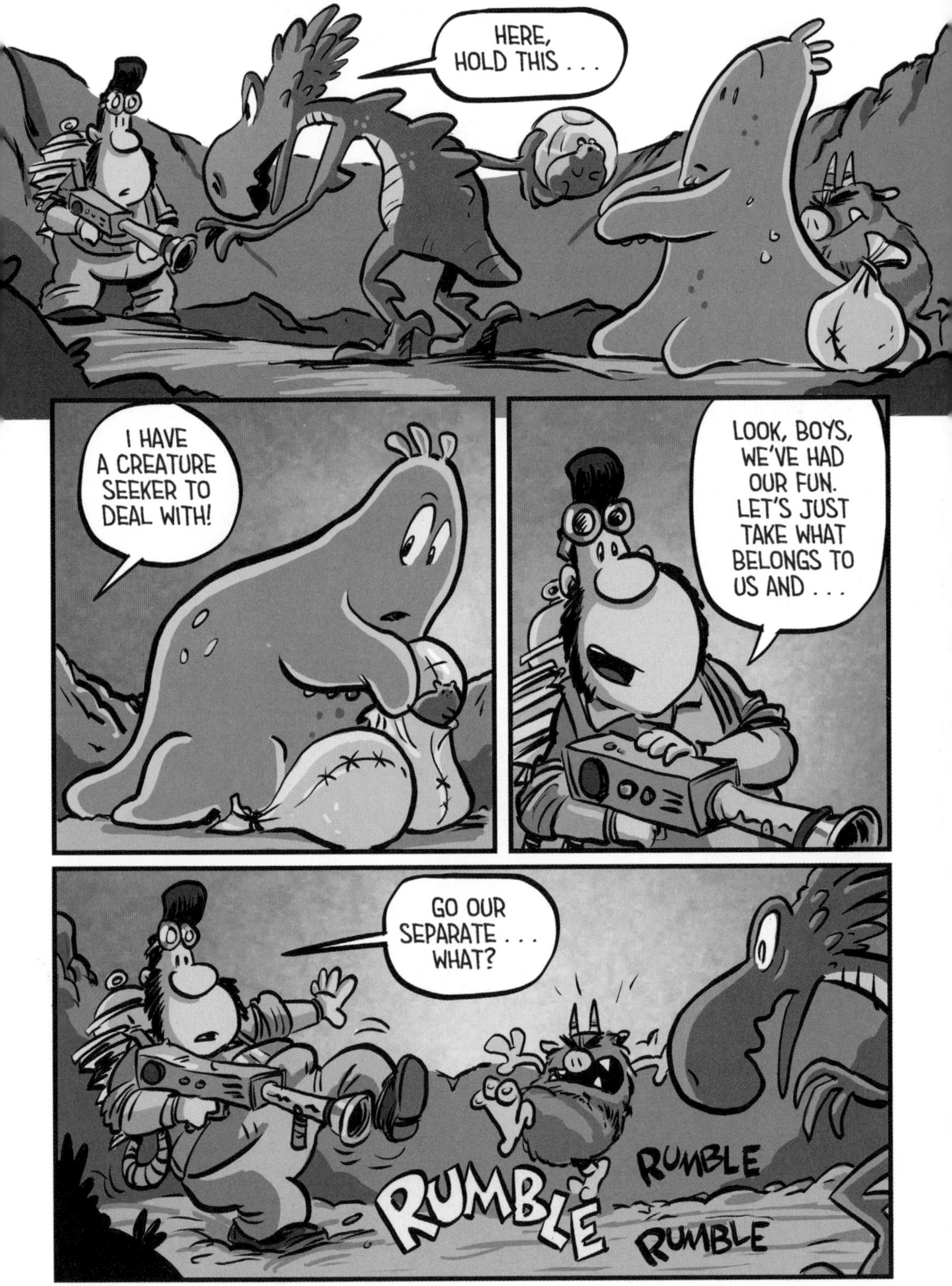
HERE, HOLD THIS . . .
I HAVE A CREATURE SEEKER TO DEAL WITH!
LOOK, BOYS, WE'VE HAD OUR FUN. LET'S JUST TAKE WHAT BELONGS TO US AND . . .
GO OUR SEPARATE . . . WHAT?
RUMBLE
RUMBLE
RUMBLE

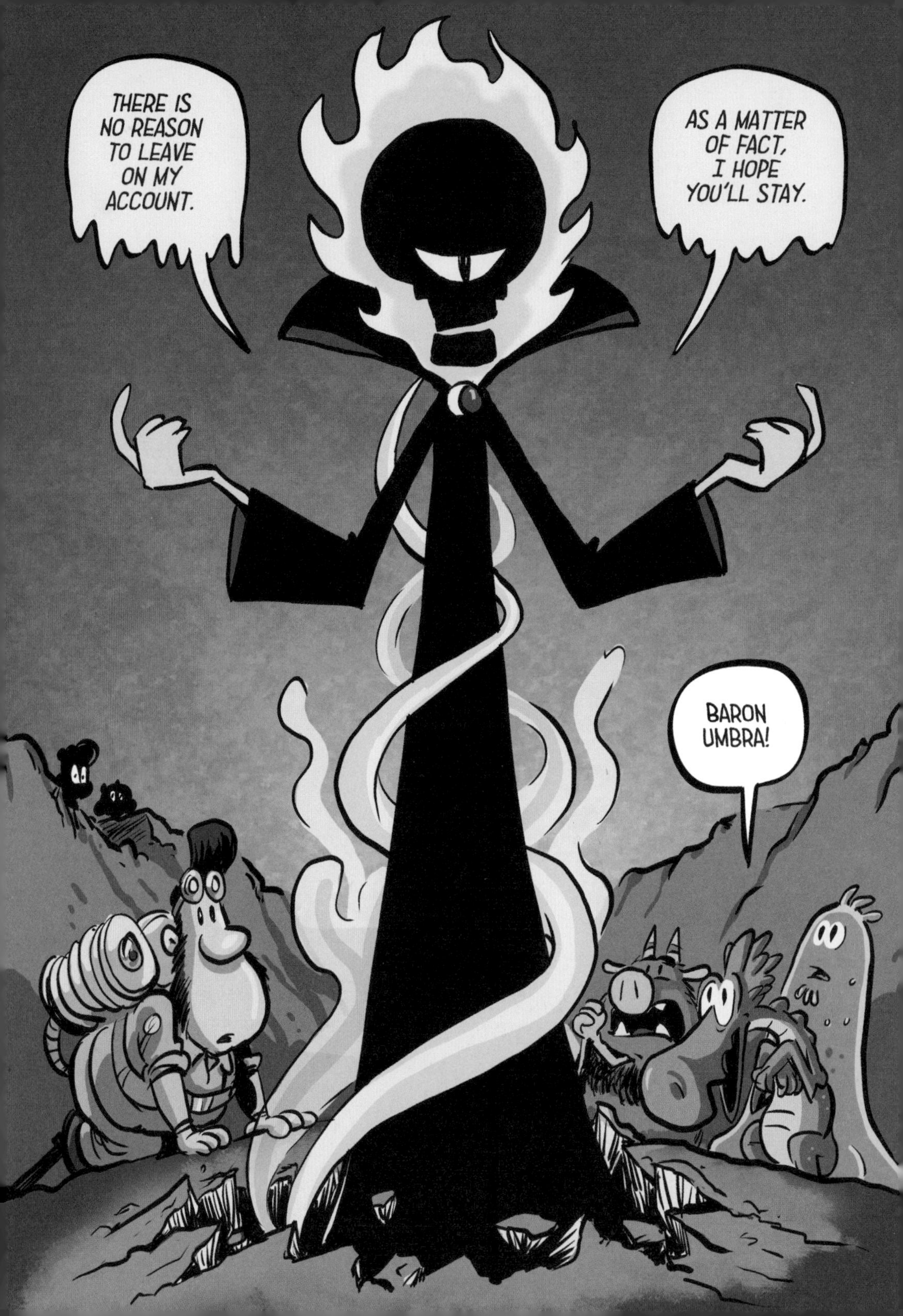
THERE IS NO REASON TO LEAVE ON MY ACCOUNT.
AS A MATTER OF FACT, I HOPE YOU'LL STAY.
BARON UMBRA!

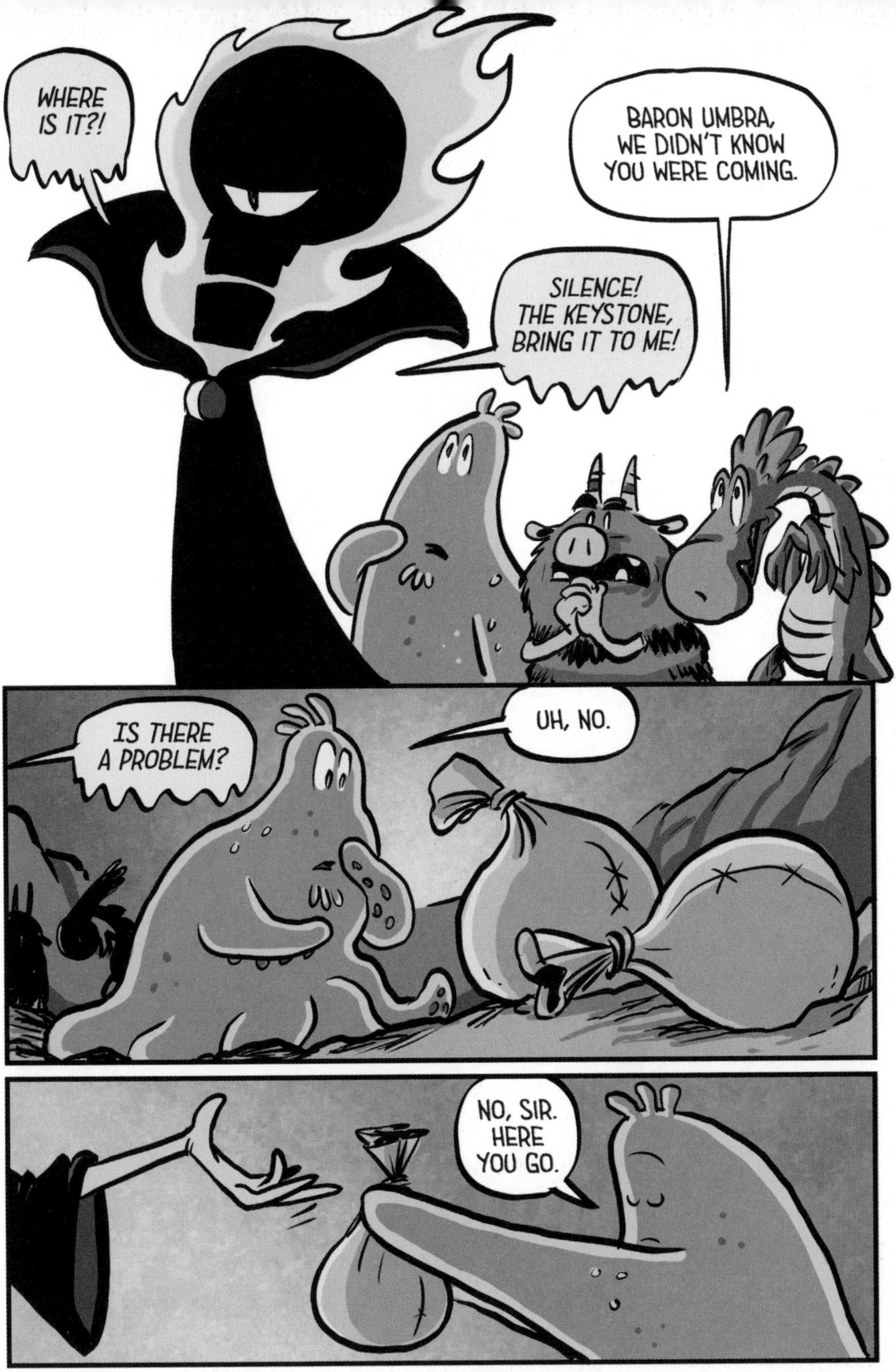
WHERE IS IT?!
BARON UMBRA, WE DIDN'T KNOW YOU WERE COMING.
SILENCE! THE KEYSTONE, BRING IT TO ME!
IS THERE A PROBLEM?
UH, NO.
NO, SIR. HERE YOU GO.

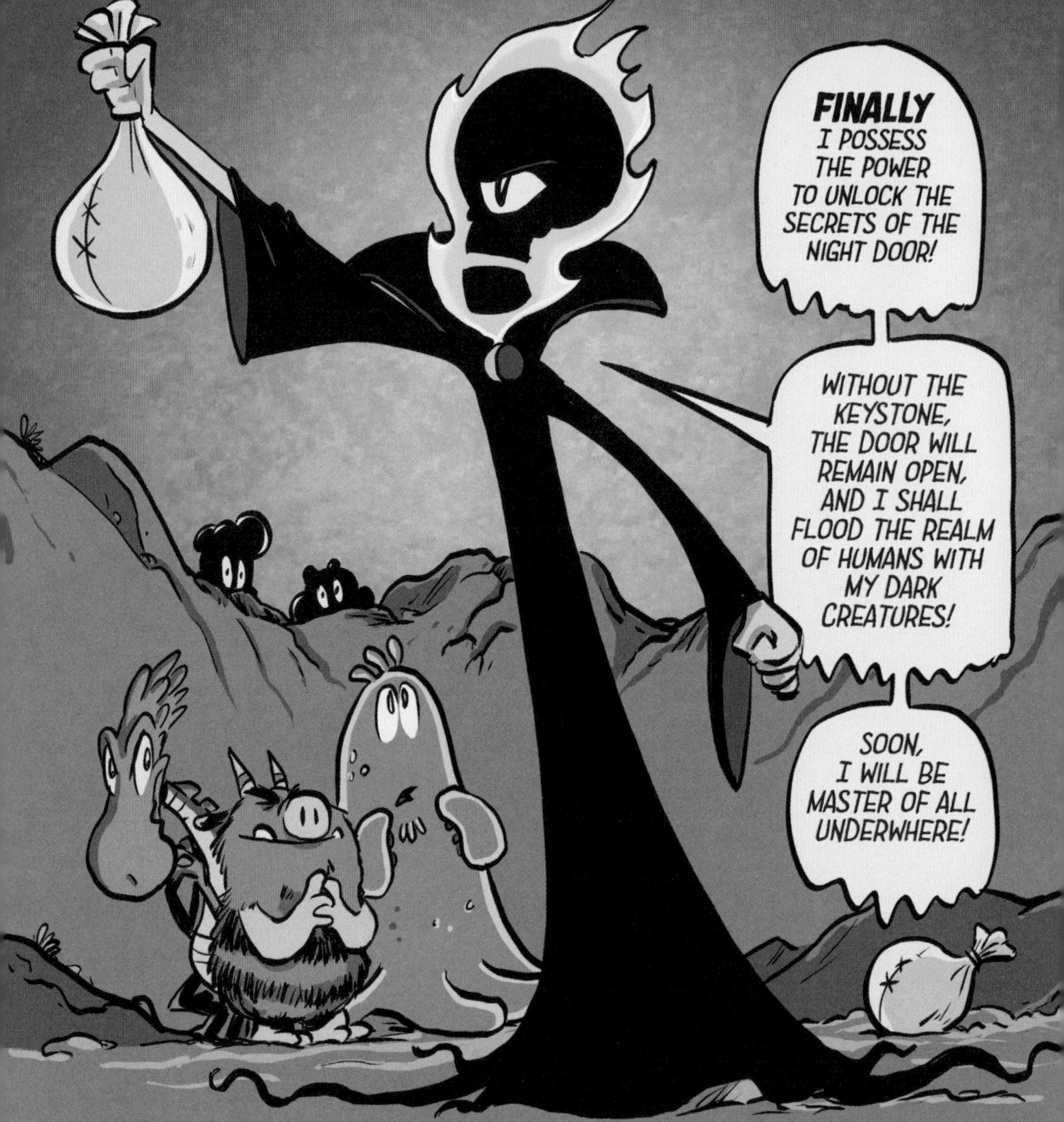
FINALLY I POSSESS THE POWER TO UNLOCK THE SECRETS OF THE NIGHT DOOR!
WITHOUT THE KEYSTONE, THE DOOR WILL REMAIN OPEN, AND I SHALL FLOOD THE REALM OF HUMANS WITH MY DARK CREATURES!
SOON, I WILL BE MASTER OF ALL UNDERWHERE!

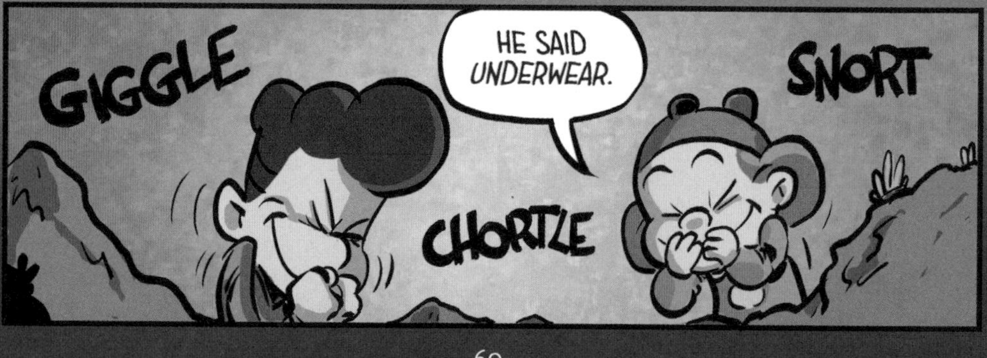
GIGGLE
HE SAID UNDERWEAR.
SNORT
CHORTLE

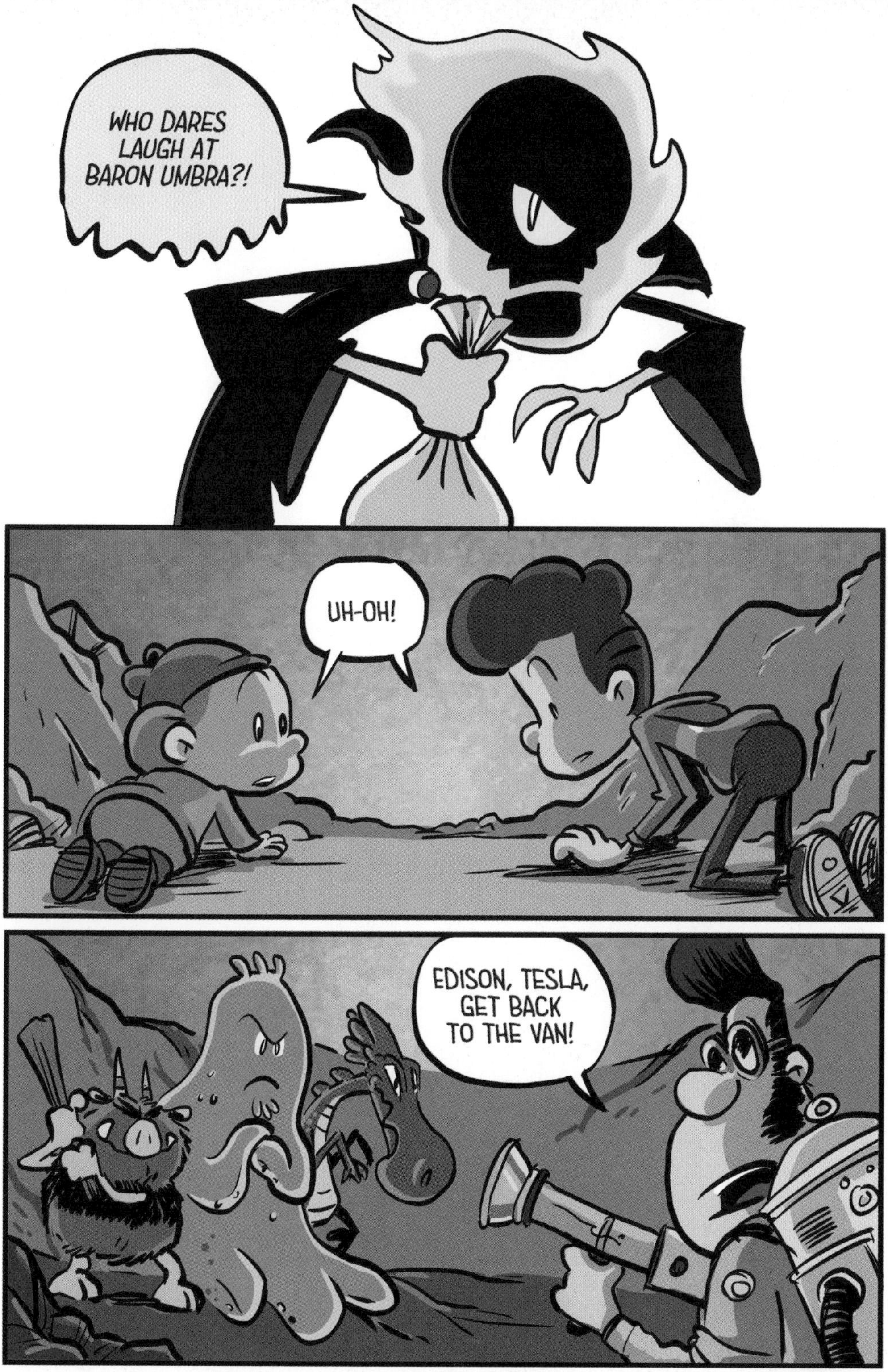

WHO DARES LAUGH AT BARON UMBRA?!
UH-OH!
EDISON, TESLA, GET BACK TO THE VAN!

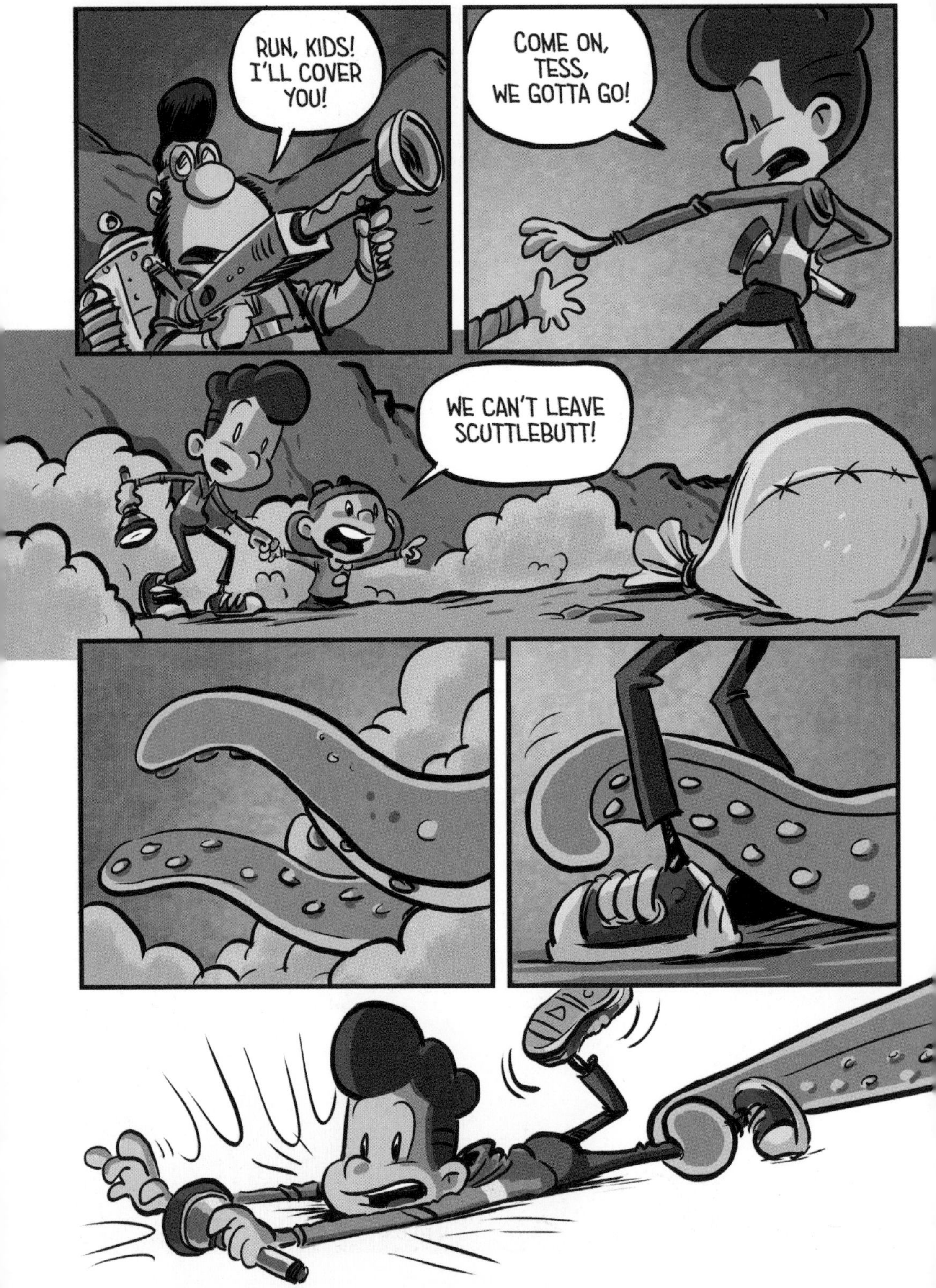
RUN, KIDS! I'LL COVER YOU!
COME ON, TESS, WE GOTTA GO!
WE CAN'T LEAVE SCUTTLEBUTT!

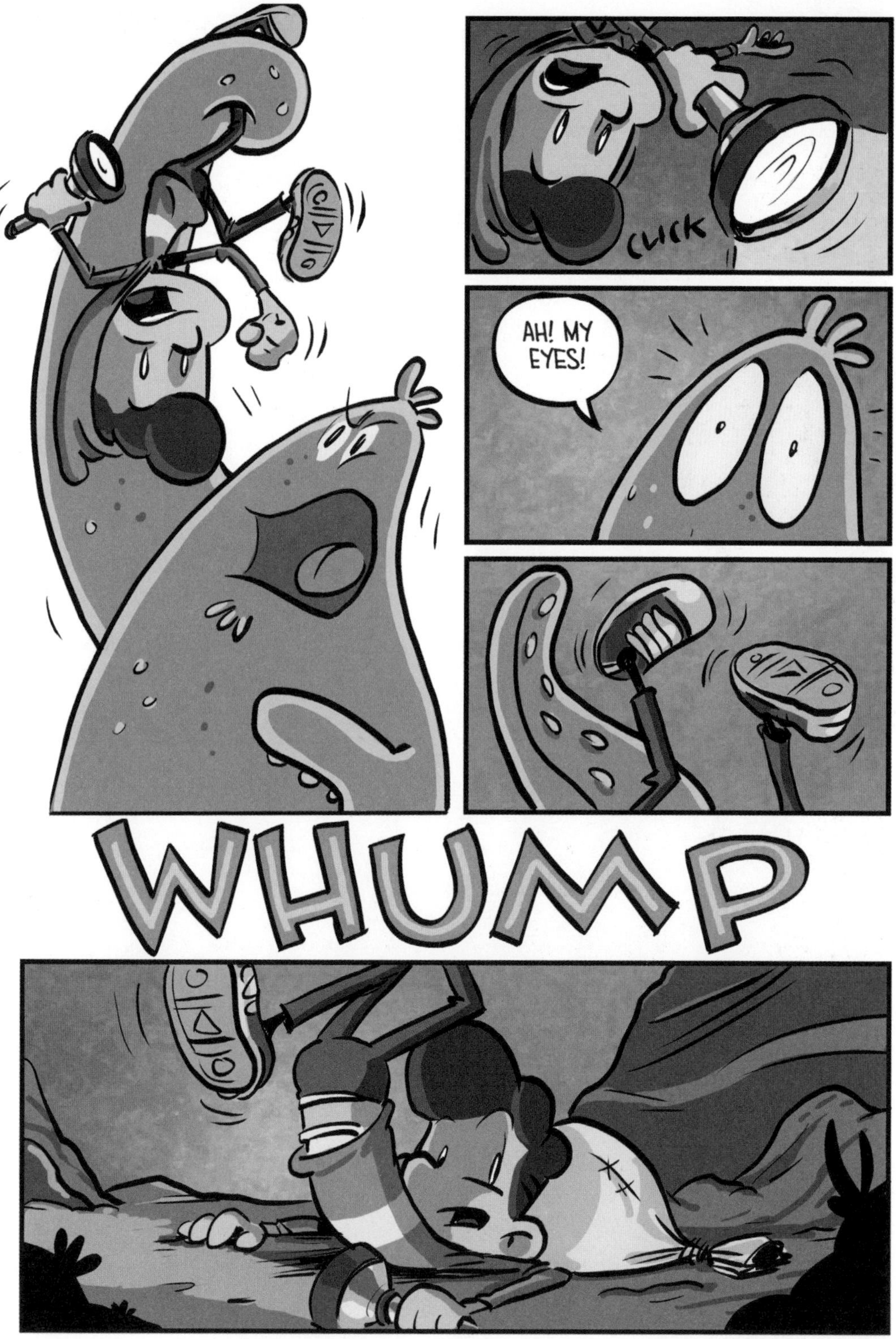
CLICK
AH! MY EYES!
WHUMP

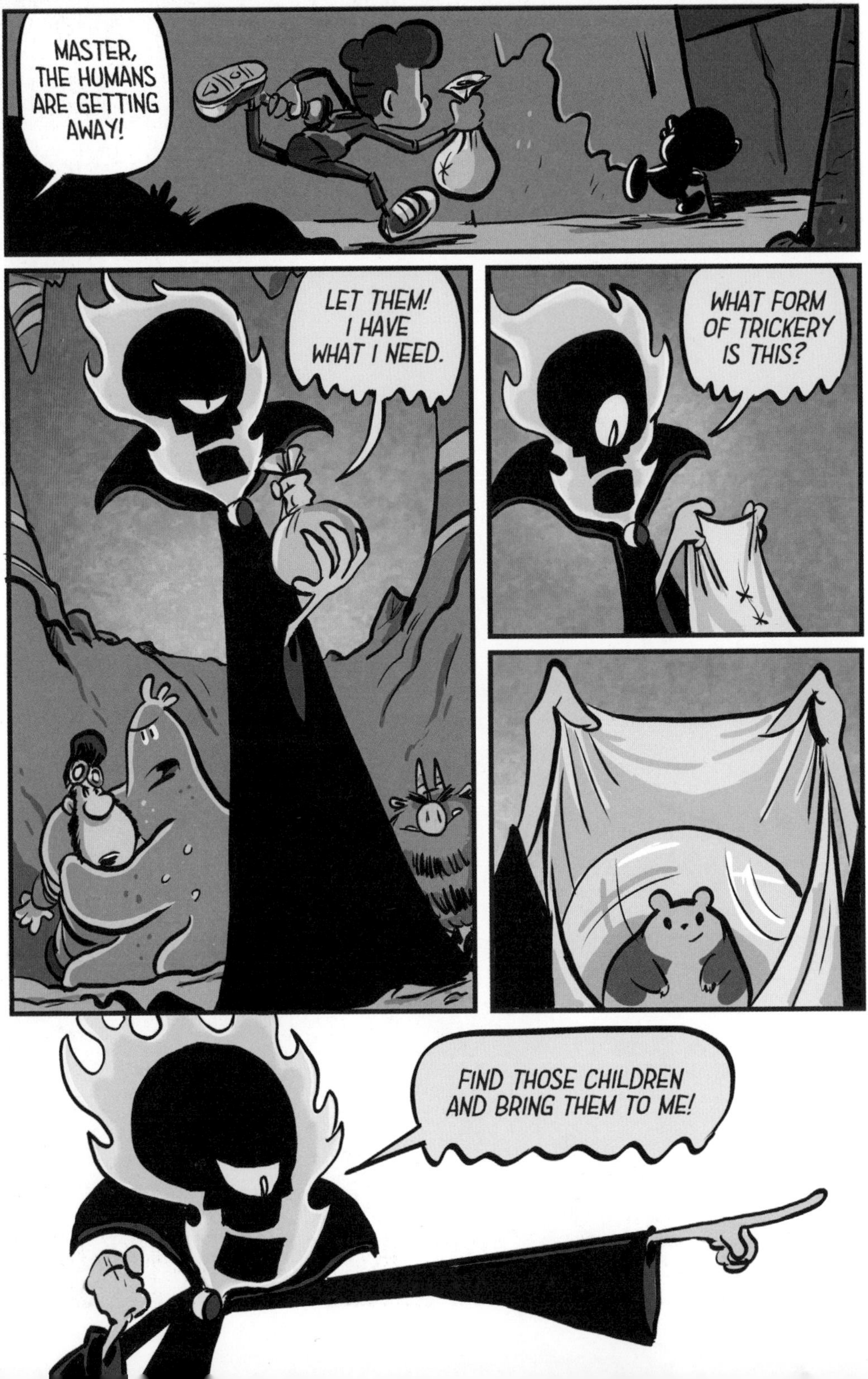
MASTER, THE HUMANS ARE GETTING AWAY!
LET THEM! I HAVE WHAT I NEED.
WHAT FORM OF TRICKERY IS THIS?
FIND THOSE CHILDREN AND BRING THEM TO ME!

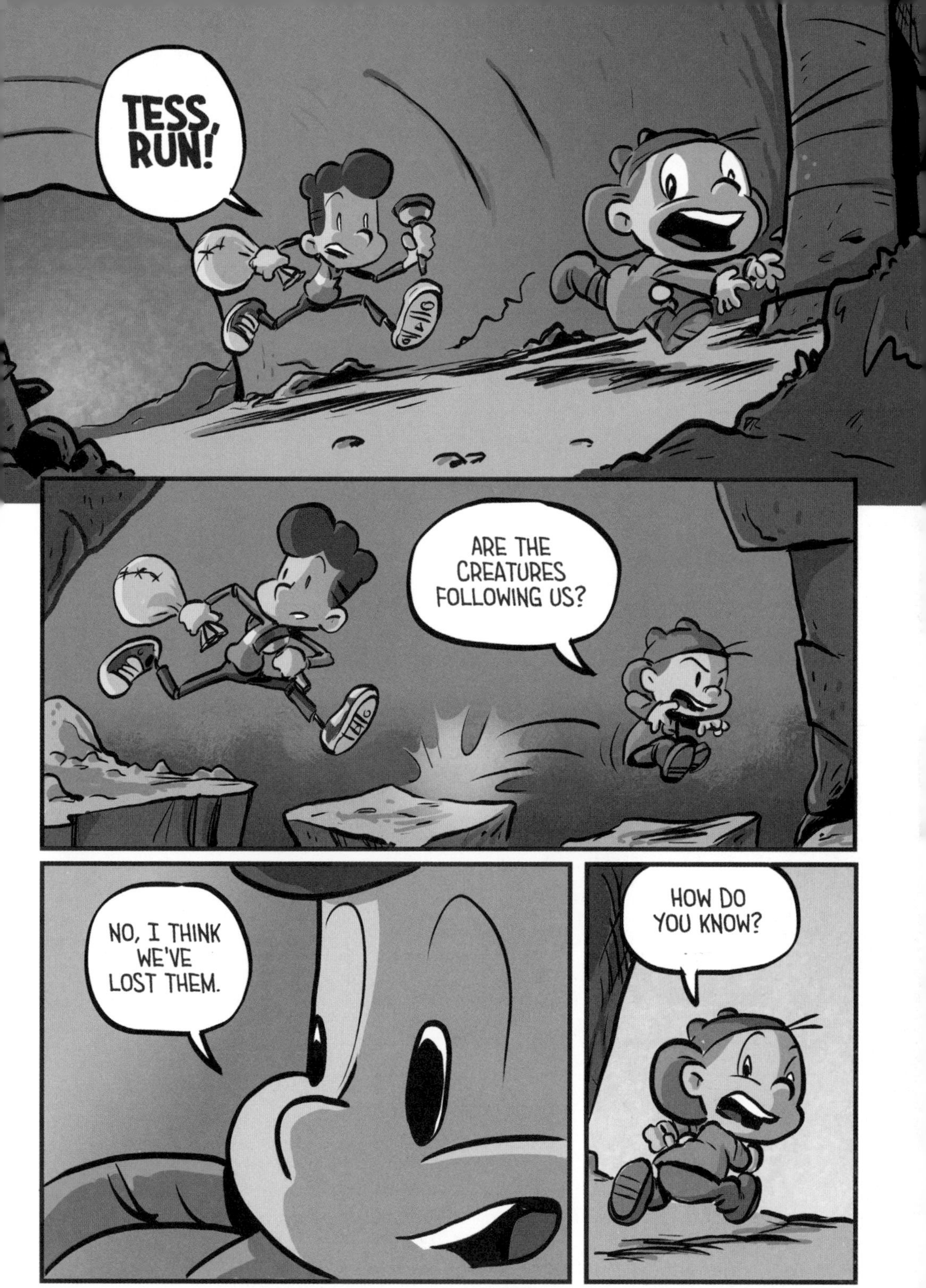
TESS, RUN!
ARE THE CREATURES FOLLOWING US?
NO, I THINK WE'VE LOST THEM.
HOW DO YOU KNOW?

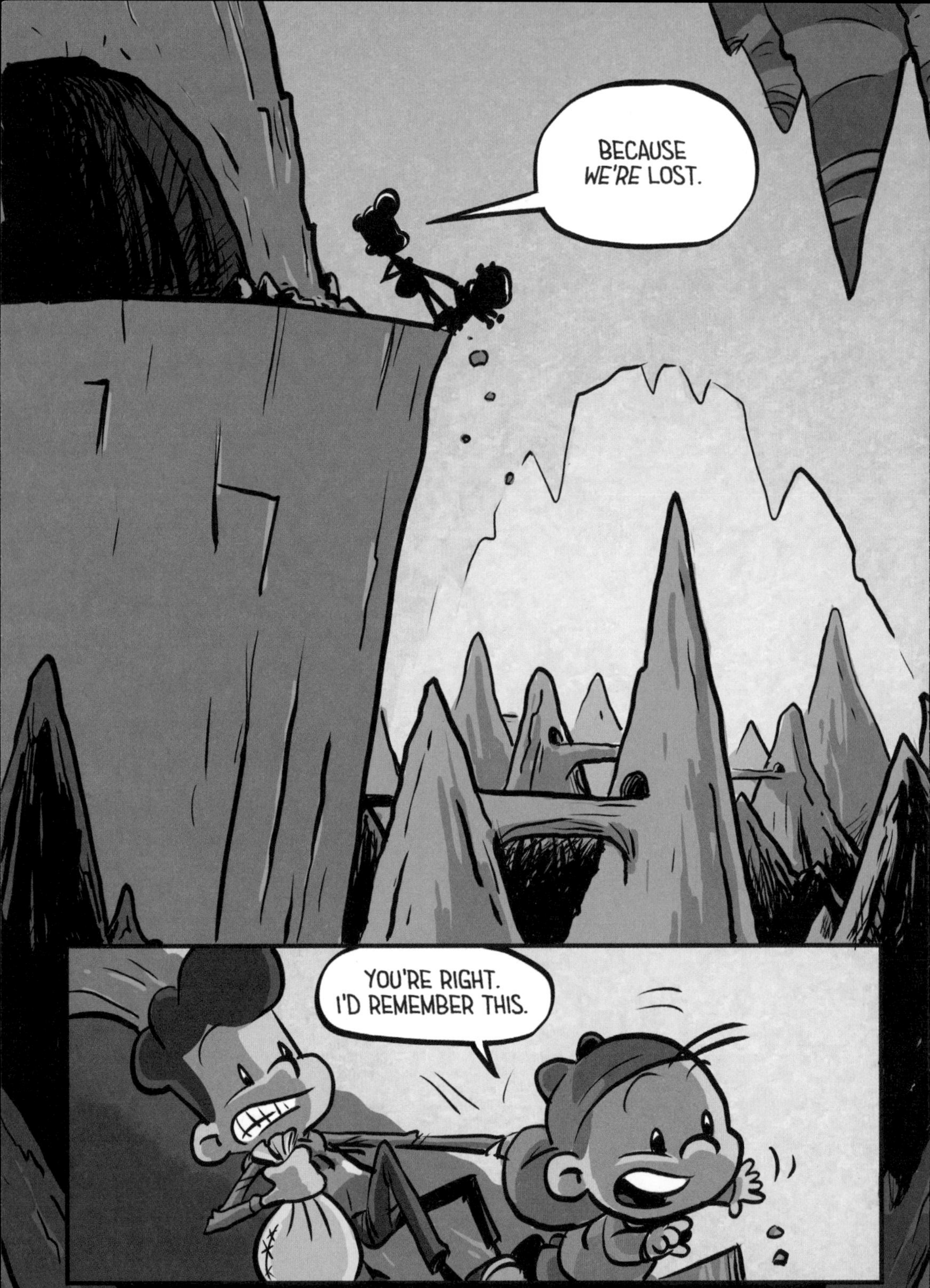
BECAUSE WE'RE LOST.
YOU'RE RIGHT. I'D REMEMBER THIS.

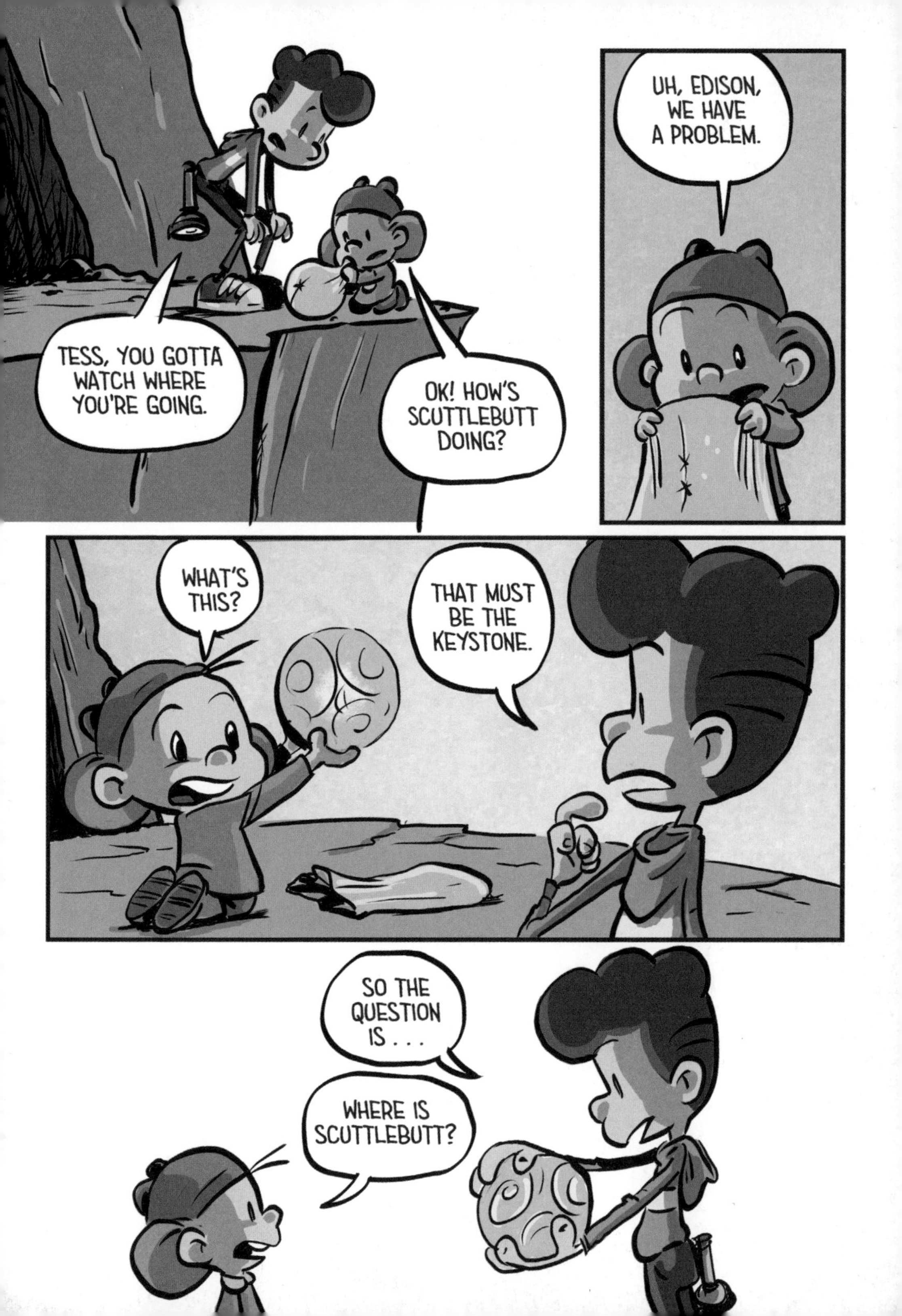
TESS, YOU GOTTA WATCH WHERE YOU'RE GOING.
OK! HOW'S SCUTTLEBUTT DOING?
UH, EDISON, WE HAVE A PROBLEM.
WHAT'S THIS?
THAT MUST BE THE KEYSTONE.
SO THE QUESTION IS . . .
WHERE IS SCUTTLEBUTT?

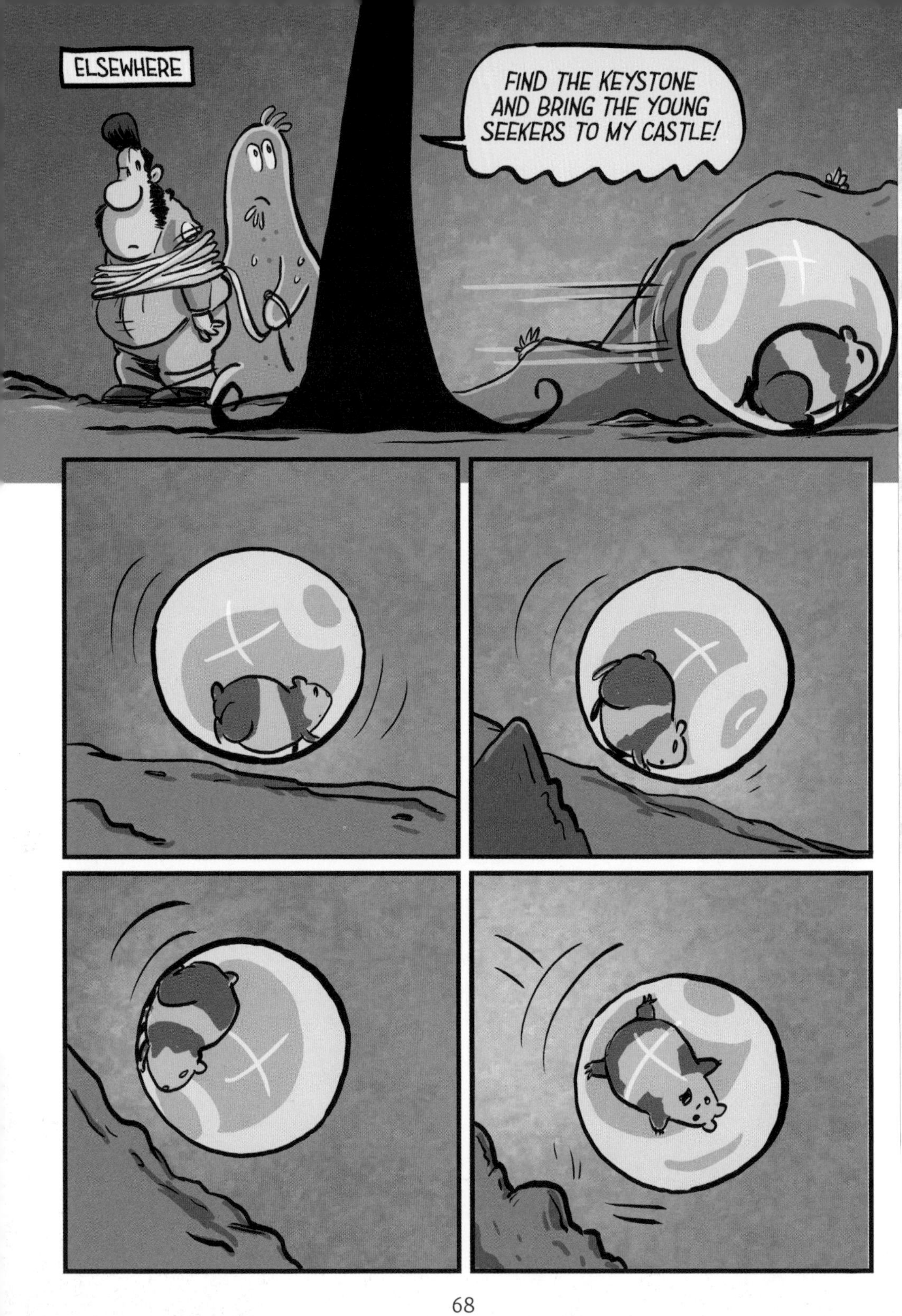
ELSEWHERE
FIND THE KEYSTONE AND BRING THE YOUNG SEEKERS TO MY CASTLE!

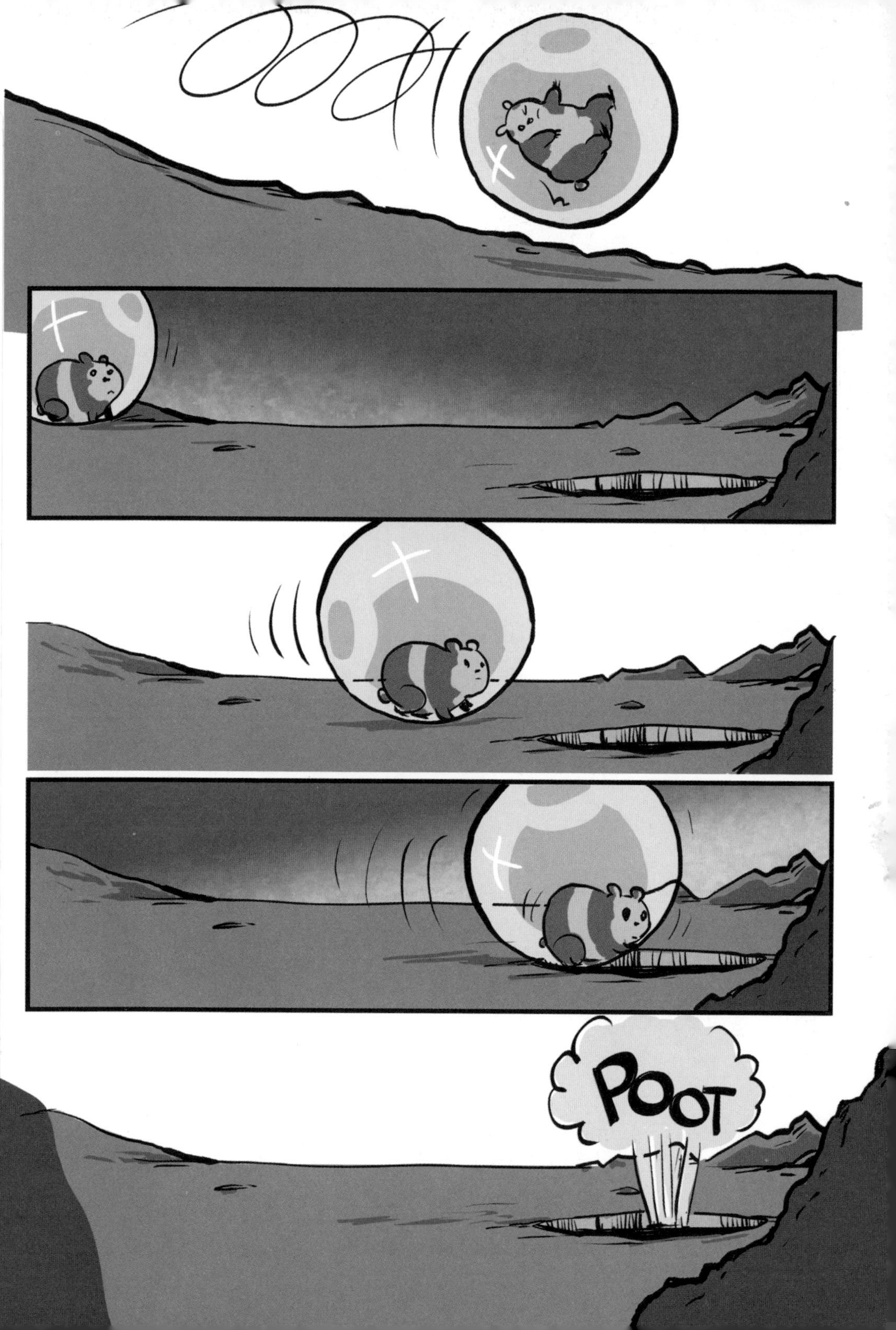
POOT

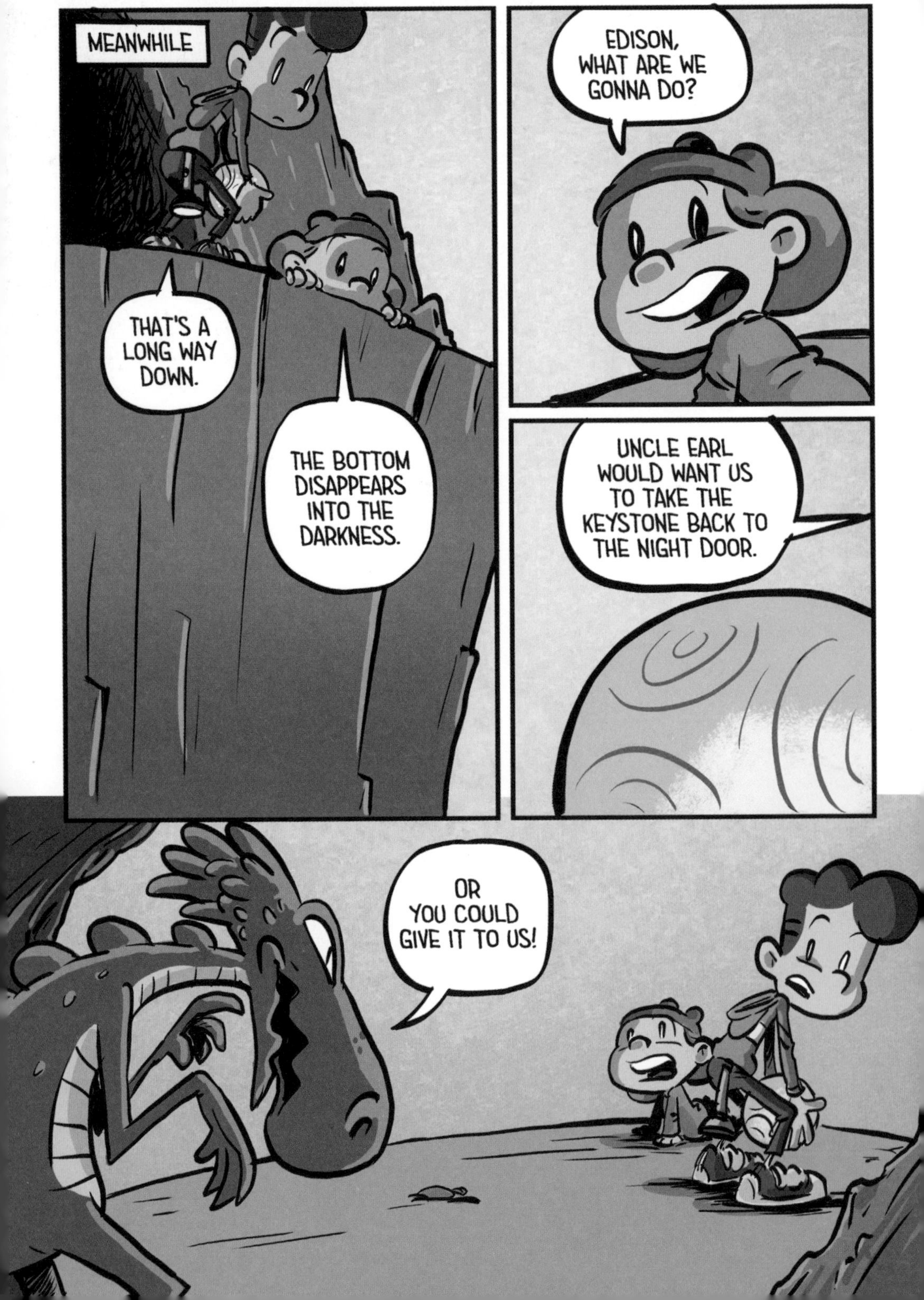
MEANWHILE
THAT'S A LONG WAY DOWN.
THE BOTTOM DISAPPEARS INTO THE DARKNESS.
EDISON, WHAT ARE WE GONNA DO?
UNCLE EARL WOULD WANT US TO TAKE THE KEYSTONE BACK TO THE NIGHT DOOR.
OR YOU COULD GIVE IT TO US!

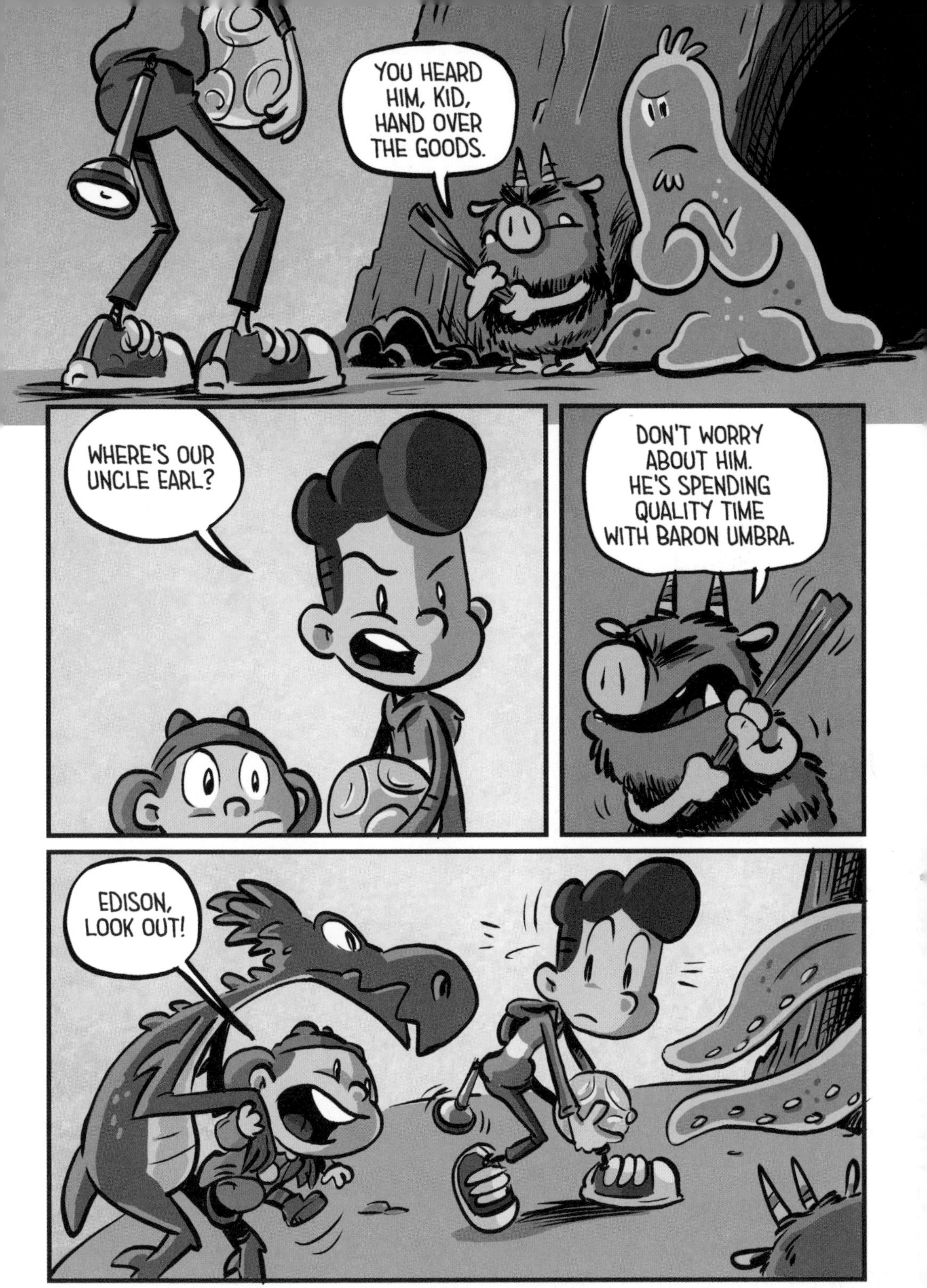
YOU HEARD HIM, KID, HAND OVER THE GOODS.
WHERE'S OUR UNCLE EARL?
DON'T WORRY ABOUT HIM. HE'S SPENDING QUALITY TIME WITH BARON UMBRA.
EDISON, LOOK OUT!

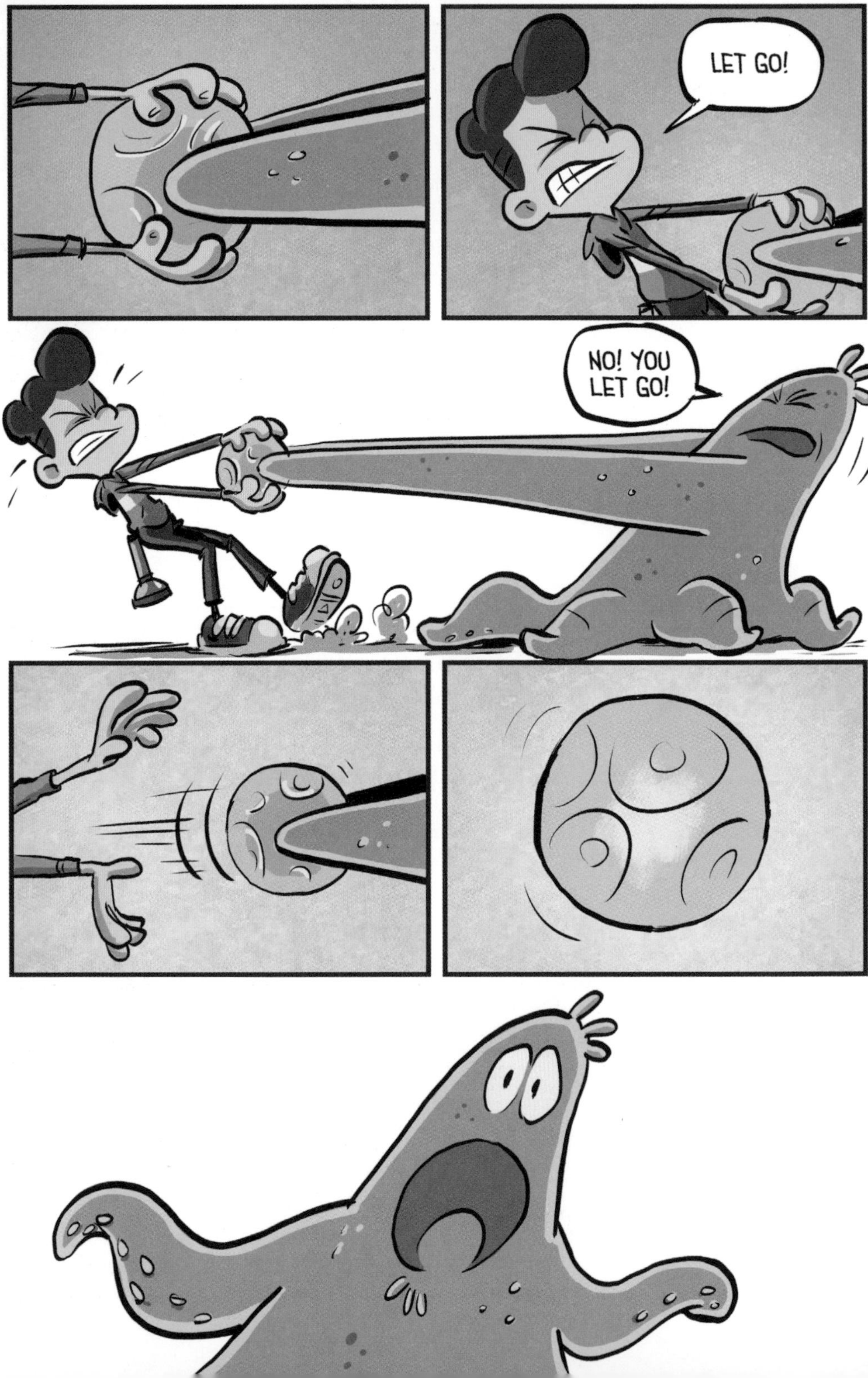
LET GO!
NO! YOU LET GO!

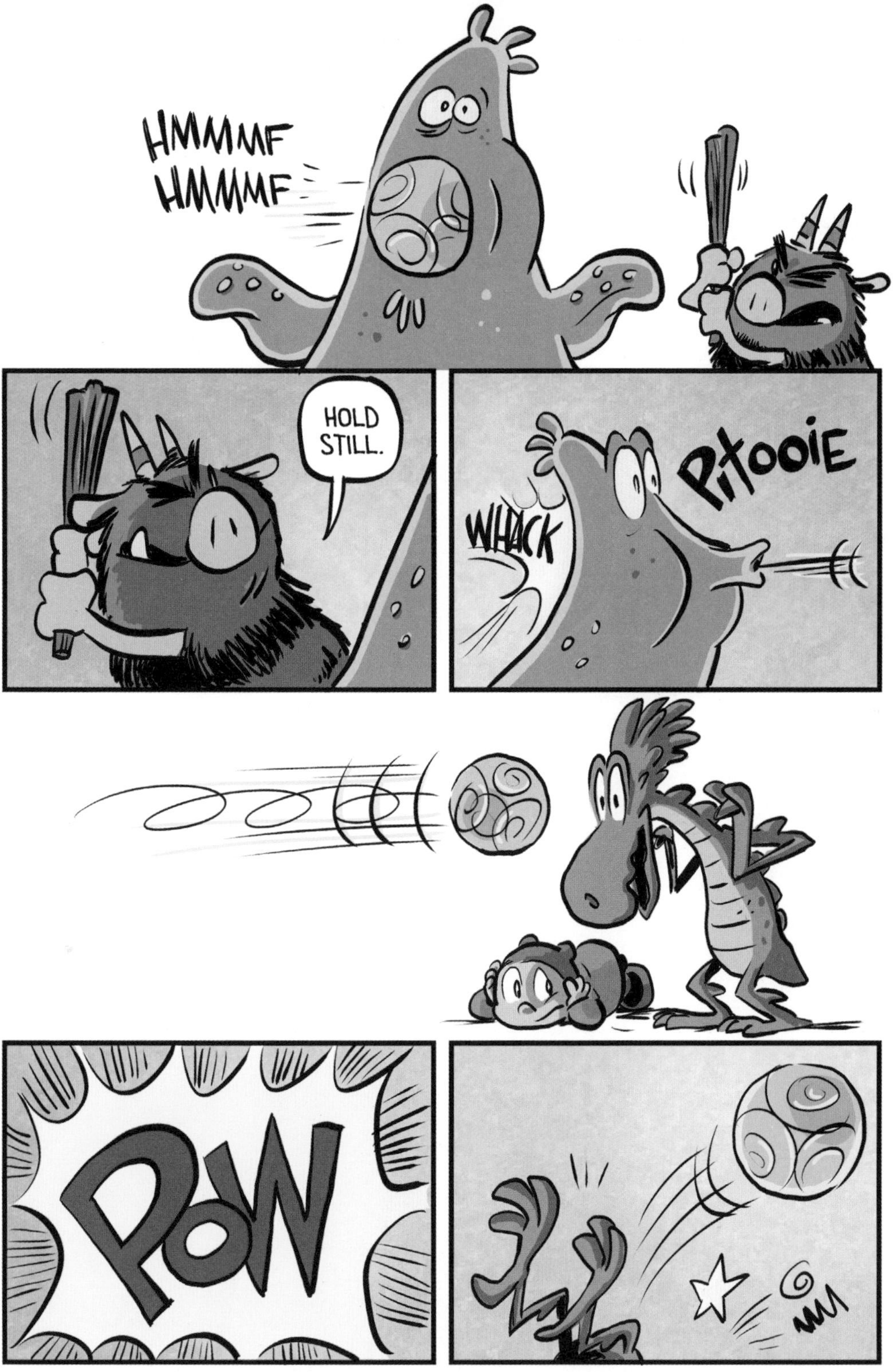
HMMMF
HMMMF
HOLD STILL.
WHACK
PITOOIE
POW

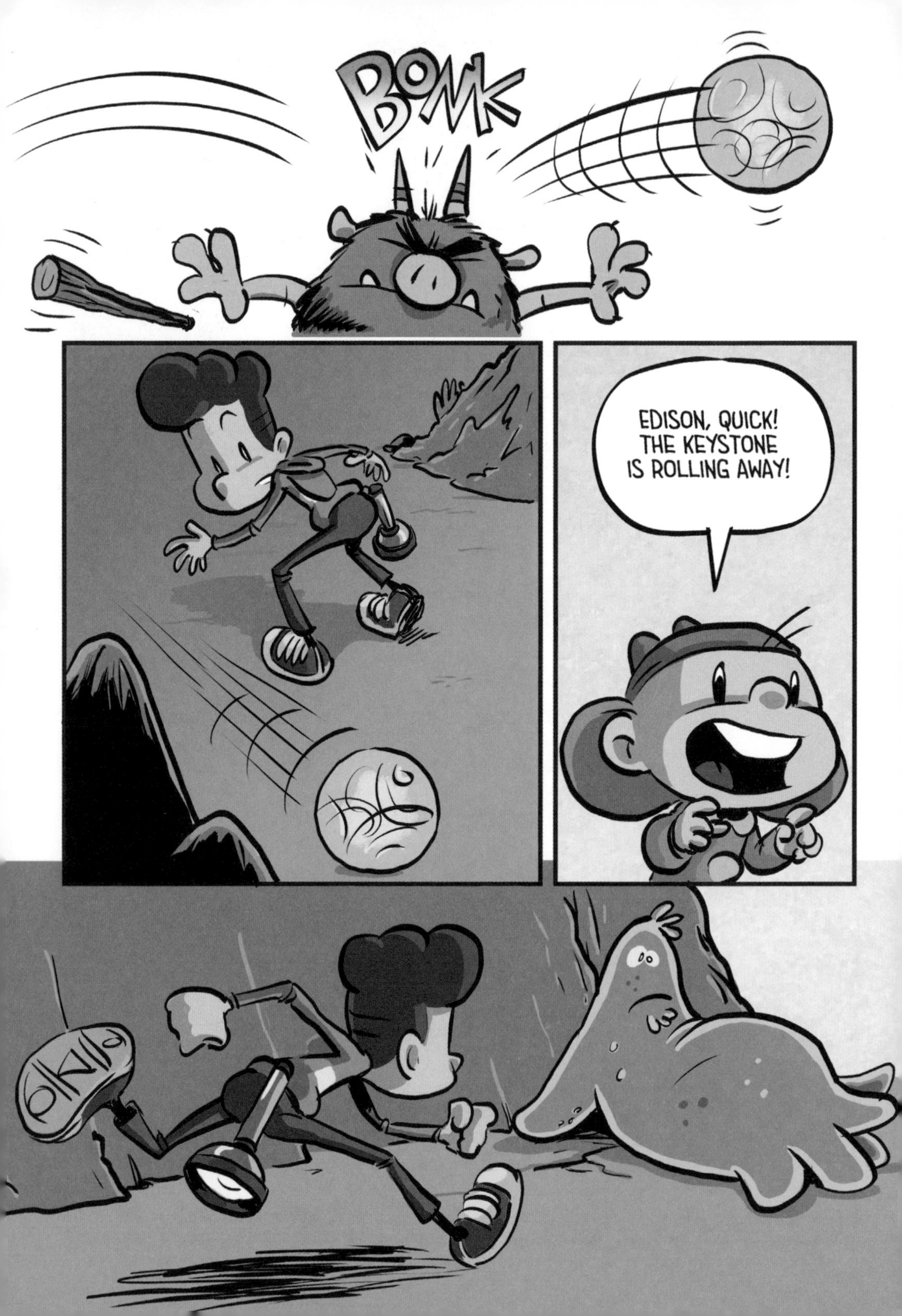
BONK
EDISON, QUICK! THE KEYSTONE IS ROLLING AWAY!

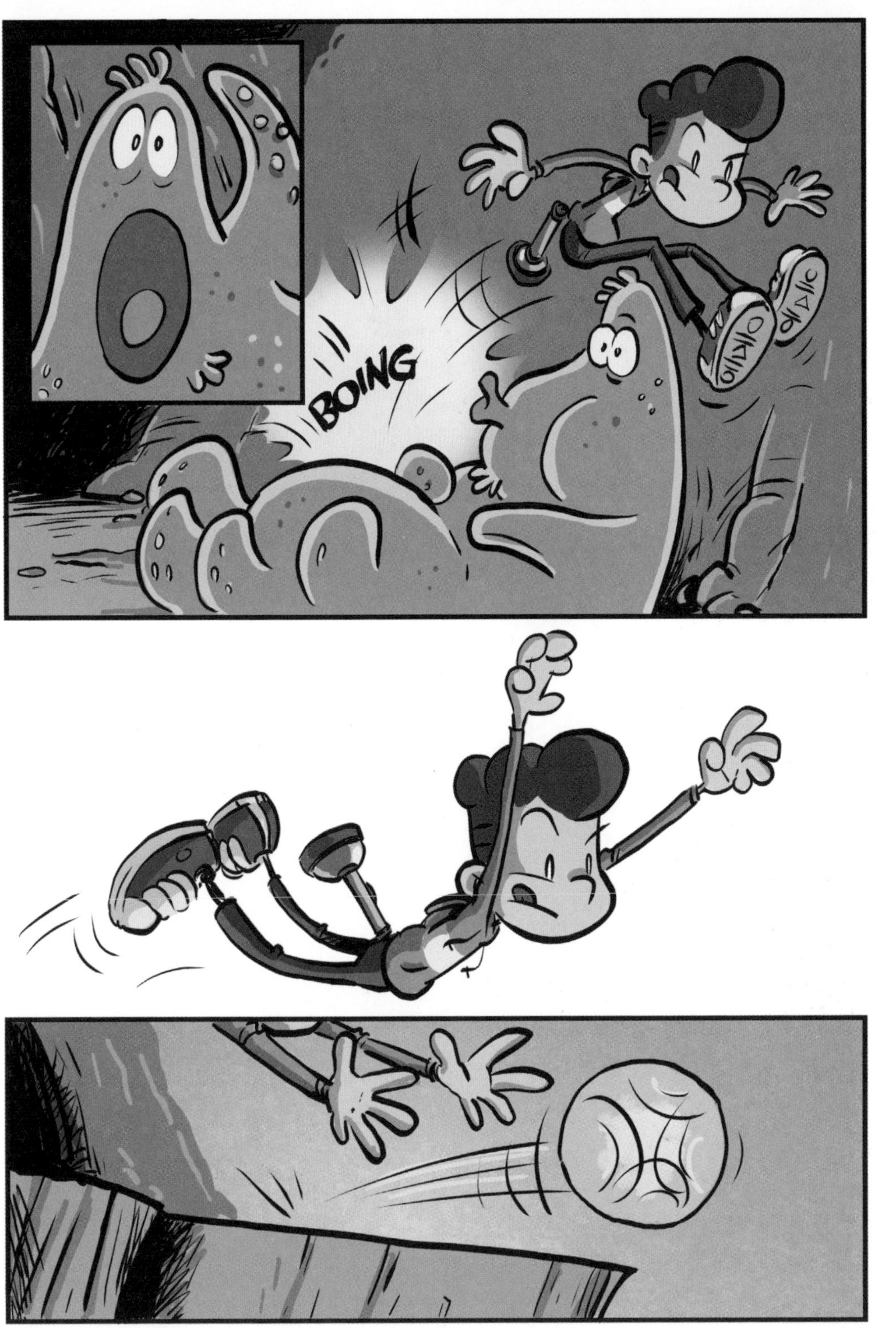
BOING

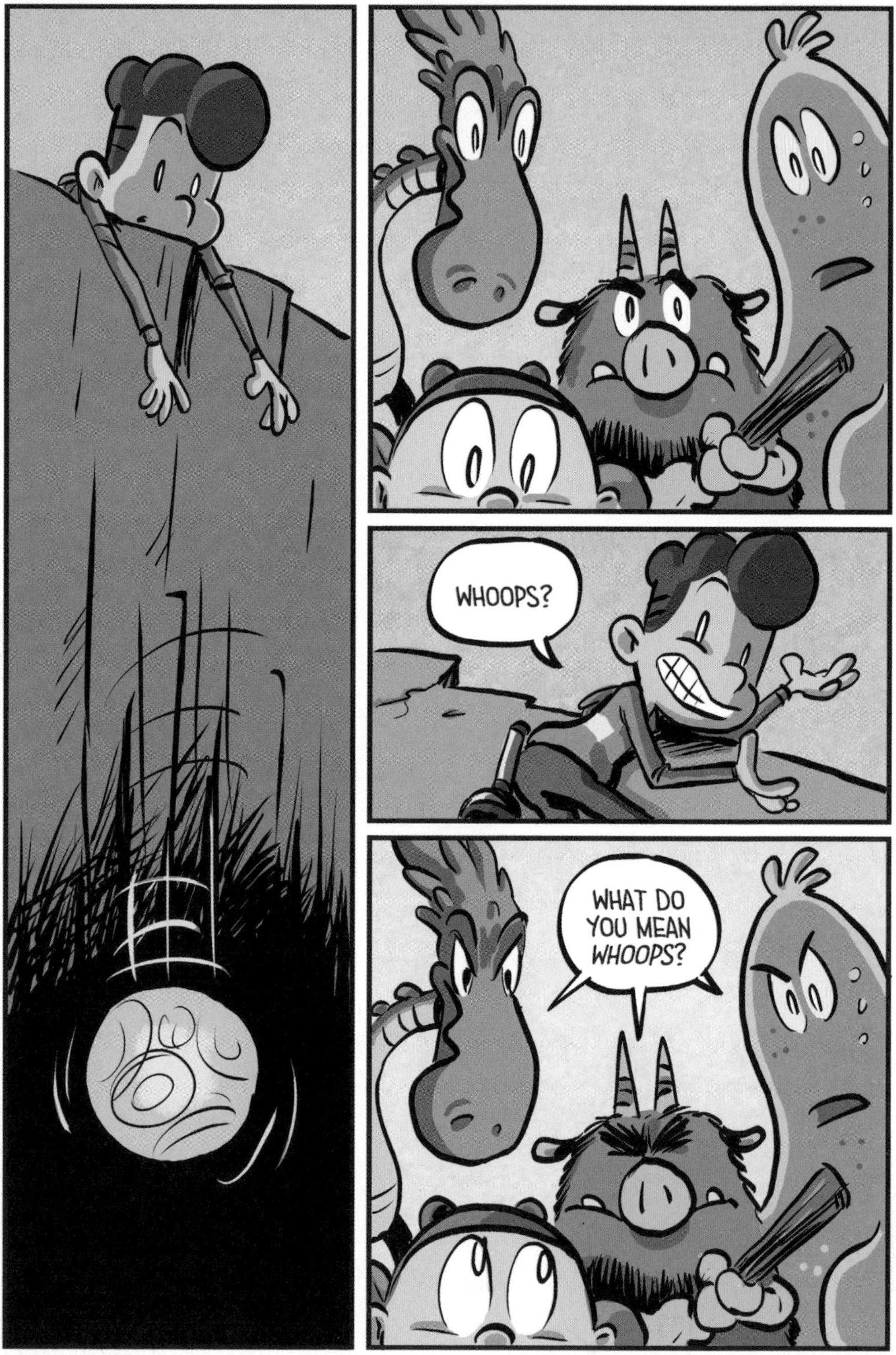
WHOOPS?
WHAT DO YOU MEAN *WHOOPS*?

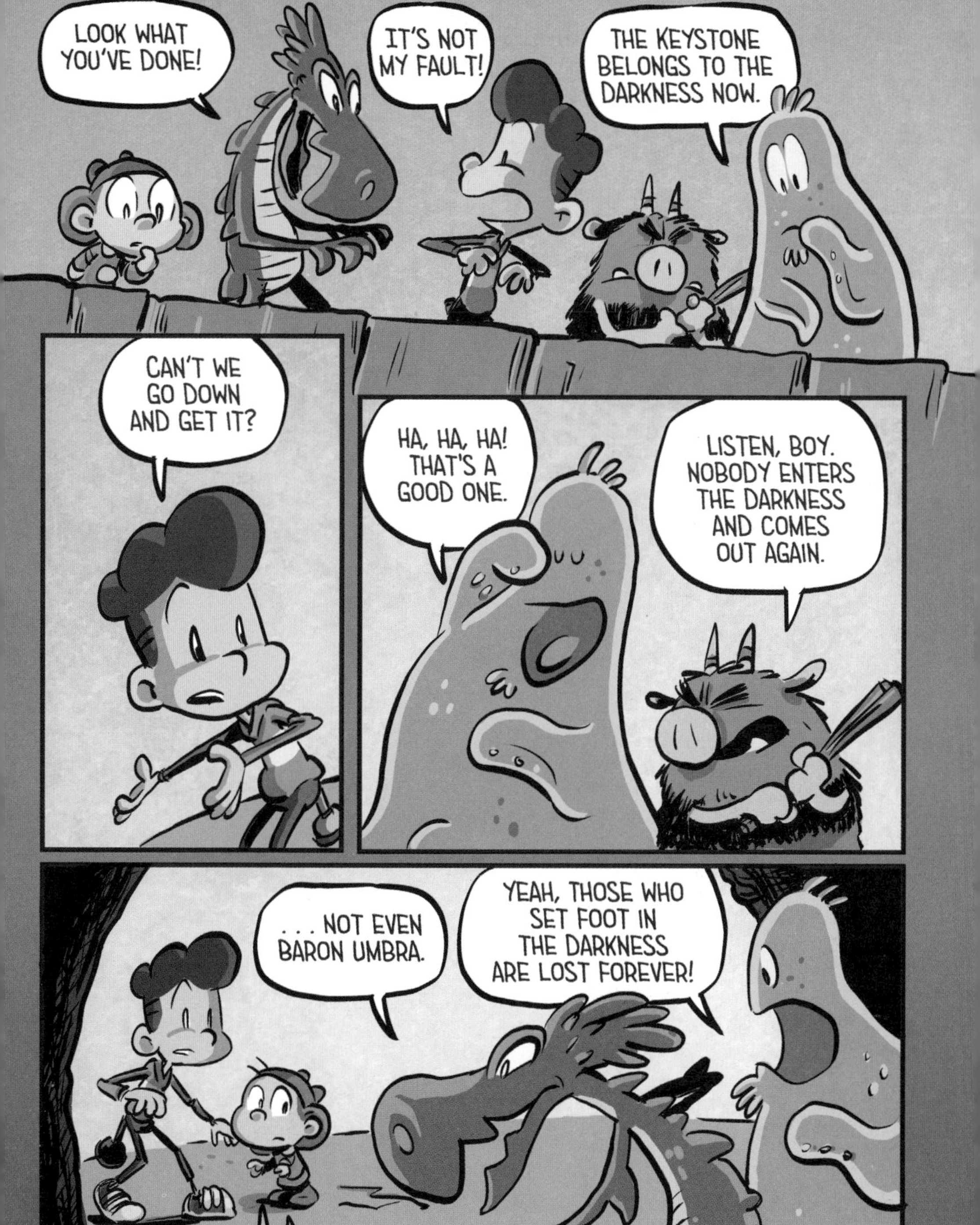
LOOK WHAT YOU'VE DONE!
IT'S NOT MY FAULT!
THE KEYSTONE BELONGS TO THE DARKNESS NOW.
CAN'T WE GO DOWN AND GET IT?
HA, HA, HA! THAT'S A GOOD ONE.
LISTEN, BOY. NOBODY ENTERS THE DARKNESS AND COMES OUT AGAIN.
. . . NOT EVEN BARON UMBRA.
YEAH, THOSE WHO SET FOOT IN THE DARKNESS ARE LOST FOREVER!

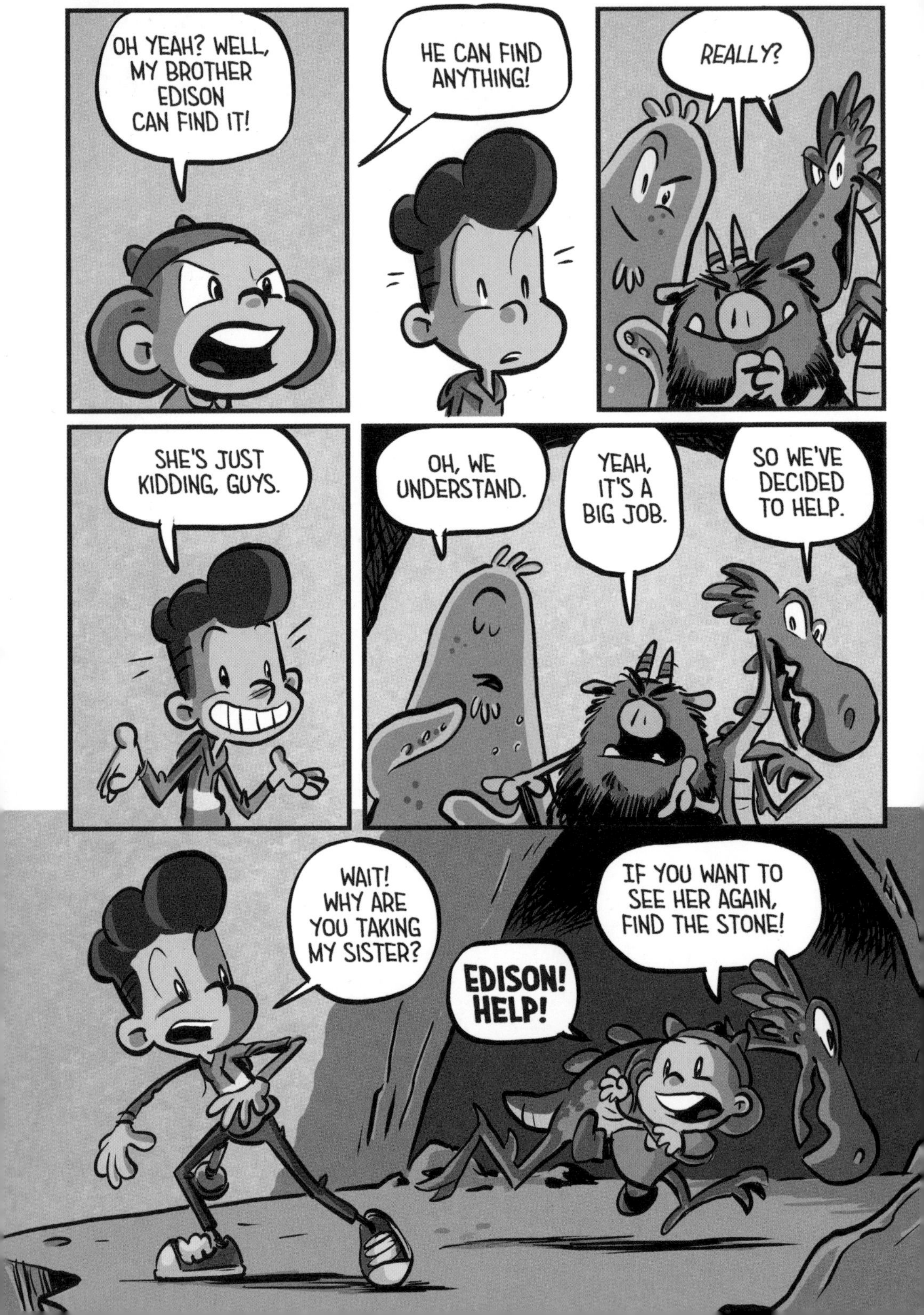
OH YEAH? WELL, MY BROTHER EDISON CAN FIND IT!
HE CAN FIND ANYTHING!
REALLY?
SHE'S JUST KIDDING, GUYS.
OH, WE UNDERSTAND.
YEAH, IT'S A BIG JOB.
SO WE'VE DECIDED TO HELP.
WAIT! WHY ARE YOU TAKING MY SISTER?
EDISON! HELP!
IF YOU WANT TO SEE HER AGAIN, FIND THE STONE!

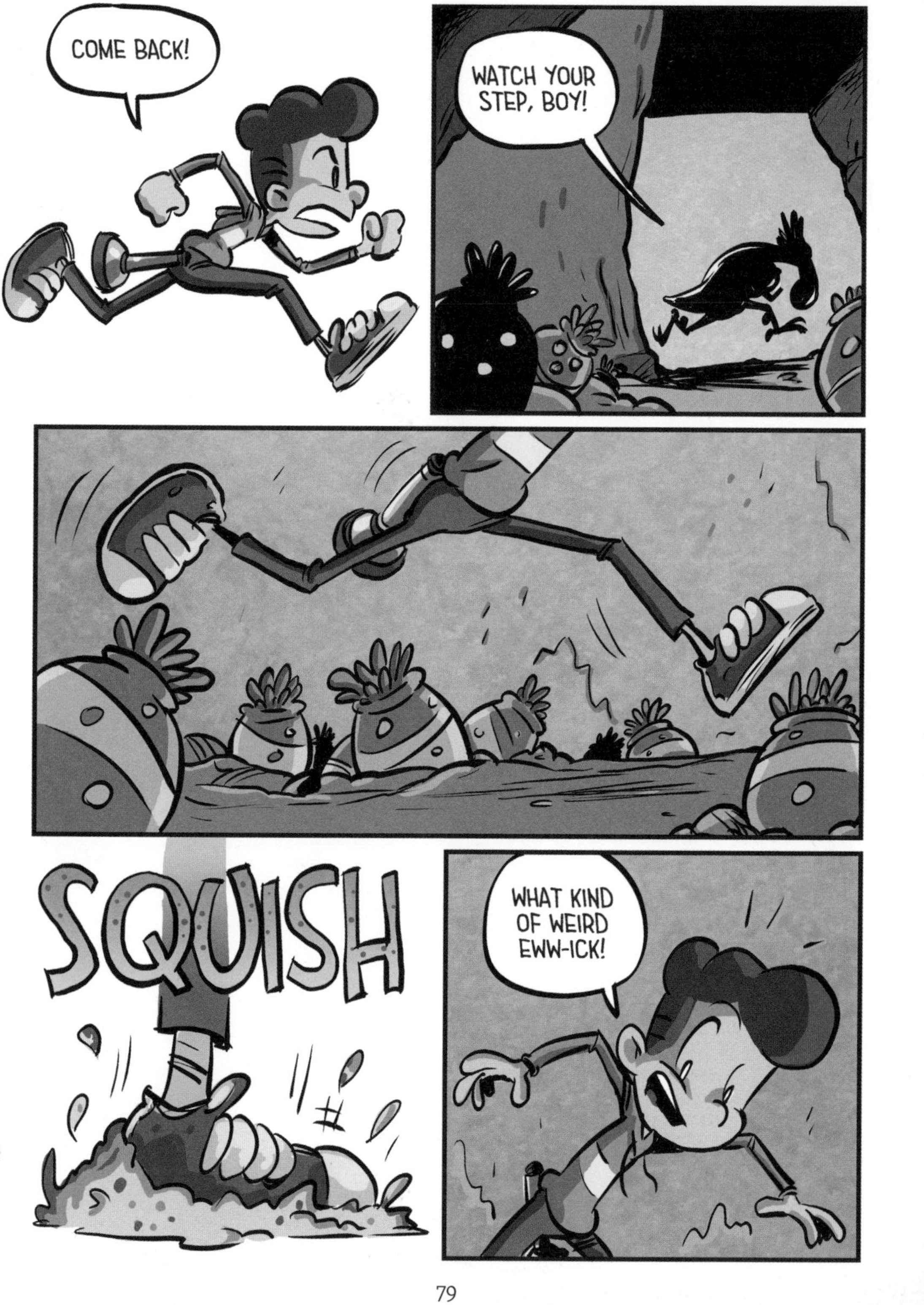
COME BACK!
WATCH YOUR STEP, BOY!
SQUISH
WHAT KIND OF WEIRD EWW-ICK!

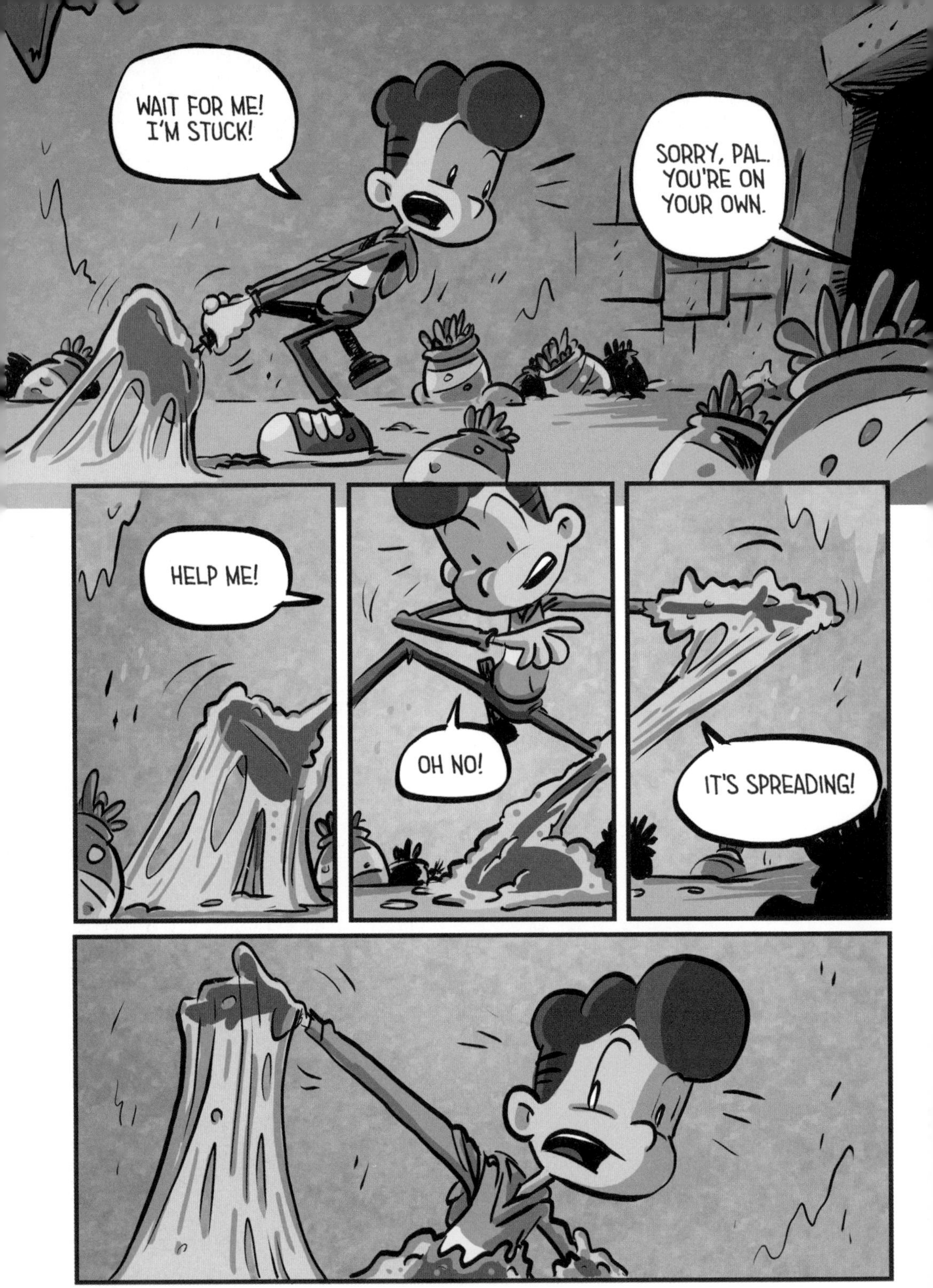
WAIT FOR ME! I'M STUCK!
SORRY, PAL. YOU'RE ON YOUR OWN.
HELP ME!
OH NO!
IT'S SPREADING!

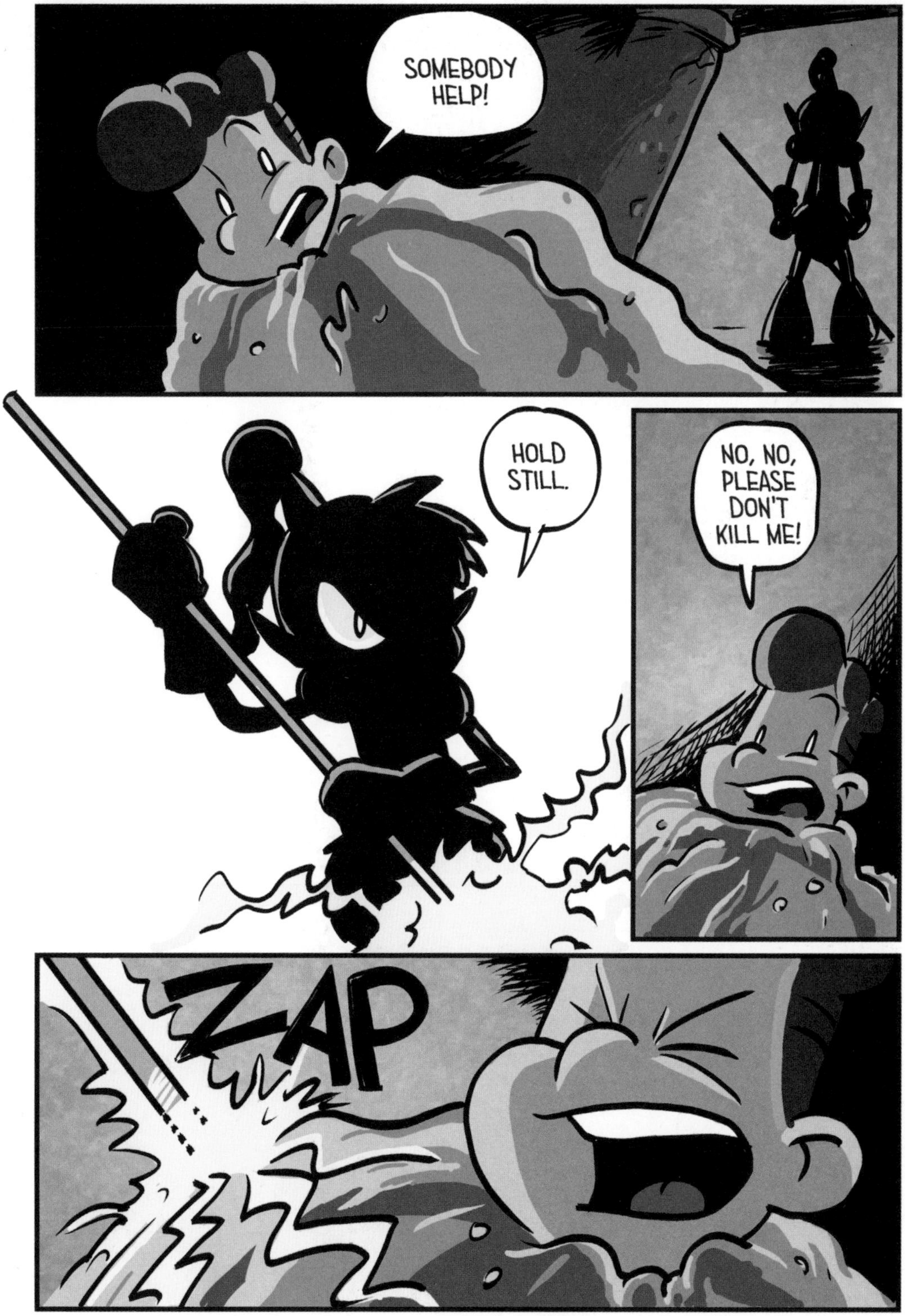
SOMEBODY HELP!
HOLD STILL.
NO, NO, PLEASE DON'T KILL ME!
ZAP

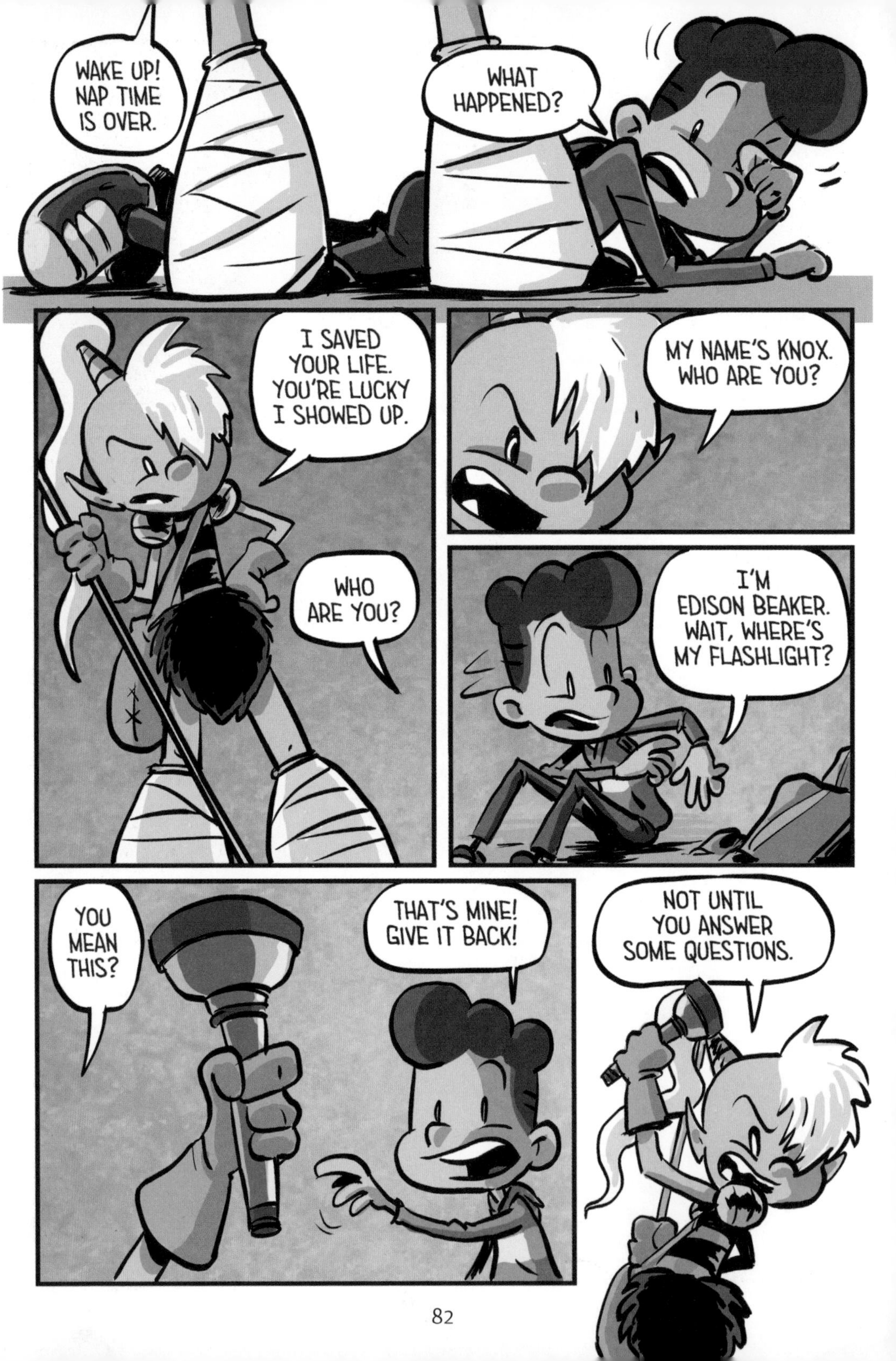
WAKE UP! NAP TIME IS OVER.
WHAT HAPPENED?
I SAVED YOUR LIFE. YOU'RE LUCKY I SHOWED UP.
MY NAME'S KNOX. WHO ARE YOU?
WHO ARE YOU?
I'M EDISON BEAKER. WAIT, WHERE'S MY FLASHLIGHT?
YOU MEAN THIS?
THAT'S MINE! GIVE IT BACK!
NOT UNTIL YOU ANSWER SOME QUESTIONS.

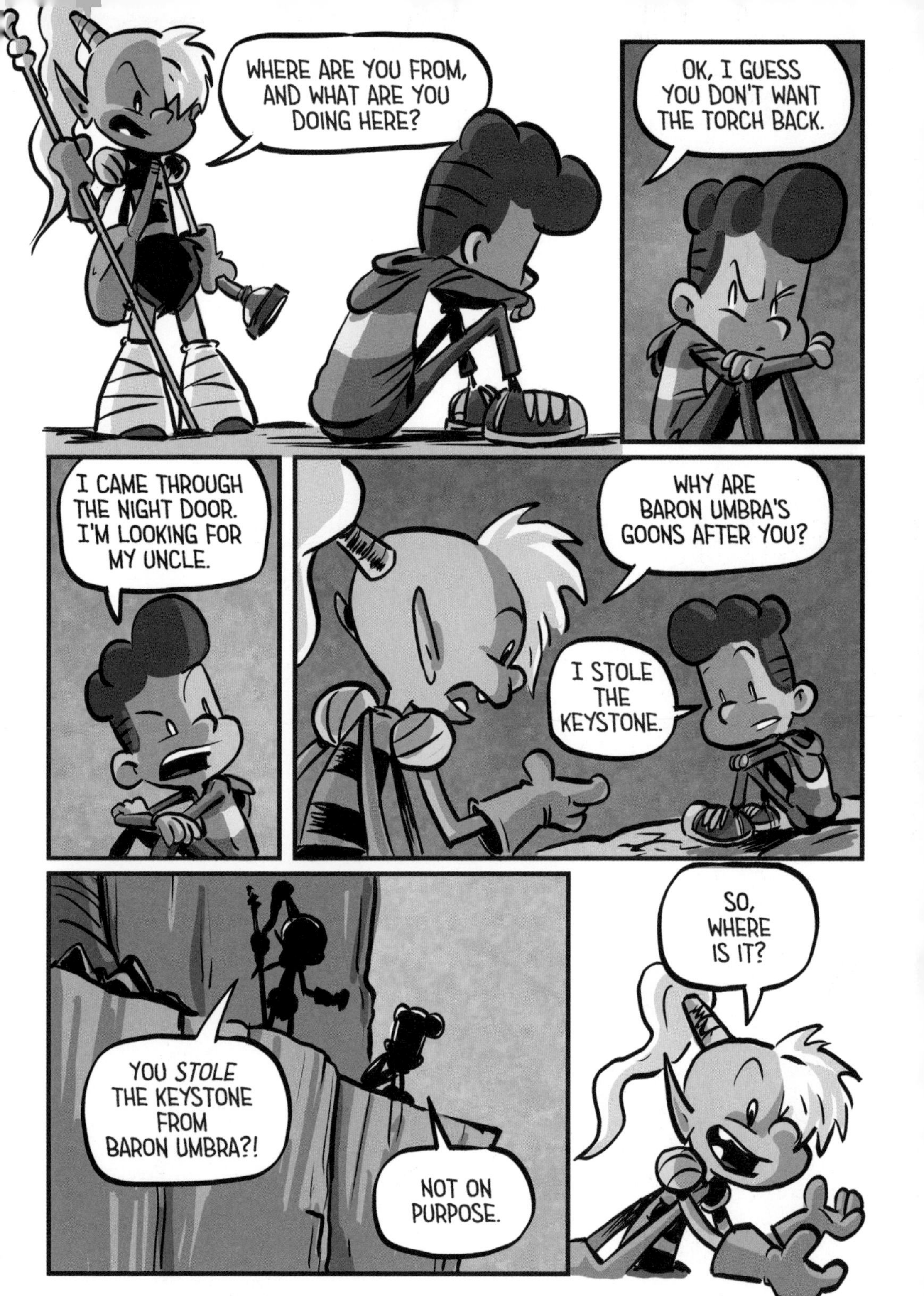
WHERE ARE YOU FROM, AND WHAT ARE YOU DOING HERE?
OK, I GUESS YOU DON'T WANT THE TORCH BACK.
I CAME THROUGH THE NIGHT DOOR. I'M LOOKING FOR MY UNCLE.
WHY ARE BARON UMBRA'S GOONS AFTER YOU?
I STOLE THE KEYSTONE.
YOU *STOLE* THE KEYSTONE FROM BARON UMBRA?!
NOT ON PURPOSE.
SO, WHERE IS IT?

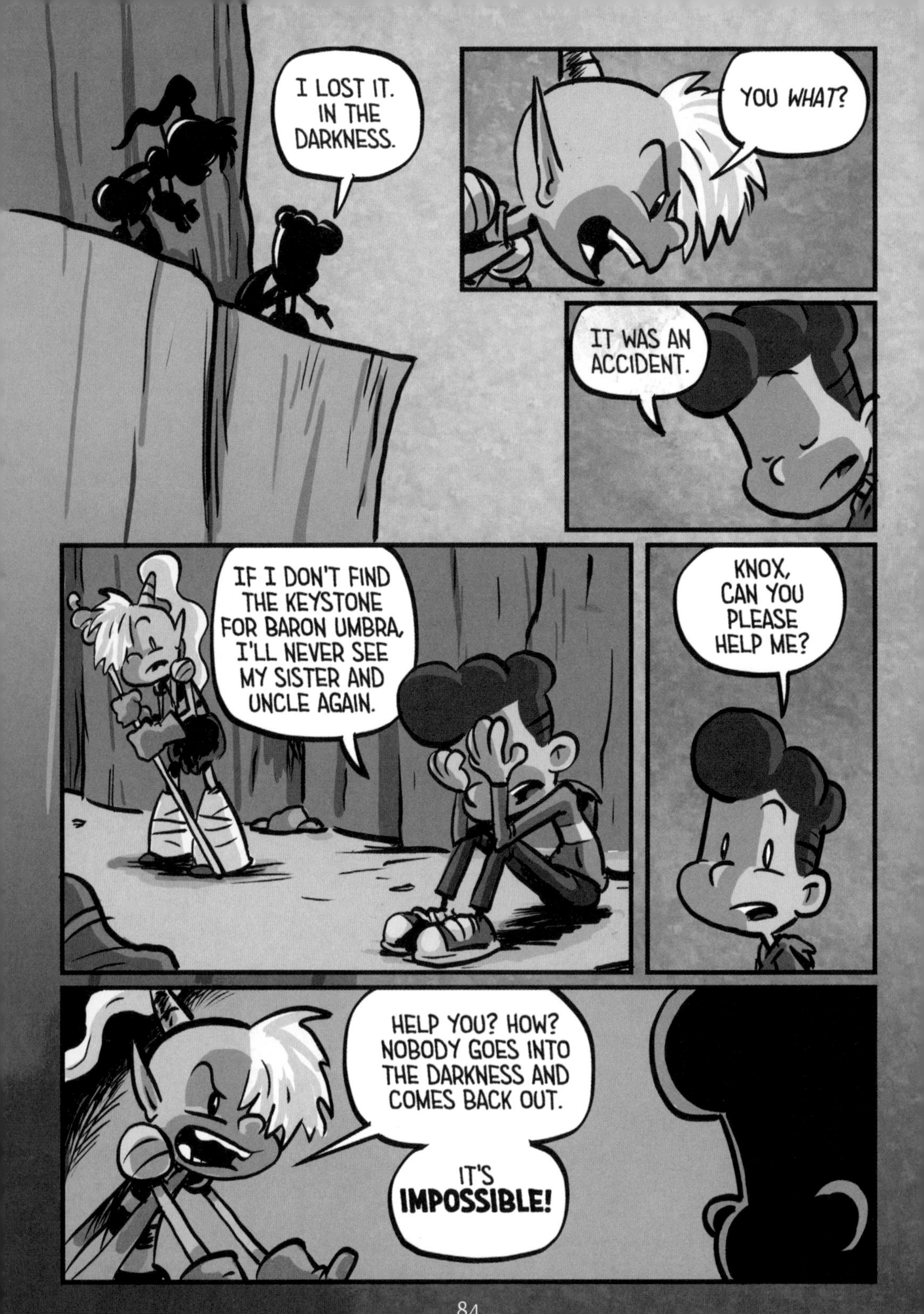

I LOST IT. IN THE DARKNESS.
YOU WHAT?
IT WAS AN ACCIDENT.
IF I DON'T FIND THE KEYSTONE FOR BARON UMBRA, I'LL NEVER SEE MY SISTER AND UNCLE AGAIN.
KNOX, CAN YOU PLEASE HELP ME?
HELP YOU? HOW? NOBODY GOES INTO THE DARKNESS AND COMES BACK OUT.
IT'S **IMPOSSIBLE!**

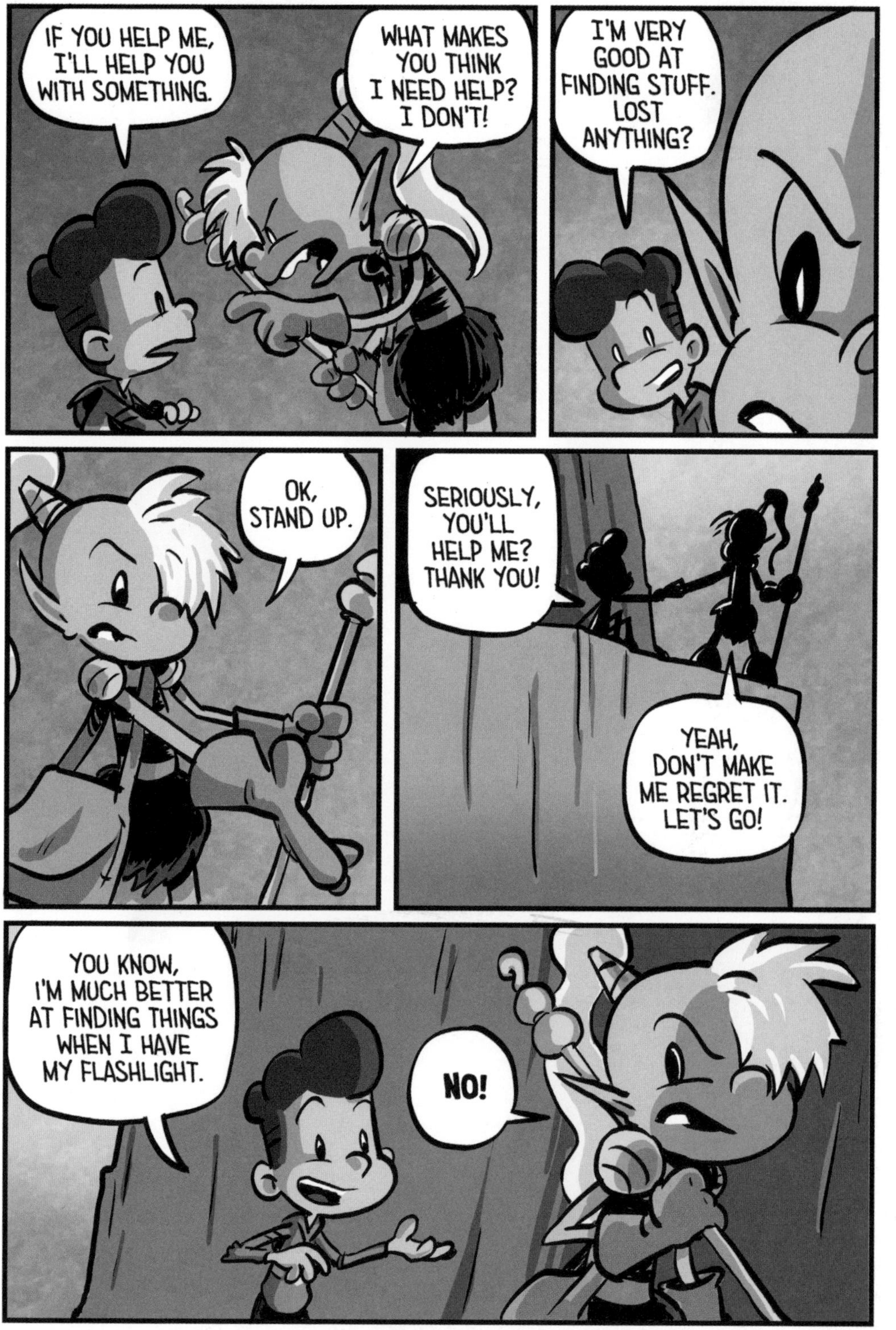

IF YOU HELP ME, I'LL HELP YOU WITH SOMETHING.
WHAT MAKES YOU THINK I NEED HELP? I DON'T!
I'M VERY GOOD AT FINDING STUFF. LOST ANYTHING?
OK, STAND UP.
SERIOUSLY, YOU'LL HELP ME? THANK YOU!
YEAH, DON'T MAKE ME REGRET IT. LET'S GO!
YOU KNOW, I'M MUCH BETTER AT FINDING THINGS WHEN I HAVE MY FLASHLIGHT.
NO!

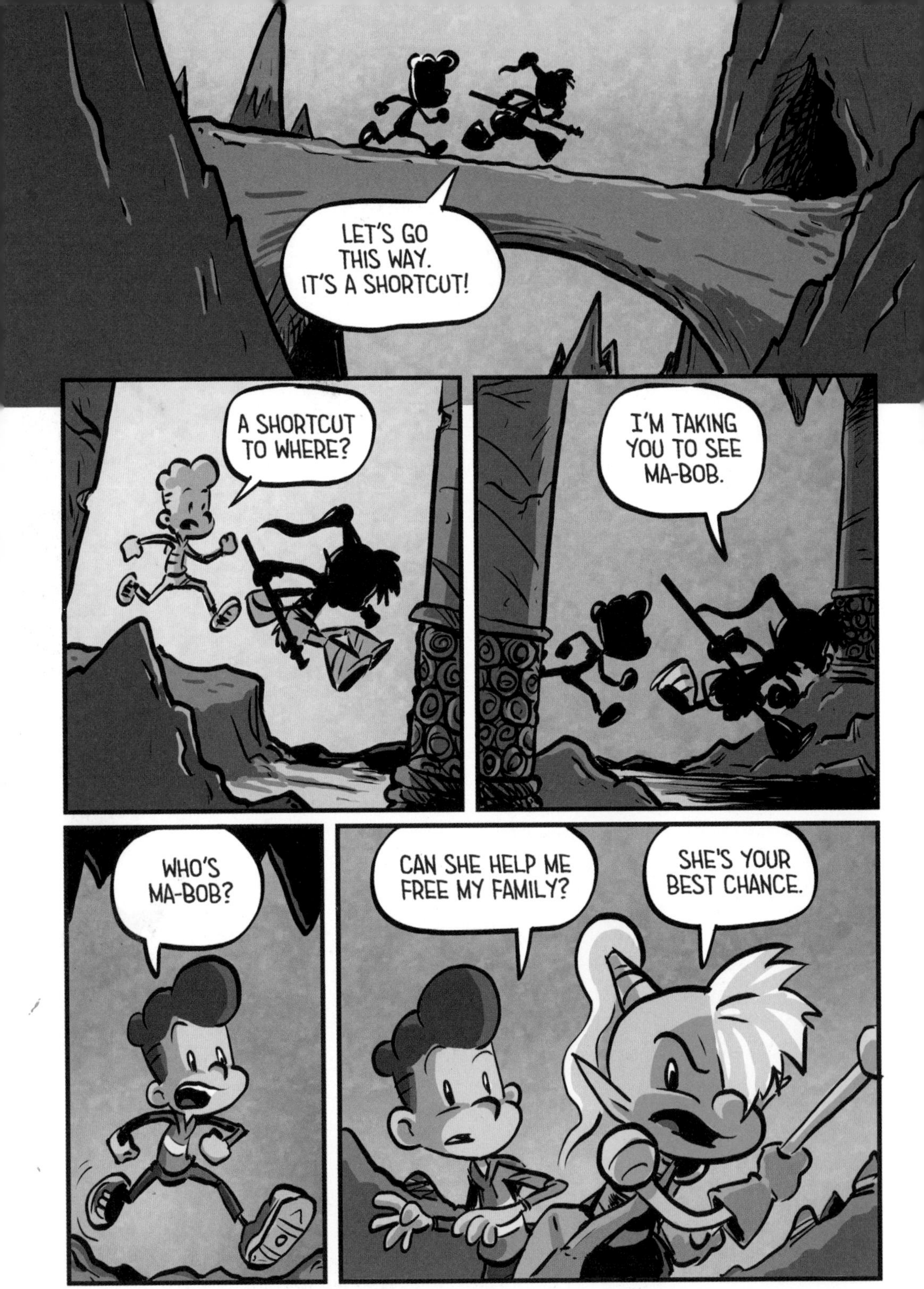

LET'S GO THIS WAY. IT'S A SHORTCUT!
A SHORTCUT TO WHERE?
I'M TAKING YOU TO SEE MA-BOB.
WHO'S MA-BOB?
CAN SHE HELP ME FREE MY FAMILY?
SHE'S YOUR BEST CHANCE.

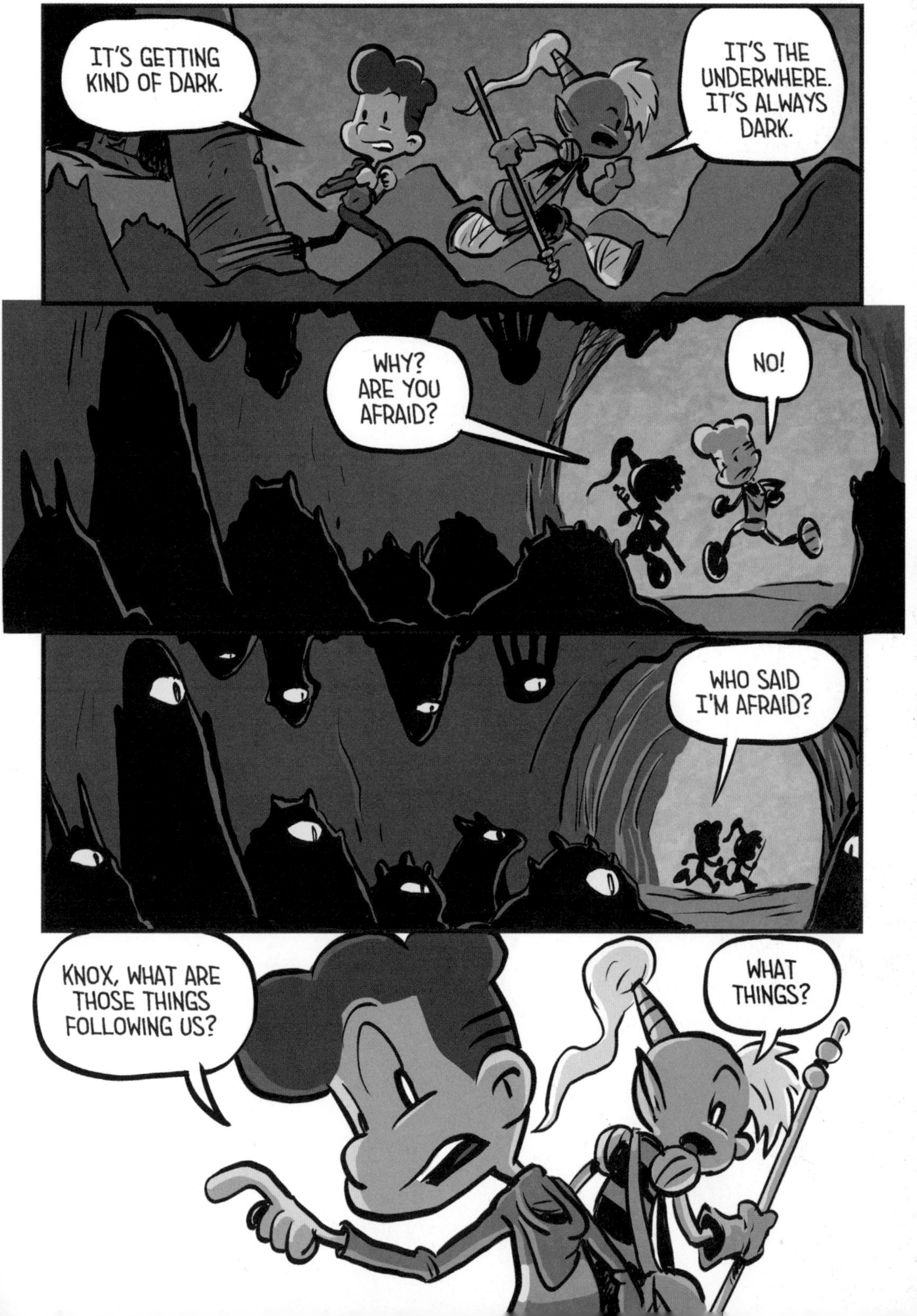
IT'S GETTING KIND OF DARK.
IT'S THE UNDERWHERE. IT'S ALWAYS DARK.
WHY? ARE YOU AFRAID?
NO!
WHO SAID I'M AFRAID?
KNOX, WHAT ARE THOSE THINGS FOLLOWING US?
WHAT THINGS?

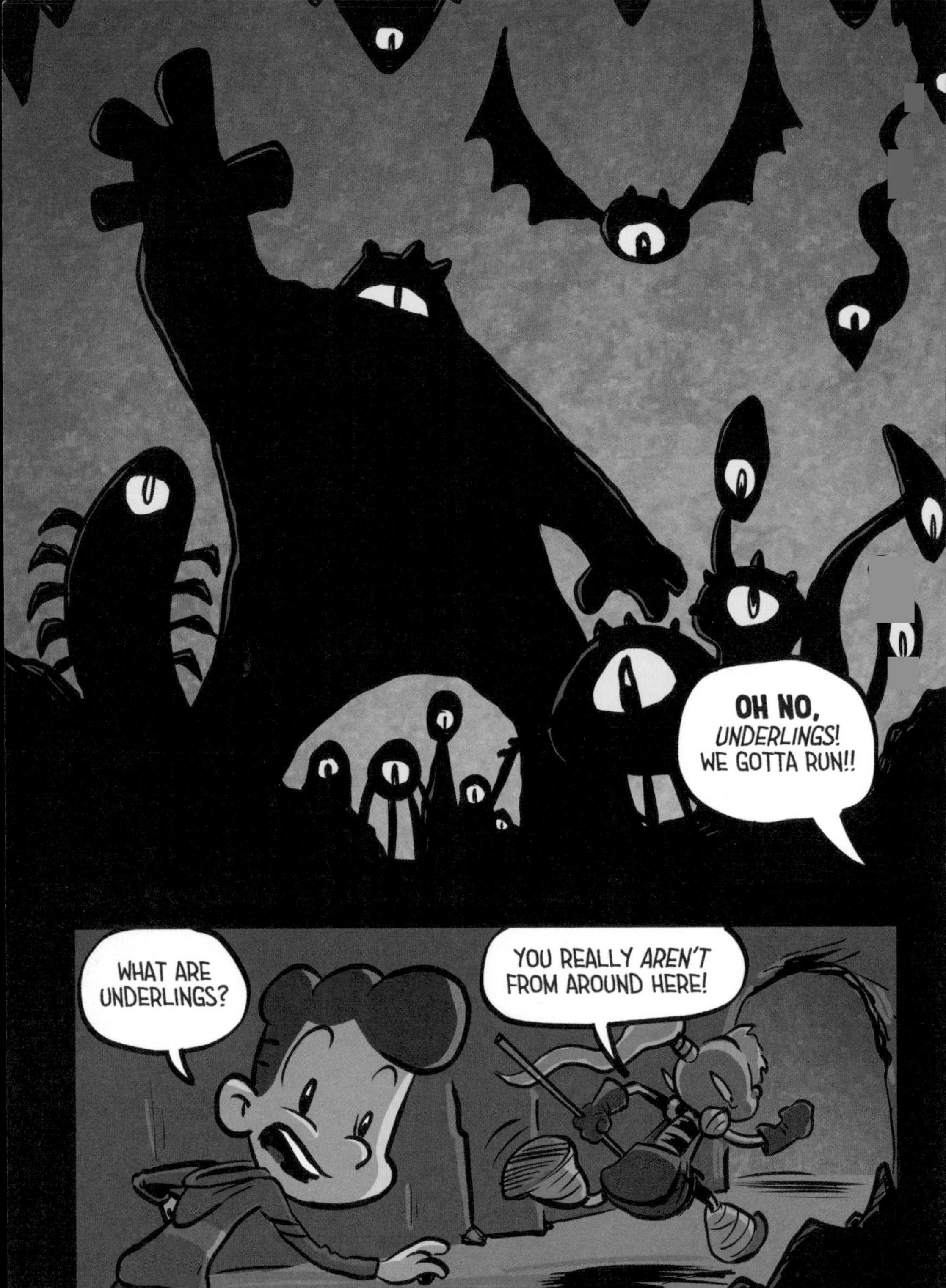
OH NO, UNDERLINGS! WE GOTTA RUN!!
WHAT ARE UNDERLINGS?
YOU REALLY AREN'T FROM AROUND HERE!

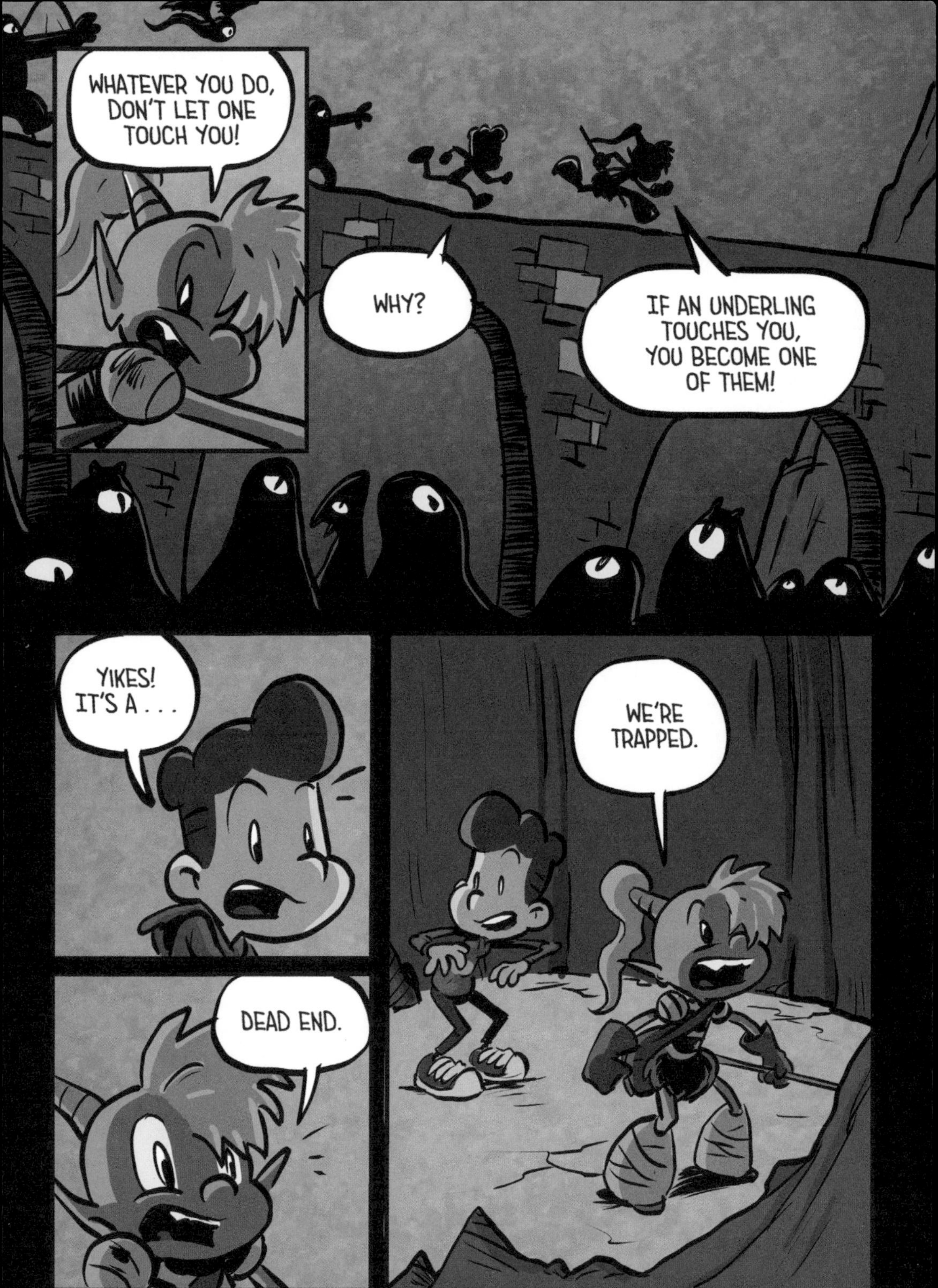
WHATEVER YOU DO, DON'T LET ONE TOUCH YOU!
WHY?
IF AN UNDERLING TOUCHES YOU, YOU BECOME ONE OF THEM!
YIKES! IT'S A . . .
DEAD END.
WE'RE TRAPPED.

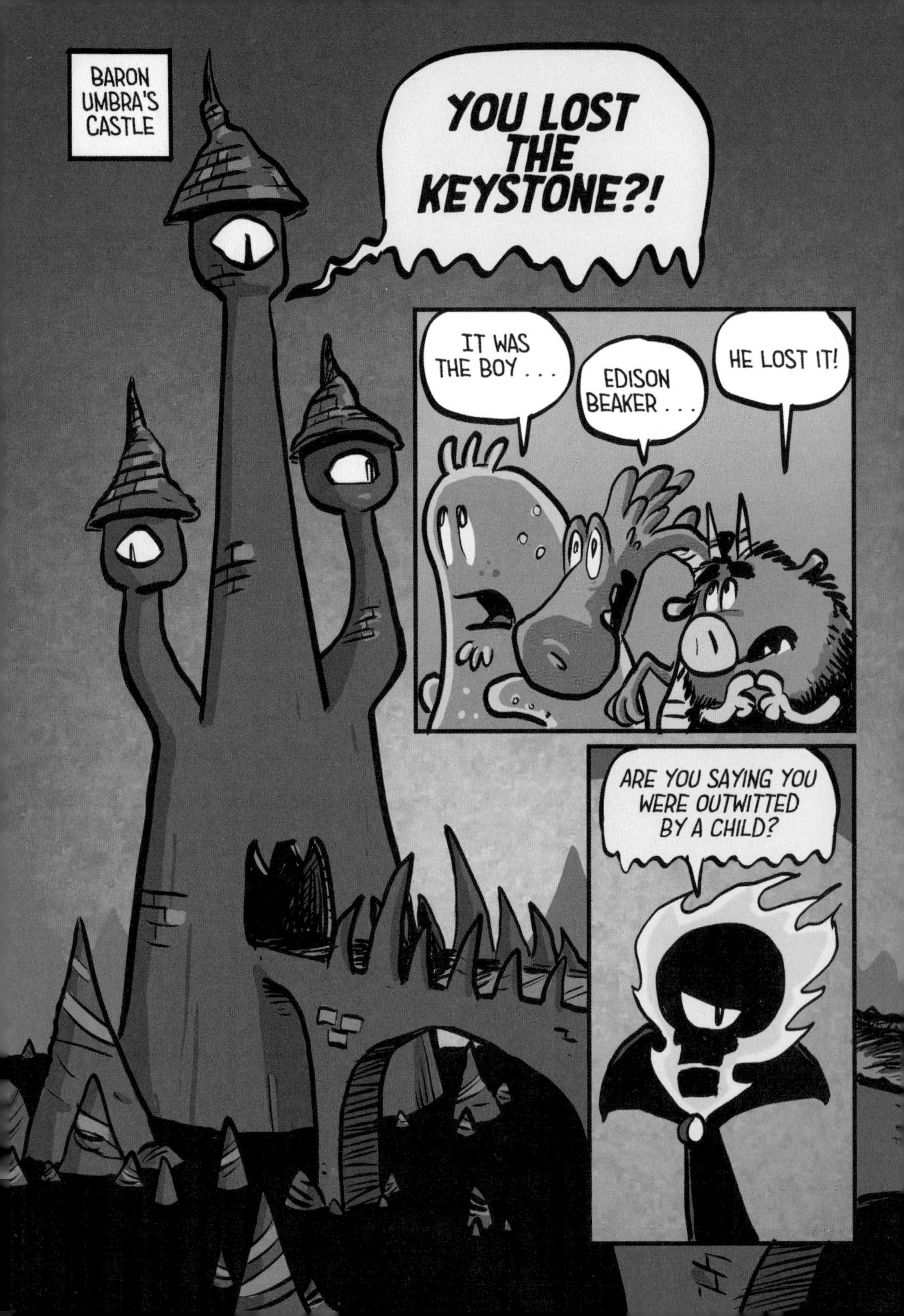
BARON UMBRA'S CASTLE
YOU LOST THE KEYSTONE?!
IT WAS THE BOY . . .
EDISON BEAKER . . .
HE LOST IT!
ARE YOU SAYING YOU WERE OUTWITTED BY A CHILD?

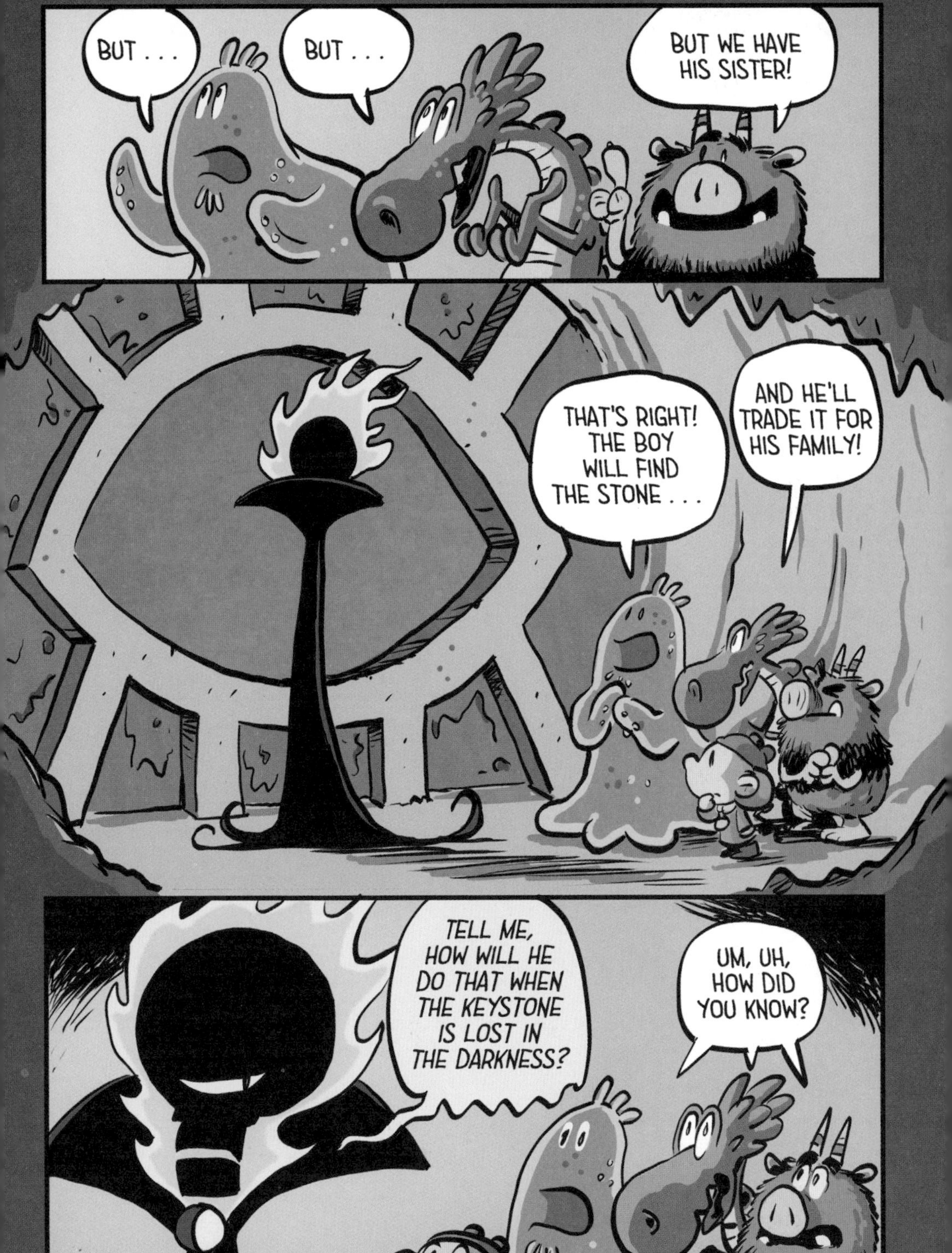

BUT . . .
BUT . . .
BUT WE HAVE HIS SISTER!
THAT'S RIGHT! THE BOY WILL FIND THE STONE . . .
AND HE'LL TRADE IT FOR HIS FAMILY!
TELL ME, HOW WILL HE DO THAT WHEN THE KEYSTONE IS LOST IN THE DARKNESS?
UM, UH, HOW DID YOU KNOW?

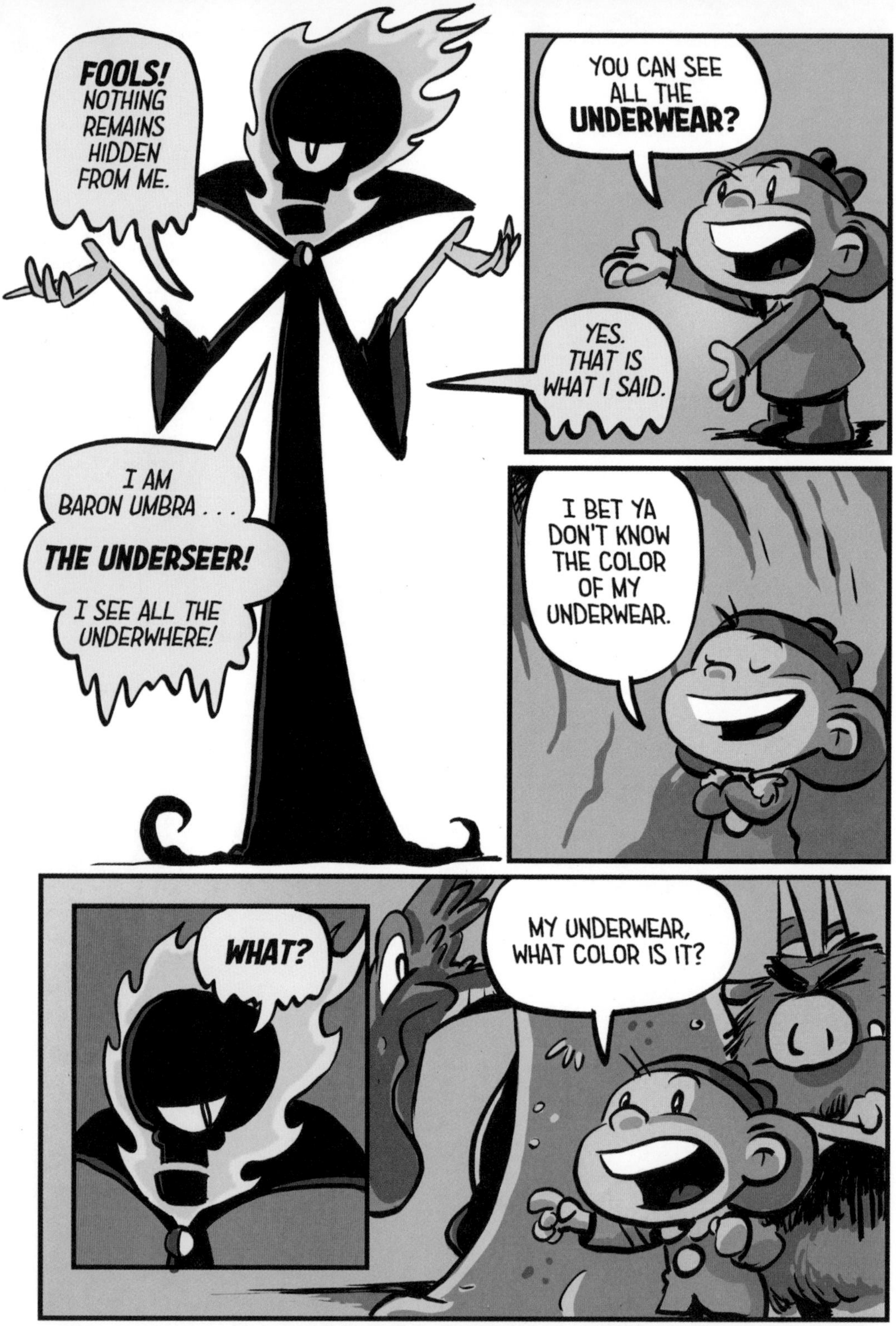
FOOLS! NOTHING REMAINS HIDDEN FROM ME.
I AM BARON UMBRA . . .
THE UNDERSEER!
I SEE ALL THE UNDERWHERE!
YOU CAN SEE ALL THE UNDERWEAR?
YES. THAT IS WHAT I SAID.
I BET YA DON'T KNOW THE COLOR OF MY UNDERWEAR.
WHAT?
MY UNDERWEAR, WHAT COLOR IS IT?

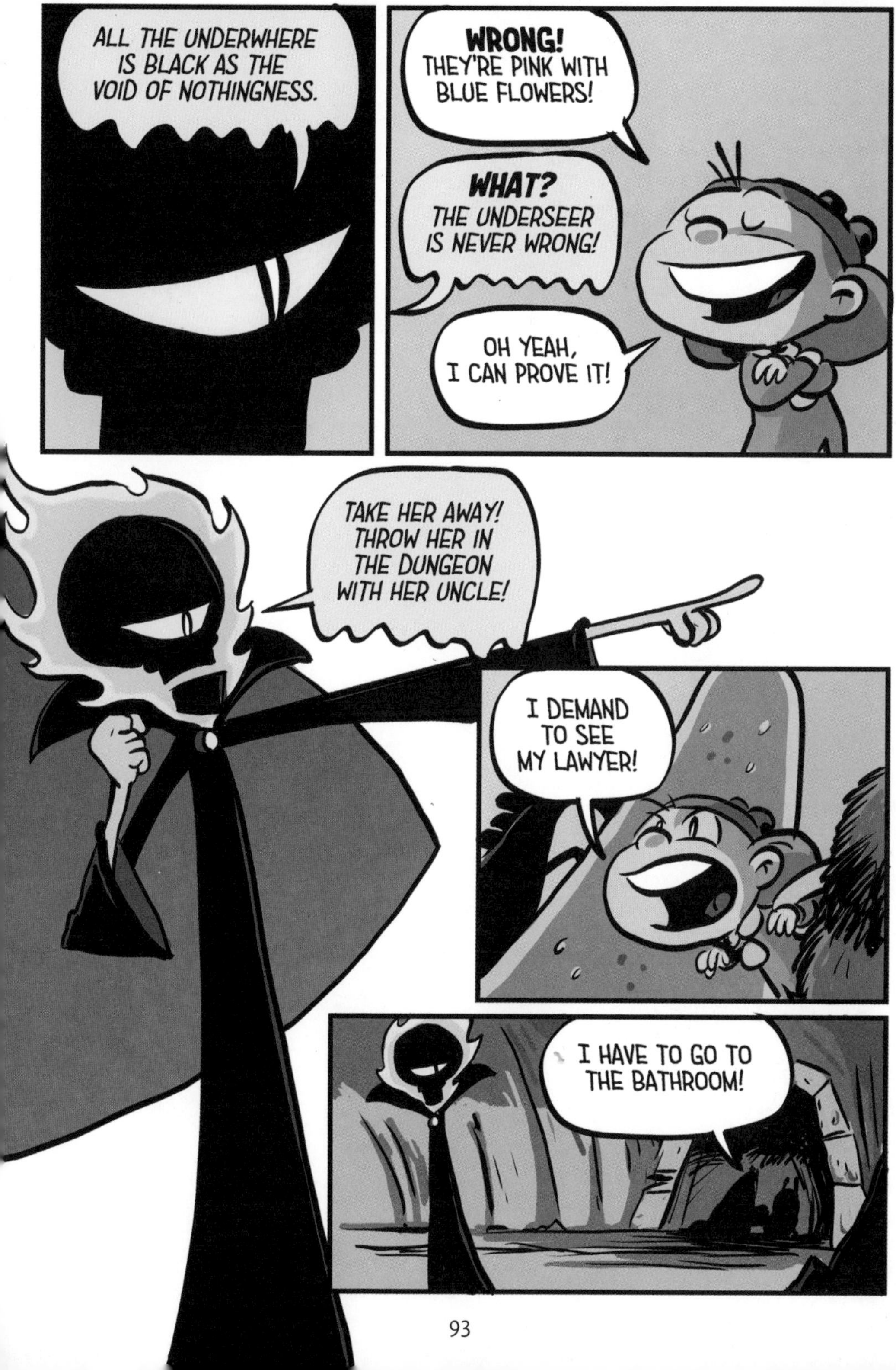
ALL THE UNDERWHERE IS BLACK AS THE VOID OF NOTHINGNESS.
WRONG! THEY'RE PINK WITH BLUE FLOWERS!
WHAT? THE UNDERSEER IS NEVER WRONG!
OH YEAH, I CAN PROVE IT!
TAKE HER AWAY! THROW HER IN THE DUNGEON WITH HER UNCLE!
I DEMAND TO SEE MY LAWYER!
I HAVE TO GO TO THE BATHROOM!

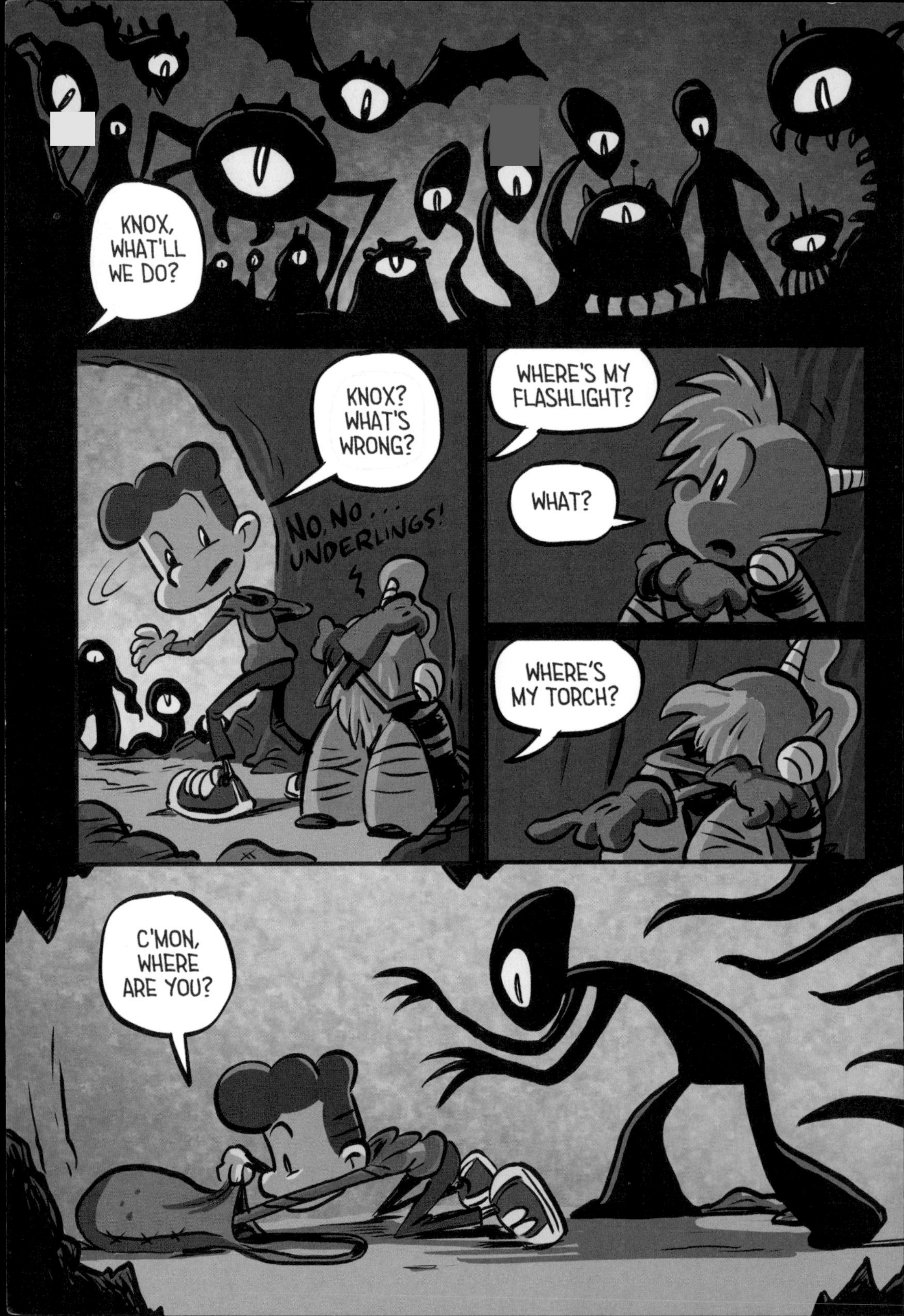
KNOX, WHAT'LL WE DO?
KNOX? WHAT'S WRONG?
NO, NO... UNDERLINGS!
WHERE'S MY FLASHLIGHT?
WHAT?
WHERE'S MY TORCH?
C'MON, WHERE ARE YOU?

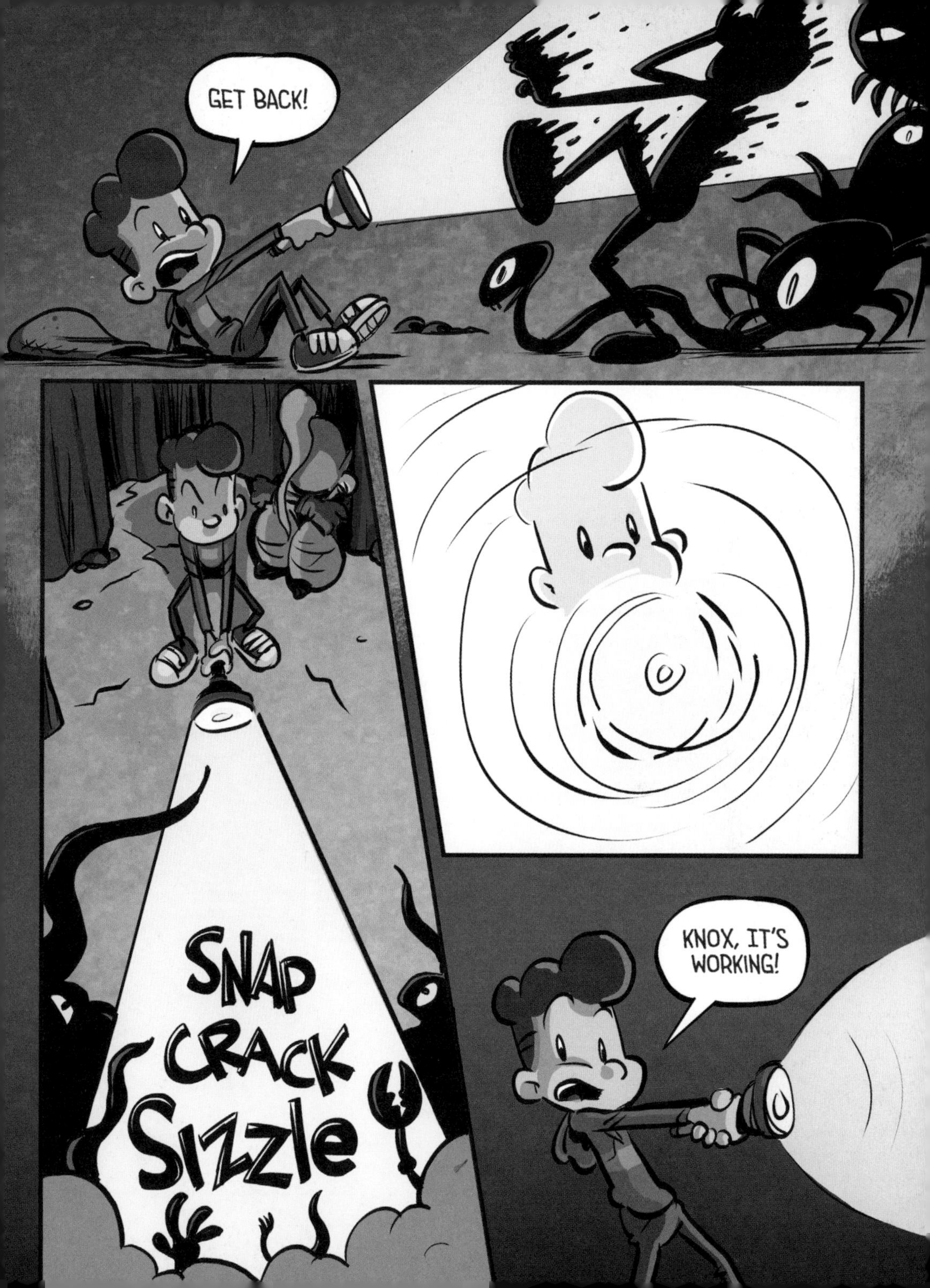
GET BACK!
SNAP
CRACK
Sizzle
KNOX, IT'S WORKING!

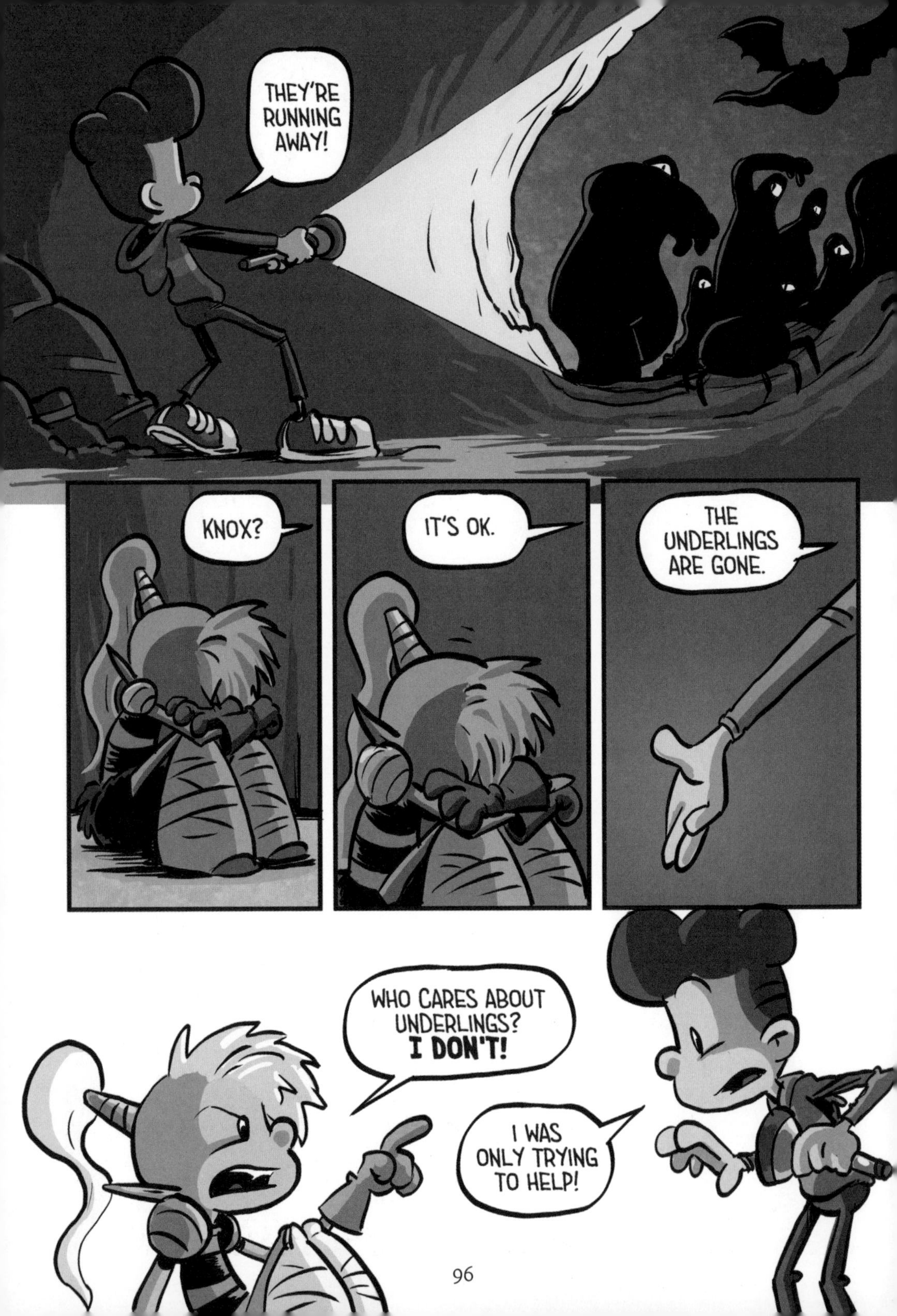
THEY'RE RUNNING AWAY!
KNOX?
IT'S OK.
THE UNDERLINGS ARE GONE.
WHO CARES ABOUT UNDERLINGS? **I DON'T!**
I WAS ONLY TRYING TO HELP!

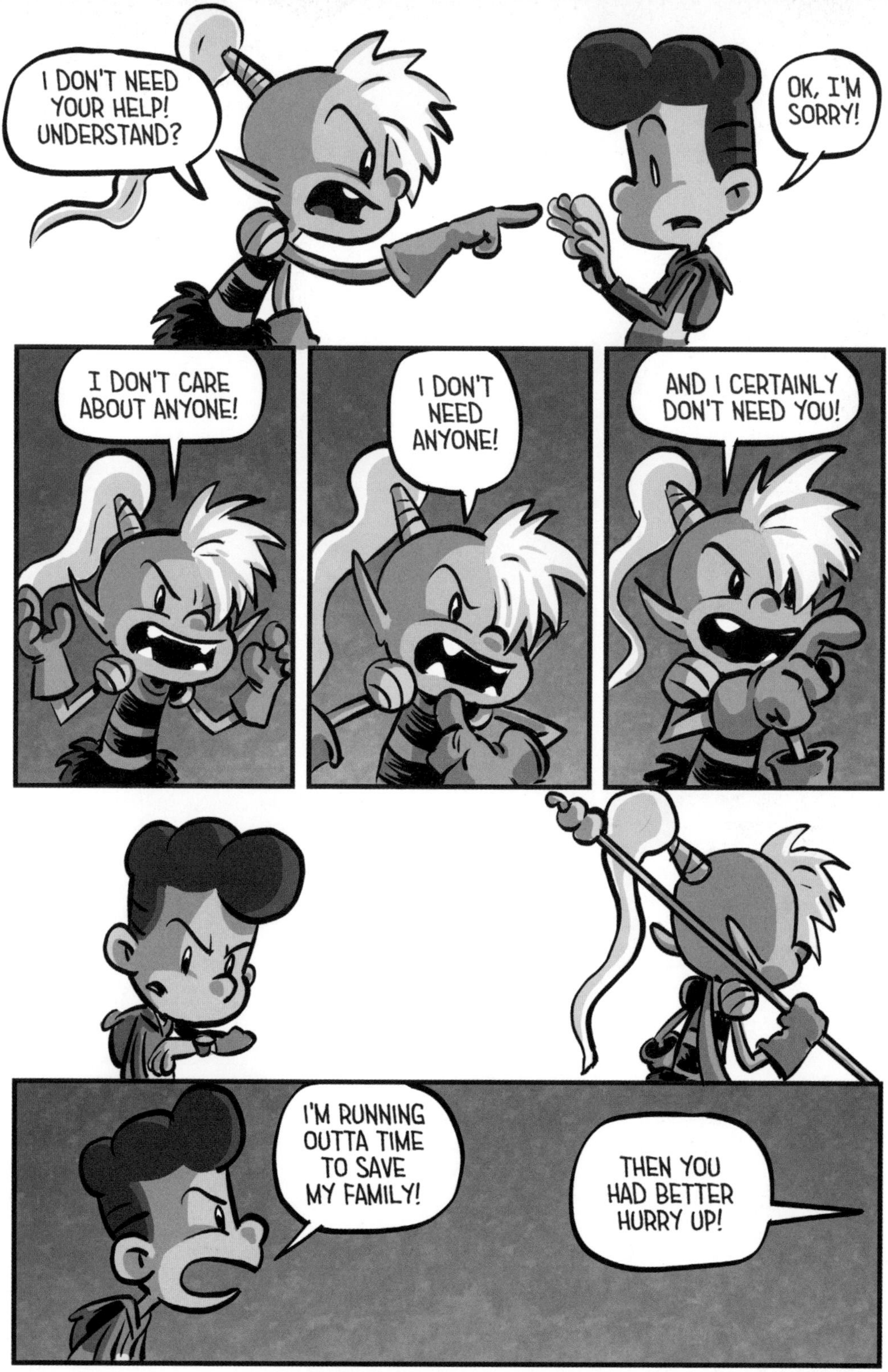
I DON'T NEED YOUR HELP! UNDERSTAND?
OK, I'M SORRY!
I DON'T CARE ABOUT ANYONE!
I DON'T NEED ANYONE!
AND I CERTAINLY DON'T NEED YOU!
I'M RUNNING OUTTA TIME TO SAVE MY FAMILY!
THEN YOU HAD BETTER HURRY UP!

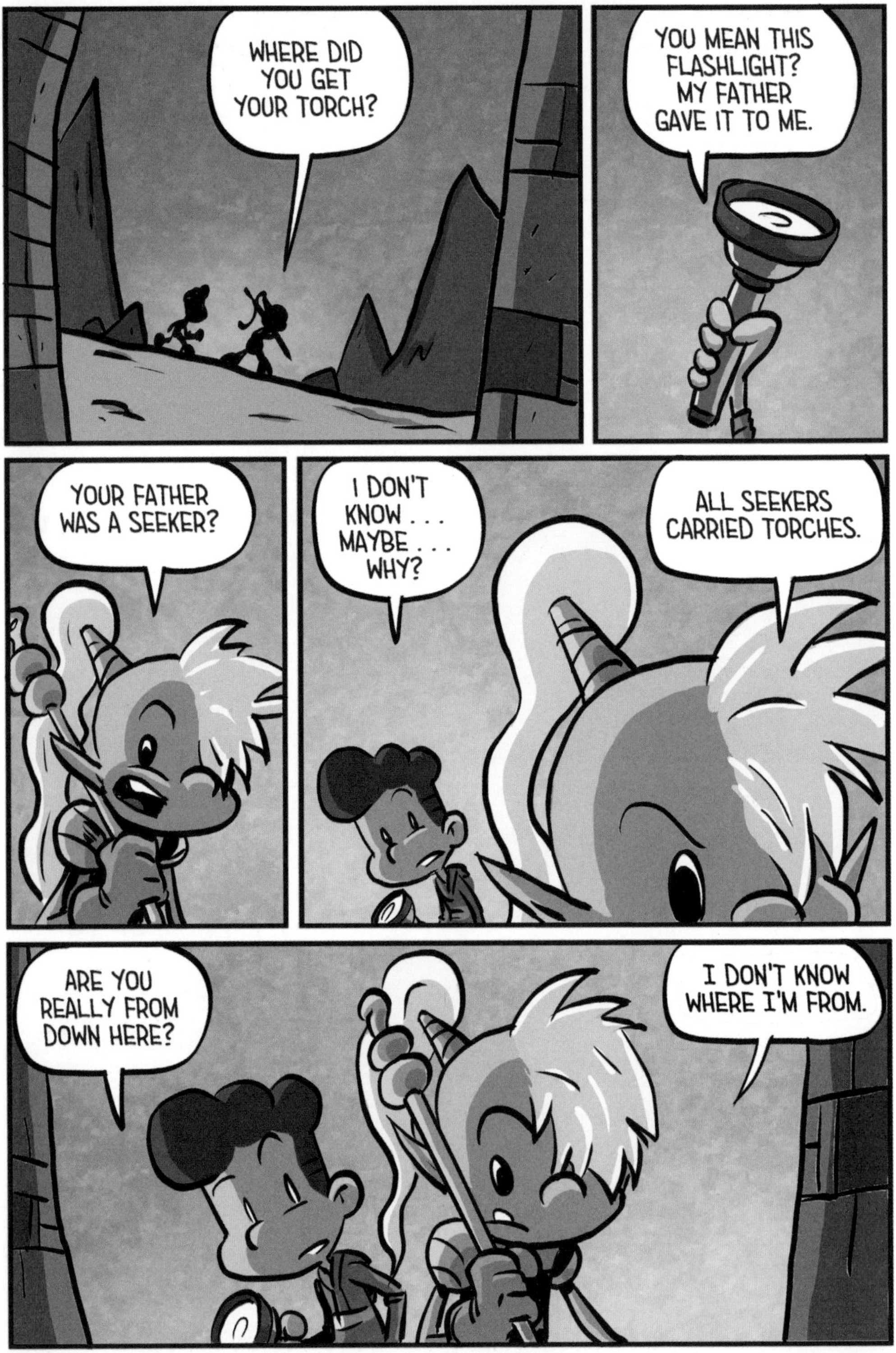
WHERE DID YOU GET YOUR TORCH?
YOU MEAN THIS FLASHLIGHT? MY FATHER GAVE IT TO ME.
YOUR FATHER WAS A SEEKER?
I DON'T KNOW . . . MAYBE . . . WHY?
ALL SEEKERS CARRIED TORCHES.
ARE YOU REALLY FROM DOWN HERE?
I DON'T KNOW WHERE I'M FROM.

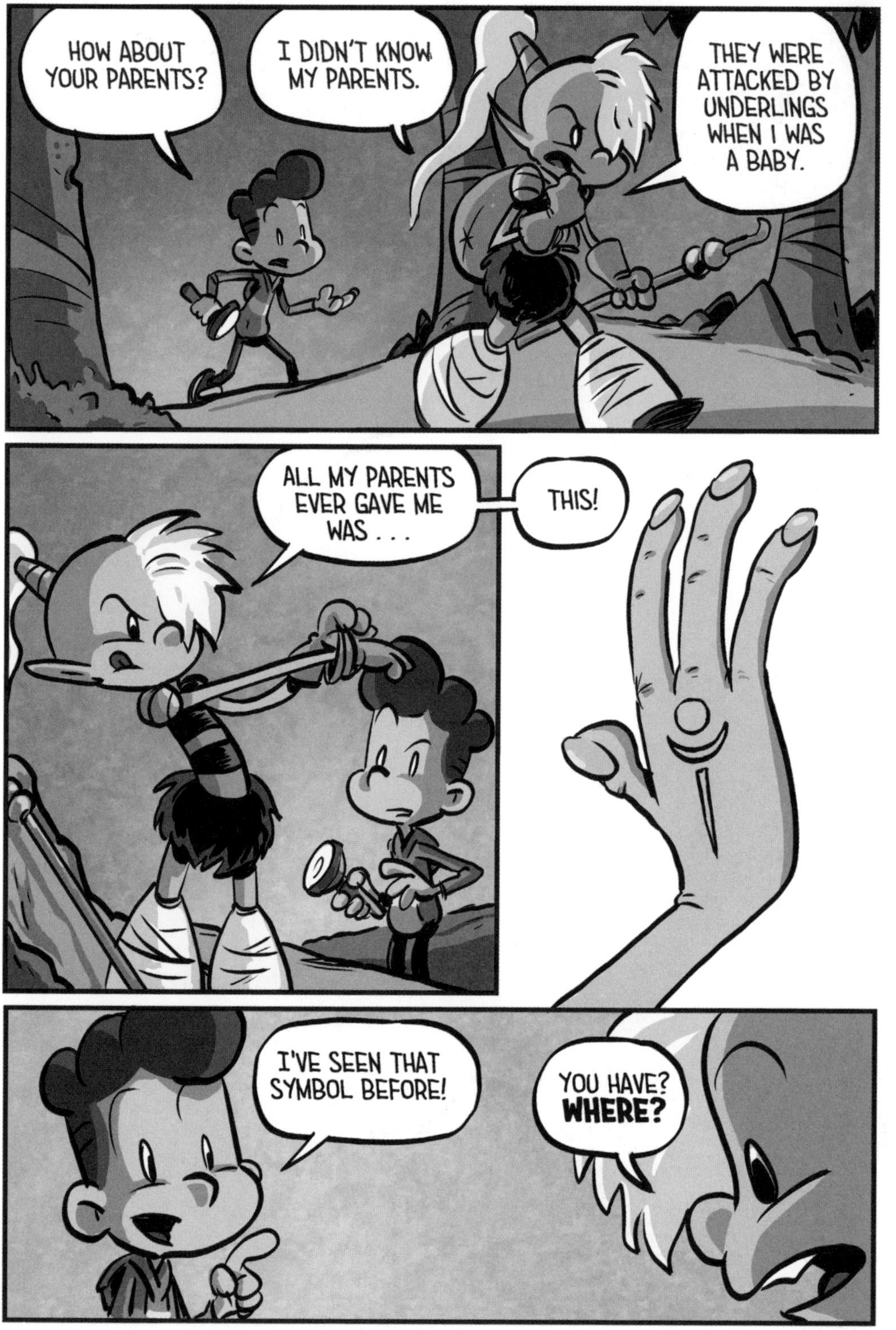
HOW ABOUT YOUR PARENTS?
I DIDN'T KNOW MY PARENTS.
THEY WERE ATTACKED BY UNDERLINGS WHEN I WAS A BABY.
ALL MY PARENTS EVER GAVE ME WAS . . .
THIS!
I'VE SEEN THAT SYMBOL BEFORE!
YOU HAVE? **WHERE?**

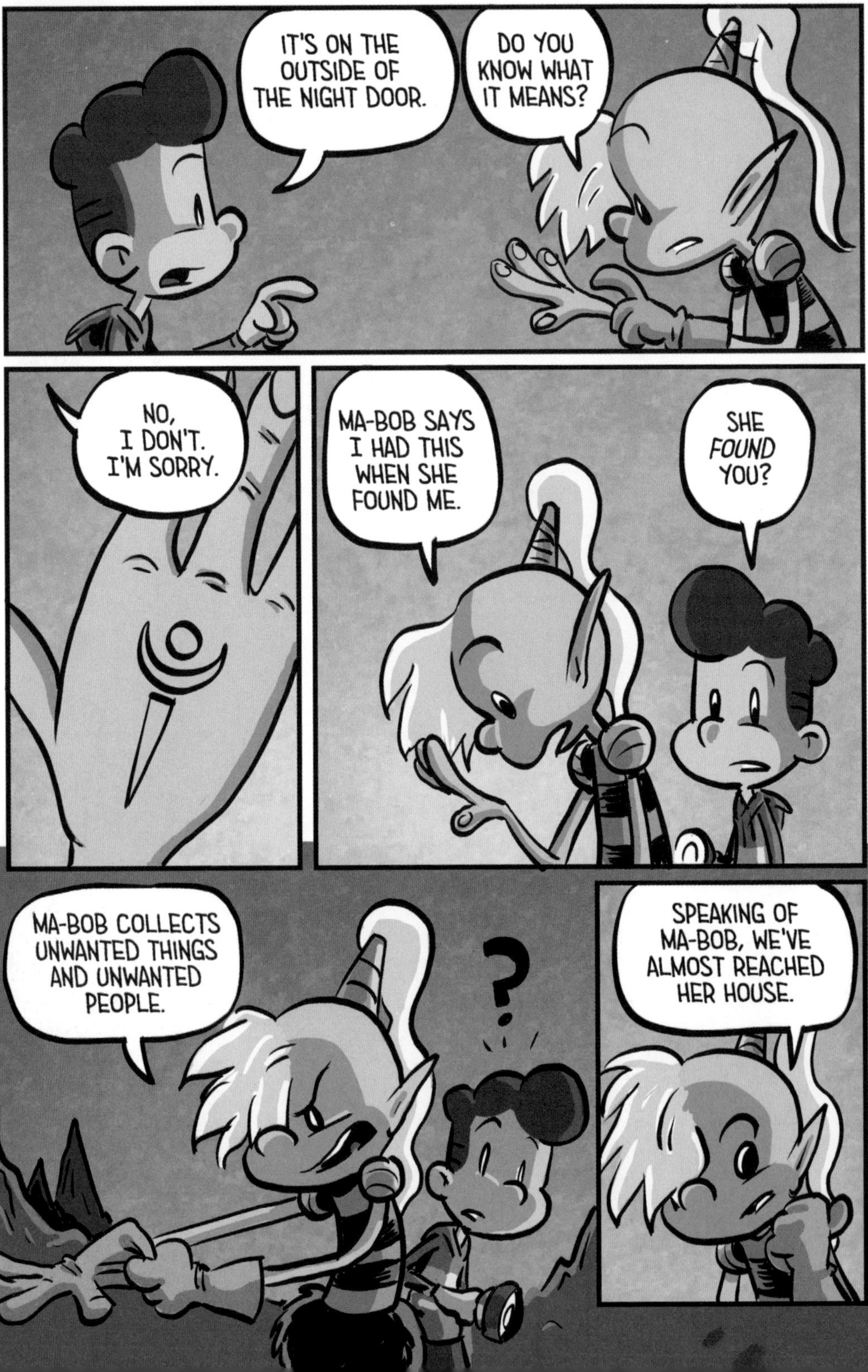
IT'S ON THE OUTSIDE OF THE NIGHT DOOR.
DO YOU KNOW WHAT IT MEANS?
NO, I DON'T. I'M SORRY.
MA-BOB SAYS I HAD THIS WHEN SHE FOUND ME.
SHE *FOUND* YOU?
MA-BOB COLLECTS UNWANTED THINGS AND UNWANTED PEOPLE.
?
SPEAKING OF MA-BOB, WE'VE ALMOST REACHED HER HOUSE.

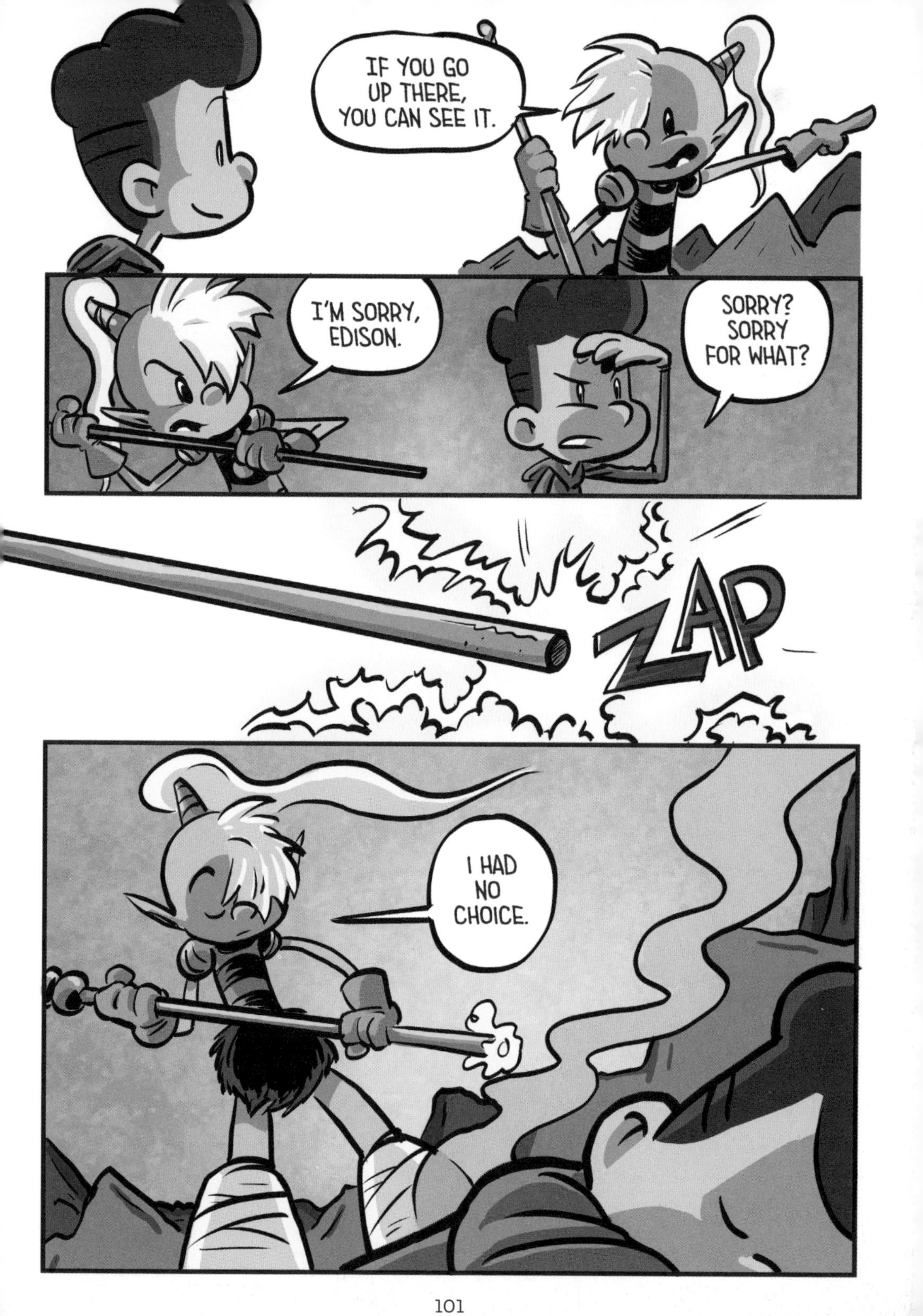
IF YOU GO UP THERE, YOU CAN SEE IT.
I'M SORRY, EDISON.
SORRY? SORRY FOR WHAT?
ZAP
I HAD NO CHOICE.

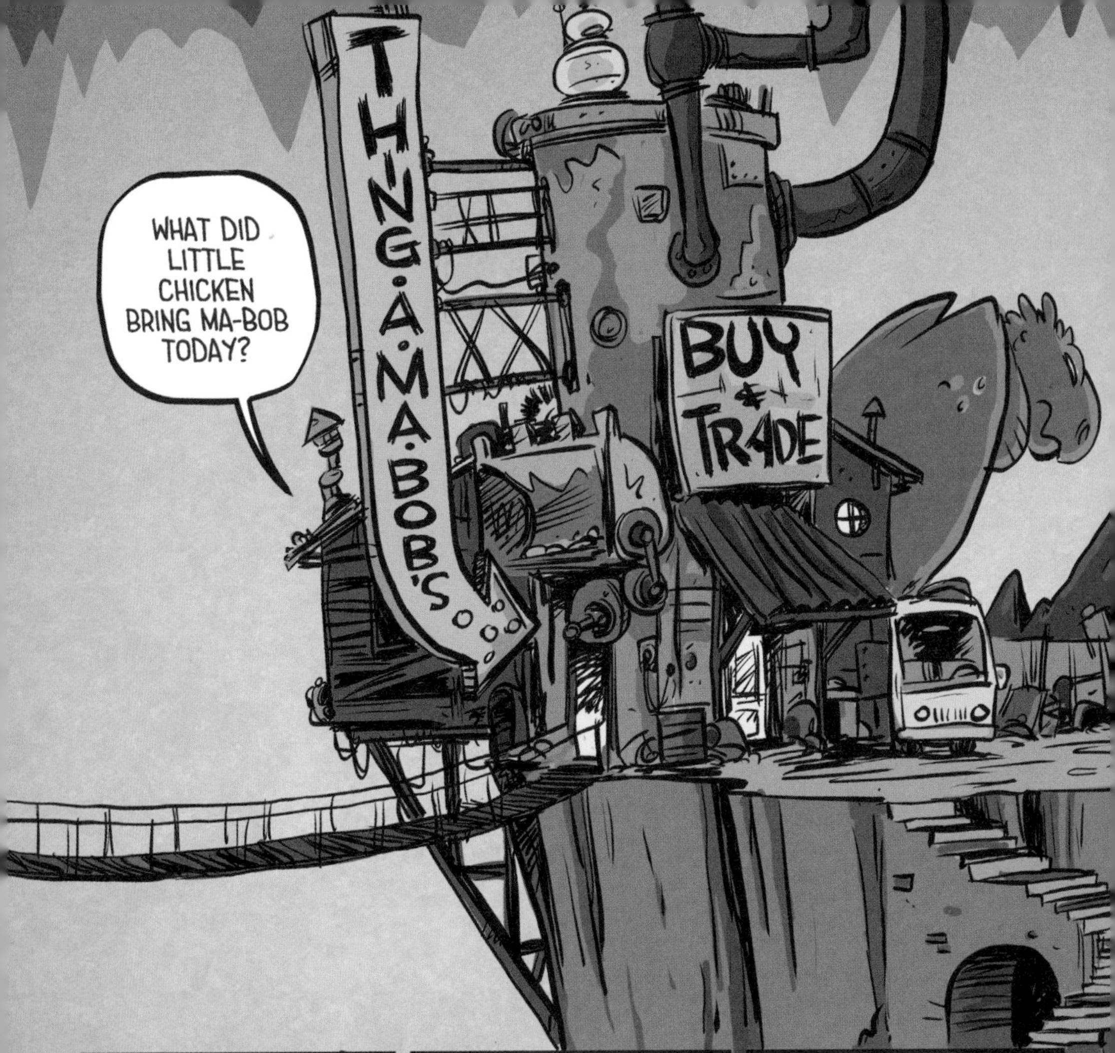
WHAT DID LITTLE CHICKEN BRING MA-BOB TODAY?
THING-A-MA-BOB'S
BUY & TRADE

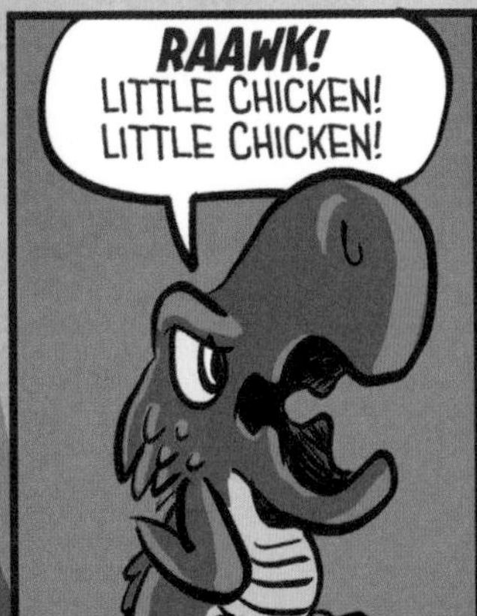
RAAWK! LITTLE CHICKEN! LITTLE CHICKEN!

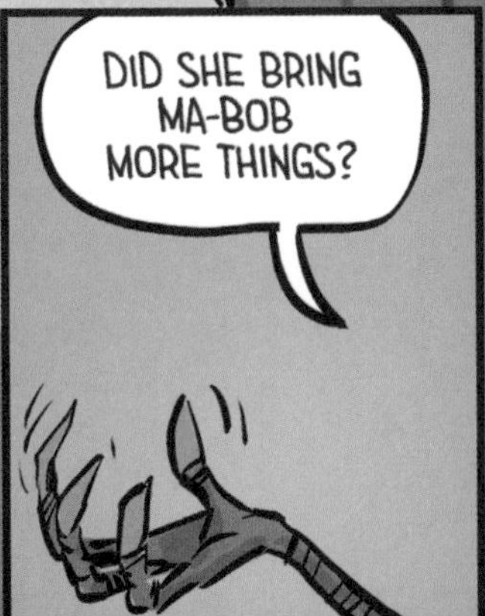
DID SHE BRING MA-BOB MORE THINGS?

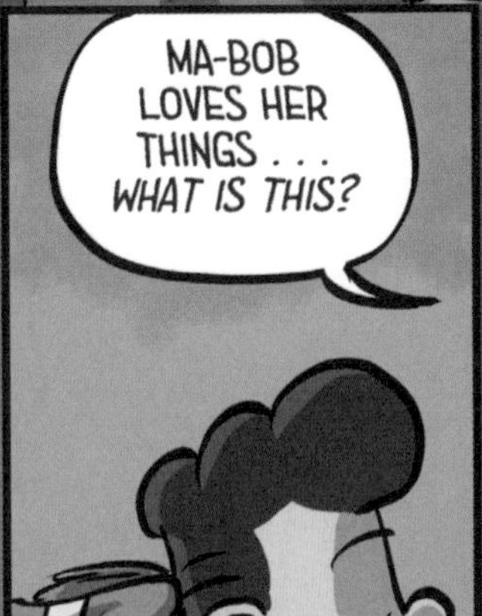
MA-BOB LOVES HER THINGS . . . *WHAT IS THIS?*

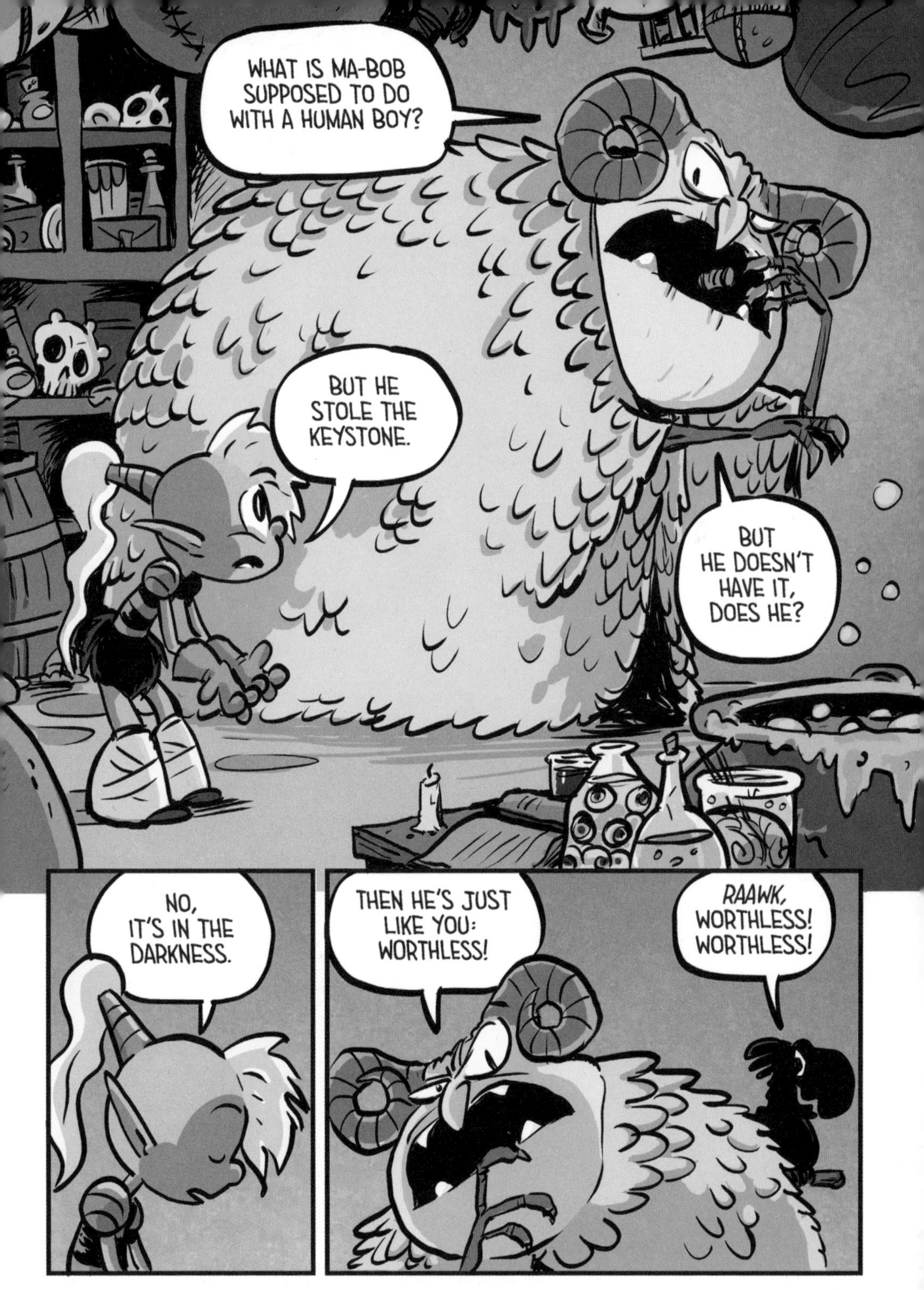

WHAT IS MA-BOB SUPPOSED TO DO WITH A HUMAN BOY?
BUT HE STOLE THE KEYSTONE.
BUT HE DOESN'T HAVE IT, DOES HE?
NO, IT'S IN THE DARKNESS.
THEN HE'S JUST LIKE YOU: WORTHLESS!
RAAWK, WORTHLESS! WORTHLESS!

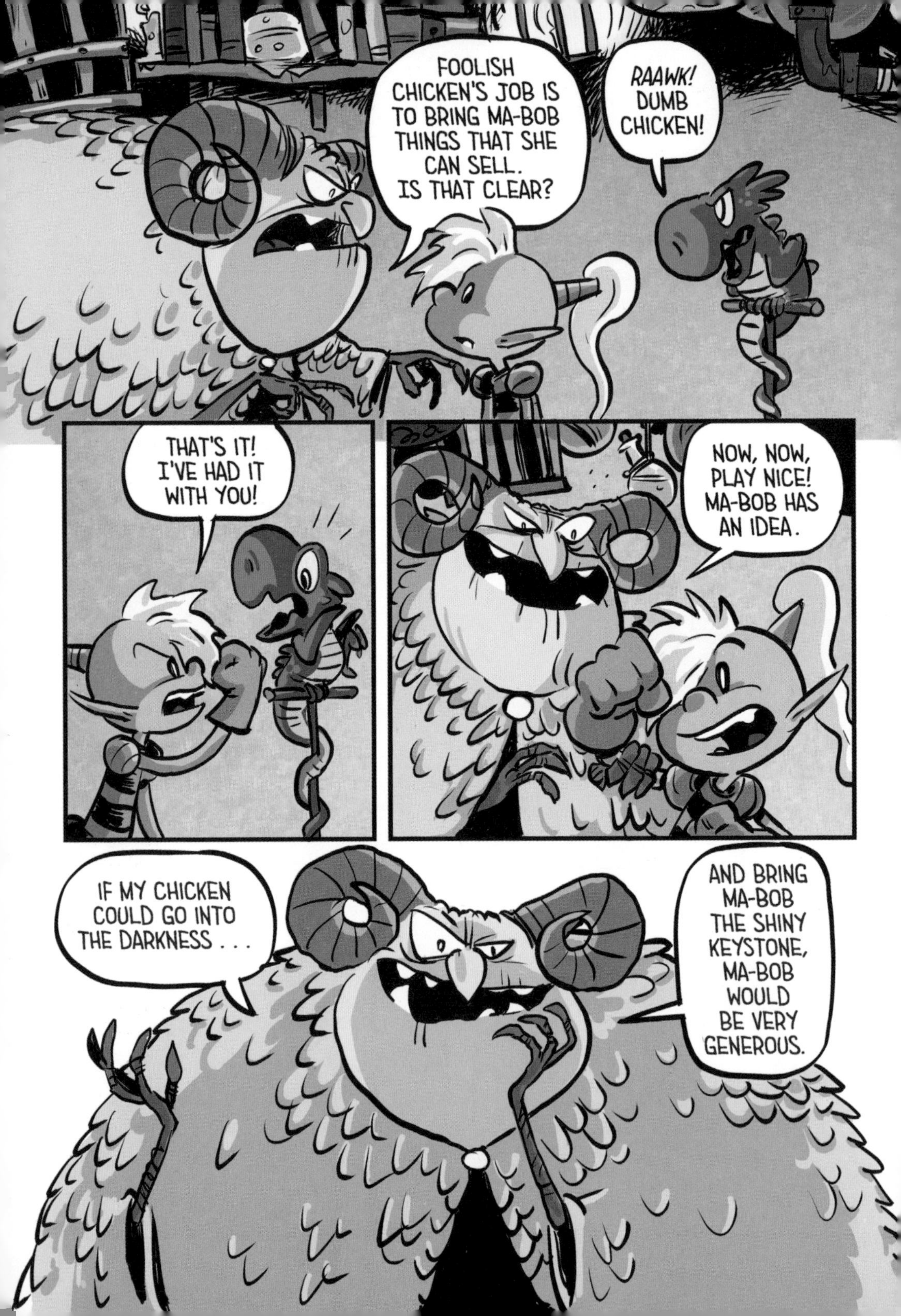
FOOLISH CHICKEN'S JOB IS TO BRING MA-BOB THINGS THAT SHE CAN SELL. IS THAT CLEAR?
RAAWK! DUMB CHICKEN!
THAT'S IT! I'VE HAD IT WITH YOU!
NOW, NOW, PLAY NICE! MA-BOB HAS AN IDEA.
IF MY CHICKEN COULD GO INTO THE DARKNESS . . .
AND BRING MA-BOB THE SHINY KEYSTONE, MA-BOB WOULD BE VERY GENEROUS.

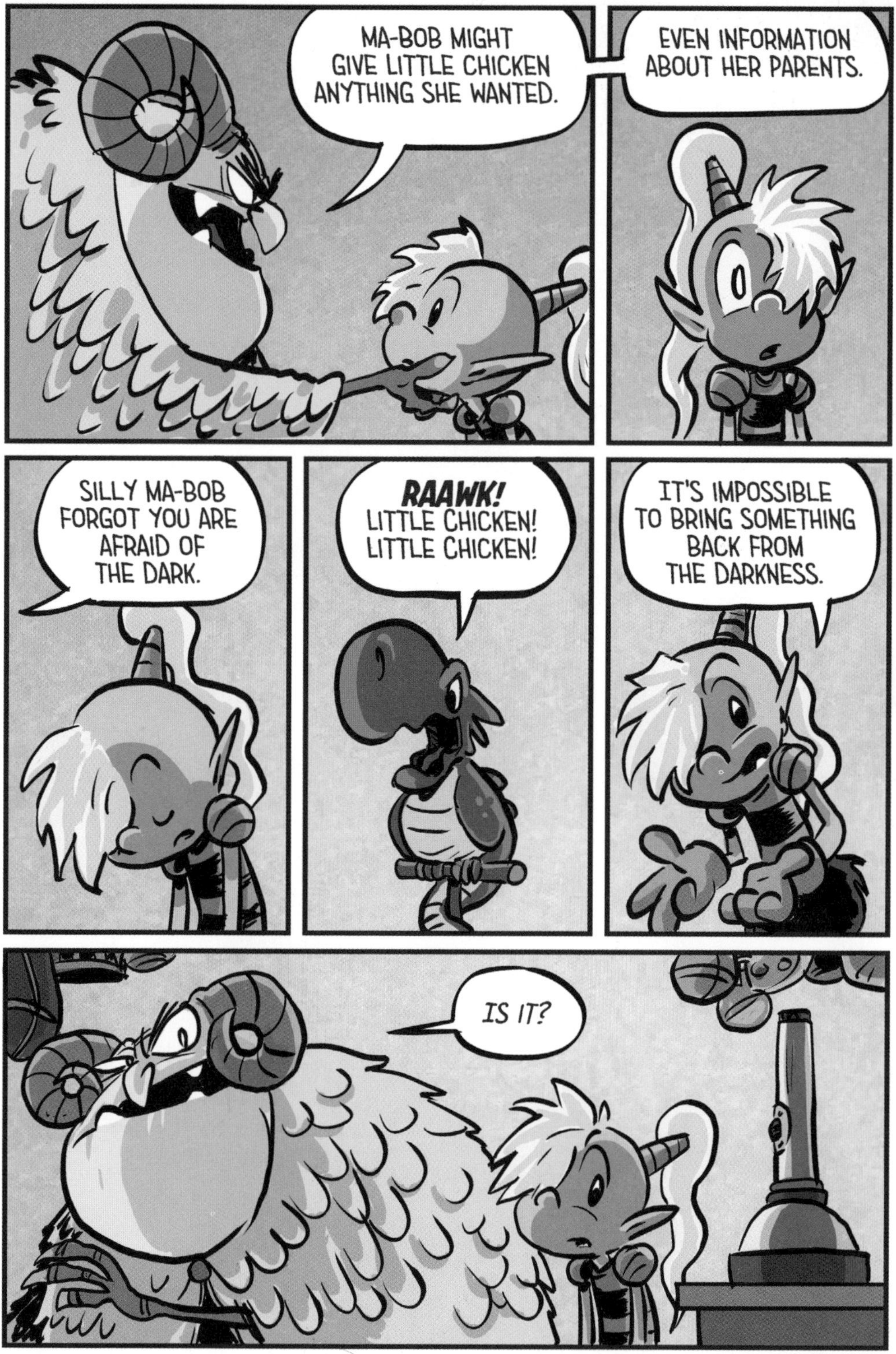
MA-BOB MIGHT GIVE LITTLE CHICKEN ANYTHING SHE WANTED.
EVEN INFORMATION ABOUT HER PARENTS.
SILLY MA-BOB FORGOT YOU ARE AFRAID OF THE DARK.
RAAWK! LITTLE CHICKEN! LITTLE CHICKEN!
IT'S IMPOSSIBLE TO BRING SOMETHING BACK FROM THE DARKNESS.
IS IT?

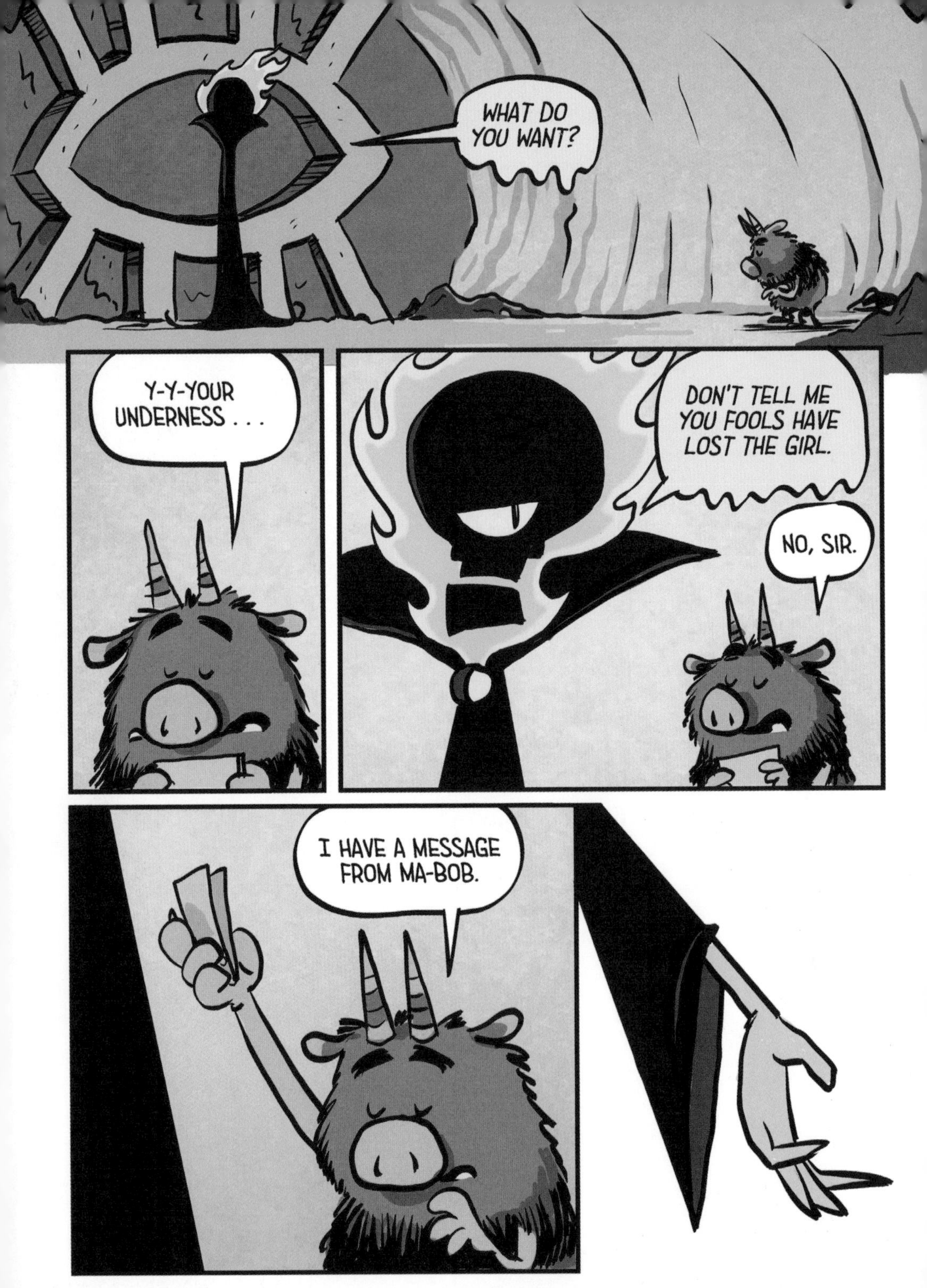
WHAT DO YOU WANT?
Y-Y-YOUR UNDERNESS . . .
DON'T TELL ME YOU FOOLS HAVE LOST THE GIRL.
NO, SIR.
I HAVE A MESSAGE FROM MA-BOB.

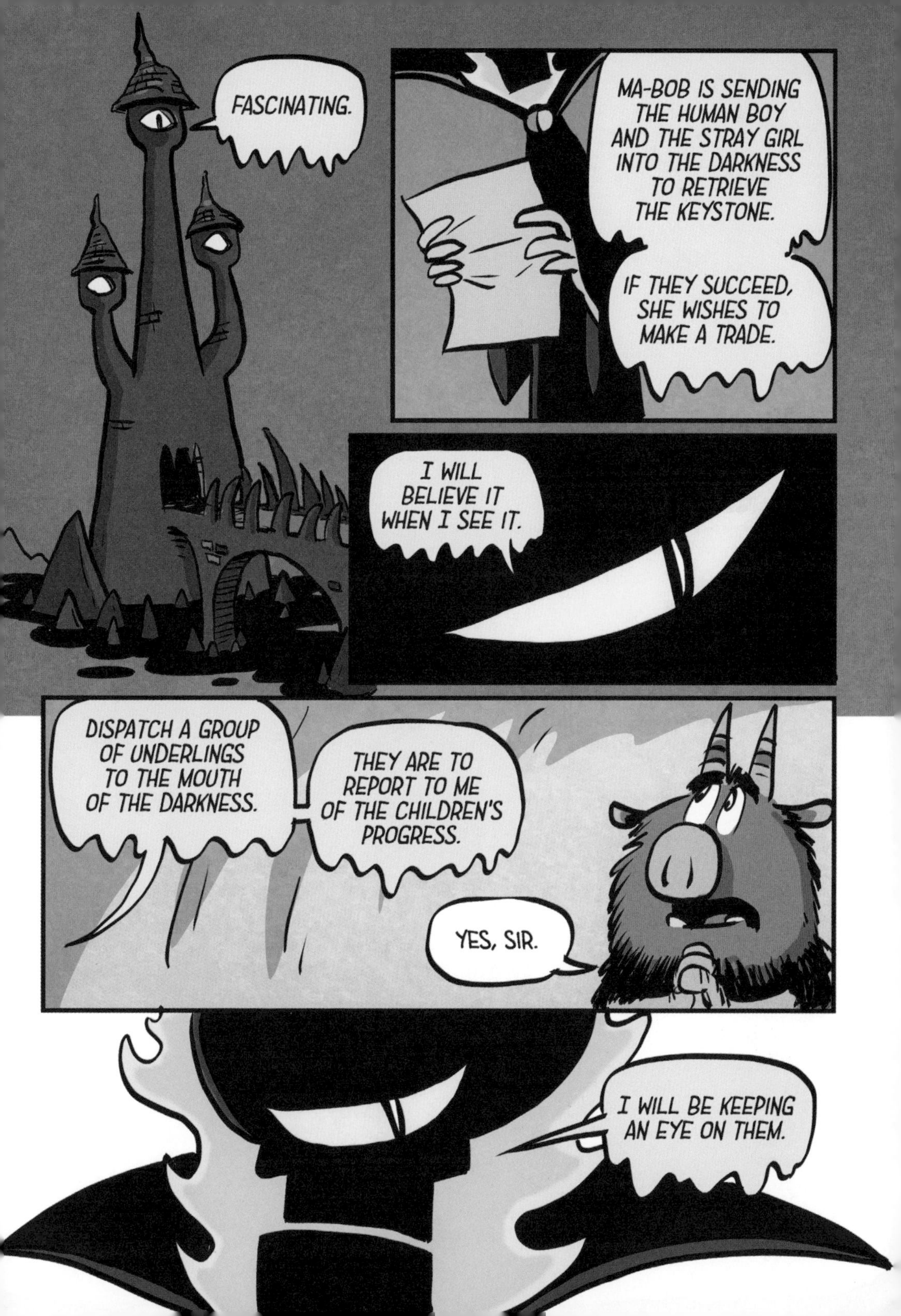
FASCINATING.
MA-BOB IS SENDING THE HUMAN BOY AND THE STRAY GIRL INTO THE DARKNESS TO RETRIEVE THE KEYSTONE.
IF THEY SUCCEED, SHE WISHES TO MAKE A TRADE.
I WILL BELIEVE IT WHEN I SEE IT.
DISPATCH A GROUP OF UNDERLINGS TO THE MOUTH OF THE DARKNESS.
THEY ARE TO REPORT TO ME OF THE CHILDREN'S PROGRESS.
YES, SIR.
I WILL BE KEEPING AN EYE ON THEM.

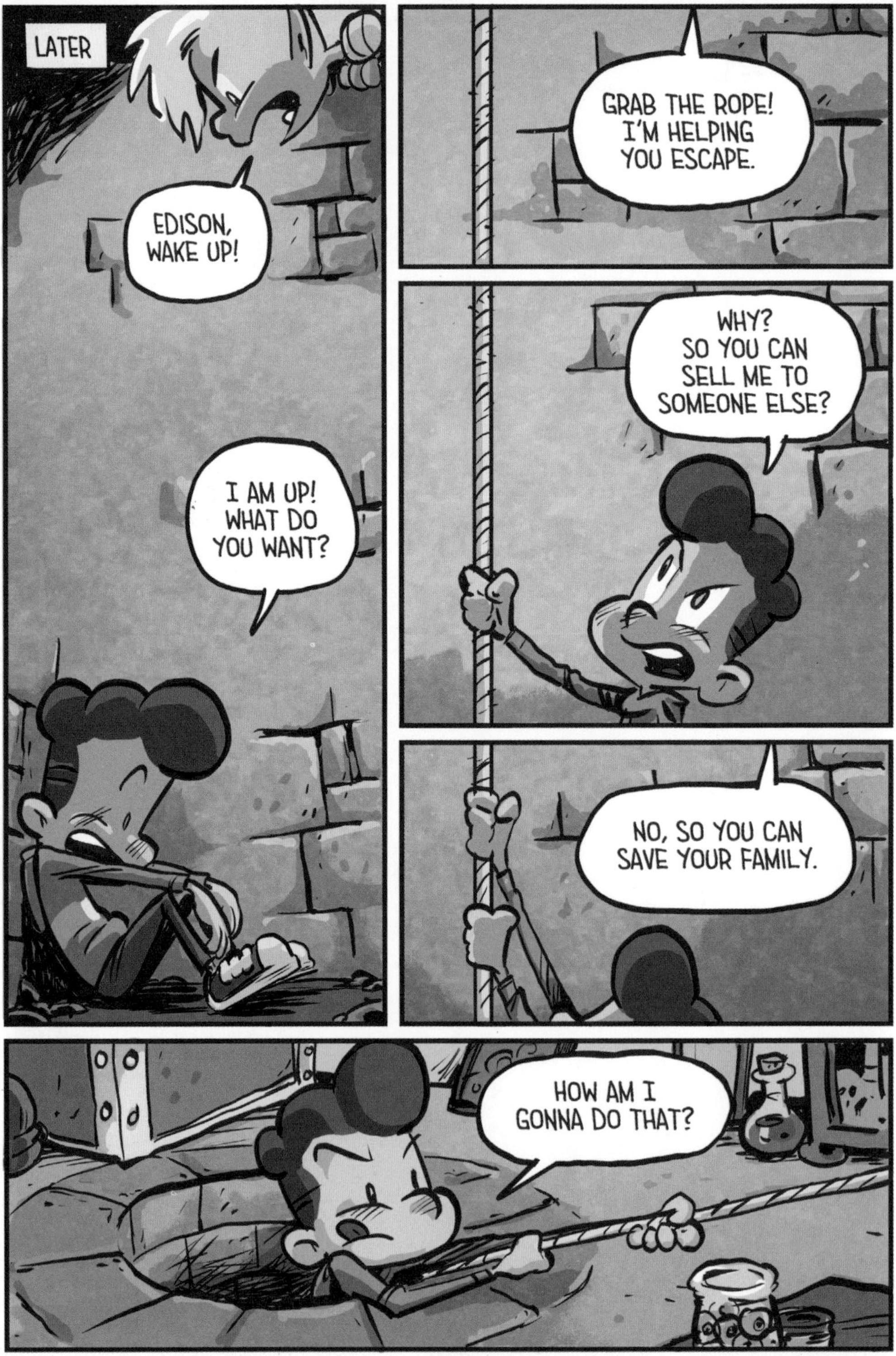
LATER
EDISON, WAKE UP!
I AM UP! WHAT DO YOU WANT?
GRAB THE ROPE! I'M HELPING YOU ESCAPE.
WHY? SO YOU CAN SELL ME TO SOMEONE ELSE?
NO, SO YOU CAN SAVE YOUR FAMILY.
HOW AM I GONNA DO THAT?

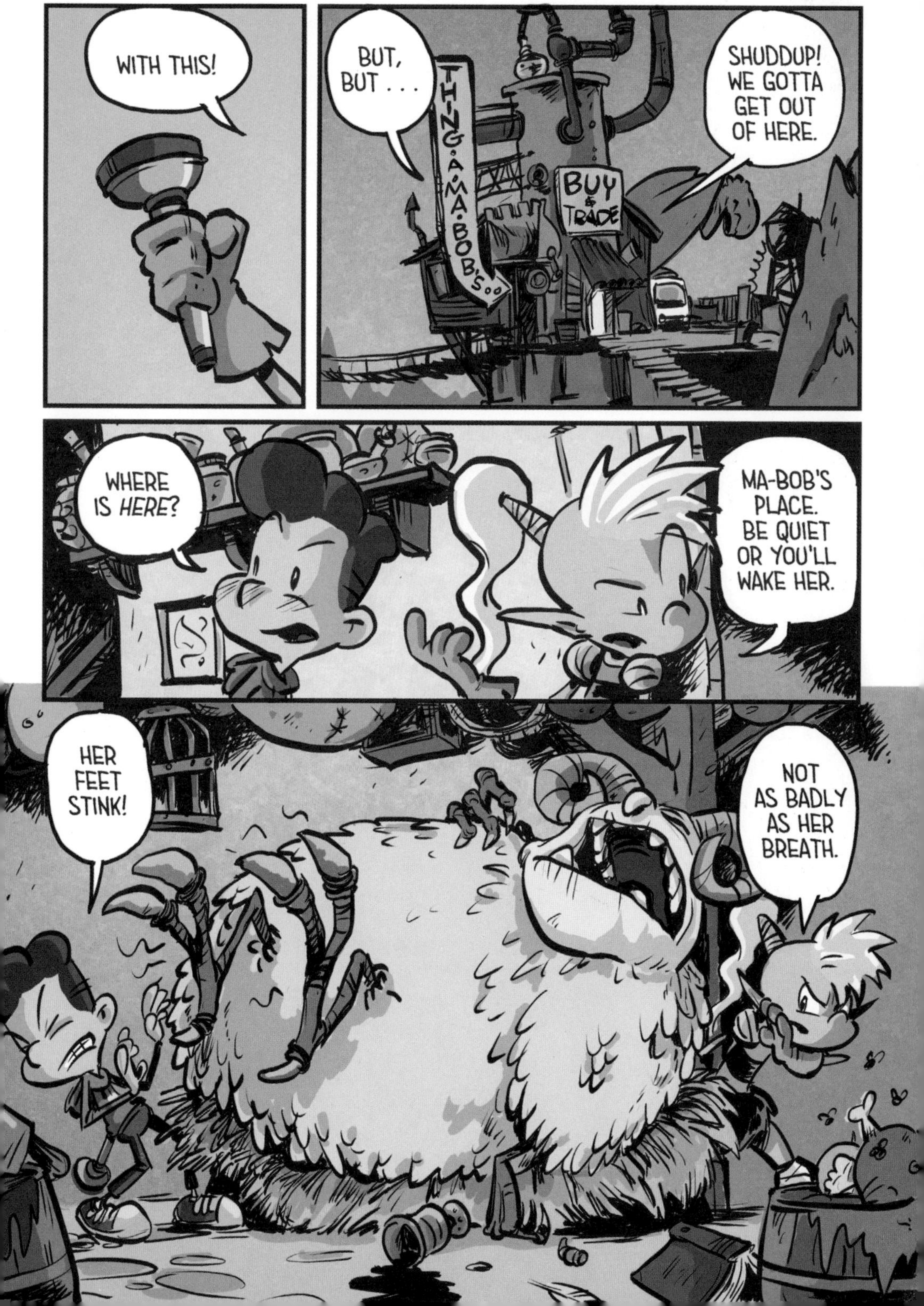
WITH THIS!
BUT, BUT . . .
THING-A-MA-BOB'S
BUY & TRADE
SHUDDUP! WE GOTTA GET OUT OF HERE.
WHERE IS *HERE*?
MA-BOB'S PLACE. BE QUIET OR YOU'LL WAKE HER.
HER FEET STINK!
NOT AS BADLY AS HER BREATH.

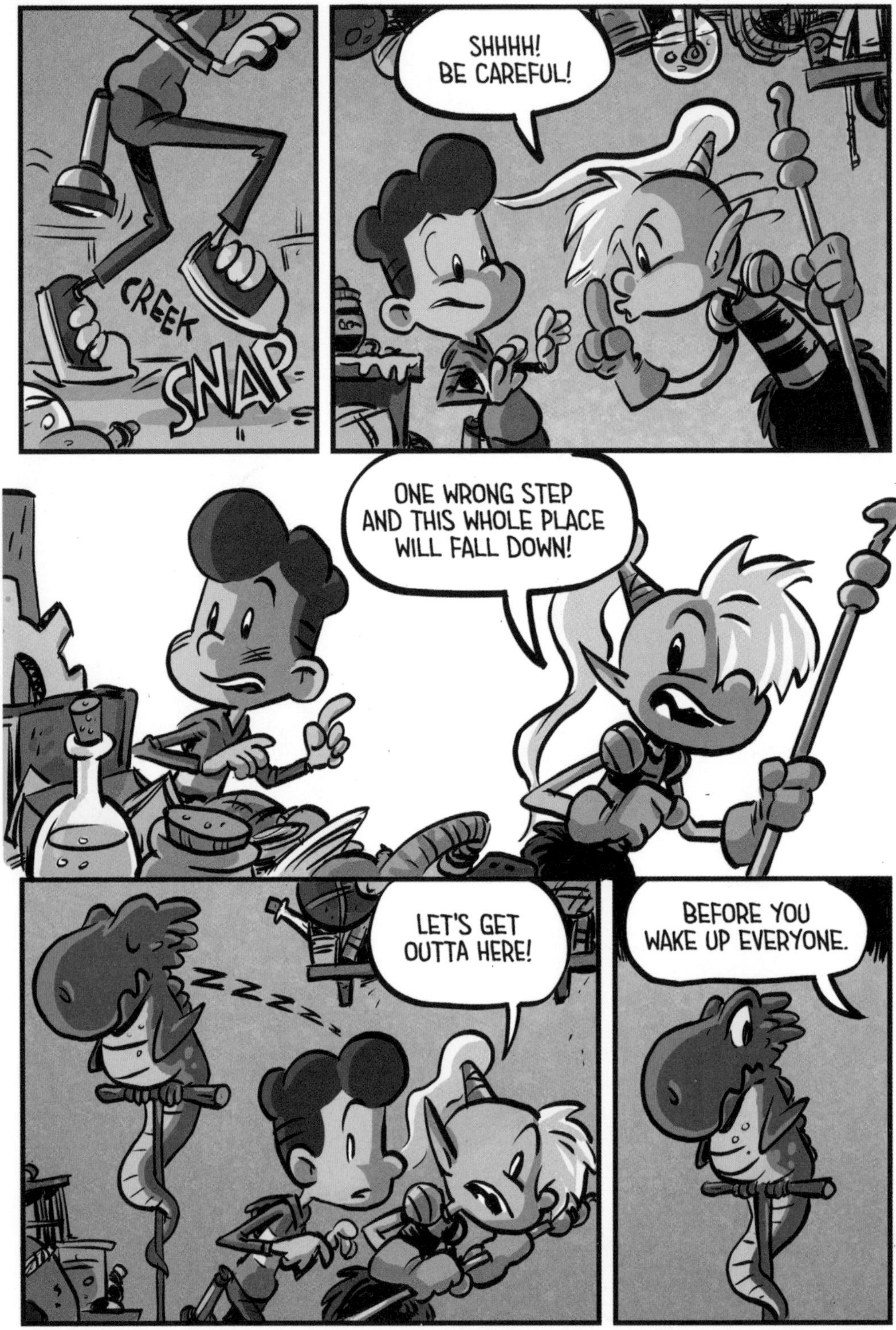
CREEK
SNAP
SHHHH! BE CAREFUL!
ONE WRONG STEP AND THIS WHOLE PLACE WILL FALL DOWN!
ZZZZZ
LET'S GET OUTTA HERE!
BEFORE YOU WAKE UP EVERYONE.

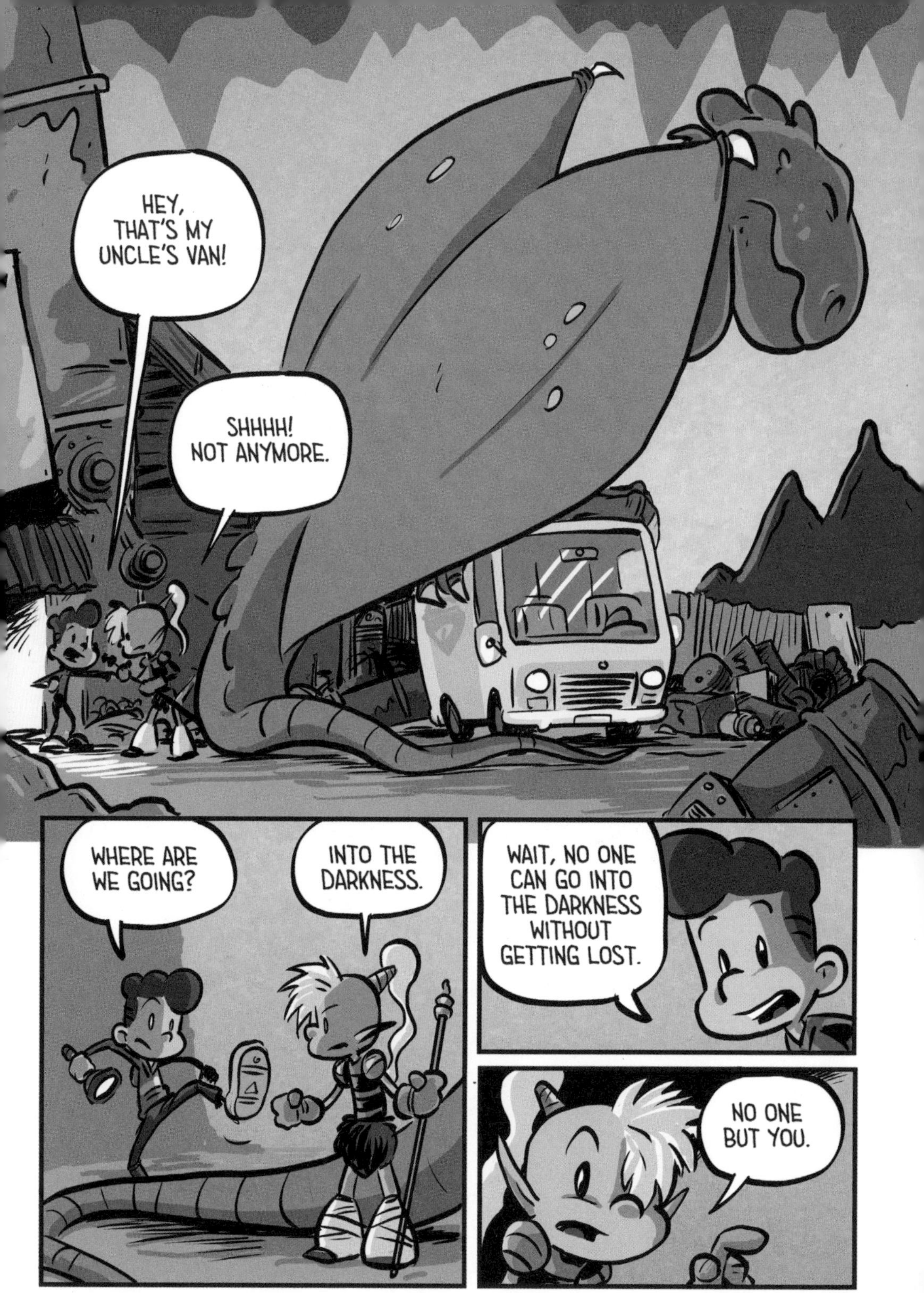
HEY, THAT'S MY UNCLE'S VAN!
SHHHH! NOT ANYMORE.
WHERE ARE WE GOING?
INTO THE DARKNESS.
WAIT, NO ONE CAN GO INTO THE DARKNESS WITHOUT GETTING LOST.
NO ONE BUT YOU.

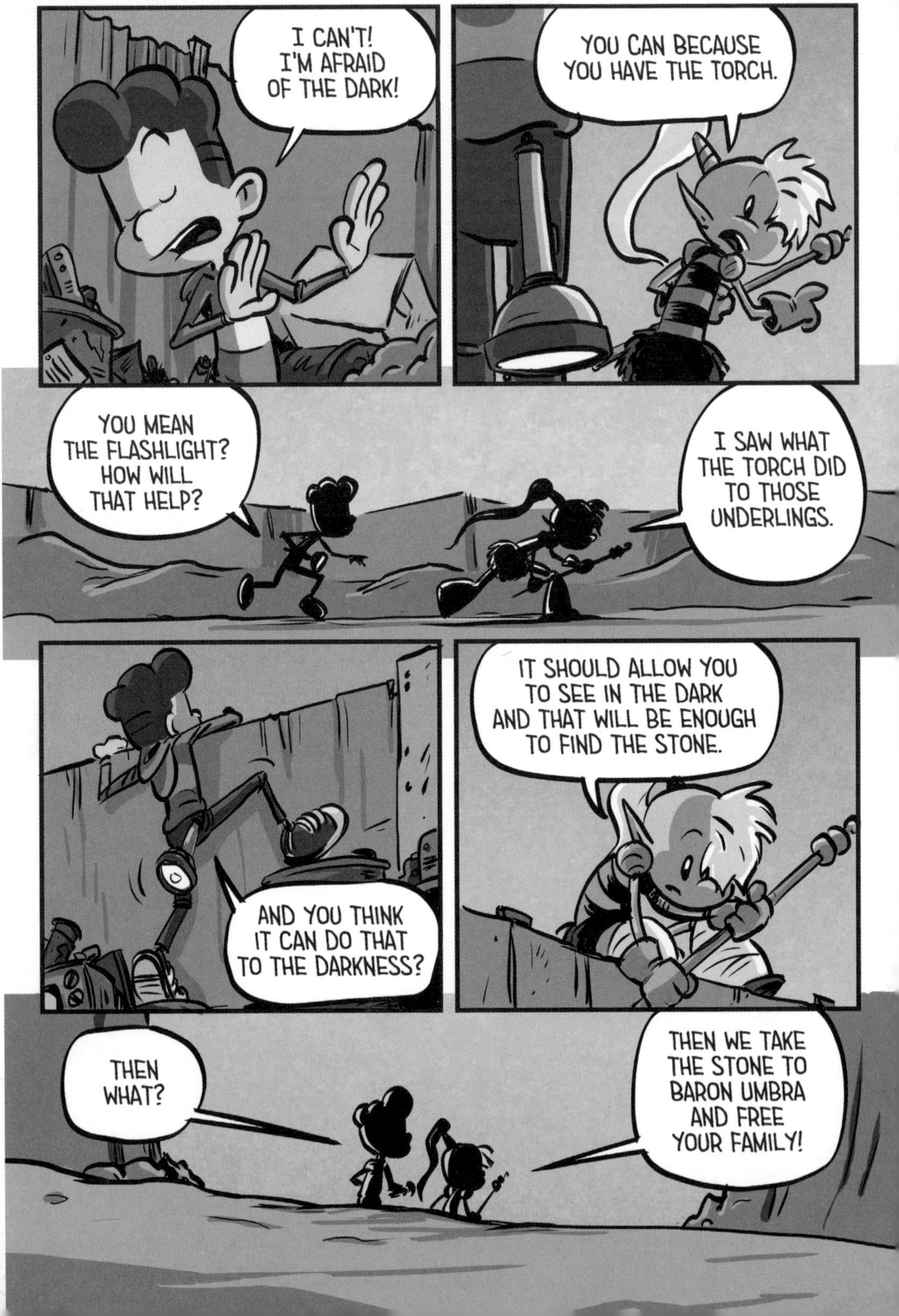
I CAN'T! I'M AFRAID OF THE DARK!
YOU CAN BECAUSE YOU HAVE THE TORCH.
YOU MEAN THE FLASHLIGHT? HOW WILL THAT HELP?
I SAW WHAT THE TORCH DID TO THOSE UNDERLINGS.
IT SHOULD ALLOW YOU TO SEE IN THE DARK AND THAT WILL BE ENOUGH TO FIND THE STONE.
AND YOU THINK IT CAN DO THAT TO THE DARKNESS?
THEN WHAT?
THEN WE TAKE THE STONE TO BARON UMBRA AND FREE YOUR FAMILY!

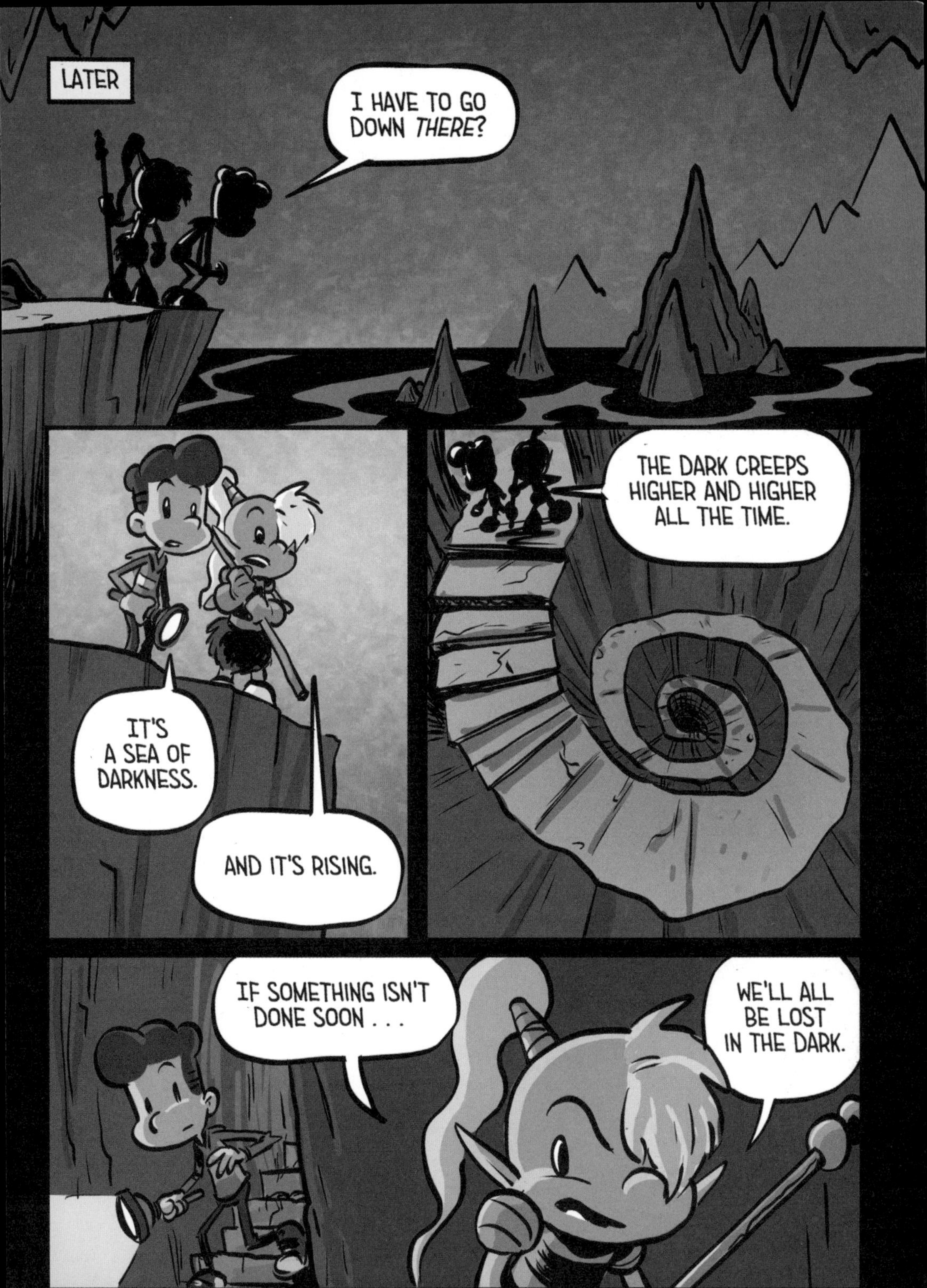
LATER
I HAVE TO GO DOWN *THERE*?
IT'S A SEA OF DARKNESS.
AND IT'S RISING.
THE DARK CREEPS HIGHER AND HIGHER ALL THE TIME.
IF SOMETHING ISN'T DONE SOON . . .
WE'LL ALL BE LOST IN THE DARK.

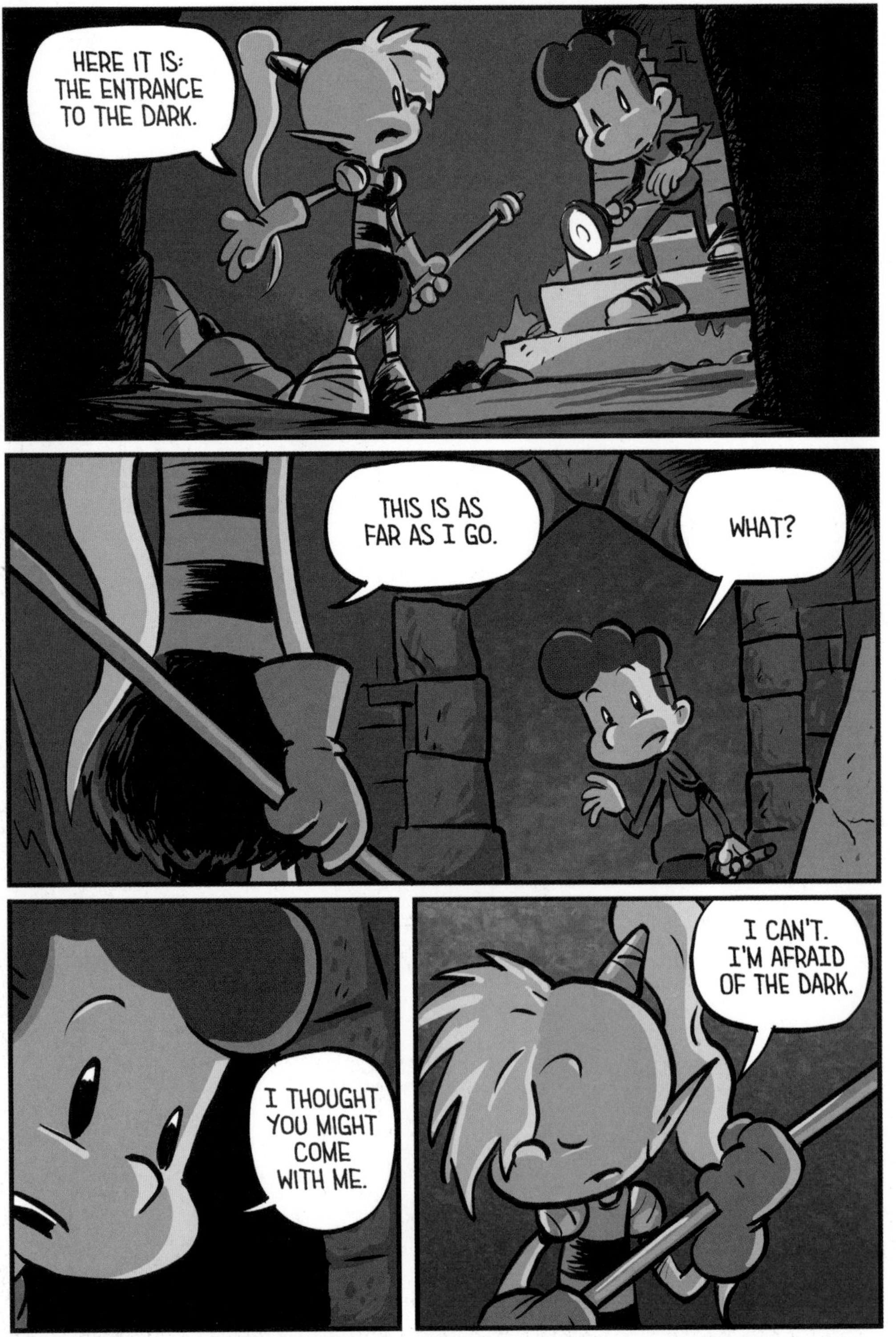
HERE IT IS: THE ENTRANCE TO THE DARK.
THIS IS AS FAR AS I GO.
WHAT?
I THOUGHT YOU MIGHT COME WITH ME.
I CAN'T. I'M AFRAID OF THE DARK.

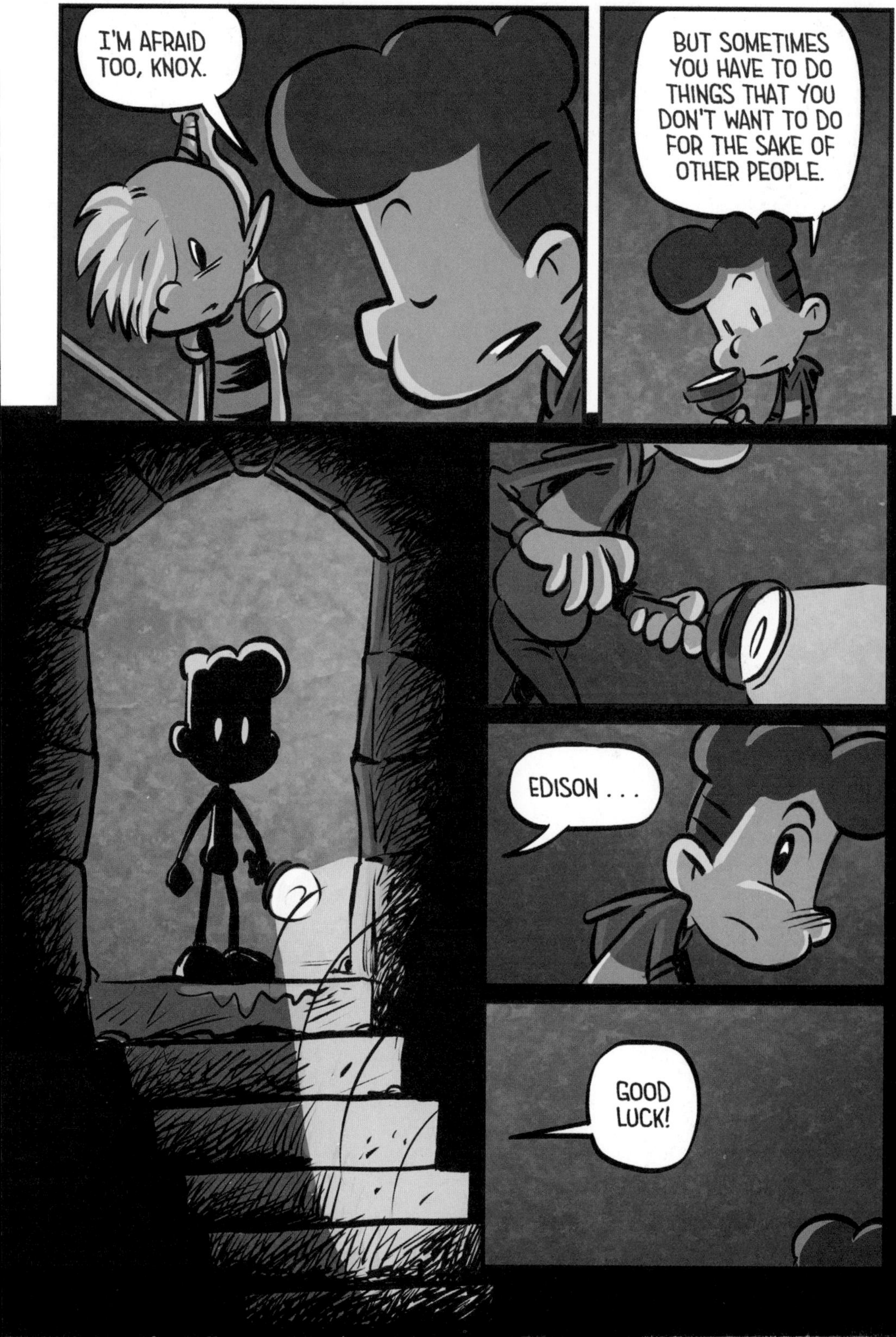
I'M AFRAID TOO, KNOX.
BUT SOMETIMES YOU HAVE TO DO THINGS THAT YOU DON'T WANT TO DO FOR THE SAKE OF OTHER PEOPLE.
EDISON . . .
GOOD LUCK!

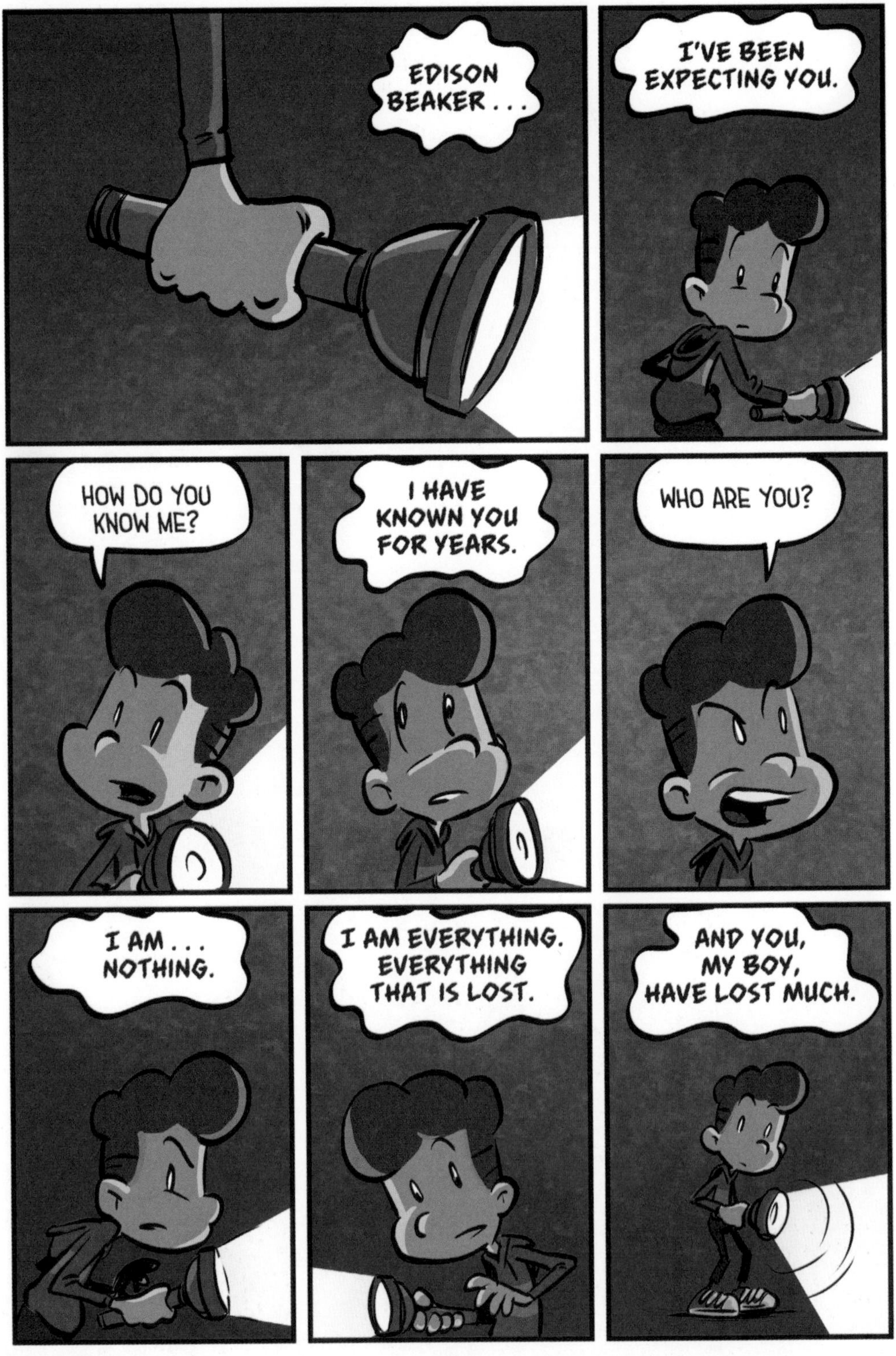
EDISON BEAKER . . .
I'VE BEEN EXPECTING YOU.
HOW DO YOU KNOW ME?
I HAVE KNOWN YOU FOR YEARS.
WHO ARE YOU?
I AM . . . NOTHING.
I AM EVERYTHING. EVERYTHING THAT IS LOST.
AND YOU, MY BOY, HAVE LOST MUCH.

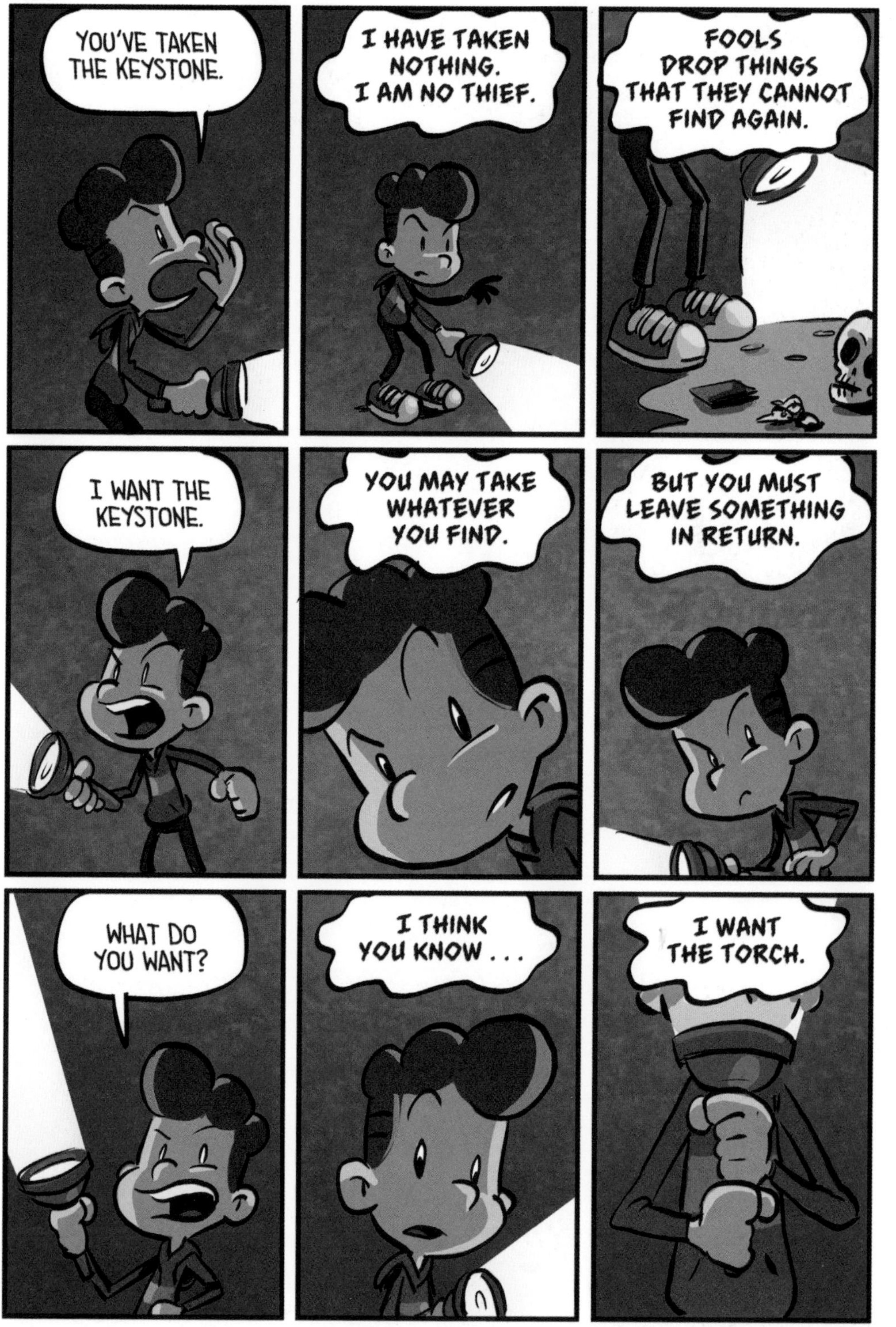
YOU'VE TAKEN THE KEYSTONE.
I HAVE TAKEN NOTHING. I AM NO THIEF.
FOOLS DROP THINGS THAT THEY CANNOT FIND AGAIN.
I WANT THE KEYSTONE.
YOU MAY TAKE WHATEVER YOU FIND.
BUT YOU MUST LEAVE SOMETHING IN RETURN.
WHAT DO YOU WANT?
I THINK YOU KNOW . . .
I WANT THE TORCH.

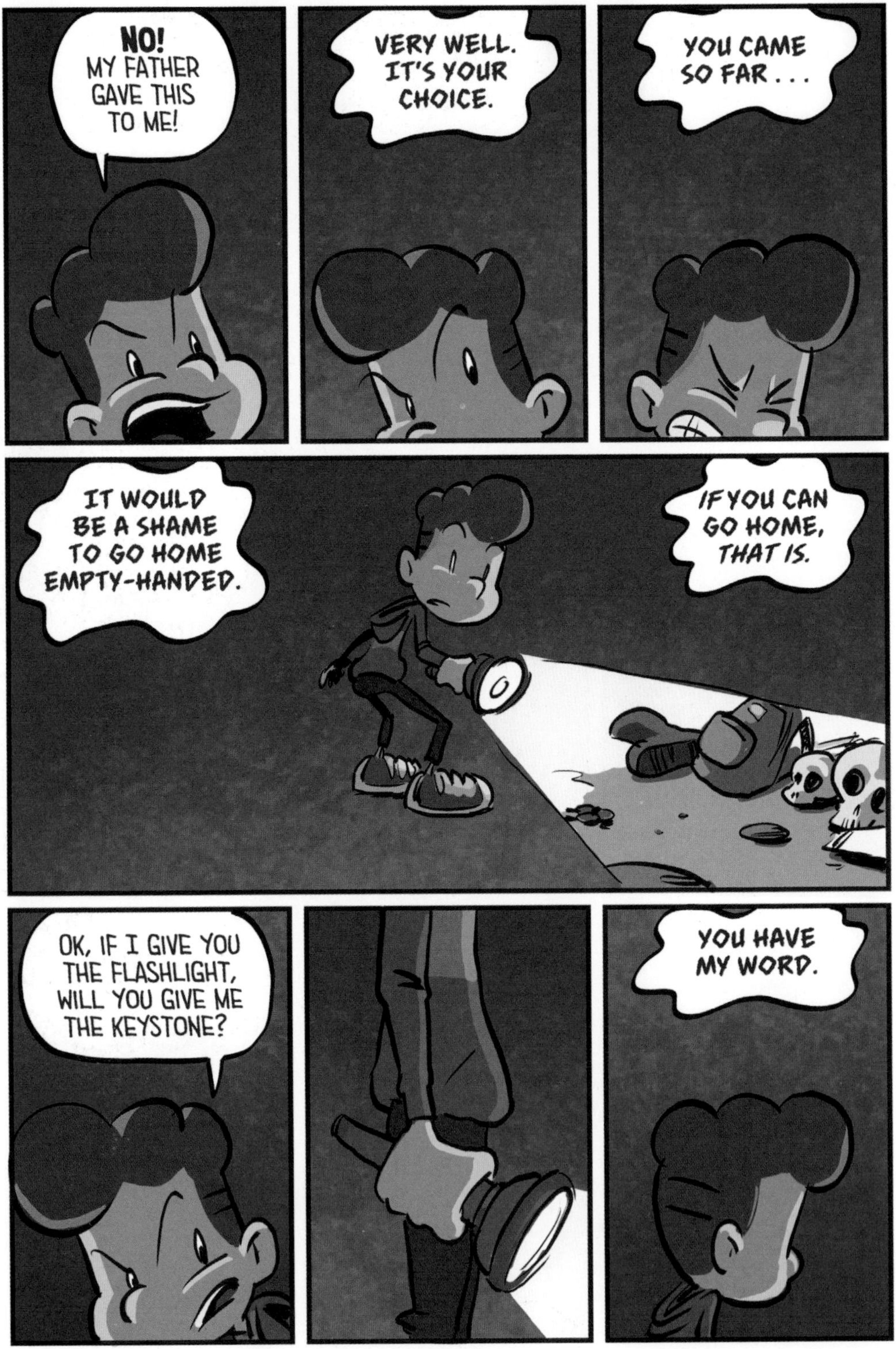
NO! MY FATHER GAVE THIS TO ME!
VERY WELL. IT'S YOUR CHOICE.
YOU CAME SO FAR . . .
IT WOULD BE A SHAME TO GO HOME EMPTY-HANDED.
IF YOU CAN GO HOME, THAT IS.
OK, IF I GIVE YOU THE FLASHLIGHT, WILL YOU GIVE ME THE KEYSTONE?
YOU HAVE MY WORD.

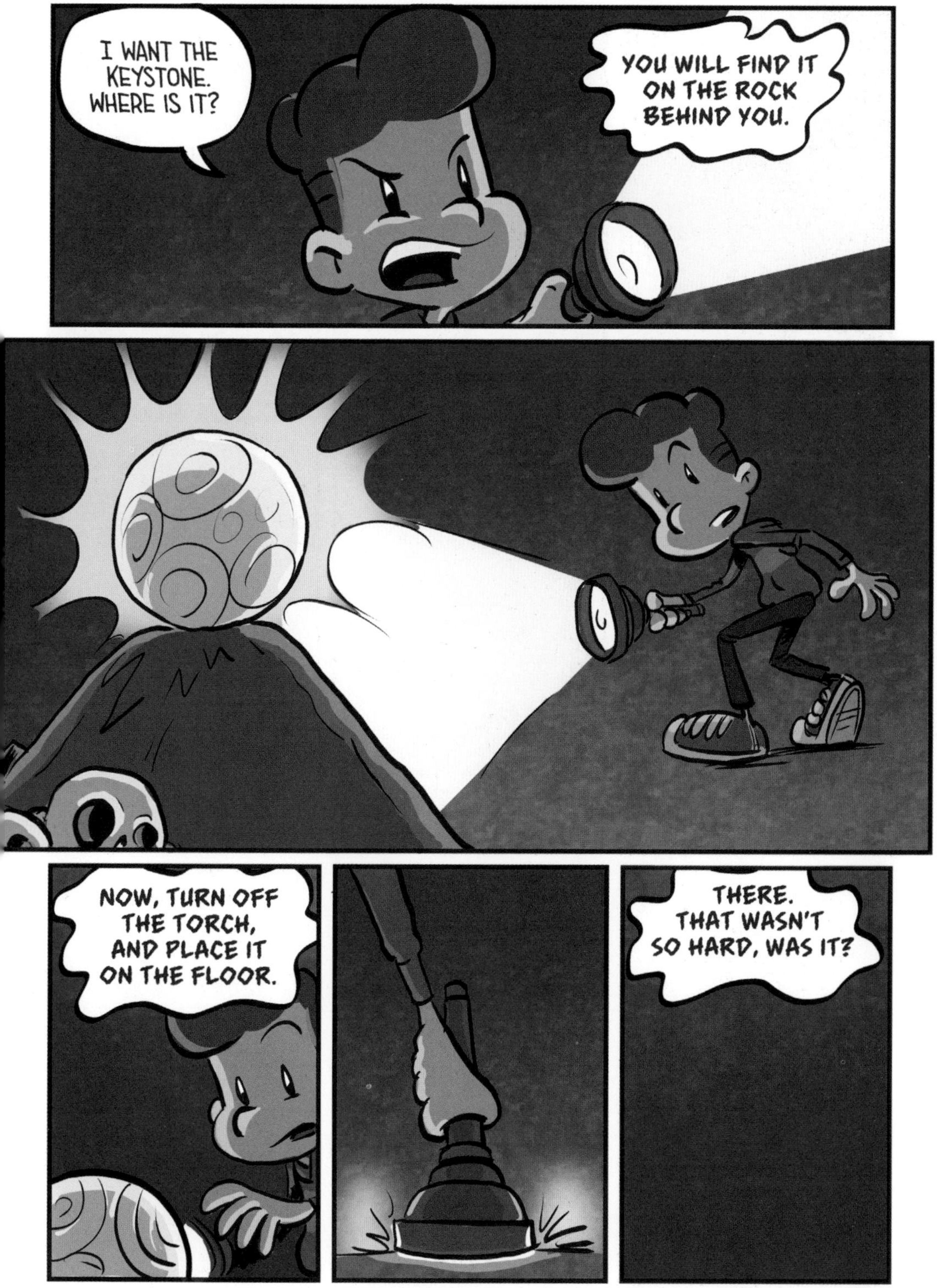

I WANT THE KEYSTONE. WHERE IS IT?
YOU WILL FIND IT ON THE ROCK BEHIND YOU.
NOW, TURN OFF THE TORCH, AND PLACE IT ON THE FLOOR.
THERE. THAT WASN'T SO HARD, WAS IT?

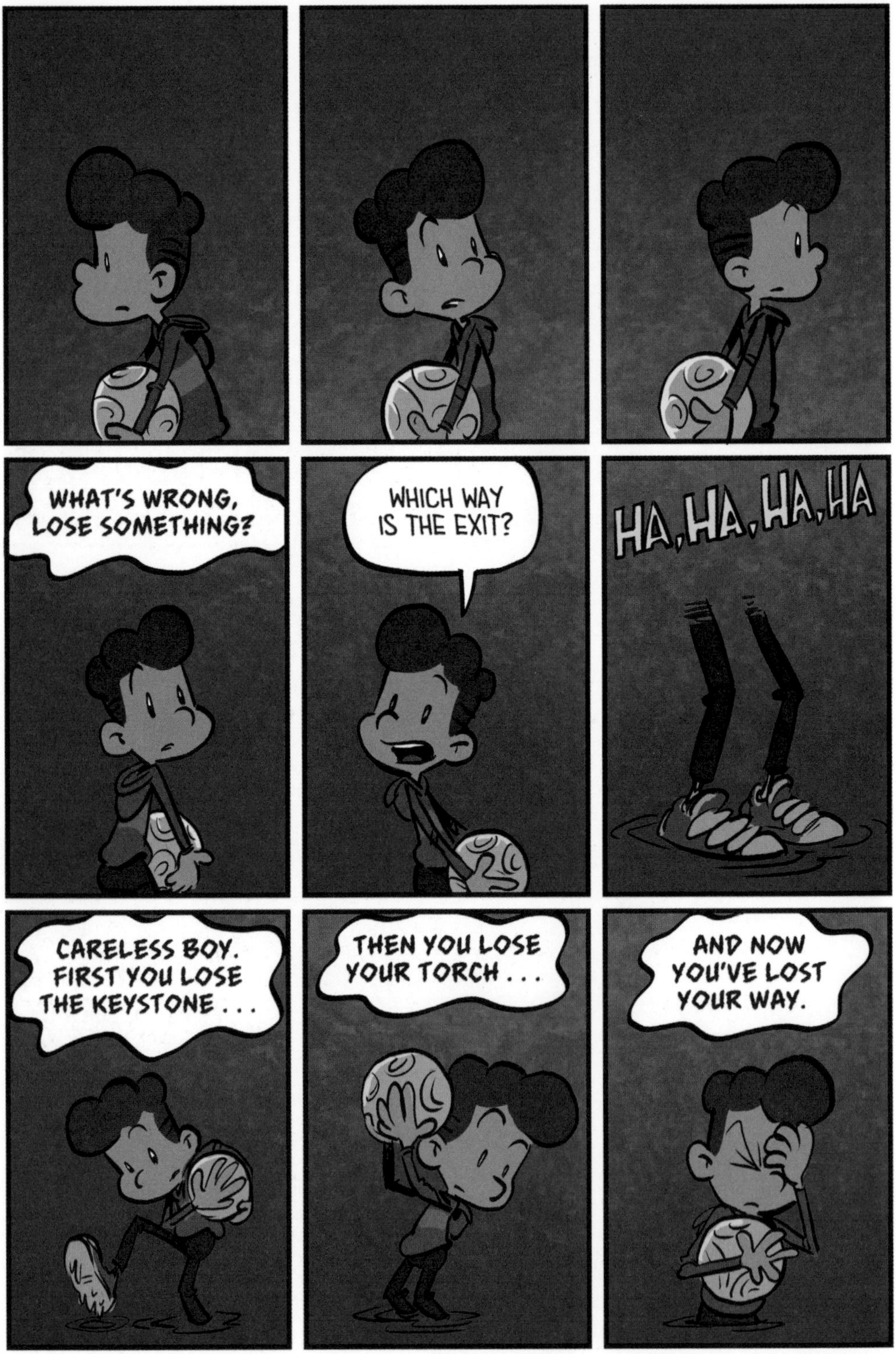
WHAT'S WRONG, LOSE SOMETHING?
WHICH WAY IS THE EXIT?
HA, HA, HA, HA
CARELESS BOY. FIRST YOU LOSE THE KEYSTONE . . .
THEN YOU LOSE YOUR TORCH . . .
AND NOW YOU'VE LOST YOUR WAY.

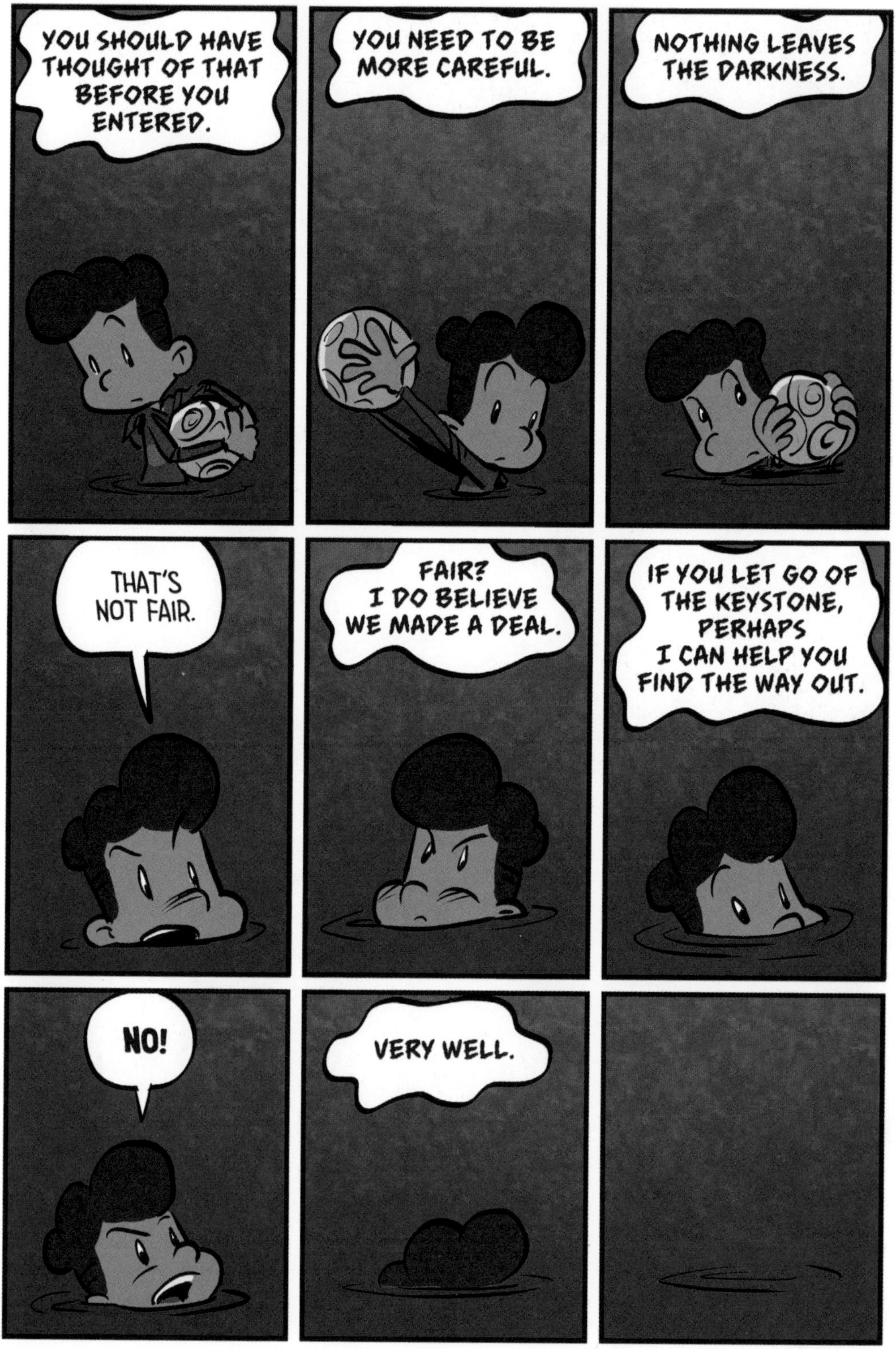
YOU SHOULD HAVE THOUGHT OF THAT BEFORE YOU ENTERED.
YOU NEED TO BE MORE CAREFUL.
NOTHING LEAVES THE DARKNESS.
THAT'S NOT FAIR.
FAIR? I DO BELIEVE WE MADE A DEAL.
IF YOU LET GO OF THE KEYSTONE, PERHAPS I CAN HELP YOU FIND THE WAY OUT.
NO!
VERY WELL.

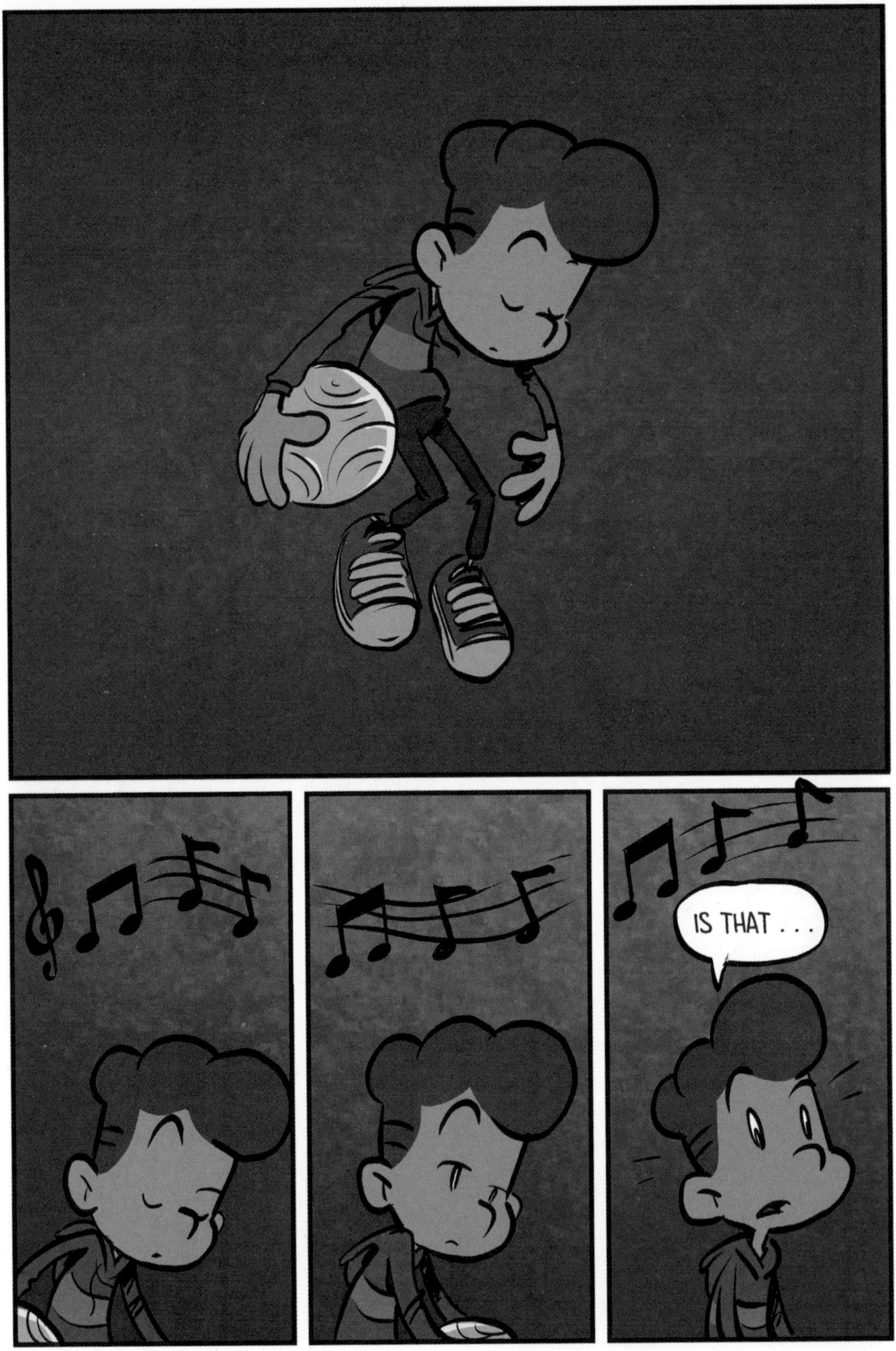
IS THAT . . .

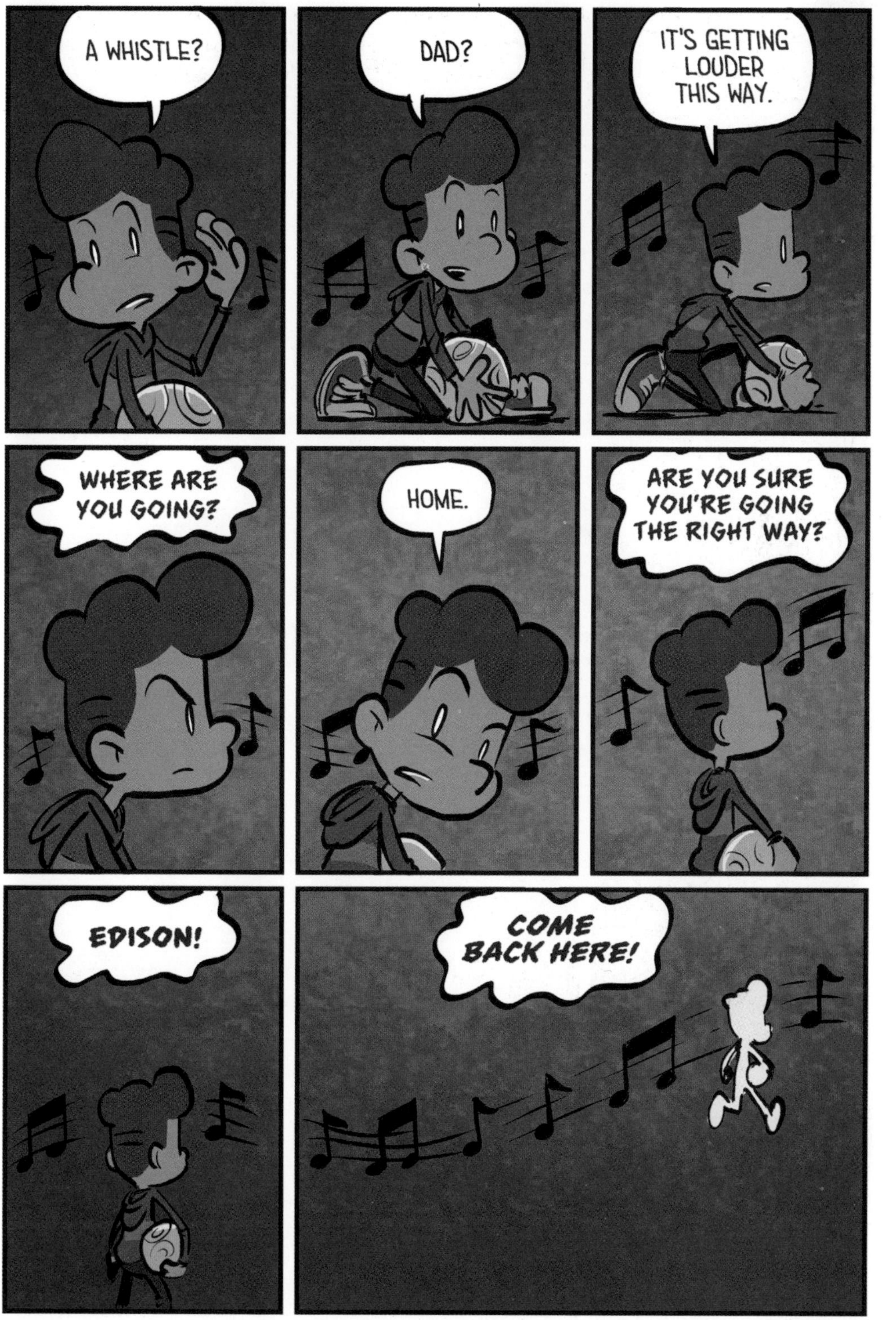
A WHISTLE?
DAD?
IT'S GETTING LOUDER THIS WAY.
WHERE ARE YOU GOING?
HOME.
ARE YOU SURE YOU'RE GOING THE RIGHT WAY?
EDISON!
COME BACK HERE!

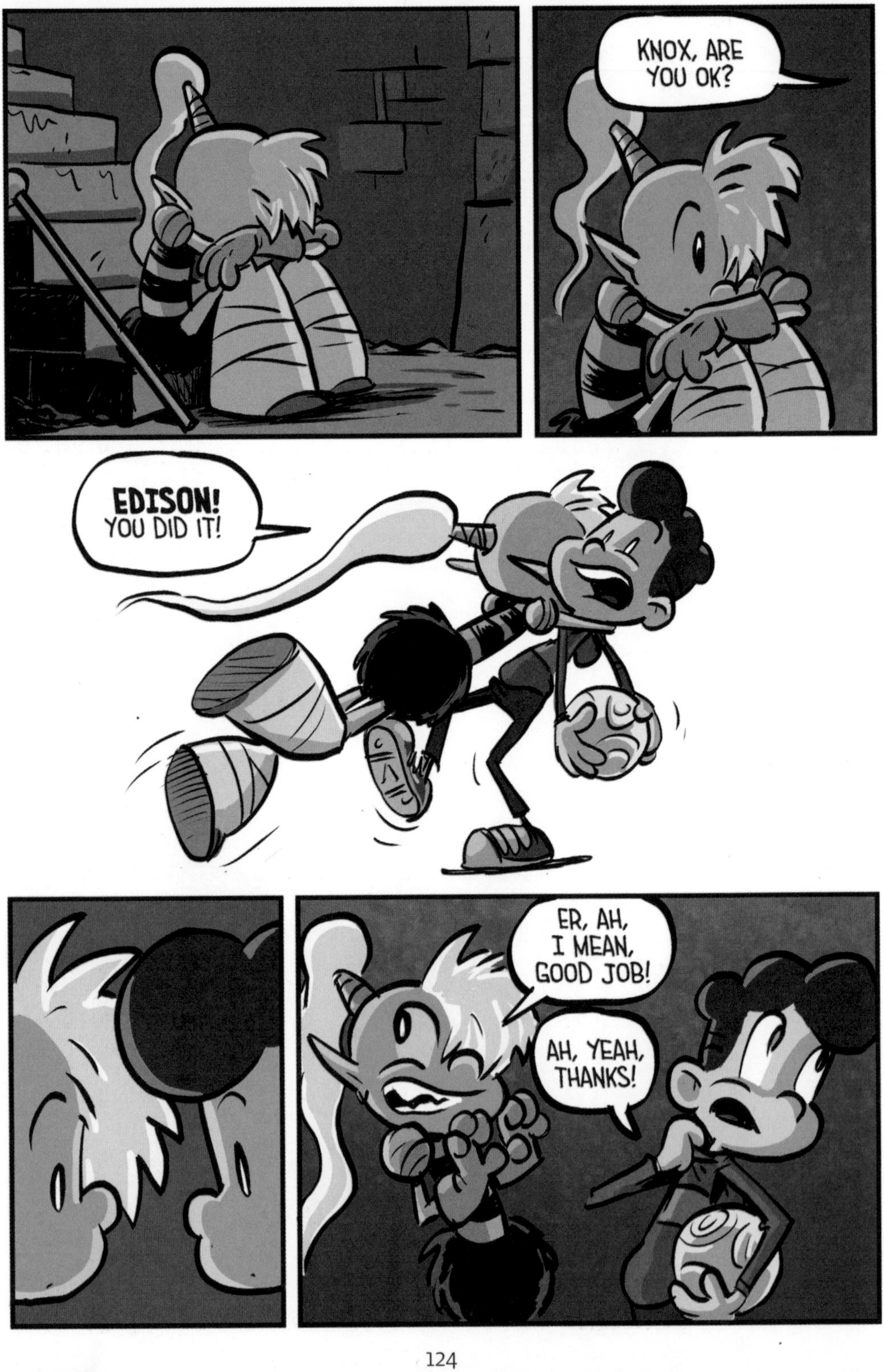
KNOX, ARE YOU OK?
EDISON! YOU DID IT!
ER, AH, I MEAN, GOOD JOB!
AH, YEAH, THANKS!

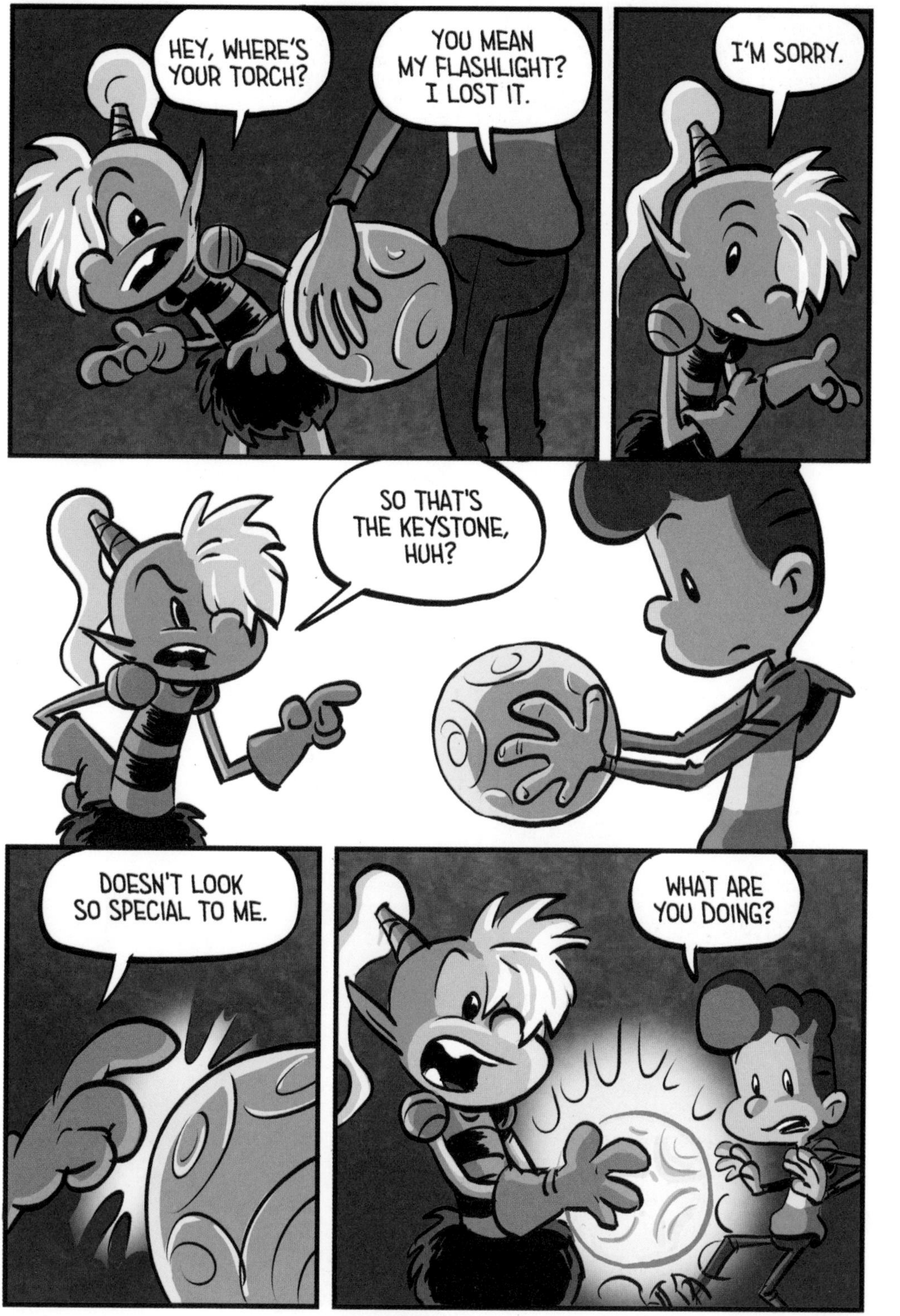
HEY, WHERE'S YOUR TORCH?
YOU MEAN MY FLASHLIGHT? I LOST IT.
I'M SORRY.
SO THAT'S THE KEYSTONE, HUH?
DOESN'T LOOK SO SPECIAL TO ME.
WHAT ARE YOU DOING?

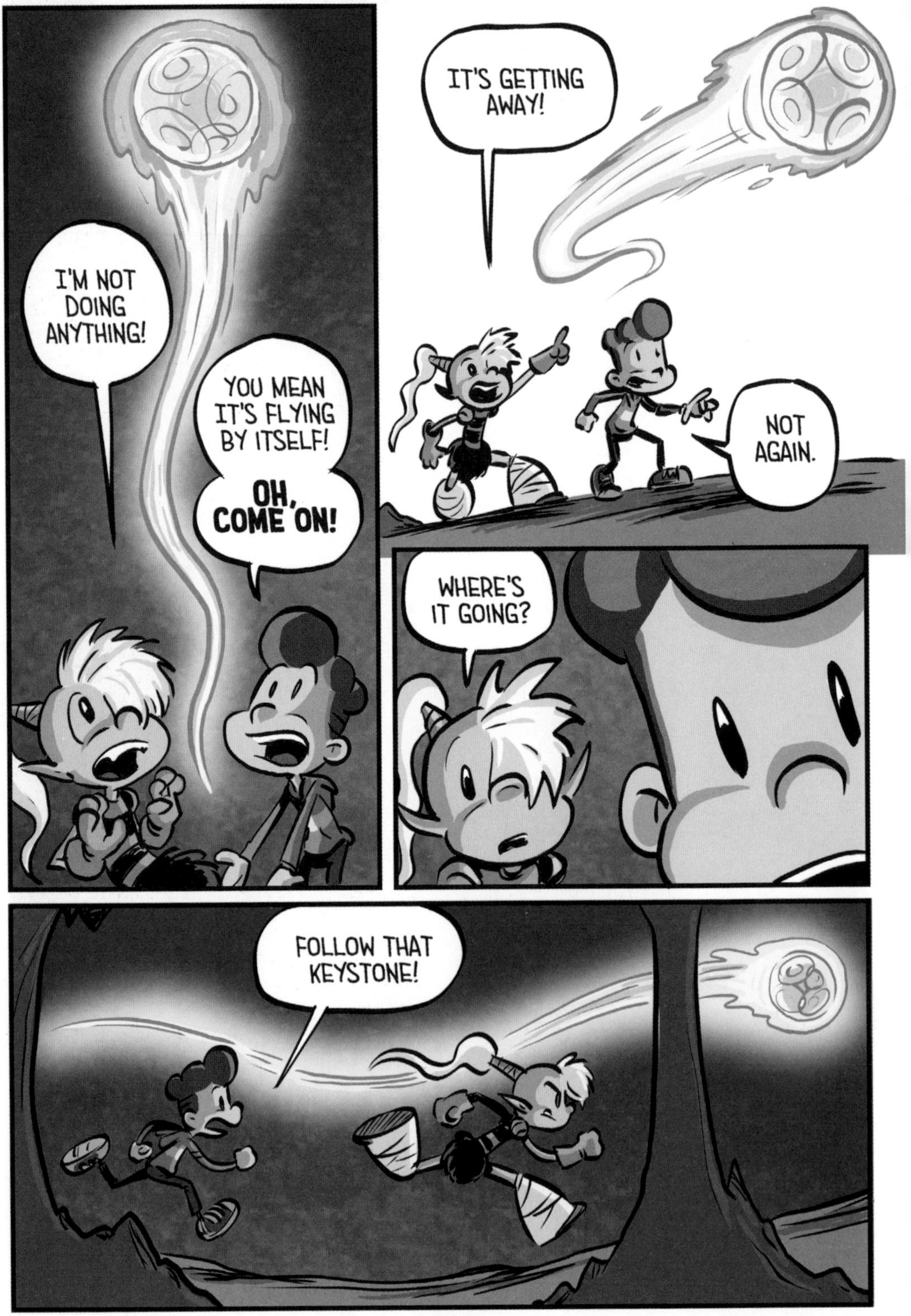
I'M NOT DOING ANYTHING!
YOU MEAN IT'S FLYING BY ITSELF!
OH, COME ON!
IT'S GETTING AWAY!
NOT AGAIN.
WHERE'S IT GOING?
FOLLOW THAT KEYSTONE!

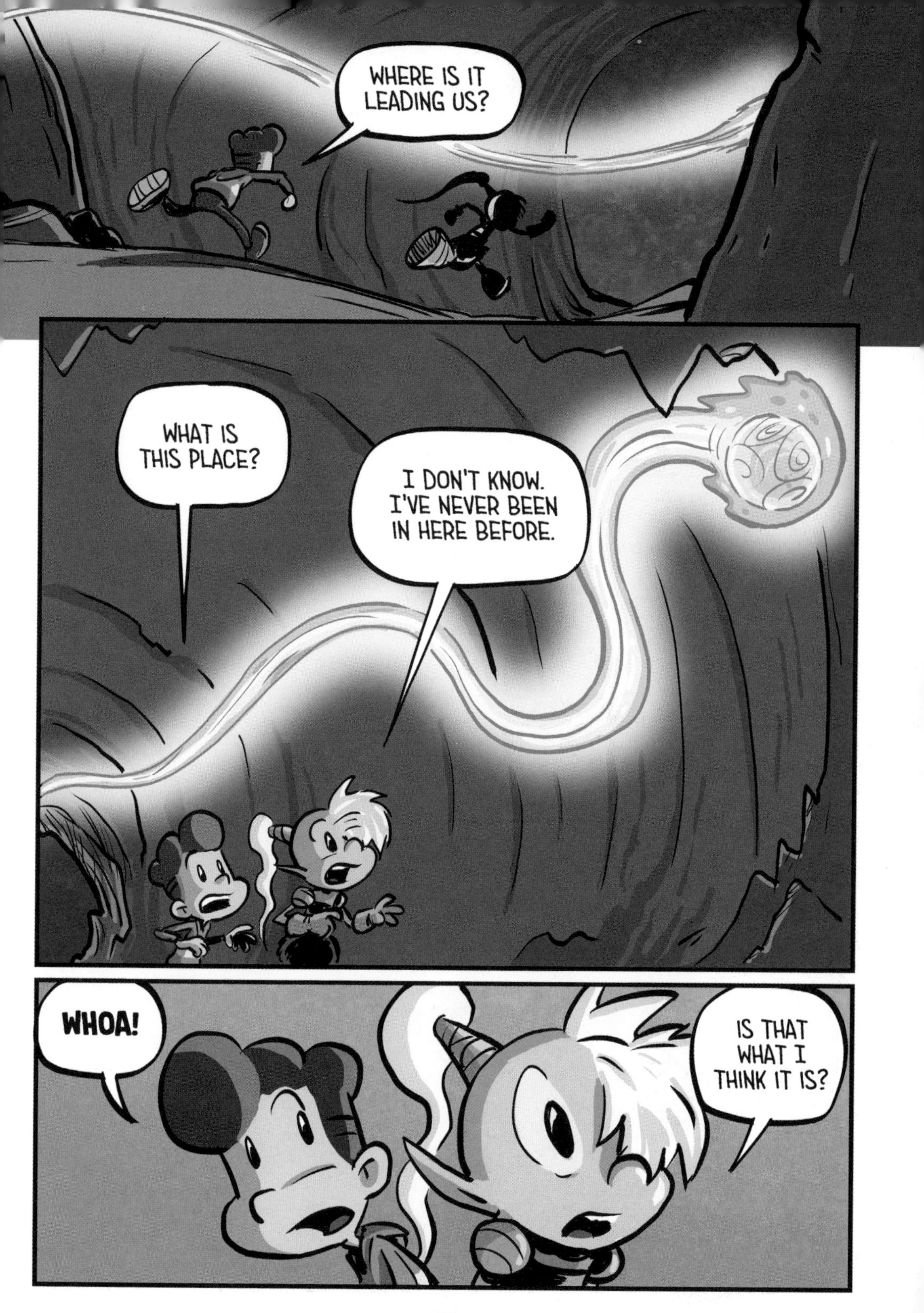
WHERE IS IT LEADING US?
WHAT IS THIS PLACE?
I DON'T KNOW. I'VE NEVER BEEN IN HERE BEFORE.
WHOA!
IS THAT WHAT I THINK IT IS?

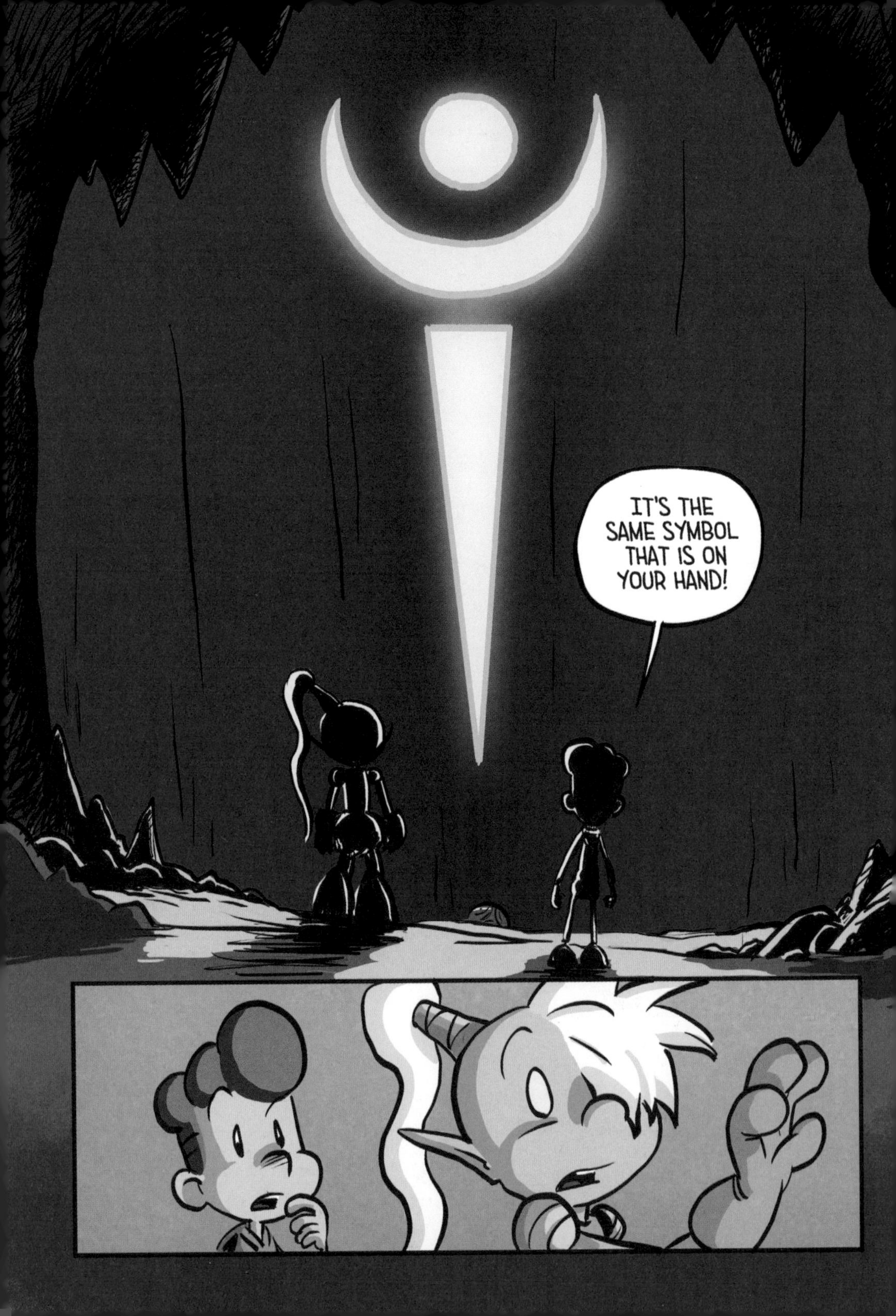
IT'S THE SAME SYMBOL THAT IS ON YOUR HAND!

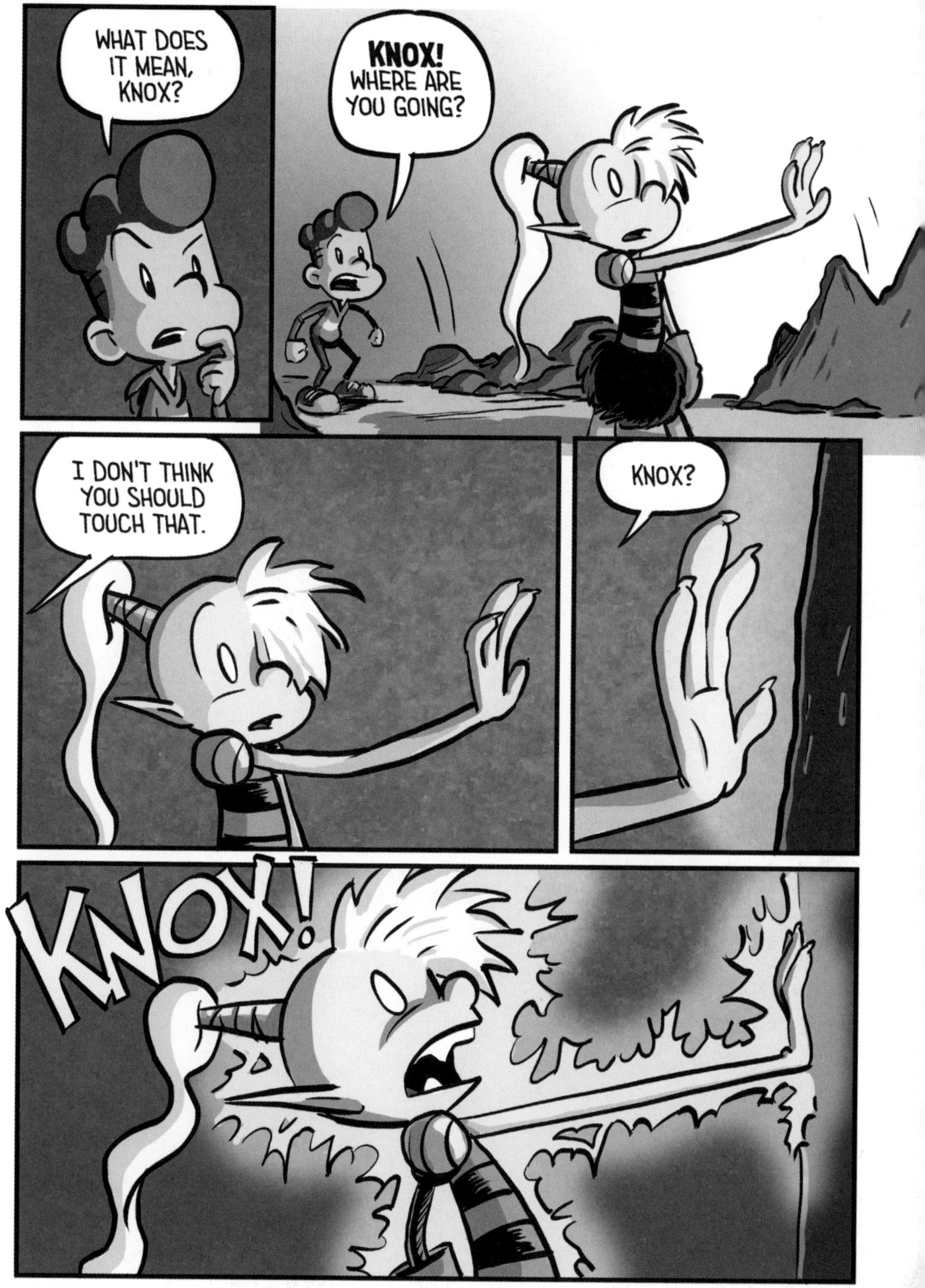
WHAT DOES IT MEAN, KNOX?
KNOX! WHERE ARE YOU GOING?
I DON'T THINK YOU SHOULD TOUCH THAT.
KNOX?
KNOX!

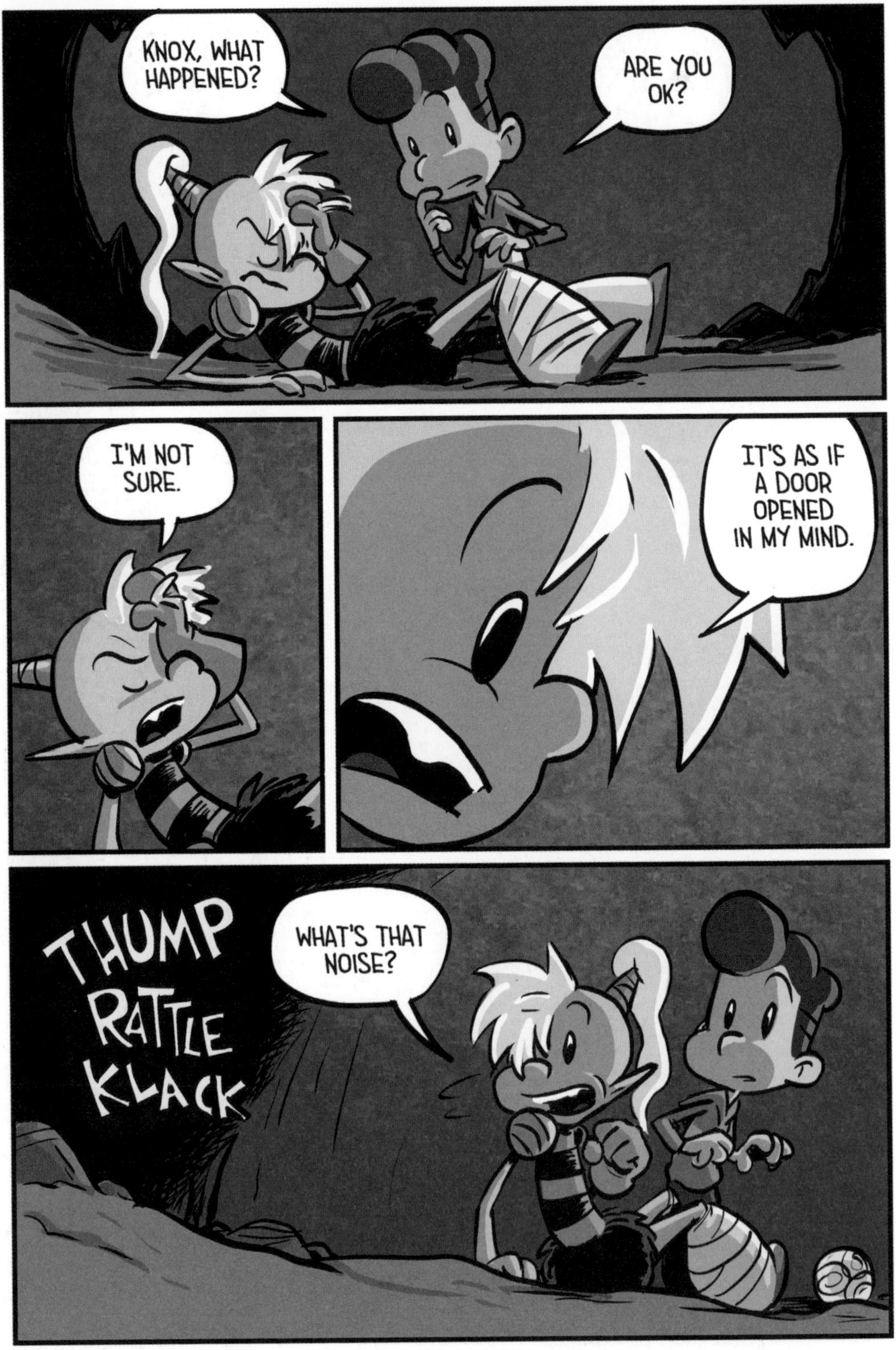
KNOX, WHAT HAPPENED?
ARE YOU OK?
I'M NOT SURE.
IT'S AS IF A DOOR OPENED IN MY MIND.
THUMP RATTLE KLACK
WHAT'S THAT NOISE?

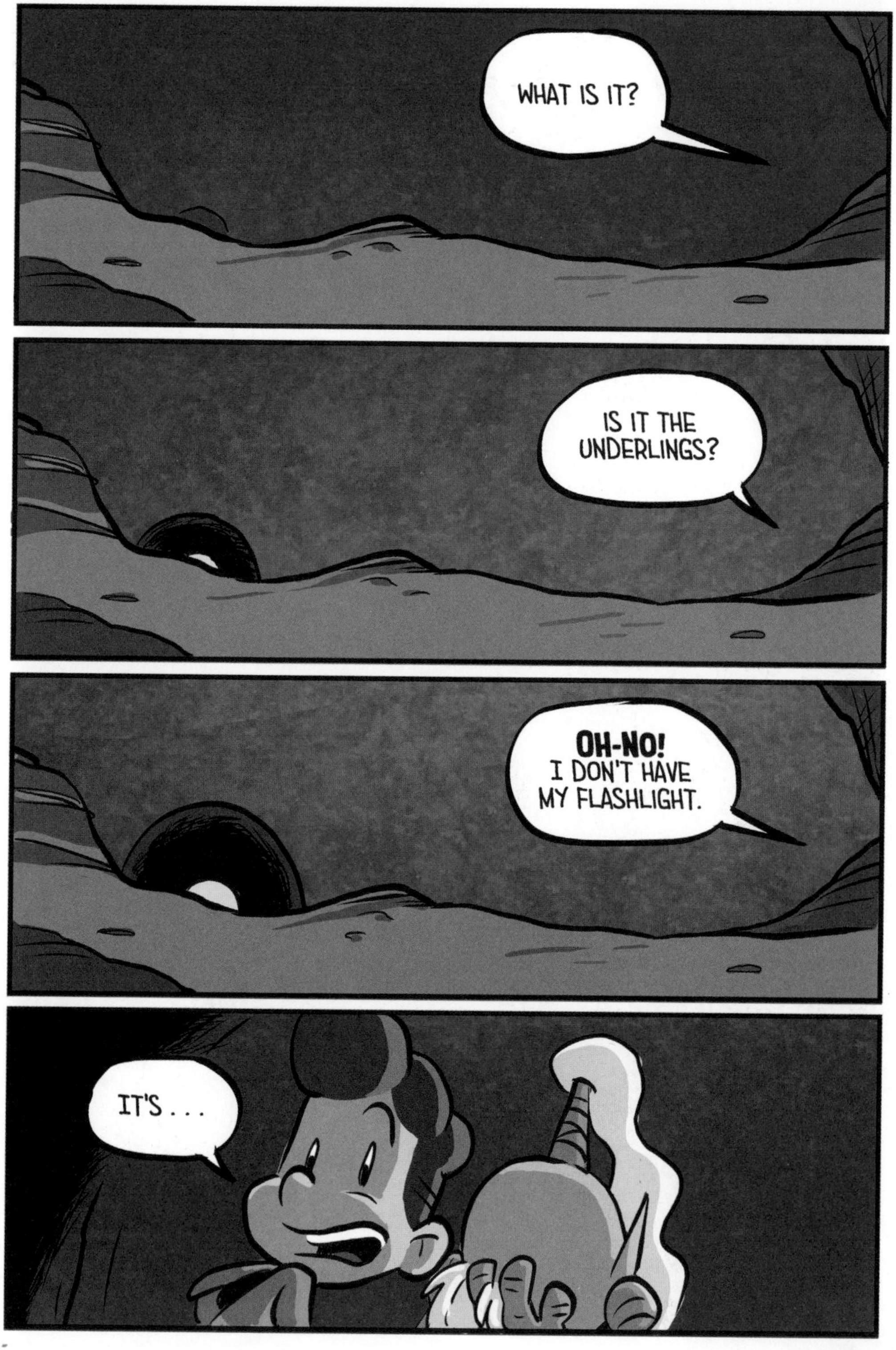
WHAT IS IT?
IS IT THE UNDERLINGS?
OH-NO! I DON'T HAVE MY FLASHLIGHT.
IT'S . . .

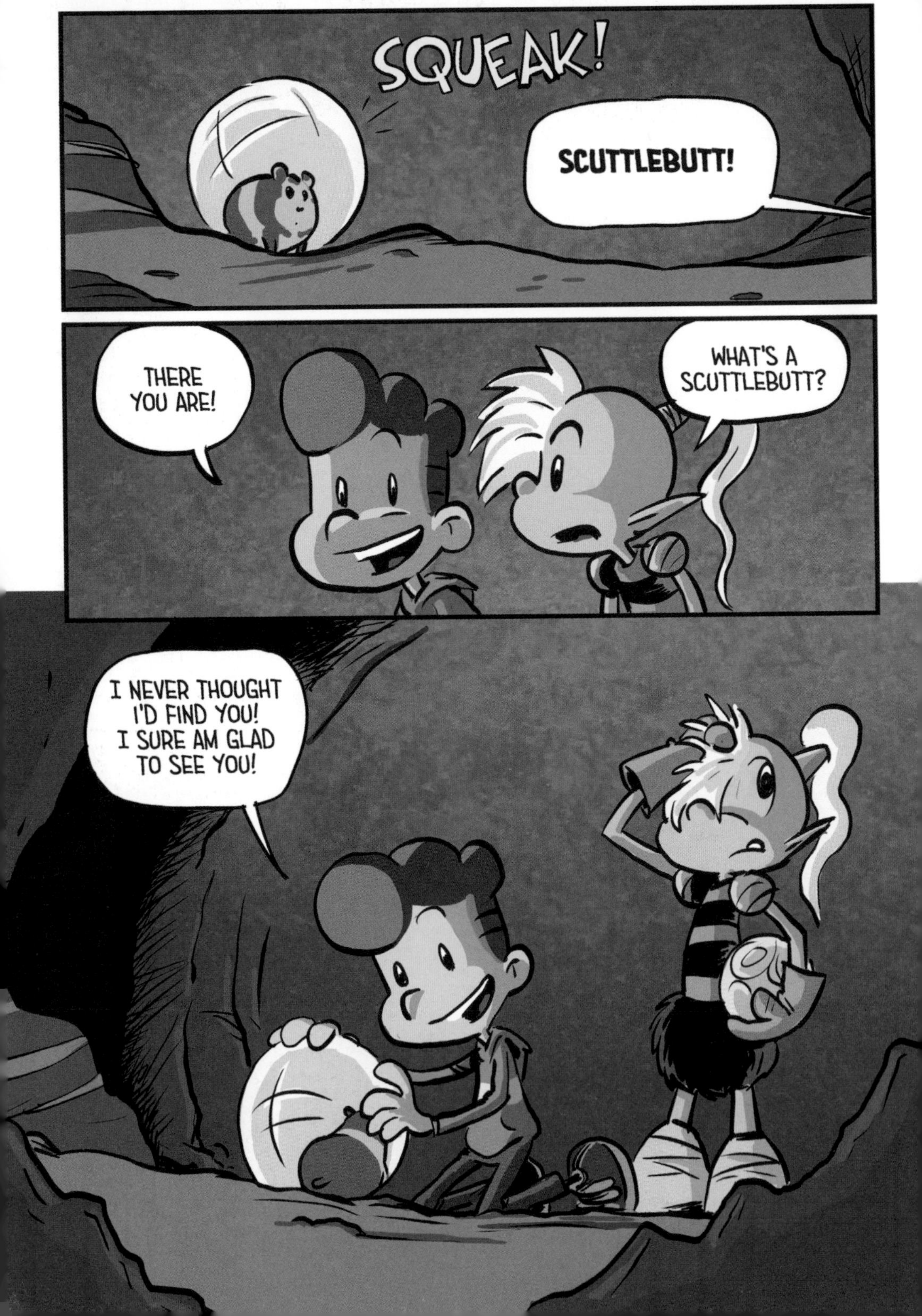
SQUEAK!
SCUTTLEBUTT!
THERE YOU ARE!
WHAT'S A SCUTTLEBUTT?
I NEVER THOUGHT I'D FIND YOU! I SURE AM GLAD TO SEE YOU!

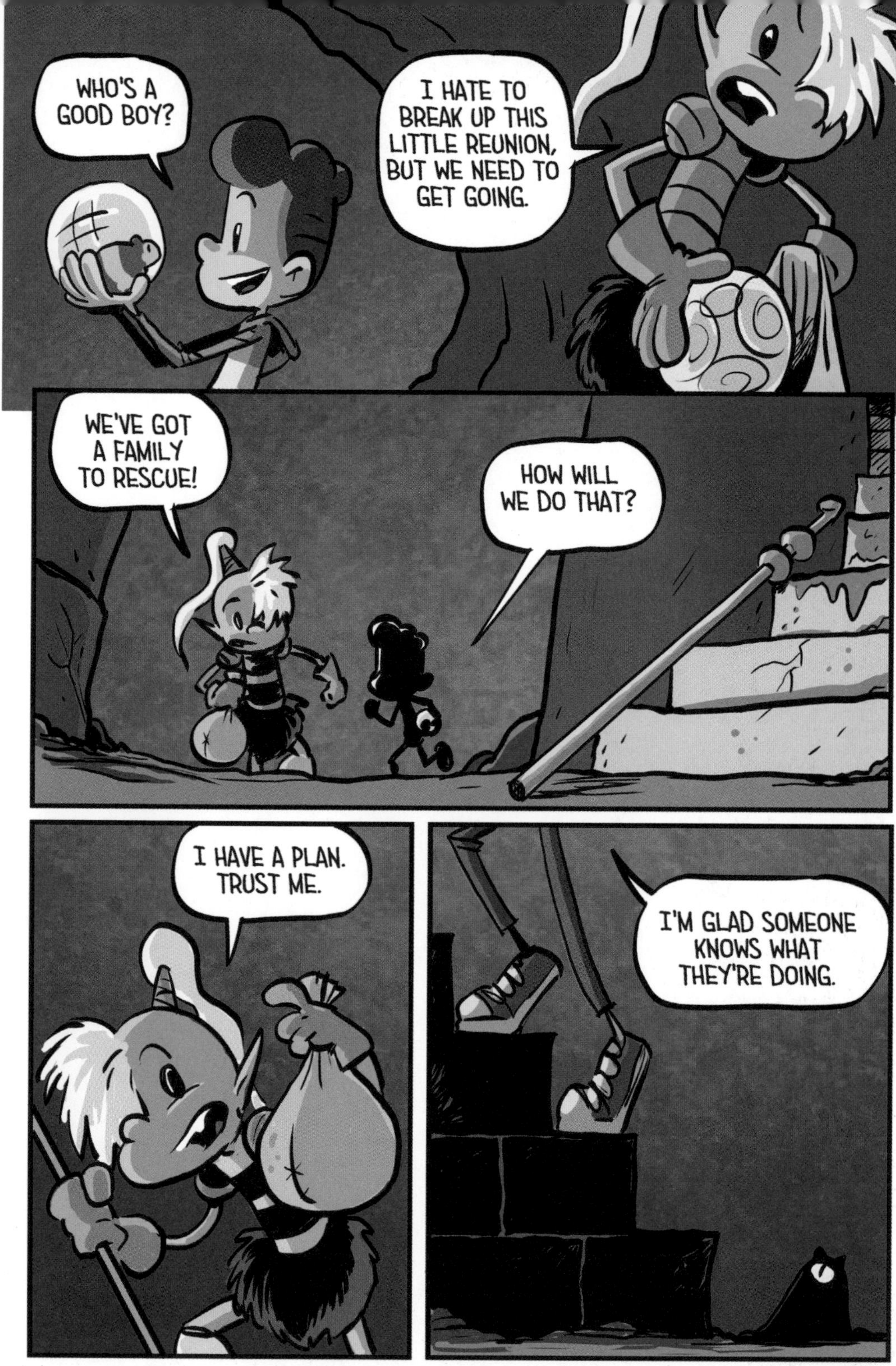
WHO'S A GOOD BOY?
I HATE TO BREAK UP THIS LITTLE REUNION, BUT WE NEED TO GET GOING.
WE'VE GOT A FAMILY TO RESCUE!
HOW WILL WE DO THAT?
I HAVE A PLAN. TRUST ME.
I'M GLAD SOMEONE KNOWS WHAT THEY'RE DOING.

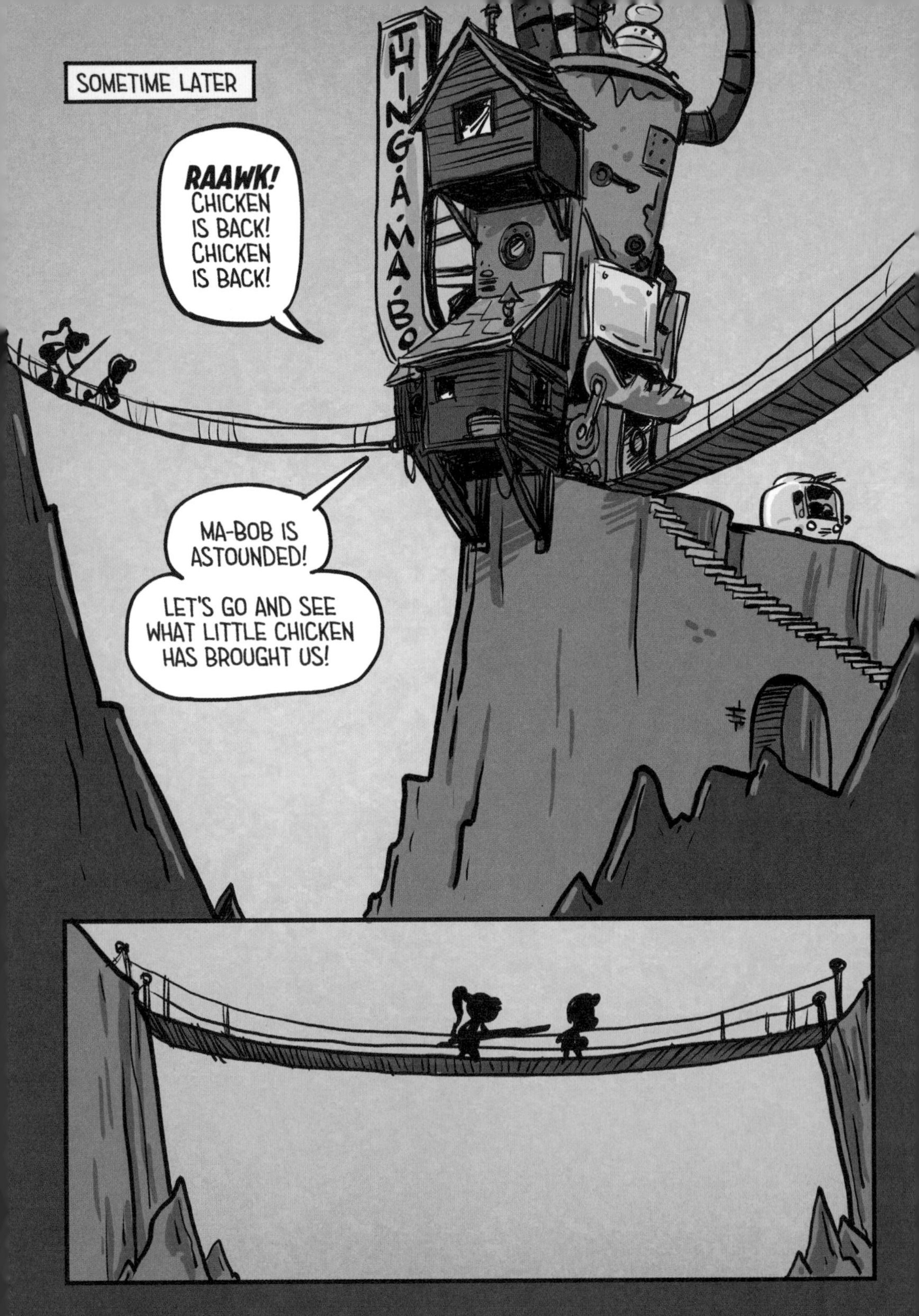
SOMETIME LATER
THING·A·MA·BO
RAAWK! CHICKEN IS BACK! CHICKEN IS BACK!
MA-BOB IS ASTOUNDED!
LET'S GO AND SEE WHAT LITTLE CHICKEN HAS BROUGHT US!

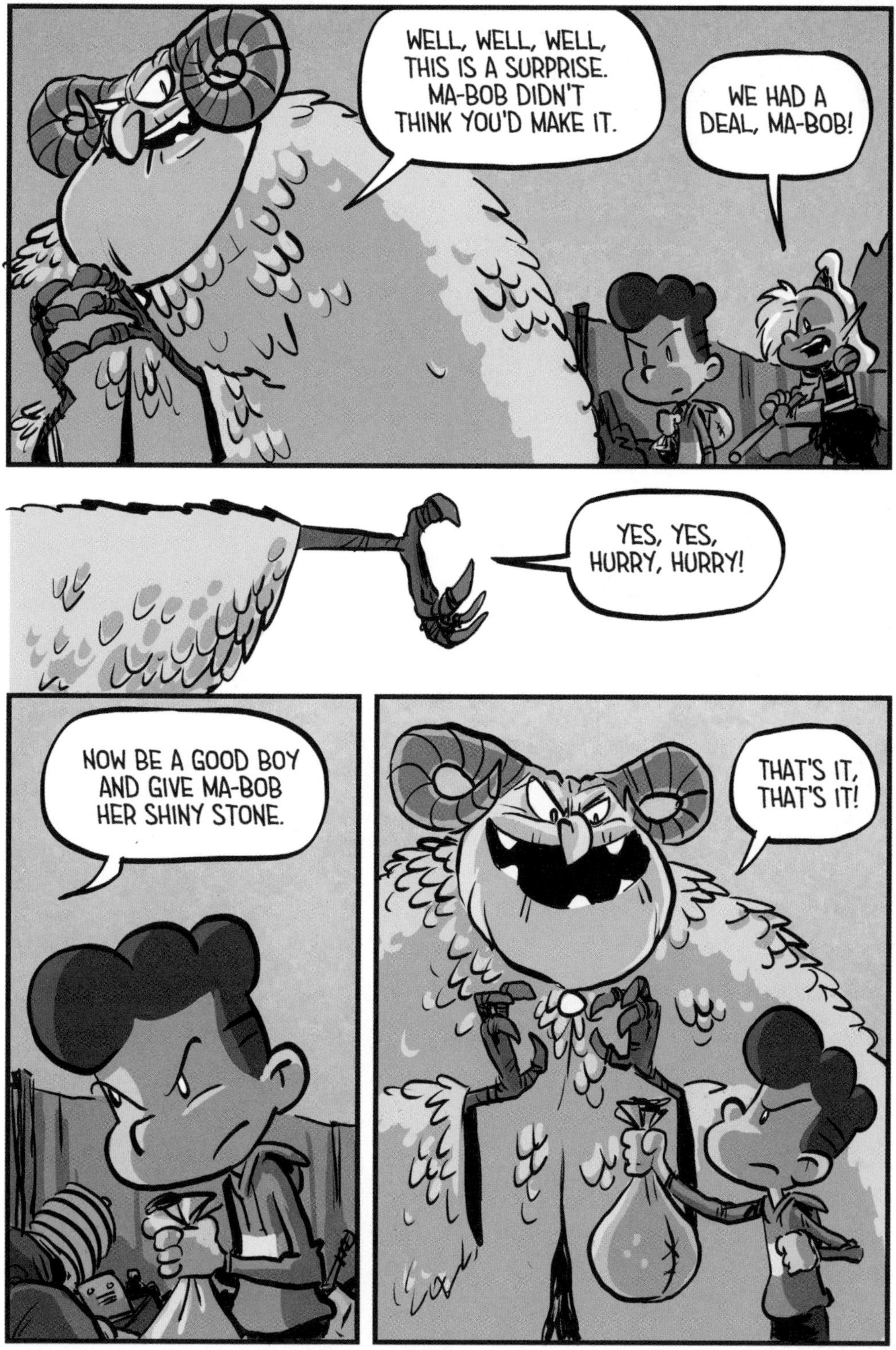
WELL, WELL, WELL, THIS IS A SURPRISE. MA-BOB DIDN'T THINK YOU'D MAKE IT.
WE HAD A DEAL, MA-BOB!
YES, YES, HURRY, HURRY!
NOW BE A GOOD BOY AND GIVE MA-BOB HER SHINY STONE.
THAT'S IT, THAT'S IT!

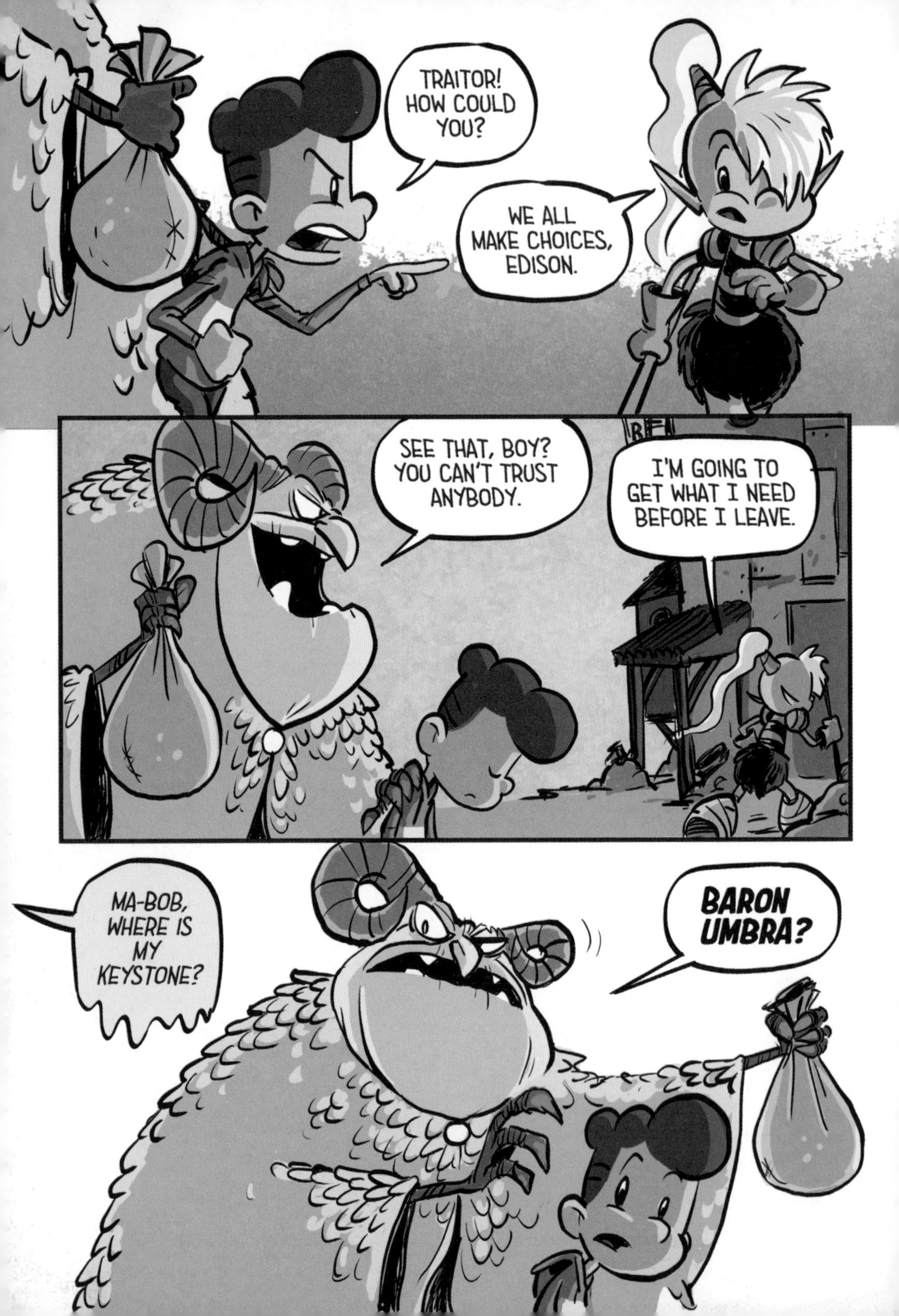
TRAITOR! HOW COULD YOU?
WE ALL MAKE CHOICES, EDISON.
SEE THAT, BOY? YOU CAN'T TRUST ANYBODY.
I'M GOING TO GET WHAT I NEED BEFORE I LEAVE.
MA-BOB, WHERE IS MY KEYSTONE?
BARON UMBRA?

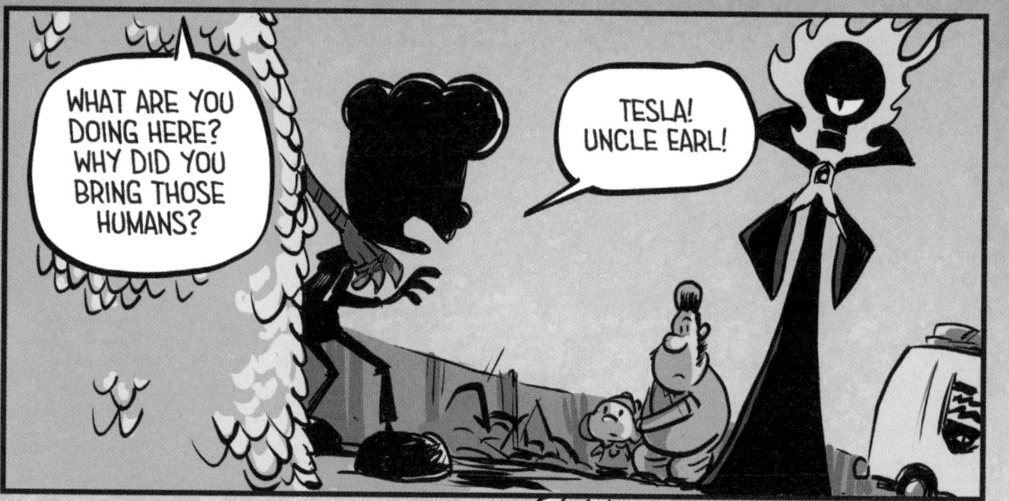
WHAT ARE YOU DOING HERE? WHY DID YOU BRING THOSE HUMANS?
TESLA! UNCLE EARL!
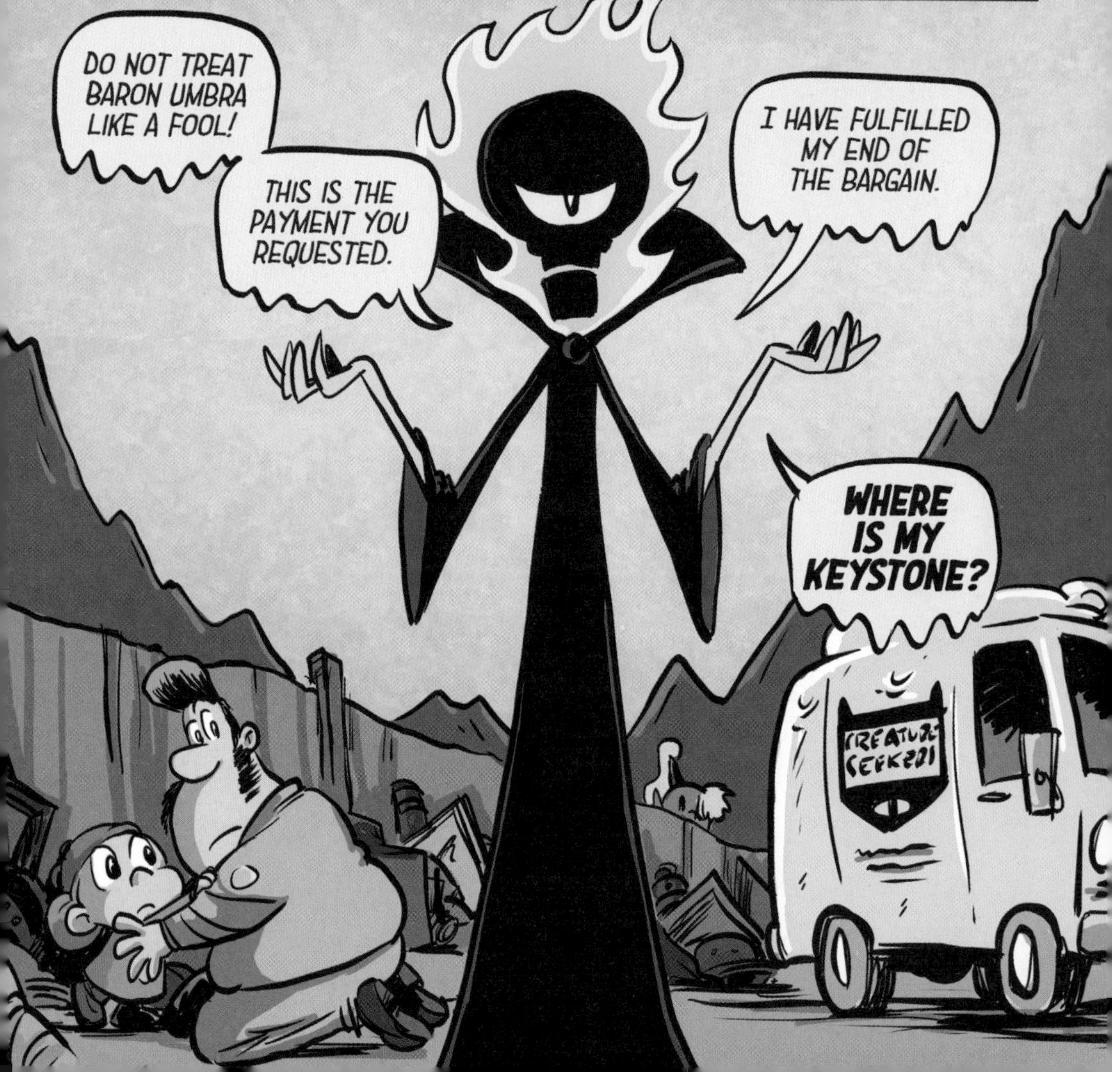
DO NOT TREAT BARON UMBRA LIKE A FOOL!
THIS IS THE PAYMENT YOU REQUESTED.
I HAVE FULFILLED MY END OF THE BARGAIN.
WHERE IS MY KEYSTONE?

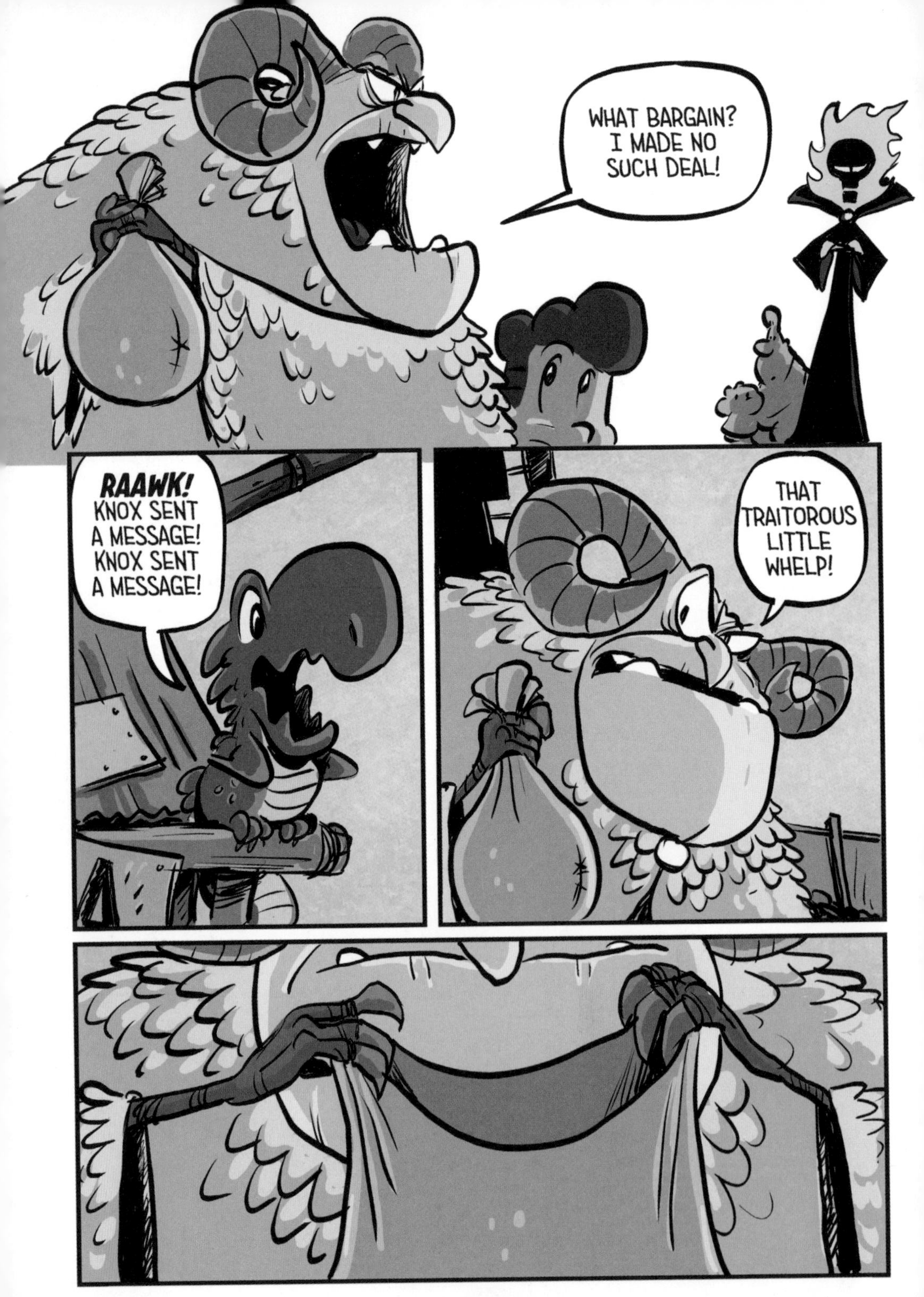
WHAT BARGAIN? I MADE NO SUCH DEAL!
RAAWK! KNOX SENT A MESSAGE! KNOX SENT A MESSAGE!
THAT TRAITOROUS LITTLE WHELP!

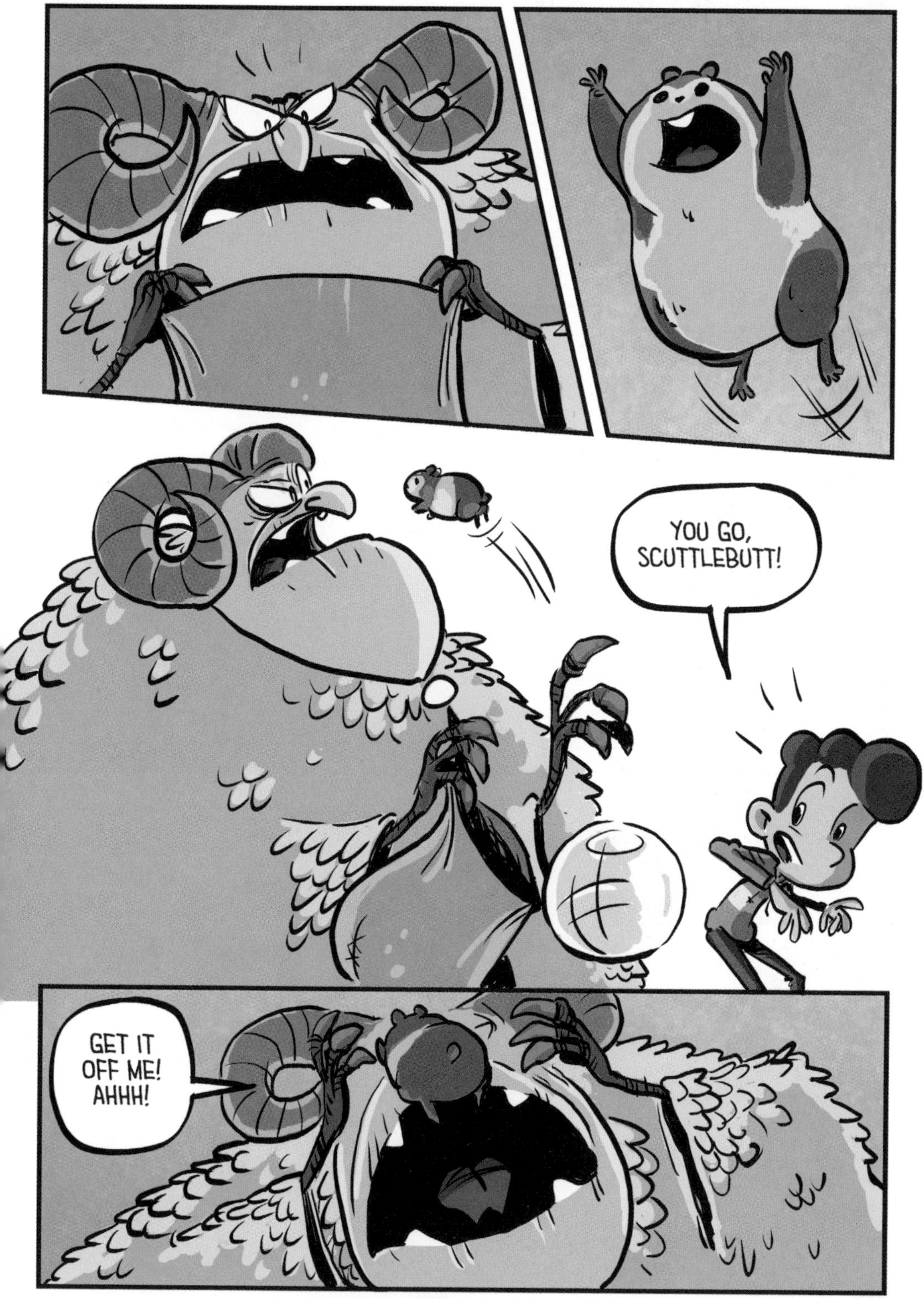
YOU GO, SCUTTLEBUTT!
GET IT OFF ME! AHHH!

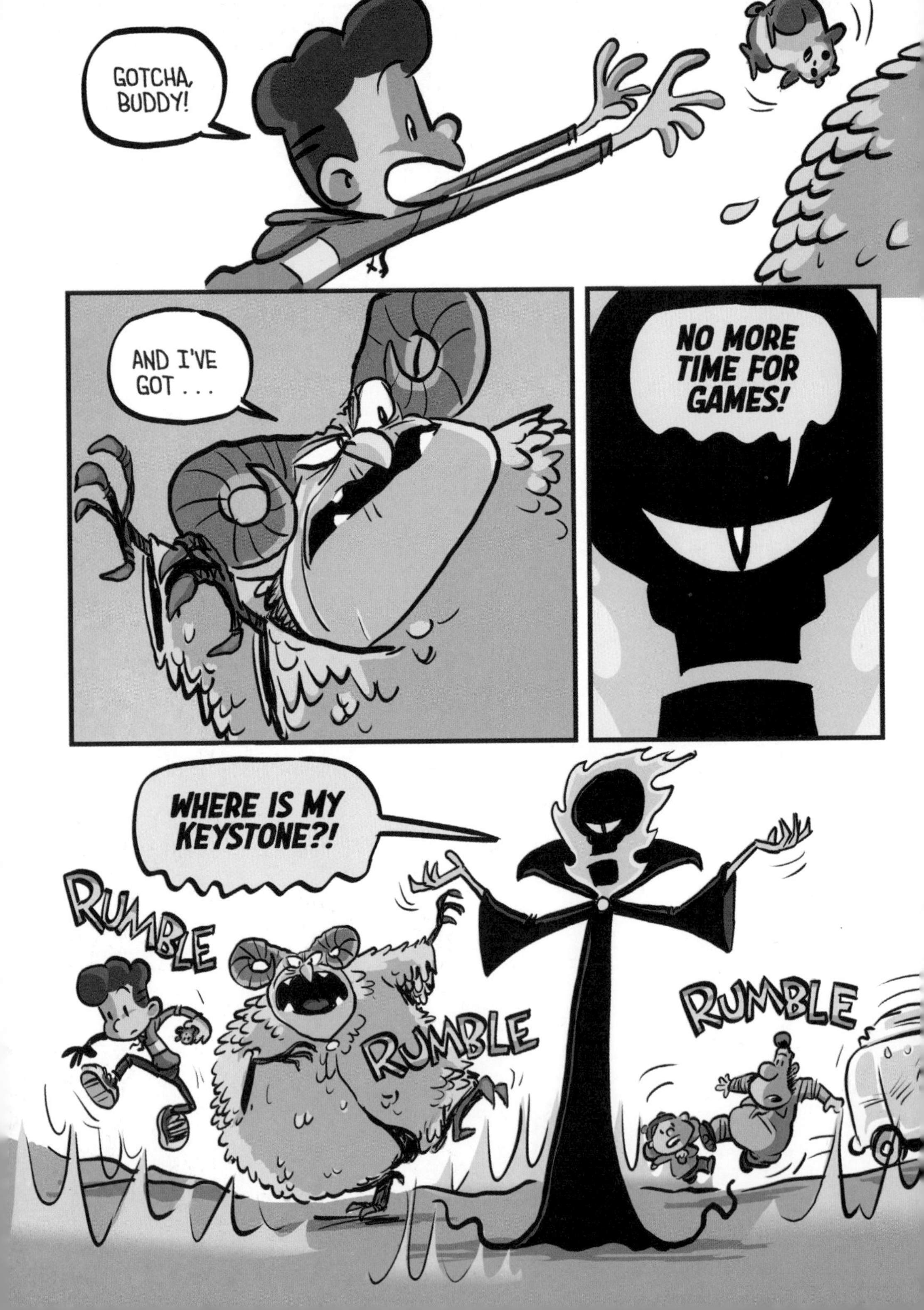

GOTCHA, BUDDY!
AND I'VE GOT . . .
NO MORE TIME FOR GAMES!
WHERE IS MY KEYSTONE?!
RUMBLE
RUMBLE
RUMBLE

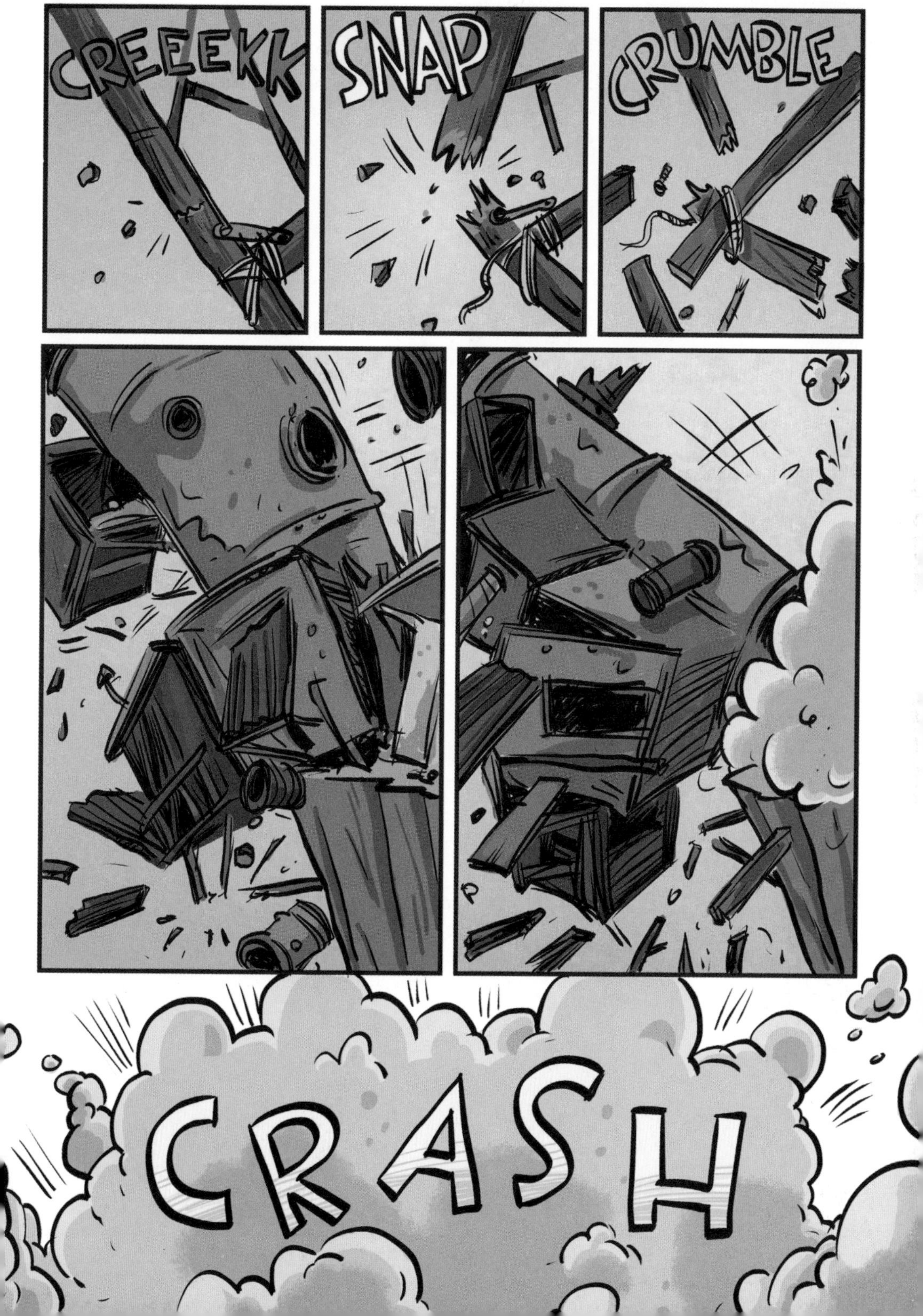
CREEEKK
SNAP
CRUMBLE
CRASH

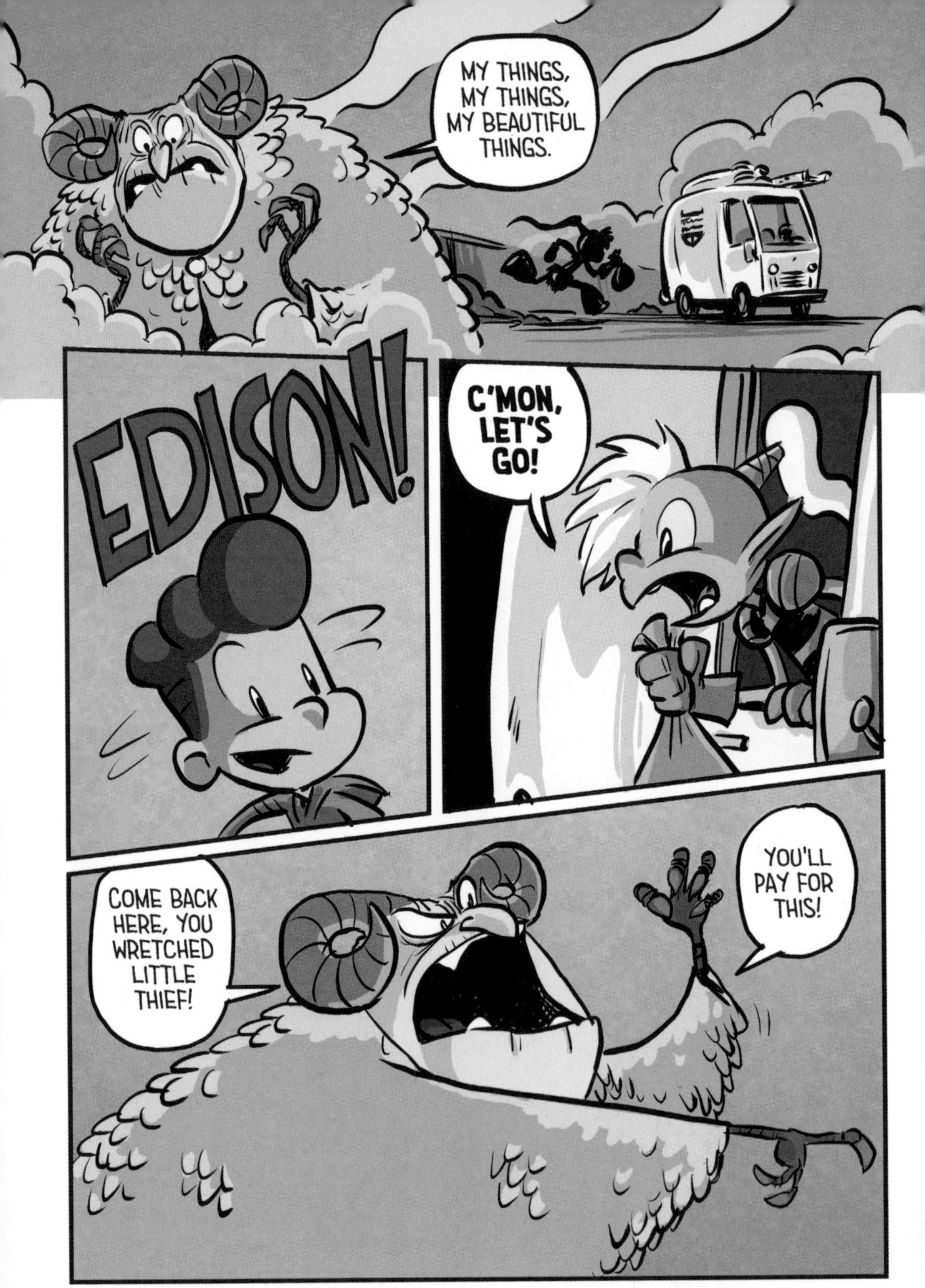
MY THINGS, MY THINGS, MY BEAUTIFUL THINGS.
EDISON!
C'MON, LET'S GO!
COME BACK HERE, YOU WRETCHED LITTLE THIEF!
YOU'LL PAY FOR THIS!

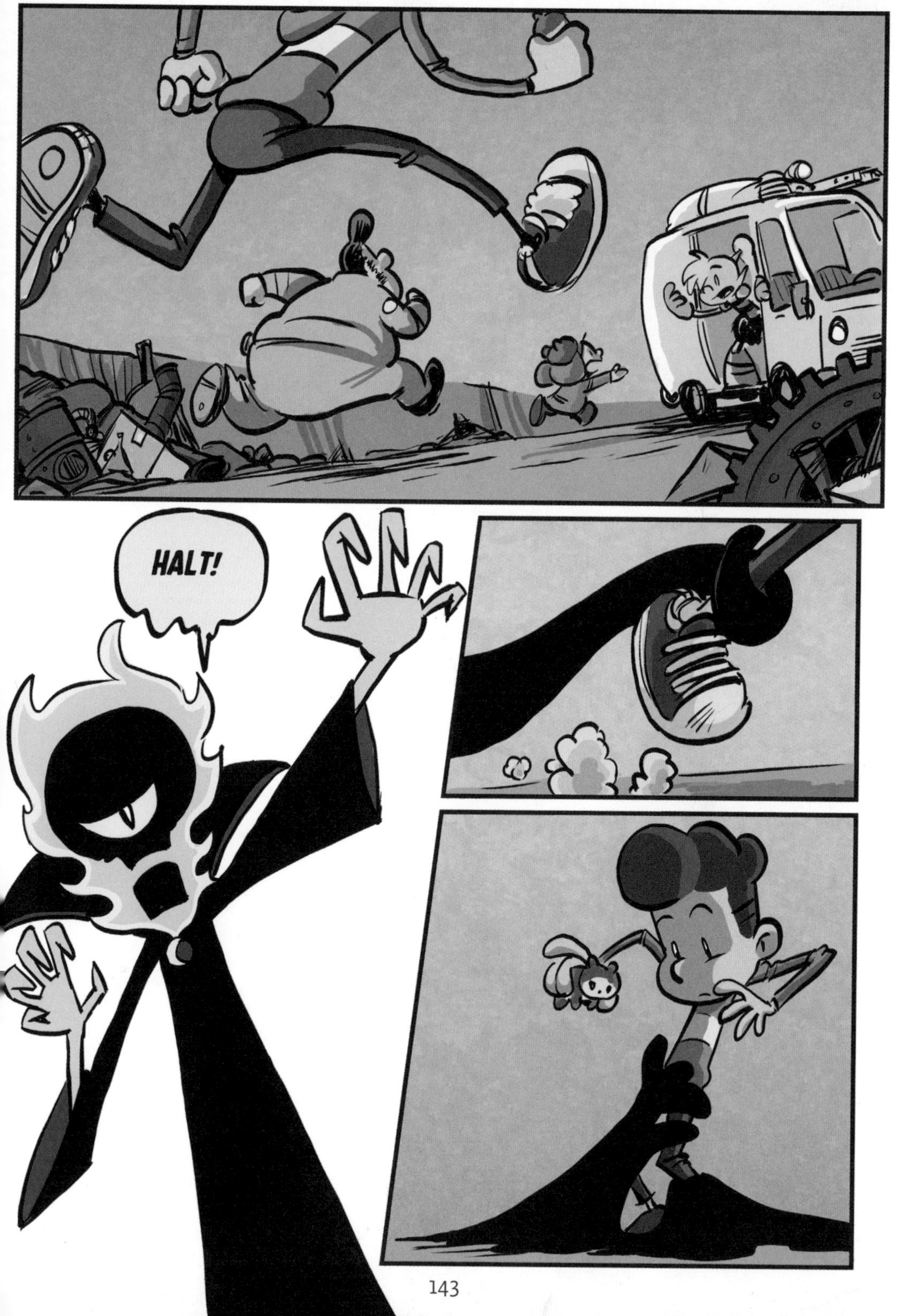
HALT!

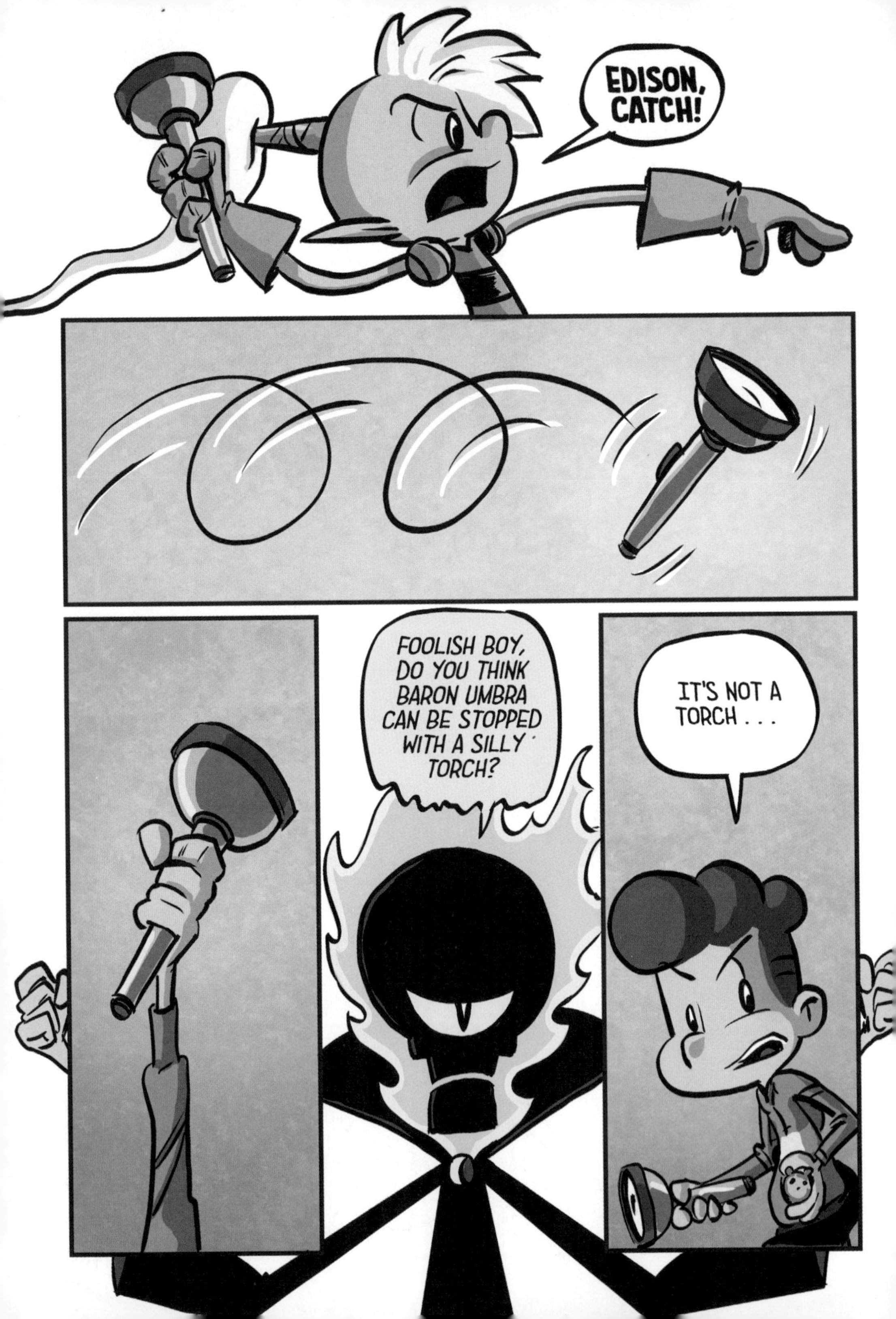
EDISON, CATCH!
FOOLISH BOY, DO YOU THINK BARON UMBRA CAN BE STOPPED WITH A SILLY TORCH?
IT'S NOT A TORCH . . .

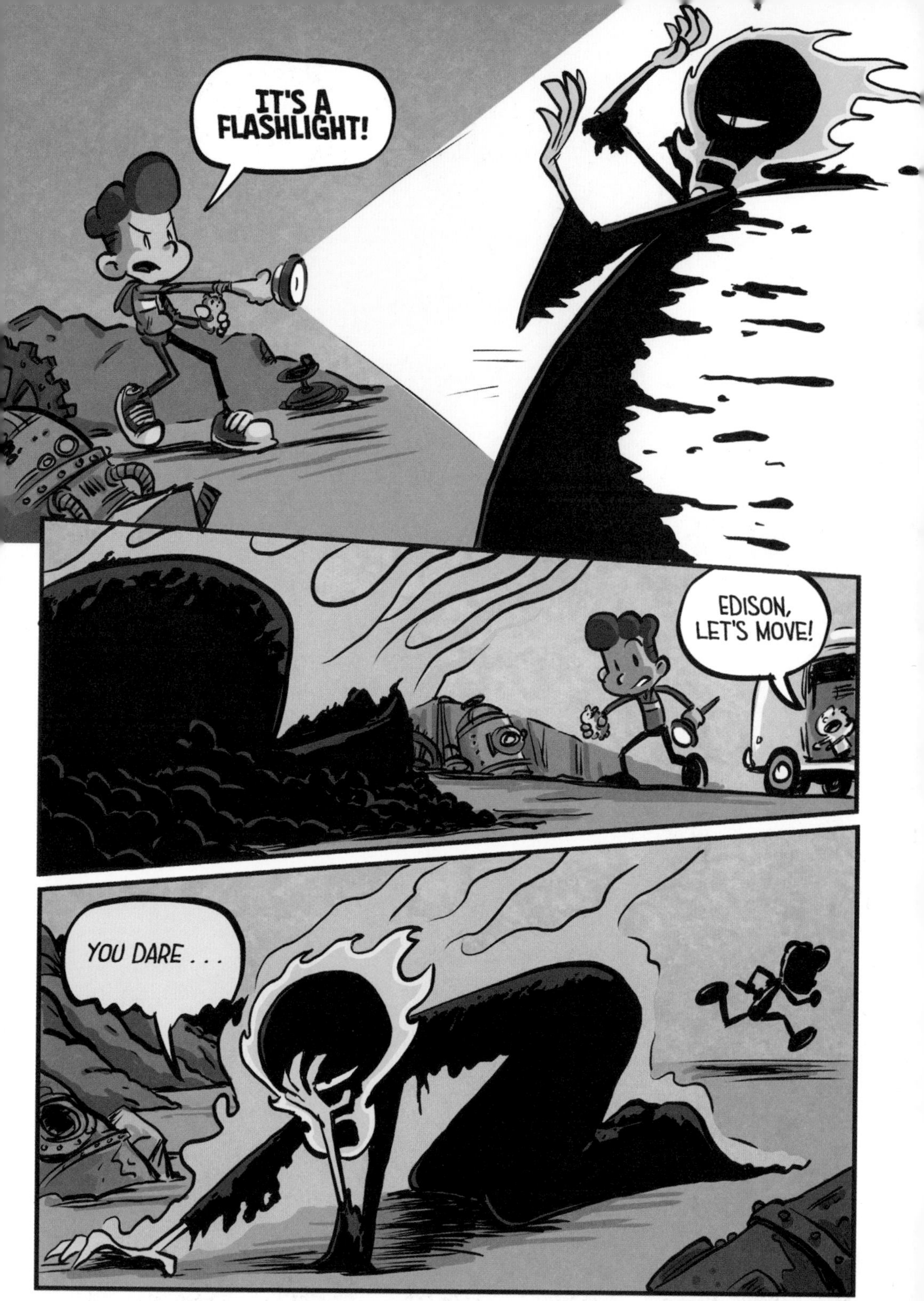
IT'S A FLASHLIGHT!
EDISON, LET'S MOVE!
YOU DARE . . .

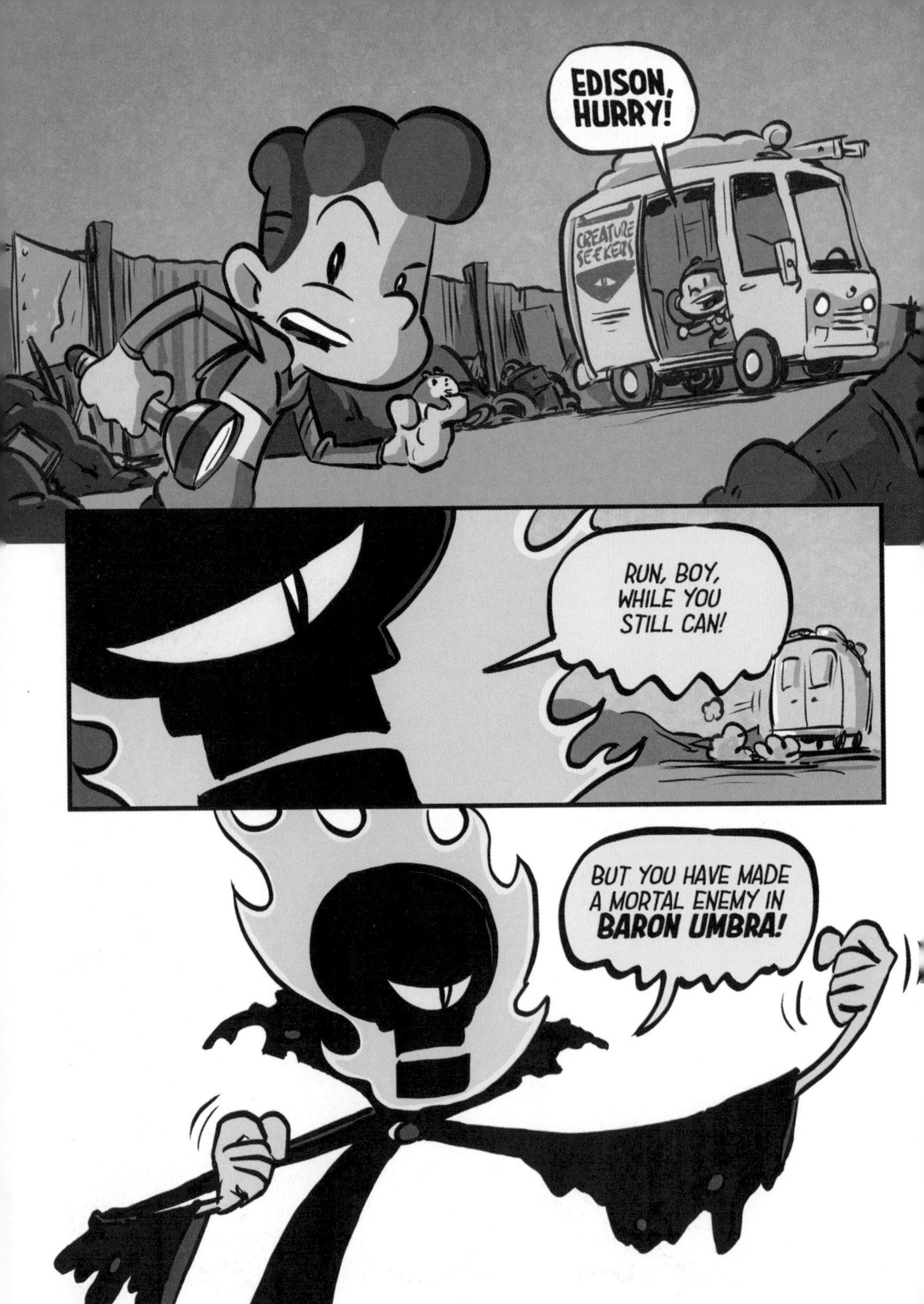

EDISON, HURRY!
CREATURE SEEKERS
RUN, BOY, WHILE YOU STILL CAN!
BUT YOU HAVE MADE A MORTAL ENEMY IN **BARON UMBRA!**

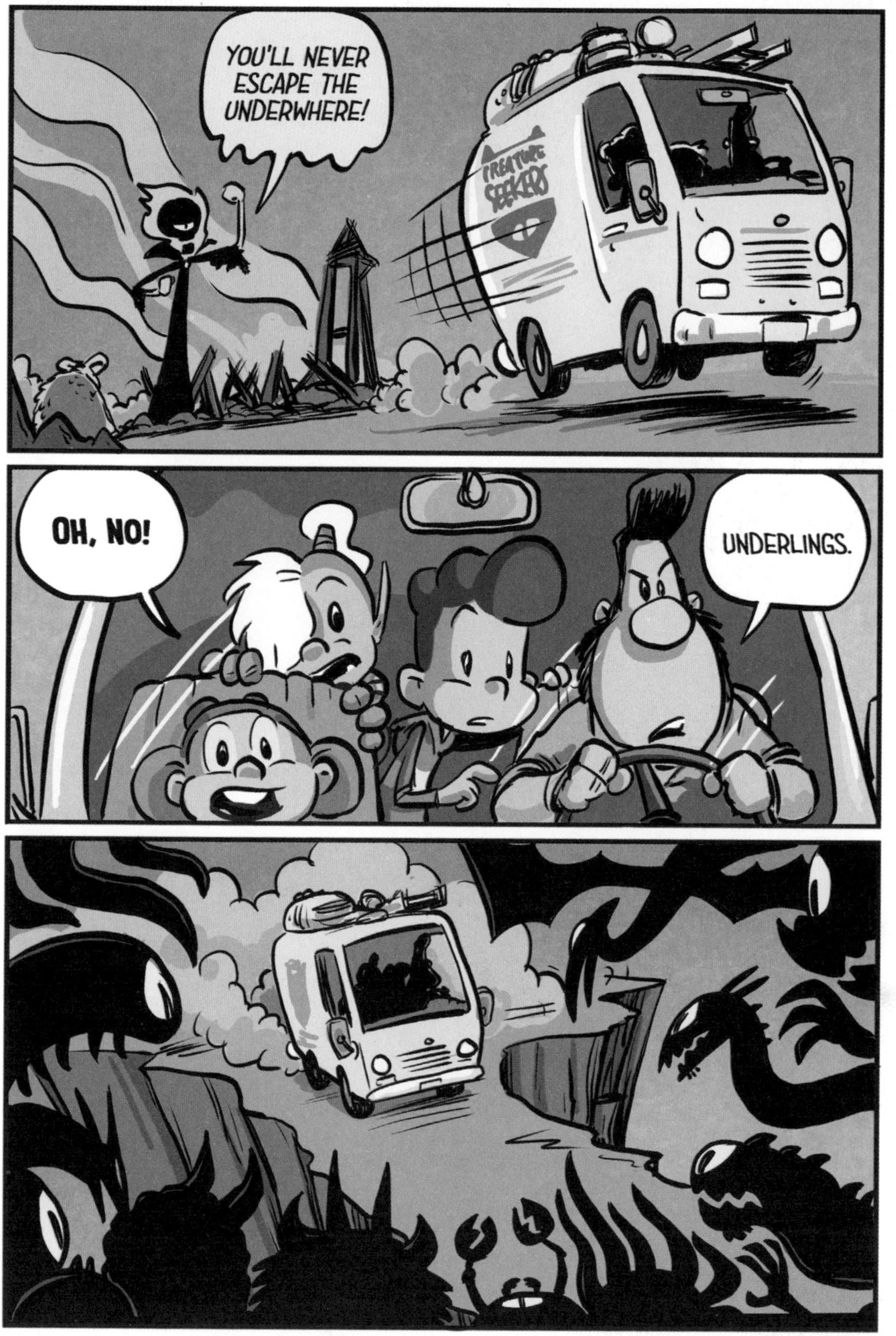
YOU'LL NEVER ESCAPE THE UNDERWHERE!
CREATURE SEEKERS
OH, NO!
UNDERLINGS.

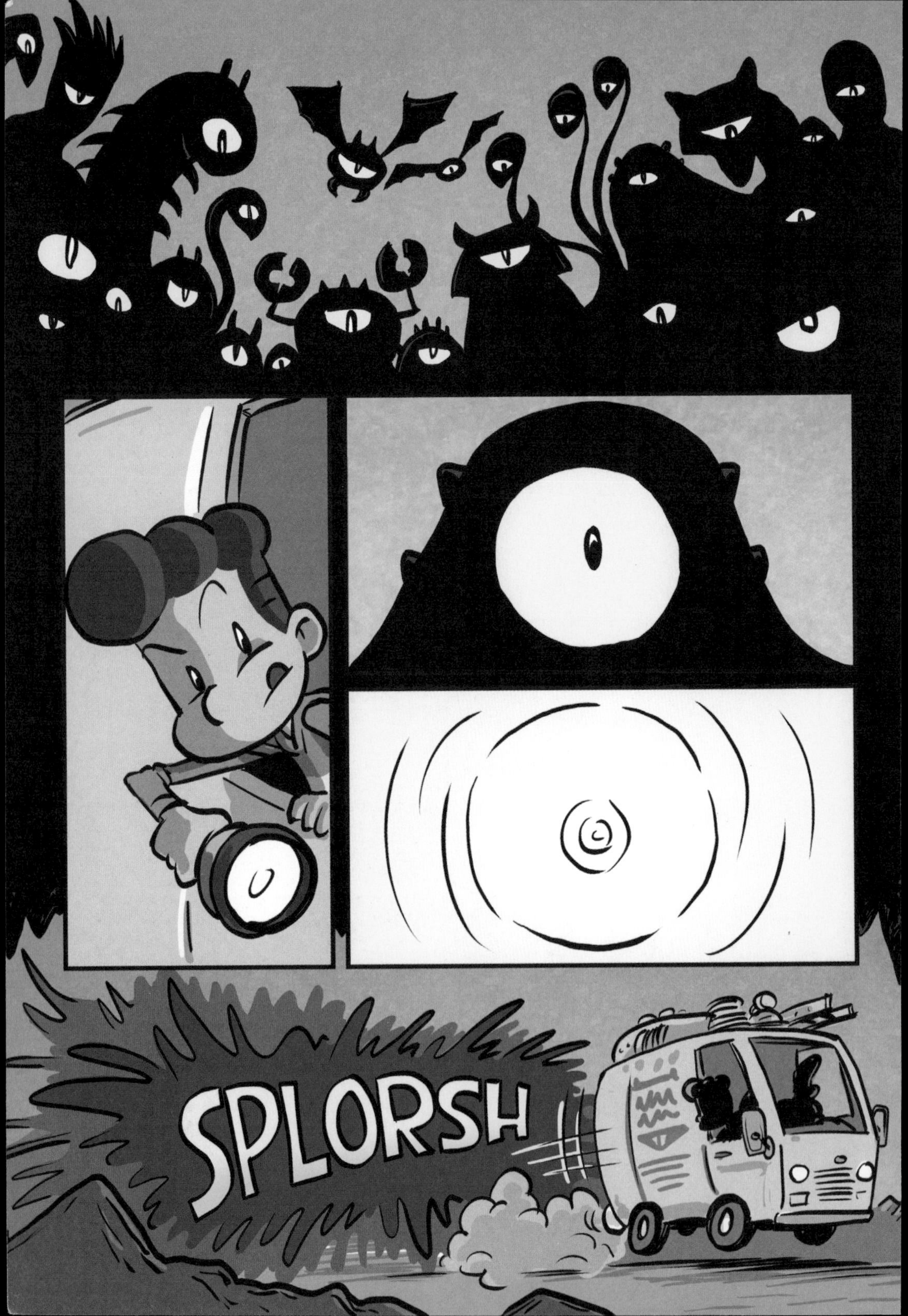
SPLORSH

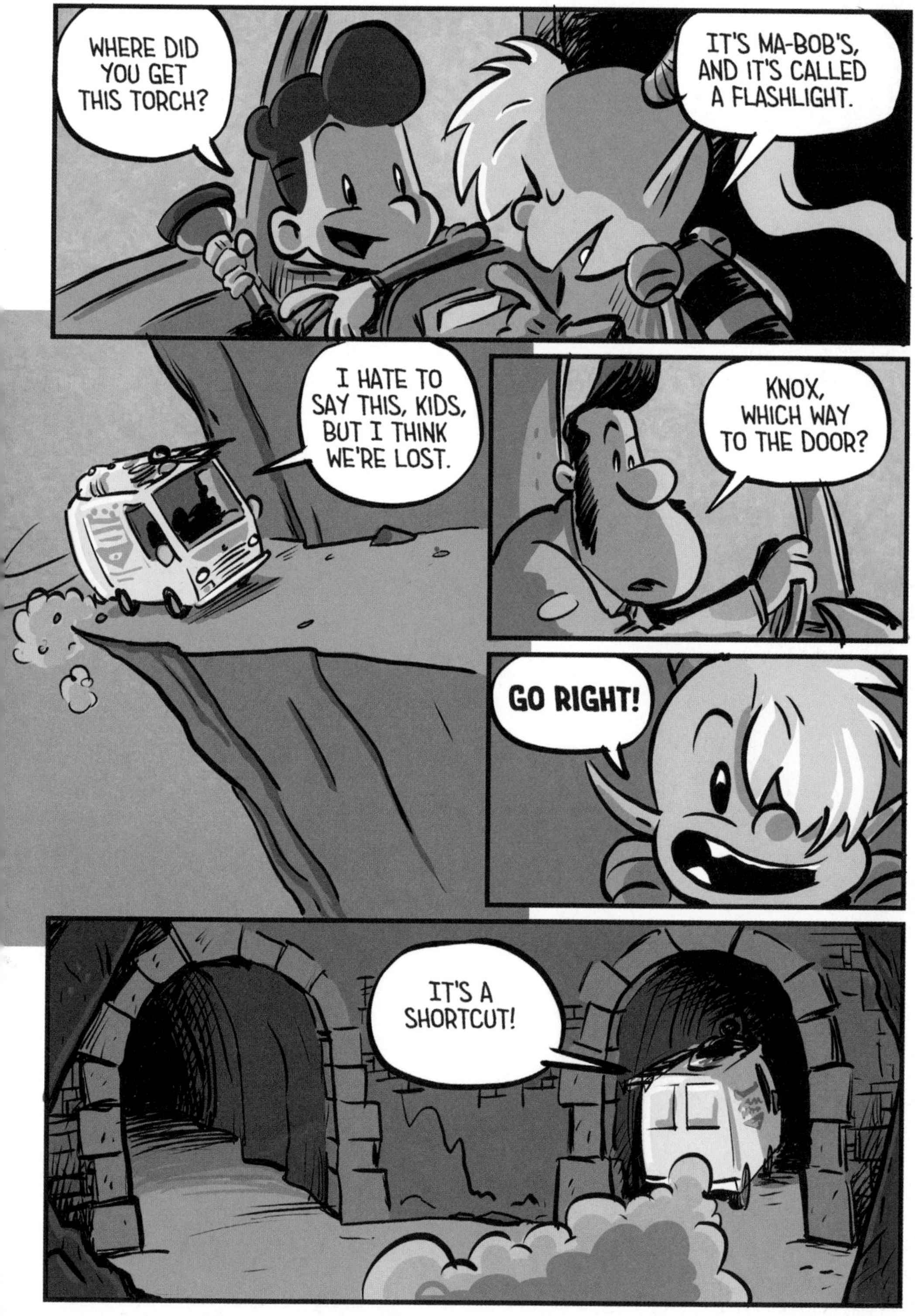
WHERE DID YOU GET THIS TORCH?
IT'S MA-BOB'S, AND IT'S CALLED A FLASHLIGHT.
I HATE TO SAY THIS, KIDS, BUT I THINK WE'RE LOST.
KNOX, WHICH WAY TO THE DOOR?
GO RIGHT!
IT'S A SHORTCUT!

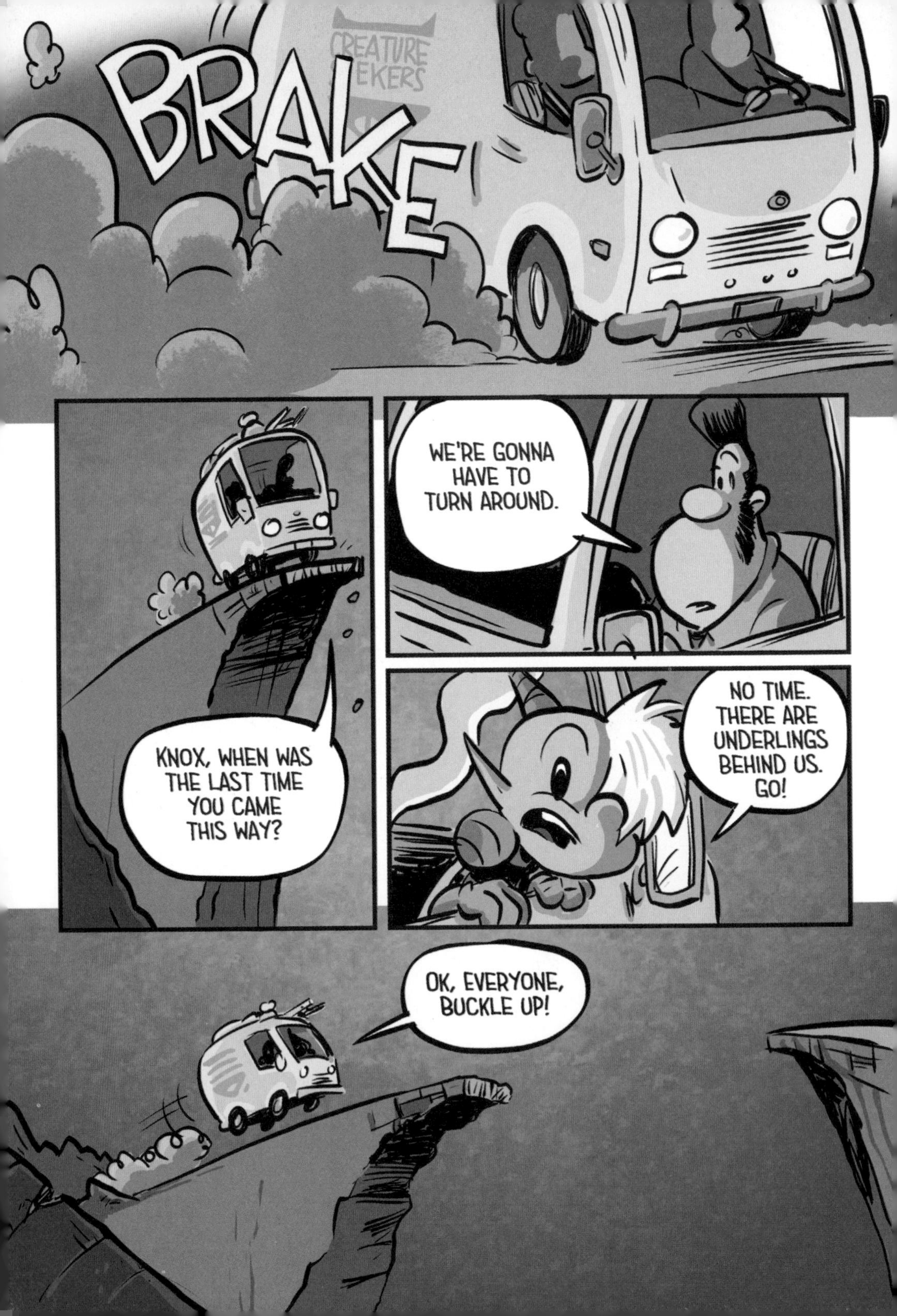
CREATURE SEEKERS
BRAKE
WE'RE GONNA HAVE TO TURN AROUND.
KNOX, WHEN WAS THE LAST TIME YOU CAME THIS WAY?
NO TIME. THERE ARE UNDERLINGS BEHIND US. GO!
OK, EVERYONE, BUCKLE UP!

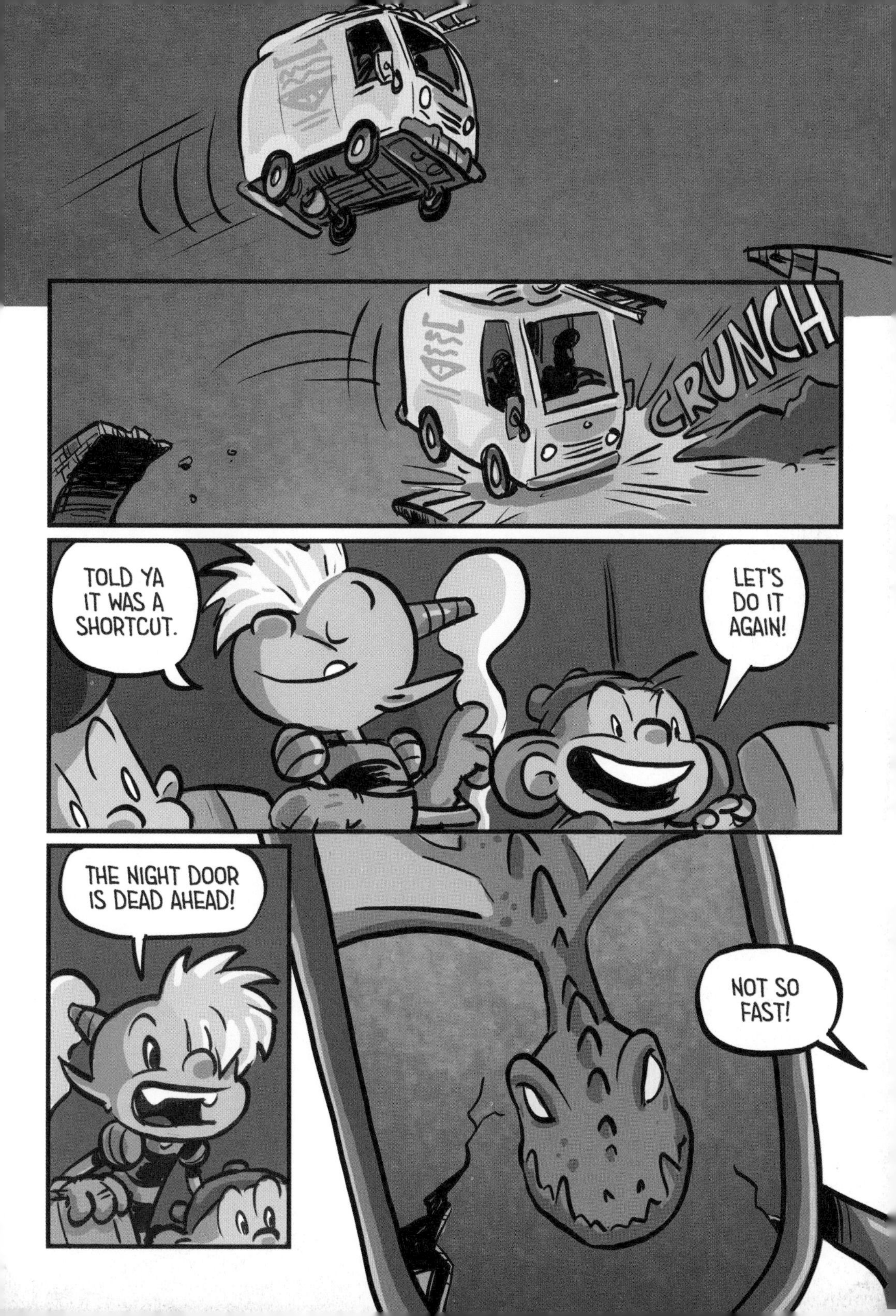
CRUNCH
TOLD YA IT WAS A SHORTCUT.
LET'S DO IT AGAIN!
THE NIGHT DOOR IS DEAD AHEAD!
NOT SO FAST!

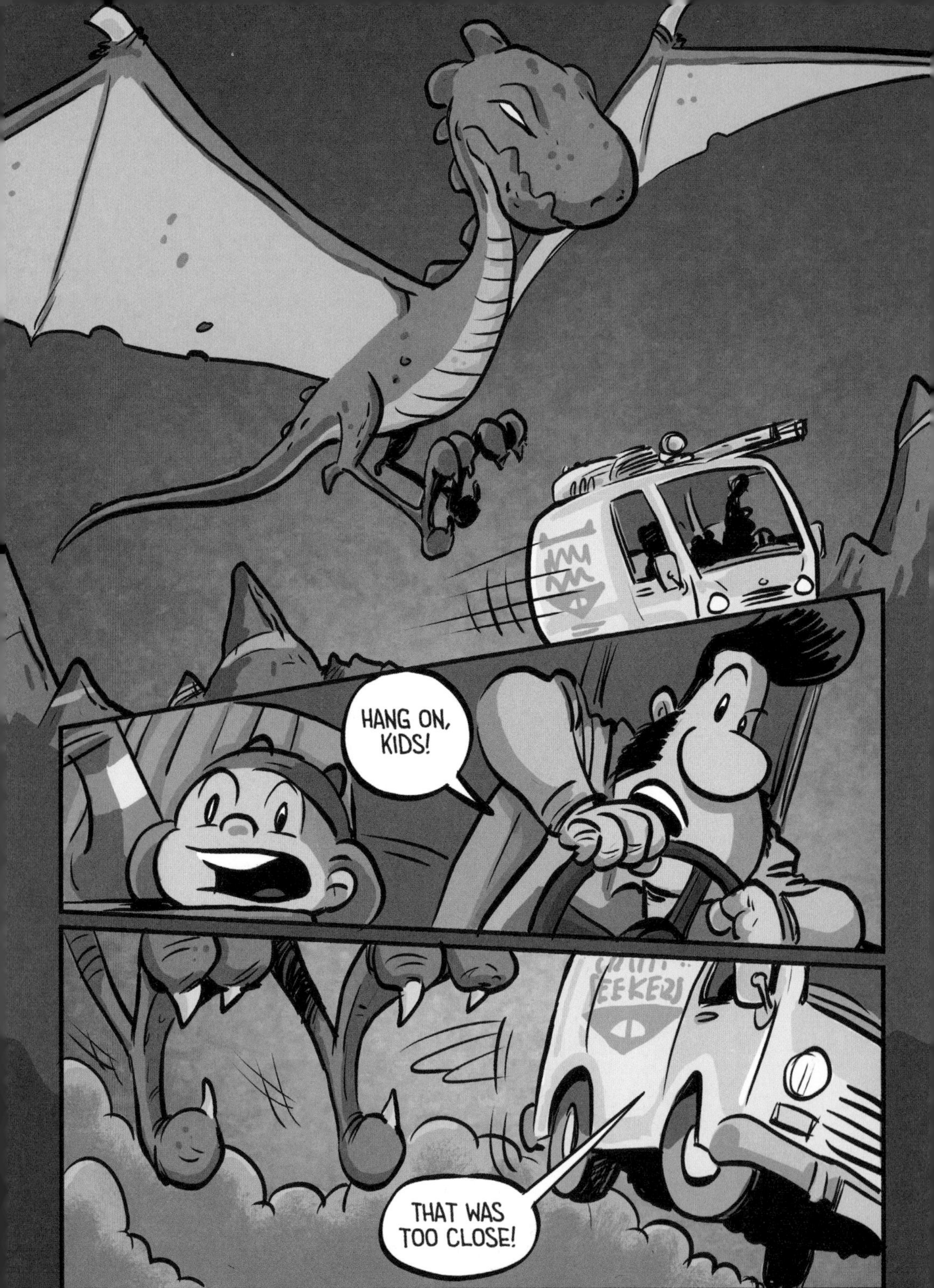
HANG ON, KIDS!
THAT WAS TOO CLOSE!

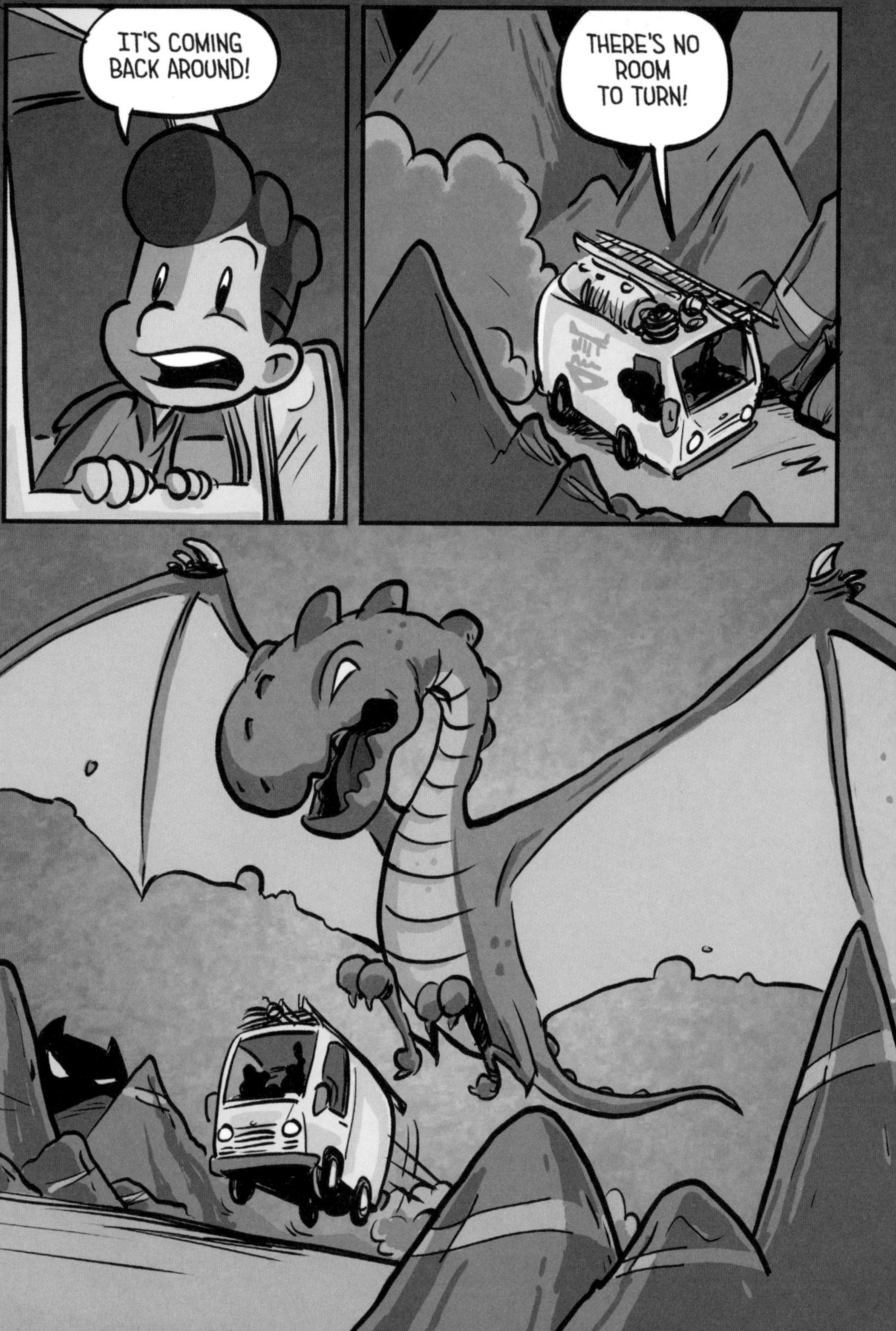
IT'S COMING BACK AROUND!
THERE'S NO ROOM TO TURN!

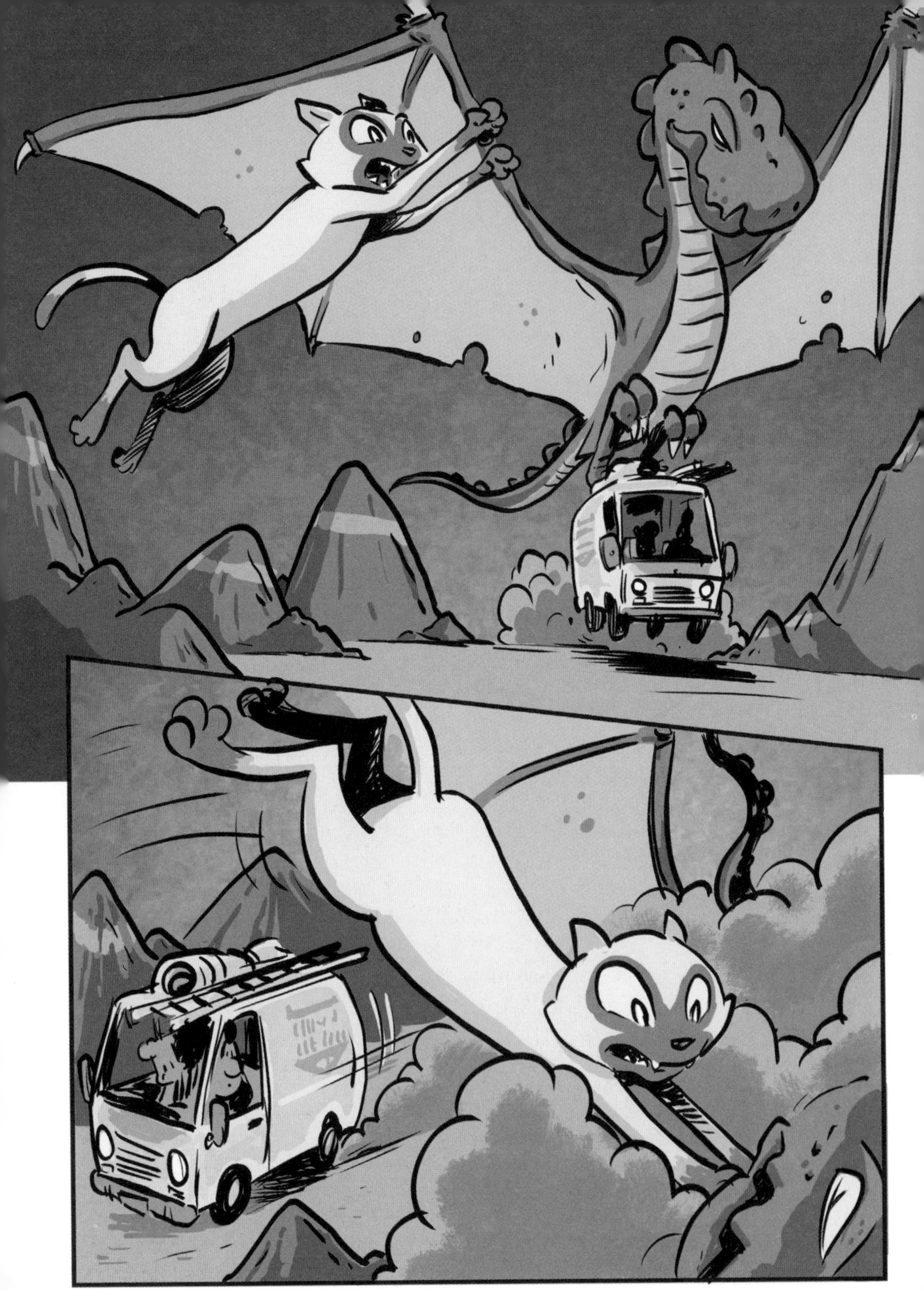

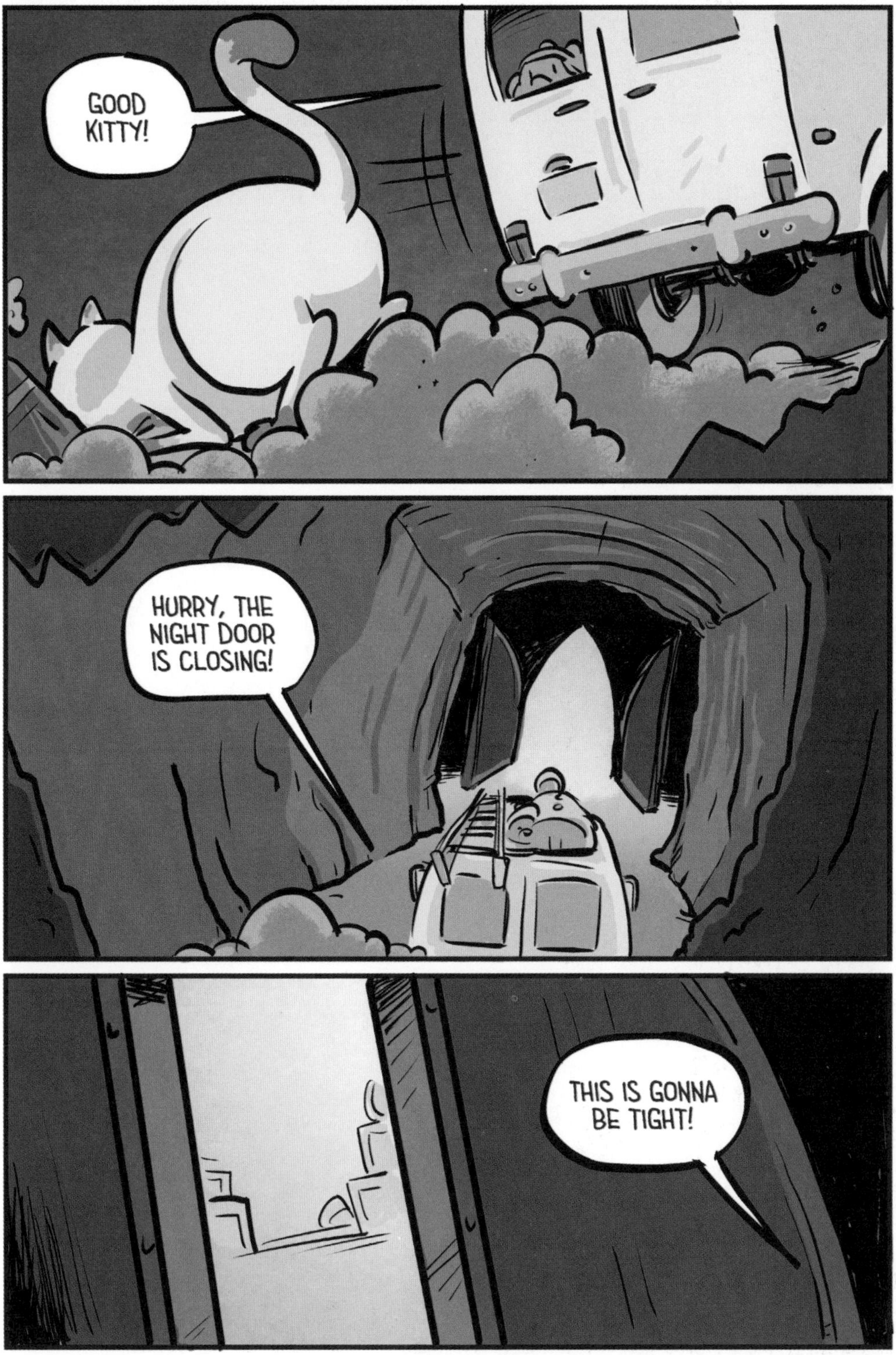
GOOD KITTY!
HURRY, THE NIGHT DOOR IS CLOSING!
THIS IS GONNA BE TIGHT!

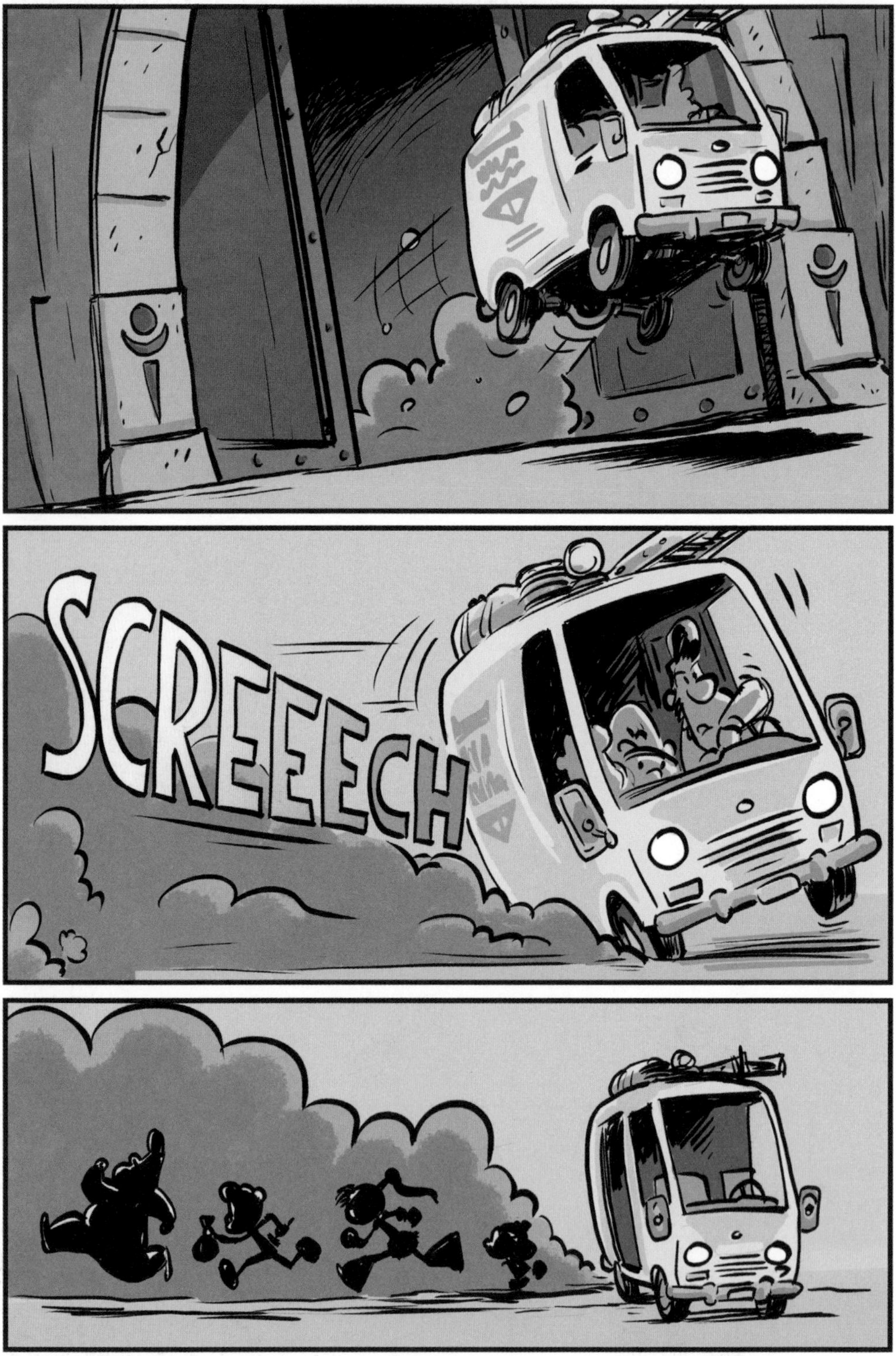
SCREEECH

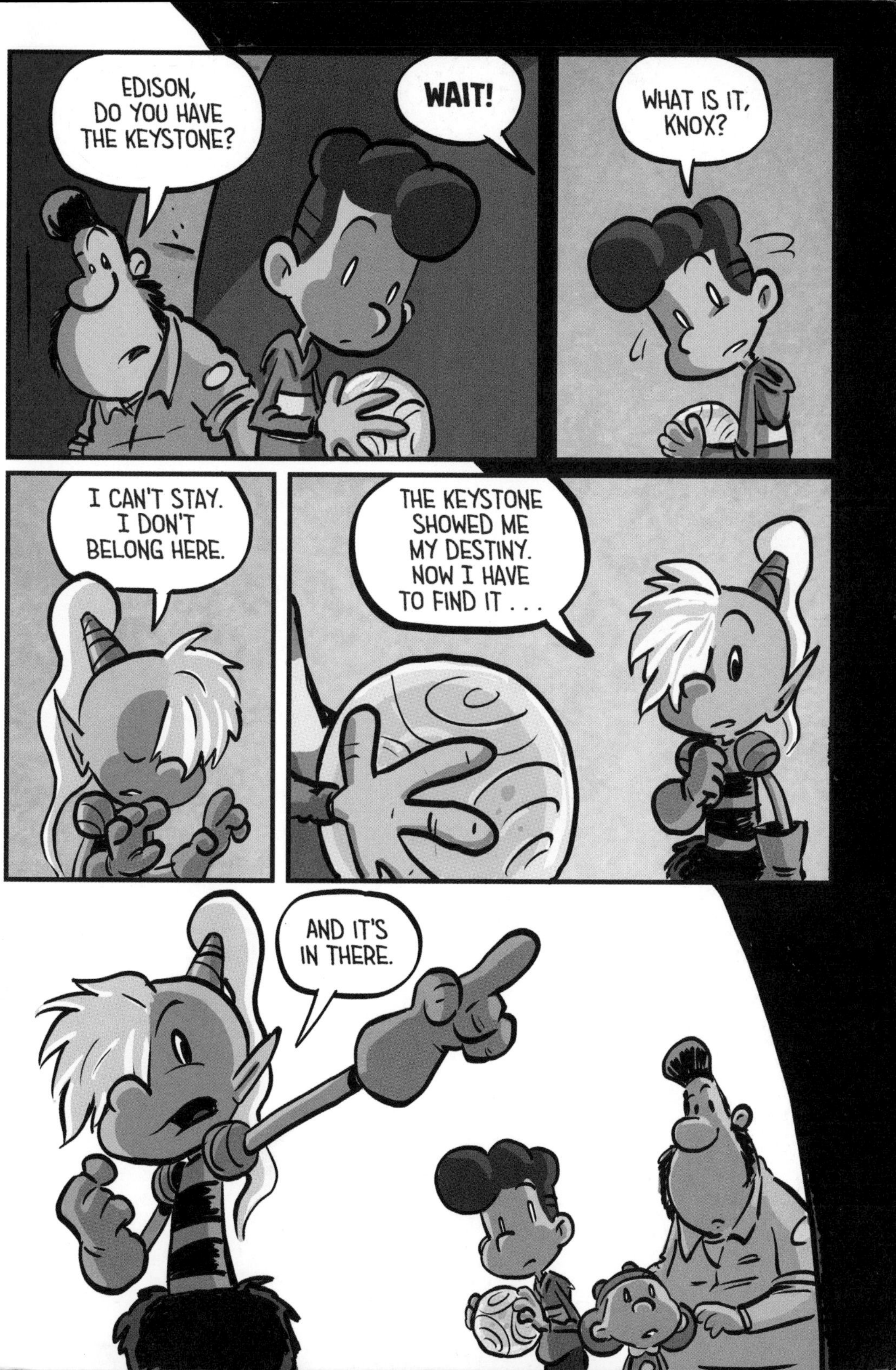
EDISON, DO YOU HAVE THE KEYSTONE?
WAIT!
WHAT IS IT, KNOX?
I CAN'T STAY. I DON'T BELONG HERE.
THE KEYSTONE SHOWED ME MY DESTINY. NOW I HAVE TO FIND IT . . .
AND IT'S IN THERE.

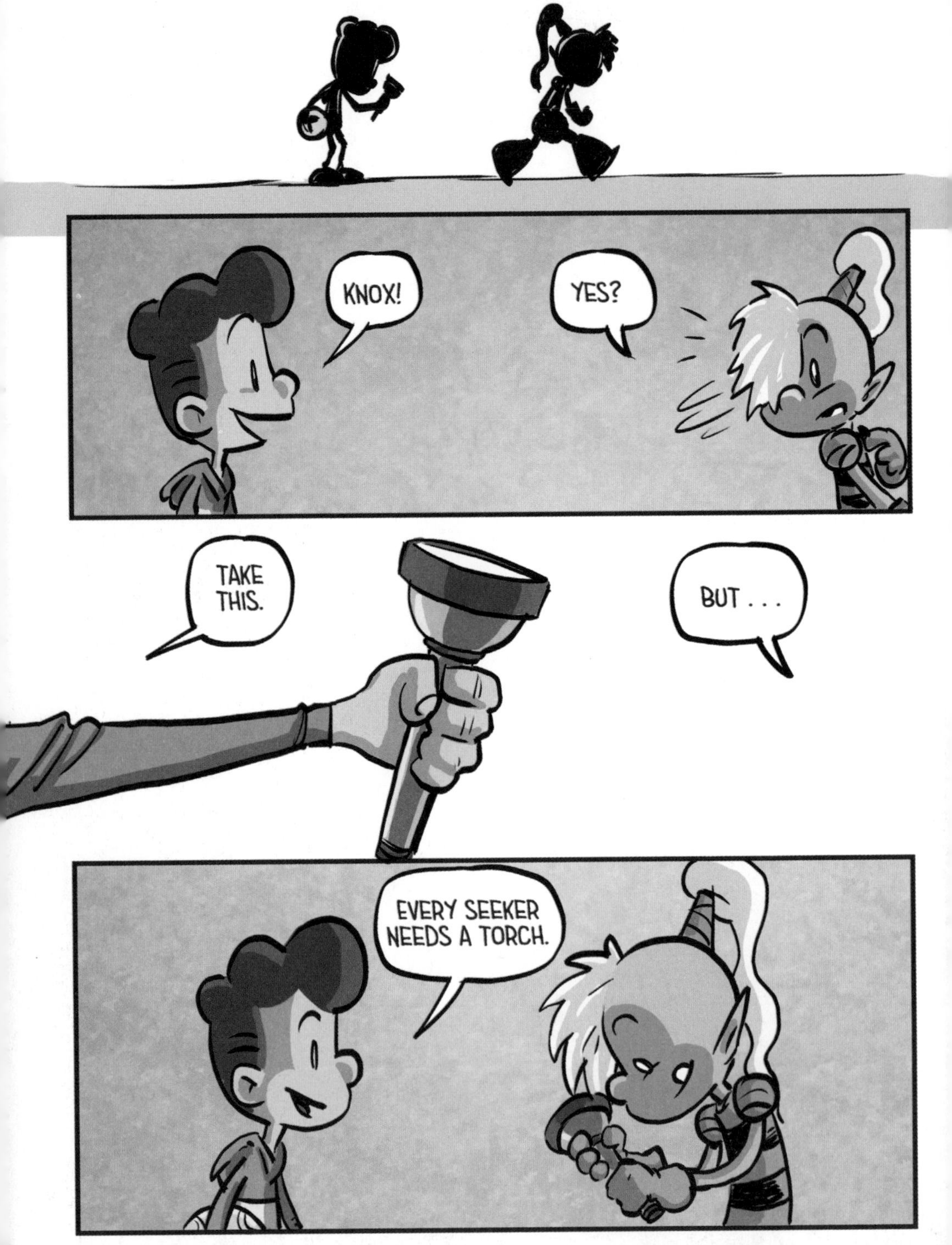
KNOX!
YES?
TAKE THIS.
BUT . . .
EVERY SEEKER NEEDS A TORCH.

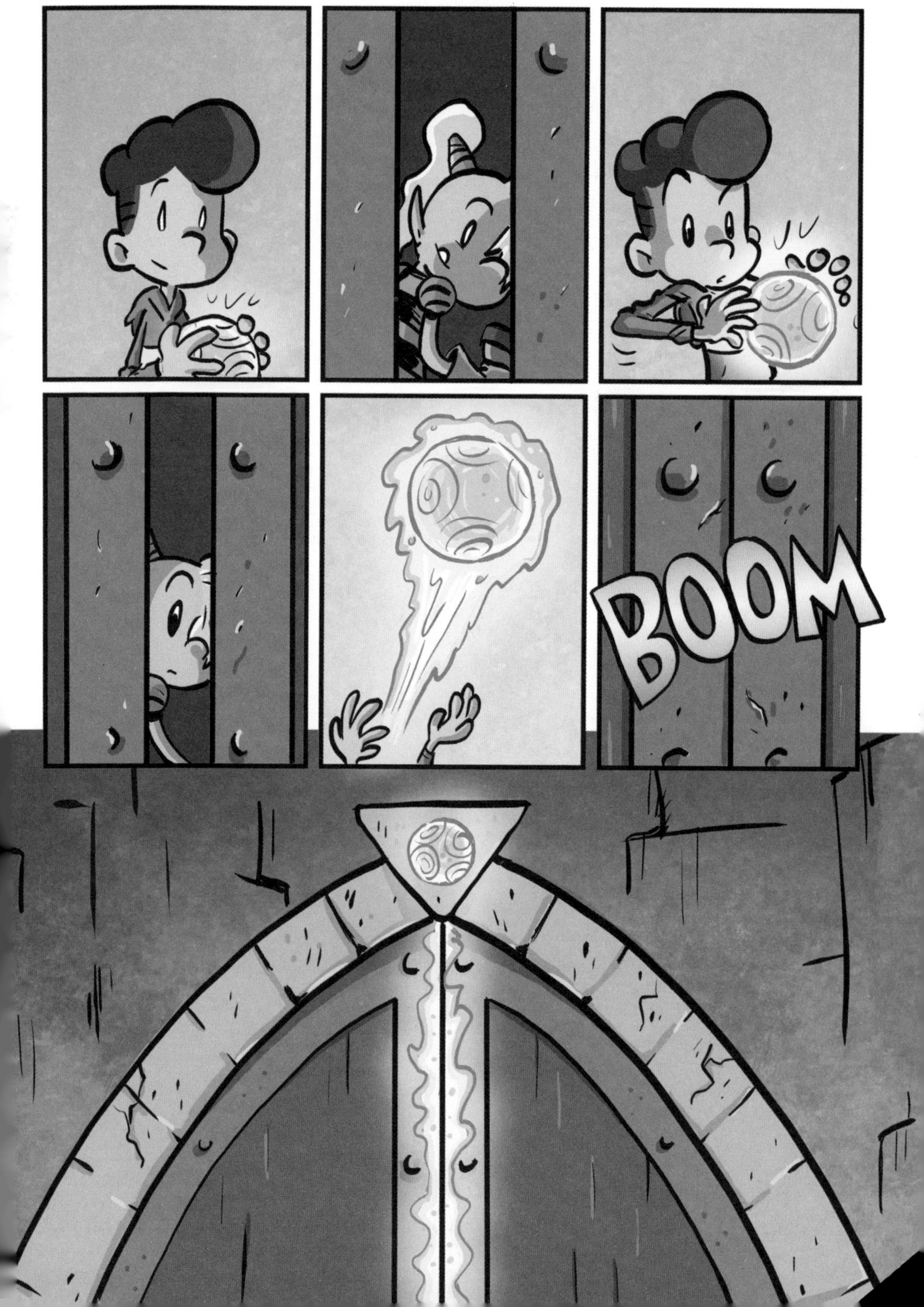
BOOM

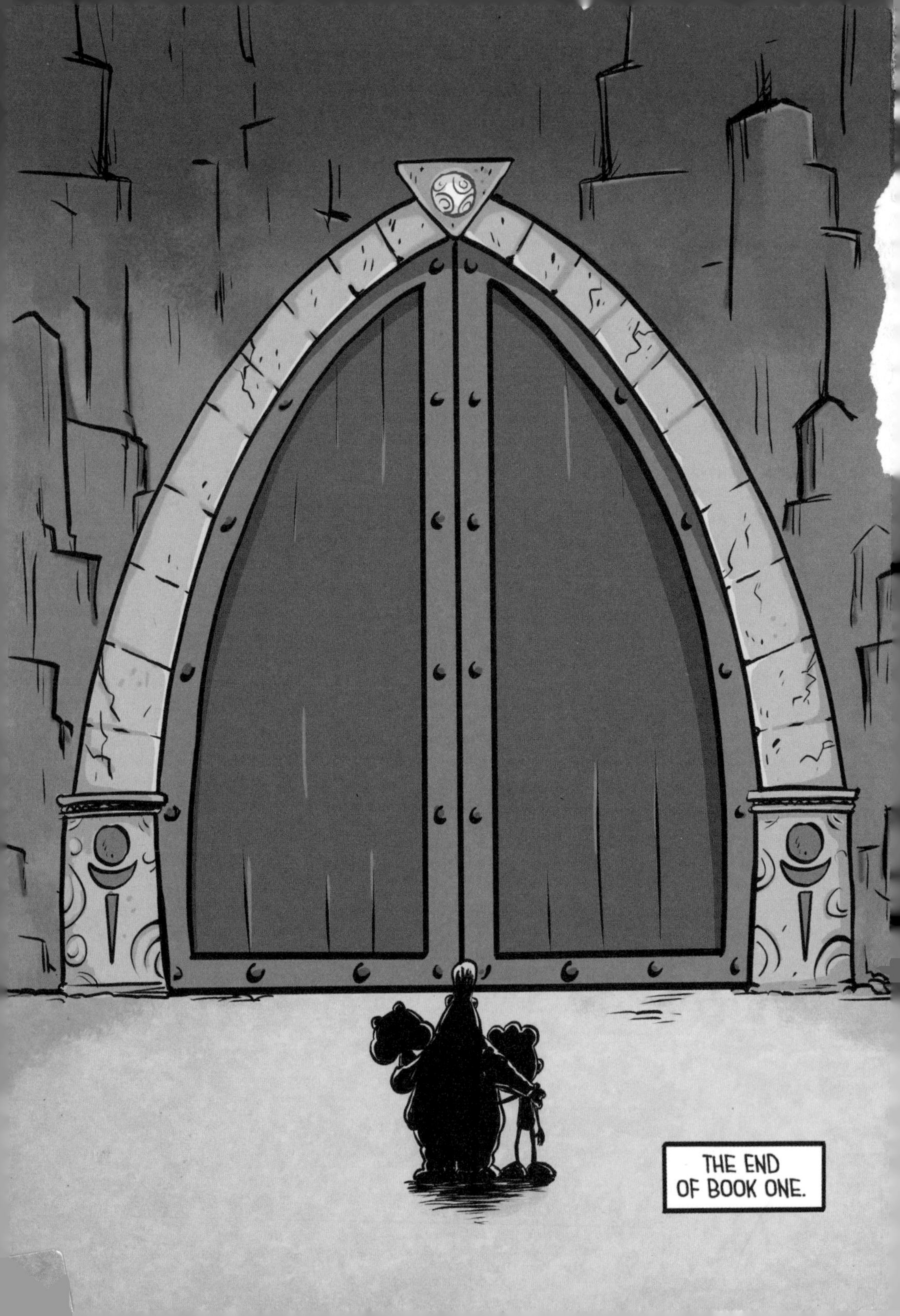
THE END
OF BOOK ONE.